Three Complete Novels
BARBARA CARTLAND

Three Complete Novels

BARBARA CARTLAND

LIGHTS, LAUGHTER AND A LADY

LOVE IN THE MOON

BRIDE TO THE KING

WINGS BOOKS
New York • Avenel, New Jersey

This omnibus was originally published in separate volumes under the titles:

Lights, Laughter and a Lady, copyright © 1981 by Barbara Cartland.
Love in the Moon, copyright © 1981 by Barbara Cartland.
Bride to the King, copyright © 1980 by Barbara Cartland.

This 1994 edition is published by Wings Books,
distributed by Random House Value Publishing, Inc.
40 Engelhard Avenue, Avenel, New Jersey 07001,
by arrangement with the author.

Random House
New York • Toronto • London • Sydney • Auckland

Printed and bound in the United States of America

Library of Congress Cataloging-in-Publication Data

Cartland, Barbara, 1902-
        [Novels. Selections]
        Three complete novels / Barbara Cartland.
                p. cm.
        Contents: Lights, laughter, and a lady—Love in the moon—
    Bride to the king.
        ISBN 0-517-11928-5
        I. Title.
        PR6005.A765A6 1994
        823'.912—dc20
                                                                94-17427
                                                                CIP

8   7   6   5   4   3   2   1

CONTENTS

LIGHTS, LAUGHTER
AND A LADY

Author's Note

❧

The Gaiety Theatre, with its wealth, its sparkle, its vivacity and its full-blooded enjoyment was a symbol of the Naughty Nineties.

The centre of London amusement, the shows were always beautifully staged and superbly dressed and, under George Edwardes' brilliant management, became unique.

Lovely as goddesses the Gaiety Girls had a grace, glamour and femininity which every man admired and desired.

"The Runaway Girl" produced on 21 May 1898, ran for 593 performances until 1900.

The authority for a ship's Captain to marry any of his passengers who demanded it, stemmed from the long voyages in sailing ships when women became pregnant and the child was likely to be born before they reached land.

CHAPTER ONE

❦

1898

"*H*AVE YOU PAID off all the debts, Mr. Mercer?" the Honourable Minella Clinton-Wood asked.

The elderly man sitting opposite her hesitated before he replied:

"The house, the furniture, the horse, and of course the estate which has been sold off bit by bit, have covered practically all of them, Miss Minella."

"How much is left?"

"Approximately," Mr. Mercer, of Mercer, Conway and Mercer replied, "one hundred and fifty pounds."

Minella drew in her breath and when she did not speak he continued:

"I have taken it upon myself to keep aside £100 for you."

"Why should you do that?"

"It is what I insist on doing," Mr. Mercer replied. "After all, you cannot live on air, and I know you have not yet decided with which of your relations you would prefer to live."

The expression on Minella's face was very revealing as she answered:

"As you are aware, Mr. Mercer, that is very difficult. Papa did not have many relatives, and Mama's are all in Ireland, and I have not met them."

"I thought," Mr. Mercer said quietly, "that you would live with your Aunt, Lady Banton, in Bath."

Minella sighed deeply.

"I suppose that is eventually what I shall have to do, unless I can get some sort of employment."

Mr. Mercer looked at her sympathetically.

He had met Lord Heywood's widowed sister who was much older than he was, and knew she was not only in ill-health but one of those people who are always complaining and finding fault.

In fact, the last time he had come in contact with her he had said to his wife:

"I do not believe Lady Banton has ever said a nice thing about anybody in her life."

"I suppose, poor thing," his wife had replied, "she thinks life has treated her badly, and of course it all started with her being excessively plain."

Mr. Mercer had laughed.

But he thought now, looking at the girl opposite him, that her being so exquisitely pretty would not make her Aunt feel any kinder towards her.

He leaned across the desk which had already been sold to pay its late owner's debts to say:

"Surely there is somebody else to whom you could go? What about that charming cousin who used to come here some years ago and ride with your father, and after your mother died helped him to entertain one of his shooting parties?"

"You mean Cousin Elizabeth," Minella said. "She married and is in India with her husband. She has not written to me, so I presume she does not know that Papa is dead."

"Could you live with her?" Mr. Mercer asked.

Minella shook her head.

"I am quite certain she would not welcome my imposing on her in India, and you know as well as I do, Mr. Mercer, that I could not afford the fare."

Because the £100 he had put aside for her would not

last for ever, Mr. Mercer admitted silently that this was the truth.

Yet he was deeply concerned as to what would happen to the girl he had known since she was a child, and who had grown lovelier year by year with nobody to admire her in the quiet, unfashionable County of Huntingdonshire.

Lord Heywood had often complained:

"Why my ancestors settled in this benighted hole, God only knows! I can only imagine that the house attracted them, for there is nothing else."

It was in fact a very attractive seventeenth century Manor, and as Lady Heywood had always said, was comparatively easy to run.

But there was nothing in Huntingdonshire to attract the sophisticated friends whom Lord Heywood enjoyed having around him except himself.

There was no doubt that Roy Heywood was born to be the centre of an admiring throng. He had a vitality and a charm about him that was irresistible.

Minella was not surprised when after her mother died her father was constantly being invited to parties in every other part of the country except that in which they lived.

There the county gentlefolk seldom gave parties anyway.

Because she was too young to accompany her father even if anybody had wanted her, she had been obliged to stay at home in the Manor and wait for his return.

Sometimes it would be a long wait, but she had learnt to be almost self-sufficient and was quite happy as long as she had horses to ride.

Until the end of last year she had also been very busy being educated.

"For Heaven's sake," her father said to her, "stuff a little knowledge into your head! You are going to be very pretty, my darling, but that is not enough."

"Enough for what?" Minella asked.

"Enough to keep a man amused, attracted and in love with you for ever," her father answered.

"The way you loved Mama?" Minella asked.

"Exactly!" her father replied. "Your mother always intrigued and amused me, and I never missed anybody or anything else as long as we were together."

This was not entirely true, for Minella could remember times when he had expressed disgust and irritation because they had no money.

He hated not being able to whisk her mother off to London, to go to Theatres and Balls, and meet people who were as gay as themselves.

Even so, the Manor House had always seemed full of sunshine and laughter until her mother died.

It had been a desperately cold winter and, however many logs were piled onto the fire, the house always seemed to have a damp chill about it.

Alice Heywood's cough had grown worse and worse until finally, unexpectedly and without warning, it turned to pneumonia and within two weeks she was dead.

To Minella it was as if her whole world had crashed about her ears and she knew that her father felt the same.

Only when the funeral was over he had said violently in a voice she had never heard from him before:

"I cannot stand it, I cannot stay here thinking your mother will walk into the room at any moment!"

He had left that same evening and Minella knew he had gone to London to try to erase the memory of her mother and the happiness they had known in the past, which haunted her also.

From that moment her father had changed.

Not that he had become morose, gloomy and introspective as another man might have done, instead he had gone back to the raffish, devil-may-care self that he had been before he married.

Because he did not want to think of the wife he had lost there were now inevitably other women in his life.

He did not talk about them but perceptively Minella was aware of them, and there were letters, some of them scented, some of them written in a flowery, extravagant, uneducated hand.

Some he tore up and threw away as if they were of no interest to him, others he read carefully.

Then a little later, as if he did not want Minella to find out, he would say casually:

"I have some business to see to in London. I think I will catch the morning train. I will not be away for long."

"I shall miss you, Papa!"

"I shall miss you, my poppet, but I will be back by the end of the week."

But at the end of the week there would be no sign of him, and when he did return Minella had the feeling that it was not because he wanted to see her but that he did not dare to spend any more money.

Even so, she did not realise until he died that he was spending so much, or had so many unpaid debts.

Roy Heywood, who as many of his friends often said, was as strong as a horse, had died by a quirk of fate that seemed quite inexplicable.

He came home late one night and as soon as she saw him Minella realised that he had not only had an amusing time in London, but a somewhat debauched one.

She had grown to know by the lines under her father's eyes and his general air of dissipation that he had been to too many parties and had far too little sleep.

Alcohol in excess had never agreed with him, and he was, she was sure, compared to his friends quite abstemious.

But from what he told her in his expansive moments about the parties he went to she had learnt that the champagne flowed like water, and the claret he drank with his friends at the Club was exceptionally good.

The combination invariably somewhat affected his health until the fresh air, the exercise he took, and of course the plain food they had at the Manor, restored him to his natural buoyancy.

As soon as he had walked into the Manor on this last occasion looking, Minella thought, dashingly raffish, but at the same time not well, he held out his hand to her and she saw it was wrapped in a blood-stained handkerchief.

"What has happened, Papa?"

"I caught my hand on a piece of loose wire, or something like it, on the door of the railway-carriage. It is damned painful and you had better do something about it."

"Of course, Papa!"

Minella had bathed his hand and saw there was a nasty jagged cut going deep into the flesh.

She could not help wondering if he had been a little unsteady when he caught the train.

Perhaps he had staggered or fallen in a way that he would never have done at other times.

Her father was always so agile on his feet, and he was usually so healthy that if hurt himself out riding or in any other way she always expected him to heal quicker than anybody else would have done.

She was therefore very perturbed the next morning when she saw that despite her ministrations of the night before, his hand was swollen and beginning to fester.

Although her father said it was nonsense and quite unnecessary she sent for the Doctor.

He had not thought it serious, but gave her a disinfectant salve to use on it which she applied exactly following his instructions.

However Lord Heywood's hand got worse and at the end of the week he was in excruciating pain. By the time he had seen a Surgeon it was too late.

The poison had spread all over his body, and only the drugs that made him unconscious prevented him from screaming with agony.

It all happened so quickly that it was difficult for Minella to realise it was really happening.

Only when her father had been buried in the quiet little Churchyard beside her mother did she realise she was completely alone.

At first, having no idea of the financial mess her father had left behind, she had thought she could stay on at the Manor and perhaps try to farm part of the estate that was not already let.

It was Mr. Mercer who disillusioned her and made her understand that such plans were only day-dreams.

The Manor itself was mortgaged, and so was at least half the land.

By the time the mortgages were paid and she had seen the huge accumulation of debts her father owed in London, she faced the truth.

She was not only alone, but penniless.

Now, looking across the desk at the Solicitor, she said:

"I do not know how to thank you, Mr. Mercer, for all your kindness. I have given you a great deal of work, and I only hope you have paid yourself a proper fee as well as everybody else."

"Do not worry about that, Miss Minella," Mr. Mercer replied. "Both your father and your mother were very kind to me when they first came to live here, and it was through your father that I acquired a great many new clients for my small and not very important family firm."

Minella smiled.

"Papa always wanted to help everybody."

"That is true," Mr. Mercer replied, "and I think that was one of the reasons why his creditors did not press him as hard as they might have done. Every one of them expressed deep and sincere regrets to me that he should have died."

As this was such a moving tribute to her father Minella felt the tears come into her eyes. Then she said:

"Papa always told me that when he could afford to take me to London, perhaps next year, his friends would look after me and give me a wonderful time."

"Perhaps they would do so now," Mr. Mercer suggested hopefully.

Minella shook her head.

"I am sure it would not be the same unless Papa was there making them all laugh at every party he attended."

Mr. Mercer knew that this was the truth, but he merely said:

"Perhaps there is some kind lady who knew your father who would be willing to be your hostess, Miss Minella, and introduce you to the Social World in which you should be moving."

"I do not think I am particularly interested in the Social World," Minella said reflectively, almost as if she was talking to herself. "Mama used to tell me about it, but I know I do not want to live with Aunt Esther, which would be very, very depressing!"

Because there was a note in her voice that sounded as if she might cry Mr. Mercer said kindly:

"You do not have to make your mind up today, Miss Minella, when we have had so many depressing things to talk about. You can stay here at least until the end of the month. That will give you time to think of someone to whom you can go."

Minella wanted to reply that she had been thinking about that already.

She had lain awake at night, unable to sleep, going over and over in her mind the Clinton-Wood relations who were still alive and repeating to herself the names of her mother's relatives whom she had never met.

"There must be somebody," she said, as she had said a hundred times before.

"I am sure there must be," Mr. Mercer said encouragingly.

He rose to his feet and started collecting the papers which were lying on the desk in front of him, to place them in the leather bag he carried.

It was old and worn, and he had used it ever since he had first become a Solicitor in his father's firm.

Although his partners and his office staff often laughed at it, he would not think of parting from something so familiar.

Minella rose too, and now they walked together over the worn carpet from the Study where they had been sitting into the small, oak-panelled hall.

Outside the front door Mr. Mercer's old fashioned gig was waiting, drawn however by a young horse which would not take long to reach the small market town of Huntingdon where his offices were situated.

He climbed in and the young groom who had been holding the horse's head jumped in beside him.

They drove off, the wheels of the gig grinding over the loose gravel of the sweep outside the front door which badly needed weeding.

Minella waved as Mr. Mercer drove away and went back into the house.

As she shut the front door behind her she thought it impossible that this was no longer her home, she did not own it, and she had no idea where to go when she left.

Except of course, and the idea was like a menacing black cloud, to live with her Aunt Esther.

She could remember every word of the letter her Aunt had written to her after her father's death had been announced in the newspapers.

There was no warmth in the sentences her Aunt had written. Then as a post-script she had penned:

"P.S. I suppose as there are so few members of our family left you will have to come and live with me. It will be an added burden, but then, as I have had nothing else in my life, I am used to them."

'A burden!'

The words seemed to haunt Minella.

With a pride she had never realised she had, she had longed to retort that she would never be a burden to anybody.

"Why should I be?" she argued with herself. "I am

young, I am well-educated, I am supposed to be intelligent. There must be something I can do to earn a living."

There was no answer to that question.

As she went back into the Study she remembered that while she was talking to Mr. Mercer she had thought that when he left she must take her father's personal papers out of the desk and destroy them.

She had no wish for the newcomers to the Manor, who had bought it for quite a reasonable sum with a great deal of the furniture too, to pry into the personal affairs of the late Lord Heywood.

Minella was well aware that when the villagers, the farmers and their few neighbours in the vicinity of the Manor talked about her father, it was either with admiration because they wished they could be as dashing as he was or with disapproval because of the way he enjoyed himself in London.

The stories of the smart fashionable people with whom he associated had inevitably reached the county sooner or later.

'It is not their business!' Minella thought.

But she knew if there were letters lying about they would read them, and if there were bills they would 'tut-tut' over them.

If there was anything like a Ball programme, a bow or ribbon, a glove or a scented handkerchief, it would feed the tales they were already repeating about her father.

She knew by the way people in the local shops eyed her when she came in through the door what they were thinking.

She had not missed the note of irrepressible disapproval in the Vicar's voice as he had read the Burial Service.

The old Vicar was a simple man, and while he had always been grateful for the generosity her father showed him and the fact that he never had to beg in vain, he had not approved of the life His Lordship had led since his wife died.

Her father had laughed when she told him the village talked of nothing else but the gaieties that kept drawing him to London.

"I am glad I gave them something to talk about!" he said. "At least it is a change from turnips, Brussels sprouts, the weather, and that the steeple is falling down."

"Oh, not again, Papa!" Minella exclaimed, knowing how much her father had already contributed towards the repairs to the Church.

"The only answer is to let it fall," Lord Heywood had said, "and as falling is what they think I myself am doing, perhaps it would be appropriate."

Minella laughed.

"They like talking about you, Papa, and I do not know what topic they would be left with if you vanished out of their sight."

But indeed he had vanished, and she felt that the conversation in the village would have to revert to turnips, and Brussels sprouts.

She sat down at her father's desk and pulled open the top drawer.

There was the usual miscellaneous collection of unsharpened pencils, pens that were unusable, stubs of cheque-books, a bent penny, and two three-penny bits in which her father had drilled a hole after they had been used in the pudding at Christmas and her mother had told him were lucky.

"I will put them on my watch-chain," he said.

But of course he had forgotten to do so.

Now they looked tarnished, and so did the buttons which had once ornamented the livery of a footman.

The previous Lord Heywood, her father's Uncle, had employed three footmen and a Butler to wait on him.

When her father came to the Manor, they had a very efficient couple to run the house, a Nanny for her, a valet for her father and an odd-job man.

First the odd-job man had gone, then the valet and

when the couple grew too old and had to retire they had been left with Minella's old nurse.

She had looked after her mother when she was a child and had been the mainstay of the house until she had died at the age of seventy-nine, shortly before her mother.

Minella often thought that if Nanny had been alive, her mother would not have become so ill, for she would have been able to warm the house better than they had.

After that there had been only daily-women.

Sometimes there were two or three of them, but although they cleaned the place conscientiously, they were always in a hurry to get back to their own families.

Now there was nobody.

After her father's death Minella had deliberately ignored the dust accumulating in the rooms they did not use.

She told herself that there was no point in spending money she could not afford, and she could manage quite well without help.

She pulled out of the drawer a piece of blotting-paper covered with ink on which her father had done various sums, threw it away and collected everything else into a tidy heap, meaning to put it into a box.

She was not quite certain what she would do with it, but she would at least keep the silver buttons with the family crest on them, and perhaps if she could not earn any money, she might even be grateful for the three-penny bits.

Then as she realised there was nothing incriminating, or anything to make any 'Nosey-Parker' curious, she shut the drawer and opened one of the side ones.

This was different and was stuffed full with letters.

She realised her father seldom answered letters, but put them in the drawer not as keep-sakes, but because he meant sooner or later to reply.

She started to open the letters systematically, tearing

up those that were out-of date and no longer of any interest.

A typical example read:

"Dear Roy,

We are expecting you to stay with us for the Hunt Ball. You know you are the only person who can make it enjoyable. We are also relying on you to bring the house-party safely down from St. Pancras . . ."

Minella did not bother to read any more but merely tore up the letter and threw the pieces into the wastepaper basket.

There were many others written in the same strain, with addresses embossed on the top of the writing-paper, and surmounted by impressive crests or coronets.

But every invitation made it clear that her father was invited, because he made the party 'go with a swing', or as one invitation, written in a woman's hand, said:

"The whole thing will be a complete failure unless you are there as usual to make us laugh and, as far as I am concerned, to make me very happy . . ."

Minella tore up the letter quickly because she had the feeling that anybody reading it would put an interpretation on the words that she did not wish them to do.

Then, because she herself had no wish to pry into her father's private affairs, she tore up one letter after another without taking them out of the envelopes or, if they were loose, without reading them.

She was just about to do the same to the last letter in the drawer when the name on the bottom of it caught her eye: *"Connie."*

She looked at it, thought she recognised the handwriting and than at second glance she was sure she did.

Constance Langford was the daughter of the Clergyman in the next village to the one in which they lived.

Her father was a clever, intelligent man who should never have accepted a country living, but should have been a Don at a University.

Her mother had persuaded him to teach Minella a number of subjects which were beyond the capabilities of the retired Governess who lived in their own village.

It had taken Minella a quarter-of-an-hour riding across the fields to reach the Vicarage of Little Welham, and the Reverend Adolphus Langford made her work very hard.

She had first gone to him when she was fourteen and had shared the lessons with his daughter Constance who was three years older.

It had been more fun learning with another girl, and Minella had been very proud of the fact that she was quicker to learn and on the whole much more intelligent than Constance.

Constance, when they were not in her father's Study, made it quite clear that she thought lessons were a bore.

"I think you are lucky to have such a clever father," Minella said politely.

"I think you are lucky to have such a handsome and exciting one!" Constance replied.

"I will tell Papa what you said," Minella laughed. "I am sure he will be very flattered."

She had brought Constance home to tea, and as her father was at home he made himself very pleasant, as he always did with everybody, and Constance had gone into ecstasies about him.

"He is so smart, so dashing!" she kept saying. "Oh, Minella, when can I come to the Manor again? Just to look at your father is thrilling!"

Minella had thought such a gushing compliment was somewhat unkind to Constance's own father.

She liked the Vicar, and found the way he taught her was efficient and stimulating, but she soon had the suspicion that Constance was being particularly nice to her so that she would invite her again to the Manor.

Because she had so few friends, Minella was only too happy to oblige.

Constance had the use of a horse when her father did not need it, and they would ride back together across the fields. When they reached the Manor, to please Constance, Minella would go in search of her father.

Usually he was in the stables or in the garden, and as it was quite obvious that Constance looked at him in wide-eyed admiration and listened to every word he spoke as if it was the Gospel, Lady Heywood had laughed and said:

"You have certainly captured the heart of the village maiden, Roy, but you must not let her or Minella be a bother to you."

"They are no bother," her husband replied good-humouredly, "and girls of that age always have a passion for the first man they meet."

"As long as she is not a nuisance," Lady Heywood said.

"If she is, I shall look to you to protect me," Lord Heywood replied.

He had put his arms around his wife and they had walked away into the garden completely happy, as Minella knew, to be together.

A year later, Constance, or rather 'Connie' as she now called herself saying that 'Constance' was too staid and dull, had gone to London.

She had written back to say that she had found herself some very interesting employment, although it seemed to Minella that her parents were a little vague as to what it was.

Only once did she remember Connie coming home, or rather coming to the Manor, and that was after her mother had died.

Her father was back from London and very depressed.

Connie appeared looking, Minella thought, quite unlike herself, and in fact so different that it was hard to recognise her.

19

She had grown slim, tall and very elegant, and was dressed so smartly that Minella stared at her in astonishment.

She had actually thought the young lady at the front door was somebody from the County calling on them, perhaps to commiserate with her father over her mother's death.

Then Connie asked:

"Do you not recognise me, Minella?"

There had been a little pause, then Minella had given a shout of excitement and flung her arms around her friend.

"How wonderful to see you!" she exclaimed. "I thought you had disappeared for ever! How smart you are, and how pretty!"

It was true. Connie looked very pretty with her golden hair that seemed much brighter than it had been a year ago.

With her blue eyes and pink-and-white complexion she looked every man's ideal of the perfect 'English Rose'.

Minella had taken Connie into the Drawing-Room wanting to talk to her and longing to find out what she was doing in London.

Then two minutes after she arrived her father had come in from riding, and after that it had been obvious that Connie only wanted to talk to him.

After a little while Minella had gone to make tea for them, leaving them alone, and only as she was leaving did Minella hear Connie say to her father:

"Thank you, My Lord, for all your kindness, and if you will do that for me I will be more grateful than I can possibly say in words."

"I can think of a better way for you to express yourself," Minella's father replied.

His eyes were twinkling and he was looking very dashing and, she thought, as if he had suddenly come alive.

"You will not forget?" Connie asked eagerly.

"I never forget my promises," Lord Heywood replied.

He and Minella walked with Connie to where she had left her pony-trap at the Blacksmith's forge.

"The reason I came here was to have my father's old horse re-shod," she explained.

She had looked, Minella noticed, at her father from under her eye-lashes as she spoke, and she had known it had only been an excuse to come to the Manor.

Then she had driven away looking absurdly smart and somewhat out-of-place in the pony-trap.

As they watched her go Minella had been perceptively aware that her father was thinking what a very small waist Connie had, and how tightly fitting her gown was.

Her neck seemed very much longer than it used to be, and she wore her hat at a very elegant angle on her golden hair.

"Connie has grown very pretty, Papa," she had said, slipping her arm through his.

"Very pretty!" he agreed.

She had given a little sigh.

"I often used to beat Connie at lessons," she said, "but she beats me when it comes to looks."

Her father had suddenly turned round to stare at her as if he had never seen her before.

He seemed almost to scrutinise her, then he said:

"There is no need for you, my poppet, to be jealous of the Connies of this world. You have the same loveliness that I adored in your mother. You are beautiful, and at the same time you look a lady, and that is very important."

"Why, Papa?"

"Because I would not have you taken for anything else!" her father said fiercely.

Minella did not understand, but because she was so closely attuned to her father she knew he did not wish her to ask him any questions. At the same time she was very curious to know what he had promised to do for Connie.

Now, feeling somehow she was intruding, and yet as if she could not resist it, she opened Connie's letter, and read:

"Dear Wonderful Lord of Light and Laughter,
How can I ever thank you for your kindness to me?
Everything worked out exactly as you thought it would,
and I have been given the job, and also I have moved into
this very comfortable little flat which—again thanks to
your 'pulling the right strings'—I can now afford.
I have always thought you wonderful, but never so
wonderful as you have been in helping me when I really
needed it.
One day perhaps I will be able to do something for you!
Until then, thank you! Thank you! Thank you!
Yours,
Connie."

Minella read the letter, then read it again. Then as she wondered what her father could have done to make Connie so grateful she read for the third time:
"One day perhaps I will be able to do something for you!"
It was too late for Connie to do anything for her father, but supposing, just supposing her gratitude might extend to her?

Connie might find her some employment which would save her from having to accept the only invitation she had received, which was to live with her Aunt Esther.

She looked at the address on the top of Connie's letter, but as she did not know London it meant nothing to her, although she had the idea that Connie was living somewhere in the West End.

"If I were in London, there must be dozens and dozens of jobs I could do," Minella told herself. "Perhaps I could look after children, teach them, or even, although perhaps Mama might disapprove, serve in a shop."

She had an idea, although she was not quite certain if

it was not just her imagination, that shop-girls were very poorly paid and had to work very long hours.

That might be true of the large shops which sold cheap goods and catered for the masses.

But there must be better-class shops which would be pleased to employ somebody lady-like.

Minella smiled to herself.

"I am sure Papa never envisaged that attribute would be commercially useful," she told herself.

But why not? Why not indeed?

It was surely better to be employed because one looked like a lady rather than common, brash, and perhaps not very prepossessing.

She went to the mirror to look at her face, thinking as she did so how very pretty Connie had looked when she had visited them nearly a year ago.

"Pink, white and gold!" Minella reflected to herself.

Then she looked at her own reflection critically.

Her face was the perfect oval her mother's had been. Her eyes were very large, and because she was slender they seemed to fill her whole face and it was difficult to look at anything else.

Scrutinising herself as if she was a stranger, she thought that her eyes were unusual, perhaps strange, because they were grey.

That was in some lights, but now they seemed to take on the colours around them, especially when the sun was shining, and there was a glint of gold in them.

At other times they were grey, the grey of a rain cloud except when her pupils expanded, and then her eyes would look dark, or rather a deep shade of purple.

"I wish I had blue eyes like Connie," Minella told herself.

She looked instead at her small straight nose, the curve of her lips, and decided she did look very, very young.

'Perhaps nobody would give me a position of responsibility,' she thought.

She wondered if there was anything she could do to make herself look older.

The way she did her hair was very simple.

It was the fashion to heap the long tresses of which every girl was very proud on the top of her head in a riot of waves and curls. Minella was aware they were often artificially contrived with hot curling-irons, and an elaborate arrangement of curling-rags took their place at night.

She however had no need of such aids, for her hair waved naturally and curled at the ends which almost reached her waist.

Because it was far too much bother when she was busy, or with her father, to do anything else, she merely brushed her hair, as her mother had taught her to do, a hundred times.

Then she twisted it into a chignon at the back of her head, and having pinned it firmly into place, forgot about it for the rest of the day.

Her father was punctilious about her hair when out riding.

"I cannot bear a woman to look untidy on a horse," Lord Heywood had said over and over again.

To be quite certain she did not upset him, Minella not only used dozens of hair-pins to keep her hair tidy out riding, but also wore a hair-net.

Her hair was not the same vividly gold colour that made Connie's head catch the eye, instead it was as pale as the first rays of the dawn.

Sometimes it appeared silver as if it had been touched by the moon, but in the sun it was the faint gold of newly ripening corn, or of the very first primroses peeping beneath their leaves in the hedgerows in Spring.

"I may look like a Lady," Minella said to her reflection in the mirror, "but rather a dull one, and I doubt if anybody in London would look twice at a little 'country mouse'."

Then, as if she could not bear to be depressed even by her own verdict on herself, she laughed.

As her laughter rang out in the empty room her whole face was transformed.

Her eyes shone and she looked, although she was completely unaware of it, very enticing. It was difficult to explain, but there was something exciting about her, as there had been about her father.

It was the excitement that Pan might have had, or perhaps one of the fairies who Minella had always believed as a child lived in the garden amongst the flowers.

It was an excitement that was as ethereal as the trees in the woods, the mists over the streams, and the stars when she could see them shining in through her window at night.

The stars had always had an attraction for her because her mother had once described to her how she was born just after midnight on New Year's Eve.

Almost as soon as she came into the world her father had opened the window to hear the Church-bells ringing in the New Year and had picked her up in his arms and carried her to listen to them.

"I remember," her mother said reminiscently, "seeing you and your father, my darling, silhouetted against the stars that filled the sky outside, and I thought how lucky I was to have two magical people here on earth belonging to me!"

"I would like to touch a star and hold it in my hand," Minella had said when she was a very little girl.

"That is what we all want," her mother smiled, "and perhaps one day, darling, that is what you will do."

"I have to believe," Minella said now, "that I was born under a lucky star, and what one believes comes true."

It was then she made up her mind.

It was daring, and something she would never have thought of in the past.

But she felt almost as if her father was beside her saying:

"Nothing ventured, nothing gained!"

"I will go to London," she decided. "I will see Connie and ask her to help me for Papa's sake."

25

As she spoke beneath her breath, but still audibly to herself, she knew it was a very tremendous, overwhelming decision, and also one that was rather frightening.

At the same time it was a risk worth taking, and what was the alternative?

Only to go tamely to the unutterable boredom of Bath and Aunt Esther.

CHAPTER TWO

MINELLA ARRIVED IN LONDON, and although it had been a slow and rather tiring journey, she had slept part of the time.

She had so much to do packing up everything in the Manor that belonged to herself, her father and her mother, that the night before she left she had fallen into bed absolutely exhausted and too tired to be unhappy.

She had made a bonfire in the garden of the things to be destroyed, and had packed everything else into the old-fashioned leather trunks she had dragged down from the attic.

The nearest farmer, who had always been fond of her father, had been kind enough to say he would store anything she did not wish to take with her.

"They'll be safe enough in the roof of one of m'barns," he said, "so don't ye go partin' with anything ye wants t'keep."

"I only wish I could keep the house," Minella replied impulsively.

"That's true, and th' village won't be the same without His Lordship galloping about, looking as if he owned th'world!"

Minella gave a little laugh.

It was a very apt description of her father, and however poor they had been, however many bills remained unpaid, her father had always seemed not only to look rich, but appeared to think life was an amusing joke.

It was an attitude he transmitted to other people, and she could understand why Connie had addressed him as the 'Lord of Light and Laughter'.

It seemed strange in a way that she should have addressed him in so familiar a fashion, but then Connie had always been, Minella felt, rather inclined to 'gush' at people.

It was something which she knew her mother thought a Lady should not do, and she had often talked to her about being restrained and self-controlled.

"It is best, dearest," she said in her soft voice, "to have a little reserve about your feelings, but at the same time to be warm, sympathetic, and of course, understanding."

"It sounds rather complicated, Mama."

"Not really," her mother answered, "and I want you to live up to your looks."

Minella had been surprised, and had not been quite certain what her mother meant.

Then she thought that once again, like her father, she was telling her she looked like a Lady, and must behave like one.

She knew that her mother's family who lived in the North of Ireland were very proud, and although they did not have much money or many possessions, they could trace their ancestry back to one of the Kings of Ireland.

"I wish you could be a Queen now, Mama!" Minella said once when she was small.

Her mother laughed, and her father who had been listening, said:

"She is a Queen! She is the Queen of my Heart, and that is a more important position than that of Queen Victoria alone on the throne of England!"

Minella had made up stories for herself in which her mother was a Queen and she was a Princess.

She had thought that one day she would meet a Prince who would look very much like her father, and they would be married and live happily ever afterwards.

But living in the Manor she saw no young men, and what little she knew of them was confined to her father's descriptions of the house-parties to which he was invited after her mother's death.

He described the friends he met at the race-meetings where he invariably lost money and at the parties he enjoyed in London, about which for some reason he was surprisingly reticent.

'I suppose I shall never have a chance of getting married,' Minella thought a little wistfully.

She knew that her mother had planned that somehow when she was eighteen she would contrive that she would go to some balls, and if it was humanly possible, be 'presented' at a 'Drawing-Room' in Buckingham Palace.

"Now I shall just have to earn my living, and forget all that," Minella told herself firmly as she packed away her mother's gowns.

Then she stopped.

Her mother's clothes were far smarter and in better condition than hers, even if they might be a little out-of-date.

Impulsively she took some of them from the huge weather-beaten trunk and put them instead into the smaller one that she was taking with her to London.

There were two very pretty Ball gowns which her mother had worn the very last time her father had taken her to London for an exciting week-end after saying he could not bear the boredom of the country any longer.

Her mother had come back looking happy and

relaxed, and even much younger than she had for a long time.

"We had a wonderful time, darling!" she said to Minella. "I am afraid we were very extravagant and Papa took me to dine out with his friends. We went to several Theatres and even very daringly to a Music-Hall!"

This meant very little to Minella who had never been to a Theatre, except once to see a Pantomime in the nearest town at Christmastime.

She had, however, listened to everything her mother had told her, and asked innumerable questions.

"Did you go to the Gaiety Theatre, Mama?" she enquired because she had heard her father talk about it.

"Yes, we went there," her mother replied, "and the Gaiety Girls are as lovely as goddesses, just as everybody says they are."

"Tell me about them, please, tell me about them!" Minella begged.

Her mother had described how they had travelled to the Theatre in a hansom cab.

"It was more exciting than going in a brougham," she said, "and we had a box, which again was very extravagant. It is difficult to explain how glamorous the Theatre is, how exquisite the scenery, and I have been humming the music ever since!"

"Did you enjoy it too, Papa?"

"Every moment," her father replied, "but I can tell you there was nobody on the stage as beautiful as your mother, even though they looked as though they had floated down from Olympus."

Because everything they told her had stayed in Minella's mind, she had said to her father when they were out riding:

"Why are the Gaiety Girls more attractive than the actresses in other Theatres, Papa?"

Her father thought for a moment. Then he said:

"I think because they have a grace and beauty and an aura of femininity which is every man's ideal. When he

29

sees them on the stage they make him feel that he is very much a man. And that, my dear, is the story of Adam and Eve since the beginning of time."

This was in fact incomprehensible to Minella, but she knew her father well enough to be aware that he liked women to be very feminine as her mother was.

He always made a point of correcting her if he thought she was behaving in any other way.

"Do not shout like that!" he had said sharply once when a boy had run across the road in front of her horse and Minella had called out to him to be more careful.

"I was afraid I might knock the silly child over," she said.

"You could have said the same thing in a much more pleasant manner."

She had looked at her father in surprise, and he had added:

"I want you to be perfect, my darling, just as your mother is, so that one day some lucky man will thank me for all the trouble I have taken over you."

"You mean the man I shall marry?"

"Of course," he replied. "Who else? And make no mistake, whoever is your husband will have gained himself a prize!"

"Suppose I fall in love with somebody who does not fall in love with me?"

"I think that is unlikely, and if I find any young whippersnapper trifling with your emotions, I will knock his head off!"

Her father spoke fiercely, and Minella had thought it thrilling to have a father who cared so much for her and was ready to fight like a Knight in her defence.

Now, she thought, her father was no longer there, and she would have to look after herself.

As the train drew nearer and nearer to London she began to think she had made a mistake.

London was very large and frightening, and from the train she could see row upon row of houses stretching away into what seemed an infinity.

"I should have gone to Aunt Esther's," she told herself.

Then logically she reasoned that if things did not work out in London as she hoped they would, there was always Aunt Esther waiting for her.

She had written a very tactful letter thanking Lady Banton for her kind invitation and saying she had not yet made up her mind exactly what she would do, but intended staying with friends for a few weeks.

She had known her Aunt would be curious, but as she gave no address there would be nothing she could do about it.

"If Connie will not help me," Minella told herself, "then I must find some cheap, respectable lodging-house while I can look around."

She was sure Connie would be able to recommend one, and if not, she thought the most sensible thing to do would be to go to the nearest Vicarage and ask the Vicar for assistance.

That was the sort of thing one did in the country, and although it might be different in London, there would be Churches, and if there were Churches there would be Vicarages and it therefore followed there would be a Vicar and who else should one turn to in time of trouble?

"I shall be all right," Minella assured herself.

At the same time there was an uncomfortable fluttering feeling inside her breast which told her she was very nervous.

The noise and confusion on the station was an ordeal in itself, but an elderly porter took pity on her and asked if he could help her.

"I have two trunks in the van," she said. "My name is Clinton-Wood."

"I'll get them for ye, Miss," he said. "Now stand 'ere where I can find ye again, and don't take no notice of anybody as speaks to yer."

He did not wait for her reply but pushed his trolley

31

towards the van and she thought it was a strange thing
to say.

Who was likely to speak to her? she wondered.

Then she thought perhaps he was speaking of pick-
pockets about whom she had read, and she held tightly
onto the leather bag that had belonged to her mother.

It did not contain a great deal of money. She was too
sensible for that, and had put most of the £100 which
Mr. Mercer had given her into the Bank.

But she had to have enough to cover her expenses,
and she knew every penny was of vital importance.

She therefore held her bag with two hands and
waited until the porter returned with both her trunks
on his trolley.

"There y'are, Miss," he said. "Now, wot do ye want to
do?"

Minella took out the piece of paper from her handbag
on which she had written Connie's address.

"I wish to go there, please. Is it far?"

The porter read the address carefully.

"It'll cost ye a shillin'," he said, "and yer give the man
two pence for his-self."

"Thank you for telling me," Minella replied. "I am
afraid of making mistakes, as I have never been in London before."

"That's wot I thought," the porter said. "Yer looked
lorst an' frightened. Why didn't ye stay in the country,
where ye belongs?"

"I have to find work."

The porter was silent for a moment as he pushed his
way through the crowds. Then he said:

" 'Ave ye got someun to 'elp yer?"

"I . . . I hope so."

"Well, yer'd better be careful," he said. "I've got a
daughter yer age, an' I'm always a-worryin' abaht her.
London ain't the right place for young, pretty girls, an'
that's a fact!"

"But we have to eat!" Minella said. "And in my case,
that means I have to work."

"Well, just ye be careful of wot yer gets up to," the porter said, "an' don't do nothing yer father wouldn't approve of."

"No, of course not," Minella agreed.

He found her an old, rather dilapidated-looking hackney-carriage with a horse which seemed too tired to pull anything.

"This'll be cheaper than one of 'em smarter ones," he said as he heaved her trunks up beside the driver.

When he opened the door for Minella to climb in she asked:

"Please, will you tell me what I should give you? I do not want to make a mistake."

"That's all right," the porter replied. "If yer didn't ask me, I'd have expected thrupence for what I've done for yer, but as it is, yer keep it. Yer're gonna need it yerself. Money soon goes in this 'ere place!"

"You are very kind," Minella said. "Thank you very much for all you have done for me."

She held out her hand and the porter shook it. Then he said:

"Remember wot I tells yer, and be a good girl!"

"Yes, of course," Minella answered.

She waved at him as the Cabby drove off and thought how kind he was.

Then she realised she must look very young and countrified for the porter to be so protective towards her.

"I hope Connie will not be ashamed of me," she murmured.

She remembered how smart Connie had looked the last time she had come home, and she thought it strange that her father had not told her that he had seen her when he was in London.

'It was unlike Papa to be so secretive,' she thought and wondered if he had any reason for it.

The Cabby seemed to drive for a very long way through the crowded streets.

Looking out of the window, Minella was fascinated by the variety of vehicles that she could see everywhere.

Most of all she found herself riveted by the smart carriages and the broughams drawn by two horses, wearing, she was sure, bearing-reins which she considered cruel.

They were driven by two men on the box, wearing crested top-hats and extremely smart liveries.

There were also the hansoms her father had described to her so often, but which she had never before seen.

She laughed at their sloping fronts with the driver high over the roof, their large wheels and the fast pace at which they could travel.

It made her feel that London was as exciting as her father had always thought it to be.

She longed to be able to travel in a hansom, but was sure it would be incorrect for a Lady to travel alone and that one should be accompanied by a very elegant man wearing a shining top-hat slightly on the side of his head.

After they had driven quite a long way down very crowded streets in which there was so much to see that Minella kept looking excitedly from side to side, they turned into a much quieter one.

The carriage stopped outside a high, rather ugly building with steps up to the front door and railings half-hiding the basement beneath it.

The Cabby got down to open the door.

"Shall I carry yer trunks in, Miss?" he asked.

"Will you wait one moment, please?" Minella asked. "I may not be able to stay here."

"That's awl-rite," he answered, "but don't be long. I wants to be orf 'home.'"

"I will be as quick as I can," Minella promised.

She ran up the steps and rang the bell thinking that Connie lived in a very grand house.

It took some minutes before a rather slovenly maid in

a dirty apron and her cap crooked on her untidy hair, opened the door.

"Yus?" she asked in an uncompromising voice.

"Does Miss Connie Langford live here?" Minella enquired.

The maid jerked her thumb upwards.

"Second floor," and without saying any more she hurried back down the narrow stairs which obviously led to the basement.

Rather surprised at such an abrupt reception, Minella climbed quickly up the stairs passing the First Floor where there were two doors, each having a card tacked onto it bearing different names.

It was then she understood that this house contained flats, and on the Second Floor must be the flat for which Connie had thanked her father.

When she got there there were two doors and she went to the first one and saw it had a card containing a man's name.

Then on the second written in Connie's own hand was the name she was seeking: *Miss Connie Langford.*

Now she felt more nervous than she had before, but realising the Cabby was waiting for her she raised the small brass knocker which was above the card.

The noise she made did not sound very effective and because she was afraid Connie would not be at home she waited for a few moments, then knocked again, this time more loudly.

Now she heard footsteps and a minute later the door opened and to her relief Connie stood there.

"What do you want?" she asked.

Then as Minella stared at her for a moment unable to speak Connie exclaimed:

"Minella! It cannot be! What are you doing here?"

"I have come to ask you for your help, Connie."

"My help? Why? Is your father with you?"

"Papa is . . . dead. Did you not . . . know?"

For a moment Connie stared at her as if she could hardly believe what she had heard. Then she said:

"Dead—I do not believe it!"

"He died a few weeks ago from a . . . poisoned hand."

"But he was—here in London—and I have never known him so—so—"

Connie stopped.

"We cannot stand here talking about it," she said. "Come in."

"I have come to London because I have to find work," Minella said, "and my luggage is downstairs."

For a moment Connie was silent. Then she said:

"You'd better tell the Cabby to leave it inside the front door."

"Yes, of course."

Minella did not wait to hear any more but hurried down the stairs as quickly as she could, feeling by this time the cabman would be growing impatient.

However he lifted her trunks off his cab and carried them up to the steps to dump them down just inside the hall on the linoleum which Minella noticed needed cleaning.

While he was doing so she got a shilling and four pennies out of her purse thinking she must give him an extra penny as he had waited so long.

He stared at the coins as if he was somewhat suspicious of them. Then he said:

"Can yer make it another twopence?"

"Yes, of course," Minella said. "You have been very kind."

He took the twopence from her, then looked up the stairs with what she thought was a disdainful glance before he said:

"If yer'll take me advice, which yer won't, yer'll find somewhere better t'stay than this!"

Minella looked at him in surprise.

"What is wrong with it?"

She thought he was about to say something, but then he changed his mind.

"Yer're too young fur this sort o' thing," he said. "Go

back to yer mother, that's where yer oughta be, an' forget London. It ain't th' place for th' likes o' yer!"

He did not wait for her to answer but clumped down the steps, climbed back on his box, and drove off without looking at her again.

As he drove away Minella gave a little sigh.

It seemed to her very strange that everybody in London seemed to think how young and foolish she was.

"It must be my clothes," she told herself, but knew it would be impossible for her to afford any others.

She had thought when her father died that she should wear mourning, but apart from one black gown which her mother had owned, which was too elaborate for her to wear in the country, she had nothing black.

After what Mr. Mercer had told her, she thought it would be an extremely stupid extravagance to spend any of her precious money on clothes.

She was acutely conscious that a few of her father's personal debts had still to be met sometime, and she felt it would seem almost like cheating to buy anything frivolous until they were paid off.

She was therefore feeling worried as she climbed up again to the second floor but just as she reached the open door where Connie was waiting she remembered once again that if she found herself in real trouble she could always go to Aunt Esther!

She was stupid to let what the Cabby had said depress her.

"Come in," Connie said, "and tell me everything from the very beginning. I can hardly believe you are here! And it is impossible to think that your father is dead!"

There was something about the tone of her voice that Minella did not miss and she said:

"I know how fond you were of him, Connie, even when you were a young girl, and I suppose I should have written to you before I came."

Connie did not say anything, but was leading the way

37

into a small but very surprisingly furnished Sitting-Room.

It was unlike any room Minella had ever seen before because it was so frilly and flouncy that it somehow seemed unreal.

A couch stood against one wall covered with cushions of various shapes and sizes, most of them frilled with lace or embroidered with sequins.

There were two arm-chairs, also frilled with cushions and the curtains which were deep pink had long fringes and were caught back at the sides of the windows with huge bows of pink ribbon.

The carpet was a riot of roses on a pale blue background while the walls, instead of being covered with pictures, had posters proclaiming what show was on at a Theatre.

Minella had time only for one quick bewildered glance at it all before Connie made her sit down in a chair and said in a serious tone:

"Have you really come here to find work?"

"I have to find some way of earning money," Minella replied simply, "or else go and live with my Aunt Esther in Bath."

"That would be the best thing for you to do."

"Oh, no, Connie! You know Aunt Esther! You met her when we were children, and I remember you saying how horrible she was because she had said your hair looked as if it had been dyed."

Connie laughed.

"Yes, I remember her. I suppose she was being prophetic. But after all, she is your Aunt."

"I know," Minella said, "but that does not make it any better."

Connie smiled.

"I understand your feelings, but tell me about your—father."

Because it hurt her to talk about it, Minella did not look at Connie as she told how her father had come back from London with an injured hand, and how it grew worse and worse until the poison spread and killed him.

As she finished speaking she looked at Connie and saw tears in her eyes.

"How could he—die?" Connie asked. "He was always so alive—always laughing and finding—everything such —fun."

"I know," Minella said, "and now I have nothing and nobody in the world except for Aunt Esther."

Connie rose and walked to the window to stand with her back to Minella.

"What do you want to do?" she asked.

Minella made a helpless little gesture with her hands.

"I really do not know, but I thought I would be able to find something in London, perhaps looking after children."

Connie did not answer and after a moment Minella said a little nervously:

"There must be work of some sort for somebody like me! After all, Connie, your father taught me, so you know I have been well educated."

"You are too young and too pretty."

"For what?"

"For London, for one thing!" Connie replied. "You might get into trouble on your own, Minella. You have always had somebody to look after you."

"I have had to be quite a lot on my own since Mama died," Minella said. "Papa kept going to London because he could not bear the loneliness of the house without her."

Connie did not speak for a moment. Then she said:

"Your father would not want you to be here."

"Why not?" Minella asked. "If he thought I was with you, Connie, or you were near me so that I could come to you if I got into difficulties, he would be glad, I am sure he would!"

Again there was a little silence, but Connie still had her back to her and Minella had no idea what she was thinking.

Then because she felt embarrassed she said:

"Listen, Connie, I do not want to be a trouble to you. If you would just suggest somewhere I could stay which would be respectable, and of course very cheap, I will look round on my own."

Connie turned from the window.

"Do you really think I would let you do that?" she asked. "Of course I have to look after you, but the difficulty is I do not know how."

"I would not want to be an encumbrance to you," Minella said humbly. "If you would just help me to try and find my feet. There must be some place for a girl like me."

"Far too many if you ask me!" Connie replied dryly. "Take off your hat!"

It seemed a strange thing to say, but Minella took off the hat which she was sure was old-fashioned, but had been the most comfortable one in which to travel.

She was wearing a pretty gown belonging to her mother and over it a cape which she had unclasped.

Now she removed both the hat and the cape and rising put them on a chair which stood just inside the door.

Then as she turned round pushing her hair which because it was so thick and curly, sprang naturally back into place, she looked at Connie apprehensively.

"You are too pretty—no, lovely!" Connie said. "It is too much responsibility."

"Oh, Connie, please help me!" Minella begged. "I will not be a nuisance, I promise you I will not."

"You do not understand," Connie answered. "What do you know about London? You can no more look after yourself in this place than a chick just hatched from its egg!"

She spoke quite crossly and because Minella felt suddenly that it was all hopeless and she should not have come here in the first place, tears came into her eyes.

"I . . . I am sorry, Connie."

Connie swept across the room and put her arms around her.

"Oh, no!" she said. "Poor little Minella! I do not want to be unkind to you, I want to help you. But it is going to be very, very difficult, and I do not know what your father would say if he knew."

For a moment Minella had hidden her face against Connie's shoulder and she felt her arms around her were very comforting.

Then she said:

"It is because of what you wrote to Papa that I am here."

She felt Connie stiffen before she asked:

"What did I write to your father?"

"I found a letter from you in his desk when I was tearing up his things in which you thanked him for helping you when you really needed it and you said; *'Someday perhaps I will be able to do something for you'.*"

Minella paused before she added:

"I thought that as you could not do anything for Papa, you might be willing to help his . . . daughter."

"I will, I swear I will!" Connie said impulsively. "But it is going to be very difficult, Minella."

Minella felt she must be speaking about money and she said:

"I will not try to cost you anything, Connie, and Mr. Mercer, who I expect you remember was Papa's Solicitor, has put aside £100 for me. If I am very careful with it, and earn something in the meantime, I am sure I can make it last for a long time."

Connie made a little sound that was a cross between a laugh and a sob, then she kissed Minella and said:

"I will try to think of something, and if I fail you, at least I will know I have done my best."

"You will help me?"

"I will help you," Connie said, "but God knows if I am doing the right thing!"

Minella flung her arms around her and kissed her cheek.

"Thank you, Connie, thank you! I knew you would not fail me, and I will do anything, I promise you, even if it means scrubbing floors, rather than go and live with Aunt Esther."

Connie laughed.

"I was not thinking of anything like that!"

Then in a more practical tone, as if she suddenly thought she was being inhospitable she said:

"As you have been travelling I expect you would like a cup of tea. Did you have any lunch?"

"Yes, I was sensible enough to realise that I must take some sandwiches with me," Minella replied, "and a woman in the same carriage who was, I think, a farmer's wife, gave me some milk to drink. It was not very nice as it was sour, but it was very kind of her."

Connie laughed but it was not an unkind sound.

Then she opened the Sitting-Room door and said:

"Come and look at the rest of my flat."

Next to the Sitting-Room was Connie's bedroom, and it was the bigger room of the two.

It was furnished in very much the same way as the Sitting-Room, full of frills and fringes.

The large bed, which Minella thought seemed quite unnecessary in such a small space, was draped with silk curtains of soft pink that were frilled and came down from a small corolla with gold angels dancing round it.

Again the curtains were tied back with huge satin bows and the pillows on the bed, Minella noticed with interest, had lace round the edges.

It was all very fantastic, but it was also exceedingly feminine and therefore something of which her father would have approved.

She thought her mother would think it was in extraordinarily bad taste, but it was so unlike anything she had ever seen before that she could not be sure.

"Now I will really surprise you!" Connie said.

She opened a door out of her bedroom and there was the tiniest bath Minella had ever seen.

It was so small that at first she did not realise it was a bath, then when she saw how proud Connie was of it she said how splendid it was to own one.

"It works on a geyser which keeps breaking down!" Connie said ruefully. "But at least I can keep clean and get the grease-paint off!"

She laughed as she spoke and Minella looked at her in surprise.

"Grease-paint?"

There was a little pause before Connie said:

"Surely you knew I was on the stage?"

"On the stage?" Minella repeated stupidly. "Do you mean you act?"

"That is a polite word for it," Connie laughed. "I am what is known as a 'Gaiety Girl'!"

Minella stared at her in utter astonishment.

"I had no idea! Do your father and mother know?"

"No, of course not, and you are not to tell them."

"As though I was likely to!" Minella replied. "They have never said what you did, which I thought was rather strange."

"You know as well as I do," Connie said, "there would be a tremendous rumpus if my father knew I was on the stage."

"I can understand that," Minella answered.

Then she gave a little cry as she said:

"Papa must have known, and he never told me!"

She thought Connie looked uncomfortable.

"I expect he was afraid of shocking you."

Then she added after a moment:

"I am not certain I did not ask him to keep it a secret."

Minella was silent before she said:

"Forgive me for asking, Connie, but I cannot help wondering. Did Papa help you to become a Gaiety Girl?"

"If you want the truth, yes, he did," Connie admitted. "He knew 'The Guv'nor' and 'pulled a few strings', and I am eternally grateful to him."

"Papa always helped everybody."

"That is true," Connie agreed, "and because he

43

helped me I am going to help you. The only difficulty is
—how?"

She did not wait for Minella to reply but went into
what seemed nothing more than a hole in the wall next
to the bathroom, but which she proudly described as
'my kitchen'.

This consisted only of a gas-ring, on which she could
boil a kettle, and Minella noticed too there was a sauce-
pan hanging on a hook on the wall.

There were a few plates, cups and saucers and Connie
started to boil the kettle searching among several tins for
the tea to put into the brown teapot which had a
chipped spout.

"Do you want anything to eat?" she asked. "I have
some biscuits somewhere."

"No, thank you, tea will be lovely!" Minella answered.

As she spoke there was a knock on the flat door.

"Oh, bother!" Connie said and walked a few paces
down the passage to open it.

Outside stood two young women and the moment she
saw them Minella felt quite certain they, too, were Gaiety Girls.

They were tall, well above average she thought, and
so outstandingly pretty that she found herself staring at
them almost rudely.

She had been so agitated arriving at Connie's flat that
she had not noticed that Connie was even more spectacular than when she had last seen her.

Her hair seemed to glow like the sun, her skin was so
pink-and-white that it reminded her of the roses in the
garden at the Manor.

Her lips were so red that Minella now realised that it
was not their natural colour.

Then she thought she had been stupid not to be
aware the last time she saw Connie that her face was
painted and powdered and she used lip salve.

Because she was in the country, it had been much less
evident than it was at the moment.

As she looked at the two young women who had just

arrived, she realised that their faces were definitely made-up and were unmistakably painted almost like the theatrical posters on the walls in Connie's Sitting-Room.

"Come in, Gertie, come in, Nellie," Connie was saying.

"We're a bit early," the one she had called Gertie replied, "but we've got some bad news for you!"

"Bad news?" Connie repeated automatically. "Now wait a minute, and I will introduce you to a friend of mine. Minella, this is Gertie, and Nellie, and they are both 'High Steppers' on the stage of the Gaiety, if you know what I mean!"

The two newcomers shrieked with laughter.

"I like your introduction, Connie! But I doubt if you thought it out yourself!"

"It was what Archie said the other night, and I thought it rather funny!" Connie admitted. "Come into the Sitting-Room. I am just making Minella a cup of tea."

"Tea?" Nellie said. "I could do with a drink! And you will want one too when you hear what we've got to tell you."

Connie was not listening, having gone into the tiny kitchen to pour the boiling water from the kettle into the teapot.

"You will find some milk somewhere," she said vaguely. "Put this on a tray and take it into the Sitting-Room, while I find the girls something else to drink."

As it was only just four o'clock Minella thought it was a strange time to be drinking.

But obediently she carried the small tray into the Sitting-Room and found a table on which to put it.

The two newcomers were standing in front of a mirror which hung on the wall between the posters and taking off their hats.

They were very different from any hats Minella had ever seen before.

Nellie's was covered with feathers, the one Gertie was

wearing had huge pink roses and lilies-of-the-valley arranged in a wreath round the broad crown.

Their hair was swept up on their heads in a mass of curls and when she looked at them Minella felt they might have stepped down on earth from a different planet.

Never had she imagined anybody could have such tiny waists or gowns fitting so tightly over their breasts.

In relation to their waists their hips seemed a magnificently rounded sweep, and their gowns billowed out at the hem showing when they lifted them a mass of lace which she thought must be on their petticoats.

They were so elegant, so graceful, that she remembered how her mother had said that the Gaiety Girls were like lovely goddesses, and thought the description was very apt.

They kept preening themselves in front of the mirror until Connie came into the room carrying a bottle of sherry and three glasses.

"My last bottle!" she said. "I must remember to tell Archie I want some more."

"He shouldn't let you get so low," Gertie said.

"He has given me a case of champagne which is what he likes himself," Connie replied, "but I do not think you want that at the moment."

"Certainly not," Nellie replied, "and it's not at all appropriate for the news we have for you."

This time Connie seemed interested.

"What are you talking about?" she asked. "What is this bad news?"

There was a little pause before Gertie said:

"Katy's ill!"

"I do not believe it!" Connie exclaimed.

"It's true. She's got a temperature of 103°!"

"Are you saying she is not going to be able to come this evening?" Connie asked.

"She can hardly see, let alone walk!" Gertie explained.

Connie sat down on the couch.

"I do not believe it! What on earth are we going to do?"

"That's what we've been asking ourselves all the time on our way here."

"It's a bit late to ask anybody else to join us who would be good enough for 'His Nibs'!" Nellie said.

There was silence before Connie asked:

"What about Gracie?"

"She's already booked and you know who with!"

"Oh, yes, I had forgotten."

"We thought of Lillie," Nellie went on, "but she's promised to dine with the Duke, and you know she's not going to give that up in a hurry!"

"No, of course not," Connie agreed, "and our host has never cared for Lillie. She is so affected, and I heard him say once that her laugh got on his nerves."

"Then what do you suggest we do?" Gertie asked, "call the whole thing off?"

"I am not going to do that," Connie replied angrily. "Archie is looking forward to it, and I know he would be furious!"

"Well, it's up to you," Gertie said. "You and Archie arranged the party in the first place, after 'Lord High and Mighty' told you to do so."

"I know that," Connie said, "and it was all so easy and straight-forward."

There was a little pause before Nellie said:

"If you ask me, he wanted a party because he finds Katy a bit of a bore, when he's alone with her."

"I think that is a very unfair remark," Connie said. "Katy suits him very well. And look at the things he has given her."

"All right, sorry I spoke!" Nellie said. "But I've a feeling in my bones that it is on the wane."

"I think you are wrong," Connie said, "don't you, Gertie?"

"To tell you the truth, I don't care one way or the other," Gertie replied. "I only know Harry was looking forward to the weekend and I wanted to have a chance to talk to him about a necklace I rather fancy."

As she spoke Connie turned to look at Minella as if she had forgotten she was there. Then she said quickly:

"This is very boring for my friend as she has not met any of the people about whom we are talking."

"She'll soon learn about the Earl!" Nellie said. "And if you are thinking of putting her in the show she'll quickly find out on which side her bread's buttered! That's if she wants to stay in it!"

Minella looked at Connie in bewilderment.

"I am sorry, dear," Connie said, "but when we get together we always talk 'shop'."

"Perhaps you would rather be alone," Minella suggested. "Shall I go into your bedroom?"

"I think it would be a good idea if you get your luggage brought up. I have just thought where you can stay, at least for the next three nights." ·

She rose as she spoke and said:

"As it happens, the room next door is available because the actor who lives there is on tour, and he gave me the key because I am watering his plants while he is away."

"If he is away you cannot ask him if he will mind my using his room," Minella said.

"Oh, do not worry about that," Connie answered airily. "If I do something for him, he will do something for me. Come on, I will open the door for you."

She went into the passage outside the Sitting-Room, picked up the key that was lying on a table and opening her front door walked across the landing to the door on the other side of it.

She opened it and Minella saw it was in darkness.

Connie crossed the room and lifted the blind and Minella was aware she was in what she had heard called a 'Bed-Sitting-Room'.

There was a couch rather like Connie's, a couple of chairs and a desk, and again the walls were covered by theatrical posters.

There were also stuck on the sides of them and be-neath them telegrams, cuttings from newspapers and a number of theatrical photographs.

"You will be comfortable enough here," Connie said, "and I shall be in the next room so you need not be afraid."

"You are . . . quite sure it is . . . all right?"

Connie smiled at her.

"Quite! Theatrical people are very generous, not like a lot of country folk who do not trust you across the doorstep in case you steal the mat!"

Minella laughed because she could not help it.

"Now, nip down the stairs," Connie said, "and shout for Ted who is in the basement, and he will carry up your luggage. Give him a penny. It is not worth any more. Then unpack what you need for the night. We will talk about things later before I go to the Theatre."

"Are you performing tonight?" Minella asked.

"Of course," Connie replied, "but I do not have to leave for another hour, so there is no hurry."

She turned as she spoke and walked back into her own flat.

As she went into the Sitting-Room Gertie and Nellie looked up at her and she said:

"Here's a nice kettle of fish! Now let us talk frankly. What are we going to do, girls?"

"We've just been talking about that," Gertie replied, "and we've come up with a solution, and a good one!"

"What is it?" Connie asked curiously.

"What about your friend taking Katy's place?" Nellie suggested. "She's pretty, and different."

"I think you are crazy!" Connie exclaimed.

"Why not?" Gertie asked. "If you ask me she's lovely in a different way from any of us, and that's the sort of thing His Lordship's always looking for!"

CHAPTER THREE

MINELLA WAS UNDOING one of her trunks to take out a nightgown and the other things she would need for the night when Connie came into the room.

Minella looked up at her apprehensively.

She had the distinct impression that Connie was going to say something that was upsetting, although why she should think so she had no idea.

Connie sat down on the couch, and said in a serious tone:

"Listen to me, Minella."

Minella, who was kneeling beside the trunk sat back on her heels.

"What is it, Connie?" she asked. "Am I in . . . the way? Do you want me . . . to go?"

"No, it is not that," Connie replied, "but I have an idea for you which you may dislike. If so, you are to say so quite frankly."

"Of course," Minella agreed, "after all, we have always been frank with each other, you and I, or at least we were in the past."

"Yes, of course," Connie said rather hastily, "but this is different."

"How?" Minella asked.

She had the feeling that something was wrong, and linked her fingers together, her eyes raised to Connie's an anxious expression in them.

She looked so very young as she did so that Connie said:

"I am sure I ought not to suggest this to you, but the girls think it's a good idea, and I do not like leaving you here alone while I am away."

"You are going away?" Minella enquired.

"Only tonight until Monday afternoon, and you would be alone in London, where you have never been before."

"I am sure I will be all right."

At the same time she thought it would be rather frightening having nowhere to go and not knowing what she could do while Connie was away.

"It is like this," Connie began, "after the show tonight we are all going to stay in the country with the Earl of Wynterborne."

"After the show?" Minella exclaimed in surprise.

"It ends about ten-thirty, and there will be a special train waiting for us at Paddington."

Minella's eyes widened, but she did not say anything and Connie went on:

"We will be at his Castle before midnight, and that is quite early—for us, anyway!"

She smiled with what seemed rather an effort. Then she continued:

"I arranged the party because he asked me to. The girls you have just met are going and there is also Beryl, who is very lovely. But the whole thing was to be a surprise for Katy."

Minella found all the names rather bewildering, but she tried to follow what Connie was saying.

"Katy is the Earl's 'Special', so to speak, but at the last moment, as you heard, she has fallen ill."

"That must be very disappointing, not only for her, but for you."

"It is," Connie agreed, "and it puts me in a fix. So what I am suggesting, Minella, is that you take her place!"

"Me?"

"Yes, you. It would not be the same for the Earl of course, but it will make us even numbers, and things would be very difficult and uncomfortable if we were anything else."

Minella drew in her breath.

"But surely he could ask one of his other friends? Or there must be lots of yours who would love to go."

"Not at the last moment," Connie replied, "and I have no time to rush around trying to find somebody. So help me, Minella, as I am trying to help you."

"Of course, I will do anything you ask me to do, but as the Earl has never met me, perhaps he will not want me as his guest."

"I am sure he will be delighted," Connie said quickly.

Minella looked down at her trunk.

"I am afraid my clothes, even though I brought Mama's, will not be very suitable."

"That is one of the things I am going to talk to you about," Connie said, "and you are not to be offended."

"Why should I be offended?"

"Because," Connie replied, "if you come to this party, and I shall be very grateful if you will, you cannot come as yourself."

Minella looked puzzled.

"You see," Connie went on, " 'Minella Clinton-Wood' has no right to be associating and certainly not staying with a lot of Gaiety Girls."

"Why not?"

"Because it is something your mother would not approve of," Connie replied.

Minella knew this was true, although she had only just thought of it.

It struck her for the first time that because Connie was a Gaiety Girl, her mother would not have wanted her to turn to Connie for help.

But then, how could she have known when she came to London that Connie was on the stage?

And why should she be any different from what she

had been when they were children together and shared their lessons.

Almost as if Connie was following her thoughts she said:

"It is not something we can argue about, Minella, and just as we cannot tell my mother and father what I am doing, you must certainly not let your host the Earl of Wynterborne know you are your father's daughter."

"Did he know Papa?" Minella asked.

There was a little silence and she thought Connie was thinking before she answered.

"I expect so. Everybody knew your father and loved him, and I am sure they belonged to the same Club."

Then, as if this was something she did not want to go on discussing, she said:

"So, if you come to Wyn Castle, you must come as my friend, and perhaps a young actress who is hoping to go on the stage at the Gaiety. They all want that."

"I know nothing about the stage."

"I know," Connie said, "but he is not likely to ask you questions about it, and you will just have to talk about other things. Anyway, men always like to talk about themselves."

Minella laughed.

"That is what Mama used to say."

"She was quite right, and the Earl has a great deal to talk about. I am told the Castle is magnificent, and his horses win all the best races."

She paused before she added:

"He is very, very rich, and very important to us because he puts a great deal of money into all George Edwardes' productions."

It was then Minella looked puzzled and said:

"George Edwardes?"

"He is the Guv'nor, as we call him, and as far as we are concerned his word is law."

She was silent for a moment before she explained:

"And the Guv'nor listens to the Earl, so there you have it in a nutshell."

"I understand," Minella said. "At the same time, Connie, I do not think I ought to go on the stage."

"You would be lucky if you got the chance!" Connie replied. "What I am asking you to do now is to act the part of an aspiring young actress for just two nights. After that, you need never see the Earl again."

"I am afraid I may make a . . . mess of things, then you will be . . . angry with me."

"You will not make a mess of anything if you do as I tell you," Connie said firmly, "and that means we have to go down to the Theatre at once."

"Am I to come with you?"

"Of course you are," Connie answered. "We have to dress you, for one thing. We cannot take you to the Castle looking as you do now."

Minella did not ask: "Why not?" because she already knew the answer.

She got up slowly from the floor and said:

"Perhaps, Connie, I should stay here. I will be all right, and I will not even go out, if you would rather I did not, but just stay inside the house until you return."

"You will do nothing of the sort!" Connie said. "Besides, have you forgotten? You are helping me! We have to take somebody with us to amuse the Earl!"

"Suppose I do not . . . amuse him?"

"You must try," Connie replied seriously. "You are not really his type, but every man likes a change once in a while, and he is not likely to be a nuisance considering he is taken up with Katy at the moment."

"A nuisance?" Minella questioned, not understanding.

"There is no time to answer a lot of questions now," Connie said abruptly, "but we have just one thing to decide, and that is what you should call yourself."

"Do I have to have another name?"

"Of course you do! The girls next door have no idea who you are, and the Earl might be aware that 'Clinton-Wood' is your father's family name."

"Then what shall I call myself?" Minella asked help-lessly.

"Let me think . . ." Connie said. "Minella . . . Minella . . . 'Minella Moore' . . . that will do. It sounds theatrical and it is also easy to remember. We all like to have names the men will not forget."

Then as she suspected there would be a question in Minella's eyes she said:

"Now remember, you are 'Minella Moore', you have only just come to London, and you must say nothing or as little as possible about yourself. Do you understand?"

"I will try to remember," Minella said humbly.

"I will get you a small case," Connie said rising from the ground, "just put in it what you need for the night, and we will find everything else for you down at the Theatre."

She left the room before Minella could say any more and for the moment she only stared after Connie in a bewildered fashion.

Then suddenly, because it was all so strange and un-expected, she gave a little laugh.

At least this was an adventure, at least this was far more exciting than setting off tamely for Bath to live with Aunt Esther!

"It is just the sort of thing Papa would have enjoyed and would make a joke about," she told herself, "and I must forget that Mama might not approve."

Quickly she knelt down again and took out a night-gown from the trunk, which was one of her mother's best and most attractive.

Her mother had kept it for the special occasions when she went to London with her father, as she had also kept a very pretty négligé of blue silk, trimmed with lace.

'At least Connie will not be ashamed of me in these!' Minella thought.

She found a pair of bedroom slippers and had put them in a neat pile by the time Connie came back into the room.

"I do not have a small case," she said, "and anyhow

you will have to pack the things we get from the Theatre, so here is a large one which will take everything,
and you had better empty your hats out of your hat-box
and bring that too."

She had gone again before Minella could answer her.
Then she heard her talking to the girls in the Sitting-
Room and she thought too they were laughing.

'I am helping Connie as she wants me to do,' Minella
thought to herself, 'and I am sure that cannot be wrong,
as Papa always helped everybody.'

By the time they reached the Theatre Minella was
feeling bewildered and even more apprehensive than
she had been at first.

She had put her small collection of things for the
night into the large case which Connie had brought her,
then was told they all had to hurry because there was so
much to do on her account.

"Come on, come on!" Connie kept saying. "You know
unless we get Natty in a good mood she will not let us
have the best gowns, and it is essential that Minella
should look the part."

"Very essential!" Nellie agreed.

Then as if to reassure Minella she added kindly:

"You'll be all right. With a face like yours anything'll
look fine on you!"

"Don't you believe it," Gertie interposed. "Clothes are
half the battle, and it's no use pretending otherwise!"

She preened herself in front of the mirror as she put
on her hat, and as she did so Connie said to Minella:

"You will have to wear a hat to go to the Theatre.
Have you got anything better than the one you came
in?"

"I am afraid you will not think so," Minella answered.
"It was one of Mama's."

"Your mother always looked lovely in everything,"
Connie smiled. "Put it on, nobody will see you if we get
there early enough."

Hurrying and shouting at Ted to come up and carry

down the case, they finally got downstairs where there was a hackney-carriage waiting for them.

The case was put up in front next to the driver, and the four girls piled in, Minella feeling that she was like a humble sparrow in a cage with three exotic humming-birds.

Because they apparently thought it a joke that they would surprise the Earl, they talked about him all the way to the Theatre.

"If you want the truth he frightens me," Nellie said.

"That's only because you're not his type!" Gertie retorted. "He's never been interested in brunettes."

Nellie tossed her head.

"That's no loss, as far as I'm concerned! I'm quite happy with Charlie. Did I tell you, he's giving me a sable wrap for the winter!"

"No!" Gertie ejaculated. "I don't believe it!"

"That's what he says," Nellie answered, "and you can be sure I'll keep him up to it. I need something warmer than I had last year."

"We were talking about the Earl," Connie said, as if she was nervous as to what Minella would make of this conversation.

"Yes, of course," Gertie said. "Now to begin with, Minella, you will find him one of the handsomest men you have ever seen. He is also cynical, disillusioned and blasé."

"A very good description," Connie laughed, "but I do not believe you thought it up yourself."

"That's what Archie said about him the other day," Gertie replied, "But what he's got to be blasé about, I don't know!"

"I'd be quite prepared to be blasé if I had his money!" Nellie said. "Even Charlie's jealous of him, especially when he won the Goodwood Stakes and beat Charlie's horse by a neck!"

She gave a sigh as if at some rather unpleasant memory, then said to Minella:

"Charlie would have been very annoyed if the party

this weekend had been called off, so we are very, very grateful to you, Minella!"

"That's true," Gertie said. "We're grateful, and Beryl'll be too, when we tell her how kind you've been."

When they arrived at the Theatre, the stage-door was, Minella thought, very disappointing.

Having heard from her father about the 'Stage-Door Johnnies' she was expecting something spectacular.

But it was only an ordinary door in a side alley and a middle aged man with a large moustache who was sitting in what looked like a box, growled "Good evening!" at them and seemed surprised that they had arrived so early.

"Where is Natty?" Connie asked him.

" 'Ow should I know?" he replied. "I expec' she's in the wardrobe room."

"Tell her we want to see her, there's an angel," Connie said, "and it is urgent, very urgent!"

Minella thought the man was about to say he was too busy, or it was not his job, but Gertie bent forward and said in a low voice:

"It concerns the Earl of Wynterborne!"

"Oh, in that case . . ."

He came out from his little office and started walking ahead of them.

As if she thought she should explain to Minella what was happening, Connie said:

"That is James Jupp. We have to keep in with him or none of our flowers ever get past him. He was a Sergeant-Major in the King's Royal Irish Hussars, and he has never forgotten it."

Gertie laughed.

"That's true! Beryl quarrelled with him once and never got any of her flowers for a week!"

They all laughed, and Minella thought they sounded like a lot of school-children dealing with a rather difficult teacher.

Then they were climbing an iron staircase, and as the walls on either side of it were badly in need of paint,

Minella thought again that the Gaiety was not as glamorous as she had expected it to be.

At the end of a long, rather dingy corridor Connie opened a door which bore her name on the outside, also Gertie's and Nellie's.

"This is our dressing-room," she said, "and it is a good thing we are all together. We do not want anybody else to know what we are doing."

"No, of course not," Nellie agreed.

The girls took off their hats, and Minella saw there was a large screen across one end of the room and a clothes-horse on which were hung a number of the most beautiful gowns she could ever imagine.

There was a long shelf which was littered with what she thought must be grease-paint and all the other things necessary for them to make-up their faces. It was in front of a mirror that was lit by lights on each side and above. In the corners of the mirror were stuck telegrams and cards, and at the end of the room by the screen was a profusion of flowers which scented the whole room.

There were baskets of orchids, lilies and carnations, and because it was the right time of year the flaming colours of dahlias.

Minella had never seen so many lovely flowers and was staring at them when the door opened and a small, middle-aged woman, very thin and dressed in grey, came hurrying in.

"Now what's gone wrong?" she asked sharply before any of them could speak. "If you've torn one of those new gowns, I think I shall kill you!"

"It's not that, Natty," Connie said. "We want your help, and we want it urgently."

"Then 'want' must be your master!" the woman said. "I've got too much to do at the moment to take on anything more."

"But you have to, Natty, because Katy is ill!"

"Ill? Do you mean she is not appearing tonight?"

"She has a temperature of 103°!"

"Well, I hope someone's told the Stage Manager," Natty said, "or there will be hell's bells to pay!"

"I am not concerned with the Stage Manager," Connie said, "but with the substitute I have found to take Katy's place at Wyn Castle tonight."

"Substitute?" Natty questioned.

"I told you we were all going away after the show, and His Lordship is not going to be pleased to find that Katy is not with us."

"Rather you than me when he finds she's missing," the woman remarked.

"That is why we had to have a substitute," Connie explained as if she was patiently trying to get her point across.

Natty's shrewd dark eyes were turned towards Minella.

"This is Minella Moore," Connie said, "and as you see, she has nothing suitable to wear."

"And you expect me to dress her?"

"Of course we do, and you know how important it is!"

Connie counted on her fingers.

"She needs two evening-gowns, something pretty for tomorrow morning, something elaborate for the afternoon, and at least one change on Monday before we come back late in the afternoon."

"I suppose you wouldn't like a steam yacht and half the jewels in Cartier's as well?" Natty said sarcastically.

"We will take anything you have got," Connie retorted, "and you can see she hasn't got a hat to her name."

As if the funny side of it suddenly struck her, Natty laughed.

"I wouldn't do this for anybody else in the world except the Earl," she said. "But as Katy's ill . . ."

Saying no more, she walked forward to stand in front of Minella and stare at her in a way that would have been an embarrassment if she had not been aware that Natty was not looking at her face, but at her body.

"She's too short for your things," she said at length.

"I know that!" Connie answered.

"Well, I suppose I can find something," Natty said at length, "but don't expect miracles!"

She walked out of the room as she spoke, shutting the door noisily behind her.

Connie clapped her hands.

"We have won!" she cried. "I thought she might be more difficult."

"One never knows with Natty," Nellie said.

Connie turned to Minella.

"You had better undress," she said, "she will be back soon, and there may have to be a few alterations to what you are to wear, and we do not have very much time."

"That's true," Gertie agreed.

Connie saw that Minella was looking embarrassed and said:

"If you go behind the screen you can hang up your own clothes there, and we can collect them on Monday when we come back."

Minella went behind the screen, found there was a clothes' rail and a chair there and began to take off her gown.

She was just hanging it up when Connie put her head round the screen to say:

"She will bring you some under-clothes as well, and they are very much prettier than what you have on now."

Minella was surprised!

She did not know that George Edwardes spared no expense where his productions were concerned.

Every Gaiety Girl not only had the most exquisite and the most spectacular gowns in London, but what they wore underneath was just as beautiful, elaborate and trimmed with real lace.

Quality was what he set out to provide, and the quality which his Gaiety Girls displayed had never been seen on the stage before.

Minella was aware of this by the time she found her-

self wearing silk stockings and a silk chemise trimmed
with real lace.

She was also given a corset which gave her such a tiny
waist that Natty muttered beneath her breath that every
gown she wore would have to be taken in.

The gowns were certainly beautiful! Natty and an as-
sistant had brought half-a-dozen for Connie's and the
other girls' approval, and every one of them seemed as
if it had been specially designed for Minella.

"No gaudy colours!" Natty said crisply. "She's too
young, and they would kill that fair hair of hers. Which
is natural, I would like to point out!"

She gave a rather spiteful glance as she spoke at Connie's golden hair, Gertie's red curls, and Nellie's dark
ones.

"I always said, Natty, you were an artist in your own
way," Connie said flatteringly.

"That's what I try to be," Natty replied, "but one
can't 'make a silk purse out of a sow's ear!' "

"If you're referring to me," Gertie said, "I shall throw
something at you!"

"You dare," Natty said, "and I'll see you don't get a
new gown until after everybody else has had one!"

Minella realised they were only joking as they sparred
with each other, but seeing how marvellous the girls
looked while Natty appeared to be nothing more than a
senior servant it was hard to understand.

She tried on gown after gown until, after travelling all
day, she began to feel very tired.

Finally she was hooked into a very elegant evening-
gown in which she was told she was to travel.

She looked at herself in the mirror, rather dismayed
at how *décolleté* the gown was, although it was swathed in
white chiffon which formed tiny sleeves over her arms.

The rest of the gown was also white, embroidered all
over with diamanté, and fitted her closely, almost like a
second skin to her body, until it swirled out from her
knees in frill upon frill of diamanté studded chiffon like
the waves of the sea.

"Surely," she said hesitatingly, "I shall look very . . . strange in the train dressed like this?"

"You'll look all right," Natty replied. "It has a black velvet cloak to wear over it trimmed with white fox, and you needn't put the ospreys on your head until you arrive at the Castle."

"Ospreys!" Minella exclaimed.

"I'll give you a chiffon scarf to wear over your hair until you get there," Natty said finally, "and you can put the ospreys in your hat-box."

"And you'll have two hats for tomorrow and two for Monday," Connie chimed in.

"And the *Koh-i-noor* for luck!" Natty snapped.

This made them laugh because the previous year, which had been Queen Victoria's Diamond Jubilee, the most exciting present she had received and which had been extolled in all the newspapers was the *Koh-i-noor* Diamond which it was said was now to be added to the Royal Crown.

It was now growing late and there was a continual noise outside the dressing-room, besides people who kept popping their heads in to say something to the girls, then disappearing again.

They were beginning to change into the clothes they wore on the stage when a dresser who was called 'Emily' appeared and was told by Connie to make-up Minella's face.

"Can't she do her own?" Emily asked.

"No, and she can't fly to the moon either!" Connie answered. "You do it now, and I will do it while we are at the Castle."

"It's always me as has extras!" Emily grumbled, and Minella said quickly:

"I am sorry to be such a bother."

"That's all right," Emily said good-humouredly, "it's a bit tricky if you're not used to it."

"Don't overdo it," Connie warned. "Natty has dressed her as what she is, someone young, and she is to appear as a rosebud, not a full-blown rose!"

"I know my job!" Emily snapped. "One thing's for sure, she's not going to look like any of you!"

"Good!" Nellie retorted. "We don't need more competition. There's quite enough about already!"

They laughed at this, then there was a tap on the door and without waiting for an answer a man put his head round.

"May I come in?"

"Oh, Archie," Connie exclaimed, "I am so glad you are here! I want you to help us."

"Always ready to oblige!"

The man who was speaking came into the dressing-room and Minella thought he looked very impressive.

He was tall, dark and she guessed his age to be about thirty-five. He wore a gardenia in his buttonhole, and two large pearl studs in his stiff white shirt.

He looked, she thought, rather as her father had done when going anywhere important, and she felt a sudden longing for him that brought the tears to her eyes.

"Now, careful!" Emily said sharply. "If your eyes water, your eye-lashes will run!"

Minella had forgotten that the dresser had put a little mascara on her eye-lashes, making her eyes look even more enormous than they were already.

When she looked in the mirror she had to admit that Emily had been very skilful.

Her skin seemed much whiter than it usually was and there was just the faintest hint of colour in her cheeks. But her face did not have the rather gaudy poster effect she had noticed on Connie and the other girls.

"Now, listen, Archie," Connie was saying. "Katy's ill and cannot come."

"Do you mean to say the party is off?" Archie said.

"No, and it is not going to be spoilt either. I have persuaded a friend of mine to come with us who I am sure will prove a very good understudy."

"Cosmo will not like it!" Archie said positively.

"There is nothing he can do about it," Connie

replied, "and it would be worse with odd numbers—you know that!"

"Yes, I suppose so," Archie agreed.

"So come and meet my friend and tell her how grateful we all are to her for 'saving the side'," Connie suggested.

She pulled Archie by the arm across to where Minella was sitting in front of the mirror and as she saw his reflection smiling at her she smiled back.

"Let me introduce you properly," Connie said. "Minella, this is Lord Archibald Connington—Miss Minella Moore!"

"How do you do!" Minella said.

"I have never met you before," Archie replied, "but I am delighted that you have been kind enough, as Connie said, to 'save the side'. There is nothing worse than a party with one woman short."

"Except when it's a man short!" Nellie flashed.

Before he had time to reply two other men joined them, and they all were told the sad story of Katy's illness and how Minella was to take her place.

Because she was not introduced to them properly it took a little time for Minella to realise that Harry, who apparently was Gertie's partner, was Sir Harold Parker, and Charlie, who was Nellie's, was Lord Skelton.

There was a knock on the door and a boy's voice called:

"Five minutes, Ladies!"

"We have to go," Connie said. "Now listen, Archie, you and the others take Minella with you in the box. She has never seen a show at the Gaiety, and it is high time she did!"

"Yes, of course," Archie agreed, "we will look after her. Don't worry, Connie."

"And you are not to frighten her! This is her first visit to London and she is finding it all rather bewildering!"

"Her first time in London? Good Heavens!" Archie ejaculated.

With a flutter of their skirts and leaving behind them

the scent of an exotic perfume which mingled with the fragrance of the flowers, Connie, Nellie and Gertie left the dressing-room to hurry down the iron staircase towards the stage.

"We had better go to the box," Archie said.

Harry and Charlie, who had been looking speculatively at Minella, as if they were wondering about her and how she had appeared so suddenly, agreed.

From the moment Minella found herself in the box in the Gaiety Theatre she felt she had stepped into a dream.

Not only was the Theatre itself far more impressive, far more brilliant and far lovelier than she had ever imagined, but once the curtain rose she knew she was seeing a vision of beauty and glamour!

She was also seeing an institution that was understandably famous all over the civilised world.

She had read somewhere, or perhaps her father had told her, that the Gaiety was not only synonymous with success, but gave London melody, laughter and glorious girls.

That was what she was watching, and it was difficult to think, but only to feel, that in some strange way she was part of the glory it portrayed.

She was seeing, although it took her sometime to be aware of it, a show that had been produced four months earlier, called: *The Runaway Girl*.

It was to be one of the greatest successes the Gaiety ever had, but for the moment Minella was not discriminating enough to be aware of anything but the beauty of every scene which took place in Corsica or Venice.

The music seemed to become part of every breath she drew, as did the exquisite dancing of two great artistes, who Archie informed her were the 'smash hit' of the show.

She was carried away by everything that was sung, every moment that was made, every word that was spoken.

Only when finally the whole audience rose to sing

'*God Save the Queen*' after an ovation that had lasted ten minutes did she feel she had come back to earth from another planet.

'Now I understand why Papa loved the Gaiety!' she thought.

There was no time for retrospection once the show was over.

Archie hustled her and the other gentlemen with him back to the stage-door and when Minella ran up the iron staircase to the dressing-room, Natty was waiting for her with the cloak she had promised.

It was so luxurious and so attractive that she felt as if she was on the stage she had just been watching.

As the other girls covered themselves in long cloaks like hers and wrapped chiffon scarves over their elaborately arranged hair, Natty said to her quietly:

"Now you enjoy yourself, and don't do anything stupid."

She saw that Minella did not understand and added:

"Nothing your father and mother'd think wrong."

"They are both . . . dead," Minella replied.

"Then be sure they're watching from up above," Natty said, "and they'd want you to remain a good girl, as I know you are now."

Minella looked at her in surprise, but before she could say any more Natty had moved away to leave the dressing-room, and Connie was saying:

"Come on, come on! If you are not hungry, I am longing for my supper!"

"You'll have to wait for it!" Gertie said. "But I bet when we get there it'll be a good one!"

"Have you ever known the Earl to produce anything but the best?" Nellie asked.

"Exactly!" Connie agreed, "and Katy or no Katy, that is what we are bringing him and he should be grateful."

Without saying any more they trooped down the stairs to where the three gentlemen were waiting for them.

Outside there were two private broughams each

drawn by two thoroughbred horses to take them to the station.

Minella found herself seated on the back seat of one brougham with Archie between her and Connie, and opposite them was Nellie and Lord Skelton.

Gertie, Harry and Beryl of whom she had caught a fleeting glimpse, were in the second brougham, with another good-looking man who was introduced to her as 'Sam'.

As they drove off, Archie said to Connie:

"You looked lovely tonight, darling. I was very proud of you!"

"Thank you."

She did not seem embarrassed, Minella noticed, by the way in which Archie addressed her, and she wondered, seeing that he was so familiar, if Connie was going to marry him.

It would certainly be a brilliant marriage, she thought, for the daughter of a country Vicar.

At the same time, she supposed Connie might feel rather uncomfortable taking Archie to the small, not very attractive Vicarage where she had often thought everything looked shabby and very threadbare.

Then, as they drove on and had almost reached the station she heard Connie say in a low voice to Archie:

"I suppose there was no trouble about your coming away for the weekend?"

"She did not like it," Archie replied, "but I said I was going to see my mother."

"Supposing she finds out?"

Because she was so close to them in the carriage Minella was aware that Archie shrugged his shoulders.

Then she heard Connie say:

"You must be careful! Wives can often make trouble when they are jealous, and who could help, Archie dear, being jealous of you?"

For a moment Minella felt she could not have heard what Connie said aright.

Then she told herself quickly it was not for her to criticise.

But surely it was very strange for Connie, who was a Parson's daughter, to be on such familiar terms with a married man?

CHAPTER FOUR

❧

WHEN THEY ARRIVED at the Castle, which appeared to Minella enormous and rather frightening, they were hurried upstairs by a Butler who handed them over to the Housekeeper Mrs. Harlow, in rustling black with the silver chatelaine at her waist.

She seemed very superior, and looked at them, Minella thought, with an expression of disdain.

She led them along a corridor which Minella was sure from what her father had told her contained the State Bedrooms, and every so often she opened a door either to the right or the left saying as she did so:

"This is yours, Miss."

Minella noticed that neither Connie, Nellie nor Gertie had adjacent rooms, and she thought, although she was not sure, that she had a sight of valets in the bedrooms beside theirs.

Then, when only she was left, the Housekeeper walking ahead of her, her black dress rustling as if she wore a silk petticoat, went to the very end of the corridor.

There was a large, impressive double door and she stepped on one side to say:

"This is where you are sleeping, Miss Denman."

For a moment Minella was surprised and was about to say there had been a mistake when she realised that must be Katy's name. She thought she should explain and as they entered the room she said:

"Actually I am not Miss Katy Denman, who is ill, and I have taken her place."

"I thought you looked very young from what I'd heard of her," the Housekeeper replied.

By this time they were in a very large and impressive bedroom.

It was so lovely that Minella could only stare around her in admiration until she realised there was a maid waiting by the dressing-table.

"This is Rose," the Housekeeper said, "who'll look after you."

"Thank you," Minella said.

"I hope you'll be comfortable, Miss—" the House-keeper paused.

Remembering not to make a mistake, Minella said.

". . . Moore, Minella Moore."

The Housekeeper gave a nod of her head to acknowl-edge the name, then without speaking left the room.

"Your luggage'll be up in a minute, Miss," Rose said, "but I understands you don't have to change."

"No, I am already wearing an evening-gown," Minella replied.

As she spoke she undid the clasp of her velvet cloak and Rose lifted it from her shoulders.

Minella unwound the chiffon scarf she had worn over her head and sat down at the dressing-table to try and raise her hair which had been flattened during the jour-ney.

"Let me do that for you, Miss," Rose suggested.

She tidied Minella's hair with skilful fingers and as she was doing so two footmen arrived with her trunk and hat-box.

They undid the straps of the trunk and opened the lid of the hat-box and when they had gone Rose said:

"Have you got anything to wear on your head, Miss?"

"Some ospreys," Minella replied tentatively.

Then as Rose took them out of the hat-box she decided she could not wear them. They were too old for her and too theatrical and she knew her mother would certainly not approve of them.

She therefore put them down on the dressing-table and said:

"They are too much. They were lent to me, but I know I would not look right in them."

Rose smiled.

"I think you're too young for ospreys, Miss, but you'll look rather bare with nothing on your head."

As she spoke Minella noticed there was a vase of exquisite white orchids standing on the dressing-table.

Even as she looked at them Rose exclaimed:

"Orchids! That's what you want, Miss. His Lordship grows some beauties in the greenhouses."

She took two from the vase and arranged them at the back of Minella's chignon.

When she had done so they certainly looked very attractive and not in any way flamboyant.

Then as Minella stared at herself in the mirror she realised as she had in the dressing-room at the Theatre that her gown was very low in front, almost indecently so, she thought.

"I am wondering, Rose," she said, "whether it would be possible to wear one or two of the others pinned to the front of my bodice? I only borrowed this gown, and I feel rather uncomfortable in it."

Rose smiled at her again.

"I'll see to it, Miss, don't you worry."

She produced a safety-pin and having closed part of the décolletage which Minella thought immodest she pinned on top of it three of the star-shaped orchids.

"That looks lovely!" Minella exclaimed. "Thank you very much, you are kind!"

As she spoke the door opened and Gertie looked in.

"Are you ready?" she asked. "Connie said I was to

71

fetch you because she's gone downstairs to break the news to our host that he's got a different guest from what he expected."

"I hope he will not be too upset," Minella said nervously.

She rose from the dressing-table and just had time to wash her hands in warm water which Rose poured out for her.

Then hurriedly she ran after Gertie who was already walking slowly down the corridor towards the stairs.

"If you ask me," Gertie said as Minella joined her, "this place is too big. I'd feel smaller than a fly if I lived here!"

Minella laughed.

She too was very impressed by the size of the Castle, but it was no less than she had expected.

Her father had explained to her so often the magnificence of Blenheim Palace where he had stayed with the Duke of Marlborough, of Chatsworth and other magnificent ancestral homes like Woburn Abbey and Arundel Castle.

She knew she would have been disappointed if after all she had heard of the Earl, the Castle had not been somewhat awe-inspiring.

She thought the suits of armour in the Hall and the flags that had been captured in battle by the Earl's ancestors were very appropriate.

The Butler met them at the bottom of the stairs and said to Gertie:

"If you'll follow me, Miss, His Lordship's in the French Drawing-Room!"

Gertie winked at Minella, then whispered in her ear:

"What it is to have a choice, instead of knowing it's the parlour or the kitchen!"

Minella laughed.

The Butler led them to where two footmen opened the double doors of what was the most attractive and impressive room she had ever seen.

She had noticed in the passages and the Hall there

was gas-lighting, but in the French Drawing-Room there were two huge crystal chandeliers lit with candles which threw their golden light over the whole room.

At the end of it were Connie, Nellie, Beryl and the four men who had come with them, besides a fifth who turned at their approach and came towards them.

Nobody, Minella thought, could have mistaken the Earl for anything other than what he was: an aristocrat and an autocrat.

He was tall and broad-shouldered and, as Connie had said, exceedingly handsome.

At her first glance at him Minella knew that the rest of the description had been accurate. He did indeed look cynical and blasé, and although he was smiling when he greeted Gertie, she thought his eyes were hard and there was no warmth in them.

"I am delighted to see you, Gertie," he said, "and looking lovelier than ever, if that were possible!"

Then he looked at Minella and Connie had come to her side.

"This is Minella Moore," Connie said. "She's been very kind to take over Katy's role at the very last minute, and she's rather nervous, so don't frighten her!"

The Earl laughed.

"I promise I will not do that."

He put out his hand and as his fingers closed over hers Minella thought there was a strength and strange kind of power in them which was unusual.

"I hope," she said, "you do not . . . mind my being an . . . uninvited guest?"

"I am delighted," the Earl said, "and of course, as Connie said, very grateful to you for saving my party from being uneven numbers."

They joined the others who were already drinking champagne, the girls chattering, Minella thought, like colourful parakeets.

Because their laughter seemed to ring out like bells and they looked so beautiful in the elaborate and glittering gowns in which they had come down from

London, Minella kept thinking that this was the sort of party her father would have enjoyed.

"No wonder he preferred it to the quietness of the Manor after Mama died," she told herself.

The Earl broke in on her thoughts.

"You are looking serious, Minella," he said, "and that is something I cannot allow."

"I was admiring your house," Minella replied quickly. "It is exactly as I thought it would be."

The Earl raised his eye-brows.

"Why?"

"I have heard so much about the great houses of England," she said choosing her words carefully, "and hoped I should have the privilege of seeing one. I am sure your pictures are magnificent!"

"Do they really interest you?" the Earl enquired. "Or is that what Connie told you to say?"

Minella gave a little laugh.

"I really am interested, and although it may surprise you, I know quite a lot about pictures, not that I have had the opportunity of seeing them, but because of what I have read."

She was thinking of the hours she and her mother had pored over the pictures that were in the old books which her grandfather had collected in the Library at the Manor.

Her father often said everything there was just a 'lot of junk', as the books were out of date and some were so old it was difficult to read them.

But the drawings which illustrated them and in the more modern books the photographs, were to Minella a delight.

"I shall certainly have to test you," the Earl remarked, "and tomorrow I will take you round my Picture Gallery."

"I would love that!" Minella exclaimed.

She thought there was a slightly mocking expression in his eyes as if again he doubted her sincerity.

When they went in to dinner she was quite certain

that he thought she, as well as the other girls in this party, were putting on a very clever act just to please him.

The Dining-Room was as impressive as the Drawing-Room.

There was a Minstrels' Gallery at one end, and the rest of the enormous room was hung with pictures of the Earl's ancestors.

On the table there were gold candelabra besides vases, cups and goblets all of gold, while the white cloth was decorated with orchids and simplex.

As they were seated and Minella found herself on the Earl's right, which she guessed would have been Katy's place, he said:

"I see that you appreciate my orchids, and may I say they could not be more delightfully displayed!"

For a moment she did not realise that he was paying her a compliment, then as she saw his eyes on the orchids at her breast she blushed a little as she answered:

"They are very beautiful! I could not resist wearing them rather than what I brought with me."

"What did you bring with you?"

"Ospreys," Minella replied, "which Connie thought you would think appropriate to the occasion."

"I think you are too young for ospreys."

Minella gave a little laugh and he asked:

"Why does that amuse you?"

"Only because everybody today has been telling me how young I am, and have in consequence lectured and looked after me."

"I am quite certain they would do that," the Earl remarked dryly.

Minella was thinking it out.

"First there was a woman in the train who very kindly gave me a drink, then there was the porter who said I looked too young to be on my own, then the cab-driver and lastly Connie."

Only when she had finished speaking did she realise

perhaps she had made a mistake in admitting she had
only come to London today and she started when the
Earl asked:

"Where have you come from?"

Minella had to think quickly because it would have
been a mistake to say she had been in the depths of the
country.

"From . . . Birmingham," she answered, as it was
the first big town that came into her mind.

"I suppose you have been on tour," the Earl remarked. "Well, I am sure now that you are in London it
would be a mistake to let you disappear back to the
Provinces."

Once again he was speaking in that dry tone which
made it difficult, Minella thought, to understand exactly
what he meant.

Instead she turned as her mother had always taught
her to do to speak to the gentleman next to her to find it
was Lord Skelton who was talking intimately in a low
voice to Nellie.

He had obviously no wish to speak to her.

The Earl must have realised what she was doing because he said:

"I think you will find at this party that everybody is
very neatly paired off with the person with whom they
want to be. So as you are my partner, Minella, you must
make the best of it."

"I would like to do that," Minella replied, "and ask
you to tell me about your horses. Connie says you have
some outstanding race-horses and you won the Goodwood Stakes."

"Are you interested in horses as well as pictures?" the
Earl enquired.

"Very interested," Minella answered, "although I
have never been to a big race-meeting, only point-to-
point meetings and the local steeple-chase which I
found very exciting."

Again, she thought, the Earl was looking at her as if

he thought she was merely pretending an interest which did not really exist.

Because that annoyed her, she talked to him about the various Classic Races that had taken place that year, all of which her father had attended.

He had naturally been at Royal Ascot with a house-party, at the Derby, and the Grand National, and he had described to her when he came home exactly what had happened.

Because she knew it pleased him she had carefully studied the Sporting papers which always came to the Manor together with the more prosaic 'Morning Post'.

As dinner came to an end there was no doubt that the Earl had found her conversation interesting and he told her a great many things she wanted to know.

She also asked him if he had a good shoot in the woods around the Castle and once again he was obviously surprised that she knew about pheasant and partridge shooting.

Minella found she had enjoyed herself very much more than she had expected to do.

She was also astonished to realise that the rest of the party was getting very noisy, obviously as a result of the amount of wine they had drunk.

A servant had poured her a glass of champagne before she was aware of it, and after she had taken only a small sip and no more the Earl said:

"If you do not like champagne, Minella, I can offer you a white wine, or a claret."

"What I would really enjoy," Minella replied, "is lemonade, or if not, some water."

He turned his head to stare at her. Then he said:

"Do you really mean that?"

"To tell the truth," Minella replied, "I have only drunk champagne very occasionally and, as I am tired, I think it would be a mistake to drink a lot tonight."

Once again there was a cynical, searching look in the Earl's eyes as if he thought she was just putting on an act.

He ordered her some lemonade while the glasses round the tables were filled and refilled, and Minella saw that Connie, who was sitting on the other side of the Earl, was looking very flushed.

She was however talking very animatedly to Archie and hardly spared a word for her host.

It seemed somewhat strange behaviour, Minella thought, after what her mother had taught her was the right way to behave, but she supposed that Gaiety Girls were different from her mother's friends.

Perhaps if her father had been here he too would have talked only to the person in whom he was most interested, ignoring everybody else.

Then at last the Earl said they should move back into the Drawing-Room.

Connie rose and as she did so kissed Archie on the cheek and said:

"Do not be long! I shall come back and fetch you if you forget me while you drink your port!"

"That would be impossible!" Archie replied.

Minella listened in astonishment.

Then Connie linked her arm through hers, and as they walked from the Dining-Room she said:

"You are being marvellous, Minella. I have never known our host to be so animated!"

She half-tripped over her gown as she spoke and there was no need for Minella to answer.

When they reached the Drawing-Room the girls chattered amongst themselves as they powdered their faces and put fresh salve on their lips.

Each one of them carried her cosmetics in a little bag hanging from her wrist.

Minella realised that she did not have one and anyway, she had no wish to touch up her face, thinking that Connie's looked rather poster-like.

Beryl particularly had eye-lashes that were half-an-inch long, which made her look like a Dutch Doll.

She did not join in as they were chattering amongst

themselves. Instead she walked round the room looking at the pictures.

She realized they were all by great French artists which was why the room was called the French Drawing-Room.

There was a Boucher that was so beautiful with its blues and pinks and a fat little cupid that made her feel as if she longed to cuddle it.

She then found a Fragonard that was so romantic she almost felt as if she could step into the garden amongst the roses and there were cupids hovering over the heads of the lovers.

She was looking at it when the men came into the Salon and the Earl immediately came to her side.

"I see you are admiring my pictures."

"They are so beautiful!" Minella replied. "I have always longed to see a real Fragonard and this one is very much more beautiful than I ever imagined they could be!"

She was silent for a moment. Then she said:

"It is so horrifying to think he stopped painting after the Revolution and died in poverty."

"Who told you to say that to me?" the Earl asked.

It was then Minella took her eyes from the picture to stare at him.

"I imagine it is Archie who has been briefing you," he said. "He has some very fine pictures of his own."

Because Minella thought it might be a mistake to admit she had never met Lord Archibald until today, she decided it would be best to say nothing.

She moved to the end of the room where there was another picture she wanted to see.

The Earl followed her. Then he said:

"Let us sit on the sofa. I want to talk to you."

A little reluctantly because there was so much more in the room she wanted to look at, Minella sat down on the satin sofa which was at the far end of the room away from the others who were standing around the fireplace.

"Tell me about yourself," the Earl said. "I have come to the conclusion you are the most brilliant actress I have ever met in my life!"

Minella looked at him and it flashed through her mind that perhaps it was because he had had too much to drink that he had said anything so extraordinary.

"Your portrayal of a young girl stepping into the magic world of the Gaiety is brilliant!" he went on. "I suppose George Edwardes discovered you and I should congratulate him!"

Minella did not know what to reply and at last she said:

"I do not . . . think anybody has . . . discovered me."

"Then it has been left to me," the Earl said, "and let me tell you, I shall certainly promote you with the same enthusiasm that you give to my horses!"

Minella laughed.

"I am not likely to win the Goodwood Stakes!"

"No, but I am quite certain you would like a part in 'The Runaway Girl'," the Earl replied.

Minella stopped herself from saying she had no intention of going on the stage, remembering that Connie said the Earl might be able to help her.

"I am looking for something to do," she said, "but I am not sure what it should be."

"I have the answer to that," the Earl replied, "and I think the best thing, Minella, is to leave everything to me."

"It sounds like a . . . good idea."

As she spoke she realised that she felt so tired that it was difficult to concentrate on what he was saying or even to sit upright on the sofa.

For one frightening moment she felt her eye-lashes drooping, and was afraid she might fall asleep.

Then with a little start she forced herself awake and was aware that the Earl was watching her.

"I think," he said quietly, "that once again you are

acting with remarkable expertise that you are very tired."

Minella managed to smile.

"I had to get up at five o'clock this morning," she said, "and so many things have happened and it has all been so . . . bewildering that although you may think it very rude . . . I am finding it hard to keep my eyes open."

"Then go to bed," the Earl said. "There will be time tomorrow to show you the rest of my pictures, and some of my horses, too."

"I would love that!" Minella exclaimed.

"Come along then," he said. "Do not say goodnight to the rest of the party, but just slip away."

Minella thought he was very understanding as that was just what she wanted to do.

The Earl took her out of the Drawing-Room through a door near where they were sitting which led into an Ante-Room through which they could reach the Hall without Connie or any of the others being aware that she was leaving.

There were two footmen on duty and when they reached the bottom of the stairs the Earl said:

"I am sure you can find your way to your room from here. Goodnight, Minella, and sleep well!"

"I shall do that," Minella answered, "and thank you for being so kind."

She held out her hand and to her surprise the Earl kissed it.

She thought it was a rather strange thing for him to do, especially as his lips were hard on the softness of her skin.

Then because she was shy she took her hand away quickly and ran up the stairs.

She did not look back because she had the feeling he was watching her.

Instead she ran along the corridor to her room, and when she reached it she found there were candles flickering by the dressing-table and the bed.

Lying where she could not help seeing it, was a piece of paper on which was written:

"Please ring when you wants me, Miss, and I'll come straight away."

It seemed rather late to summon anybody, but because it was obviously expected of her Minella rang the bell and a few minutes later Rose came into the room.

"You're very early, Miss!" she said.

"I am so tired!" Minella answered.

She did not speak any more, but let Rose unhook her gown and release her hair.

Then she slipped into the nightgown that had been her mother's and got into bed.

Almost as her head touched the pillow she fell asleep and did not even hear Rose blow out the lights and leave.

※※※※※

Minella awoke in the morning with a feeling of excitement.

Never when she left the Manor had she expected to find herself in such an exciting place.

She was quite certain that today would be full of surprises and she knew there were a thousand questions she wanted to ask the Earl.

She rang the bell and when Rose came hurrying to answer it she said:

"You're very early, Miss!"

"Actually I thought I was late. I am usually up long before this," Minella replied.

"Nobody else is even awake," Rose replied. "It was nearly three o'clock before the other young ladies came up to bed."

"I was lucky to get away so early," Minella smiled.

She got up and washed and Rose helped her into a

very elaborate gown that Connie had approved of for her to wear in the morning.

Minella thought her mother would have considered it ridiculously overdressed, but that was what the other girls would wear, and Minella knew she must do the same.

As she was dressing she noticed that Rose was yawning and she said to her:

"Oh, you are tired! It was abominable of me to disturb you so late. I promise I will not do so again."

"Oh, it's not you, Miss," Rose replied. "It's my baby."

"Your baby?"

"Yes, it sounds strange, but I used to be second house-maid here. Then I got married, so I only come in when there's a party, so to speak."

"I understand," Minella said, "and you have brought your baby with you."

"My husband's a game-keeper, Miss, and at this time of the year he's out protecting the pheasants from the foxes. So I had to bring my two children with me and I hardly got a wink of sleep last night."

"I am sorry," Minella said. "May I see him?"

"You don't want to do that, Miss. It's a bother for you."

"No, I would love to," Minella answered, "and I wonder if you have tried giving him honey? Mama always told the people in the village to give their babies honey when they were teething. You will find it will quieten him during the day and help him sleep really well at night."

"I've never heard of that!" Rose exclaimed. "But of course I'll try him on it."

"Let me come and look at your son," Minella said.

"He's right at the end of the corridor, Miss. The Housekeeper's been kind enough to let me have a room on this floor. It means I don't have to come so far to wait on you."

Minella insisted on seeing the children, and Rose led her right across the front of the house to a room that was certainly not one of the grand Guest-Rooms, but was not a servant's room either.

In it there was a baby in a cot who was crying, and a very pretty little girl of three was sitting on the floor playing with some bricks.

"This is Elspeth," Rose said proudly, "and this is Simon."

She picked Simon up out of the cot as she spoke. He stopped crying noisily and merely whimpered.

"Go and get some honey for him quickly," Minella said. "I am sure they will have some in the kitchen, and I will stay with the children."

Rose was about to argue. Then as she was obviously worried about her son she put him back in the cot where he instantly began to cry again, and she ran from the room.

Minella picked the boy up and walked up and down patting him on his back and rocking him until he stopped crying and whimpered quietly.

Her mother had looked after the people in the village because the old Vicar was an unmarried man.

The mothers had come to her with their troubles and children's ailments and any accidents that took place.

Minella therefore was quite used to nursing babies, binding up wounds, or playing with one child while another member of the family required her mother's attention.

When Rose came back they gave Simon a spoonful of honey which he obviously appreciated and it certainly made him stop whimpering.

"I never thought of it, Miss, I didn't really!" Rose said. "It seems silly now when almost everybody on the estate has a hive in their garden!"

"Do not forget to give Simon a drink of water," Minella said, "as well as any milk you are giving him. He will be thirsty, but you will see the honey will make him much quieter, and tonight you will be able to sleep."

"You're very kind, Miss. That's what you are!" Rose said.

Having seen the children Minella hurried downstairs thinking she might be late for breakfast, but when she entered the Breakfast-Room the only person present was the Earl.

He was surprised to see her, especially when she said:

"I am sorry if I am late, but Rose told me I was too early."

"You are early, but not too early," the Earl replied. "In fact we are the only people downstairs."

"Do you mean to say that all the men are sleeping late too?" Minella asked.

She was surprised because her father always got up early in the country as she did, and usually they rode before breakfast.

"I expect they have good reason for being tired!" the Earl remarked.

Minella wondered what that reason could be.

She could understand that Connie and the other girls after a performance at the theatre and making the long journey by train might be exhausted, but it seemed odd for the men to be so tired.

She did not, however, say this to the Earl.

She merely chose what she wanted to eat from a long row of silver dishes on a side-table and sat down at the table opposite him.

She ate a good breakfast of bacon and eggs and enjoyed the Jersey butter and several spoonsful of the large comb honey that she chose in preference to the homemade marmalade and several jams.

She thought the Earl was watching her with a twinkle in his eyes which she had not noticed before.

As she finished he said:

"Now you are receiving your reward for having been so abstemious last night! I am sure there are several aching heads upstairs who wish they had followed your example!"

Minella remembered that her father never felt well after drinking a lot of champagne, and she said:

"Perhaps it is very gay to drink wine, but that can

85

mean, as Byron said: *'sermons and soda-water the day after'*!"

The Earl laughed.

"Come and admire my horses," he suggested.

"That is what I was hoping you would ask me to do," Minella replied.

She got up from the table and followed him to the door.

Only when they reached the Hall and she thought he hesitated did she say:

"Are you expecting me to wear a hat?"

She had never worn one at home because it had seemed ridiculous to put on a hat to go into the garden or to groom the only two horses they had left in the stables the last year. "No, of course not, not unless you want to," the Earl replied. "I like the way you do your hair."

Minella put her hand up to her chignon almost as if she had forgotten it was there.

"I am afraid it looks very ordinary beside Connie's and the others," she said, "but I never seem to have time to bother about anything more elaborate."

She did not see the look of surprise in the Earl's eyes, but started to ask him about the horses and the races in which he was entering them.

They reached the stables which were magnificent, and Minella went from stall to stall running out of expressions of praise.

Never had she imagined she would see and touch such wonderful examples of perfect horse-flesh.

Then the groom who accompanied them said to the Earl:

"What time are you wishing to ride, M'Lord? There's a horse ready saddled for Your Lordship."

Minella gave a little exclamation as she realised that the Earl was wearing riding-breeches.

"Oh, I have kept you from your ride," she said, "how terrible of me! I am sorry."

"There is no need to apologise," he replied. "I suppose you would not like to accompany me?"

Minella gave what was a cry of joy.

"Can I really do that?"

Then her face fell.

"I had forgotten . . . I have no riding-habit with me. I never thought . . . I never dreamt there would be a . . . chance of riding when I came here."

The Earl thought for a moment. Then he said:

"I am quite certain Mrs. Harlow the Housekeeper can provide you with one, as you are about the same size as my sister."

"Could she really?"

There was a look of excitement on Minella's face that seemed to light her eyes and give her a radiance that was almost like the sunshine.

"We will go and see about it," the Earl said good-humouredly, and turning to the groom said:

"Saddle another horse as well as mine, and have them at the front door in a quarter-of-an-hour."

Then he added:

"*Remus* will suit this young lady best."

"Oh, please," Minella interposed. "Could I not ride *Saracen*?"

She looked in the stall at the black stallion that she had liked particularly and who was looking back at her through the bars.

She saw the Earl hesitate before he asked:

"You are quite certain you can manage him?"

"Quite certain."

He seemed about to argue, then almost as if he thought he would teach her a lesson if she was mistaken, he said:

"Very well, put a saddle on *Saracen,* and I will ride *Crusader*. I doubt if any other horse will keep up with him."

The groom did not reply, but Minella had the feeling that he wanted to do so.

'I will show them,' she thought to herself with a spirit

of defiance. 'It is ridiculous because I am supposed to be a Gaiety Girl that I should not be able to ride properly.'

The Earl walked back with her to the Castle and told a footman to tell Mrs. Harlow he wanted to see her immediately.

By the time the Housekeeper had brought a habit to her bedroom Minella had already undressed and was waiting for it.

It was a beautifully cut habit from Busvine, who Minella knew was the best tailor of hunting clothes.

She tied the starched stock very neatly, arranged her hair with dozens of pins, exactly as her father liked, and put a small bowler, which Mrs. Harlow had also provided, firmly on her head.

The riding-boots which had also belonged to the Earl's sister were a little large, but quite comfortable.

When she was ready, having dressed more quickly than she had ever done before, she picked up the white knitted gloves and thanking Mrs. Harlow ran from the bedroom.

"It might have been made for her, its fits so perfectly!" Mrs. Harlow said to Rose, who had also been helping Minella dress. "She wears it like a Lady, I'll say that for her!"

"She's different from the others," Rose said. "Ever so kind she was about the baby."

"I expect it's just her way of sucking up to His Lordship!" Mrs. Harlow said. "All actresses are the same—no better than they should be!"

As Minella reached the front door she saw that not only were the horses waiting outside, but the Earl was already mounted on *Crusader*.

He was having a little trouble in controlling him which meant that *Saracen* was also moving restlessly.

"I feel you ought to ride something quieter," the Earl said as Minella appeared.

She pretended not to hear him and hurrying to the stallion's side mounted to the groom's astonishment without any assistance.

It was something she always had to do at home so that she never even thought about it. Only as she placed her leg over the pommel did the groom nearest to her hurry to arrange her skirt.

By this time *Saracen* was emulating *Crusader* and showing his impatience to be off.

He was not only pulling at his bridle, but bucking a little to show his independence, then as Minella held him with a firm hand the Earl rode ahead and she followed.

Never in her wildest dreams had she thought she would ever ride a horse that was so magnificent.

She was determined to show the Earl he was wrong in thinking *Saracen* would be too much for her and that once again she was putting on an act by pretending she could ride anything so spirited.

There was no chance of speaking as they rode at a sharp pace across the Park keeping out of the way of low branches.

Then once they were on open ground they gave the horses their heads.

Only when they had galloped for nearly half-a-mile did they pull in their animals, and the Earl said with a note of astonishment in his voice:

"How in the name of Providence did you ever learn to ride like that?"

Minella laughed and it was a very joyous sound.

"I knew you thought I was being over confident, but I have ridden ever since I was old enough not to require a pram."

"I am surprised, and also may I commend you on your appearance! Your borrowed plumes become you," he said with his eyes on her neat hair and the skilful way she had tied her stock.

They rode for another ten minutes without speaking. Then he said:

"I find you mystifying, Minella, and also very intriguing."

"Why am I puzzling you?"

"Because you are not in the least what I should have expected you to be."

"I am glad about that," Minella said, "otherwise you would undoubtedly be bored as everybody has told me you always are."

The Earl did not reply and she said looking back at the Castle which they could see in the distance:

"How could you be bored when you have so much?"

"I suppose like all women you think that money and position makes for happiness," the Earl said mockingly.

Minella shook her head.

"I am not as foolish as that, but I think they help. Lack of money can be very frustrating, especially for a man."

The Earl raised his eye-brows.

"What about a woman? I am sure you would find it very frustrating not to have your beautiful gowns, and of course your admirers to pay for them."

Minella turned her face towards him and without thinking said sharply:

"I would certainly not allow anybody to pay for my clothes! That is something . . ."

She stopped suddenly.

She had been about to say: "no Lady would do," then remembered she was not supposed to be a Lady but a Gaiety Girl, and to deny it would let Connie down.

She realised she had made a mistake and one it was impossible for the Earl to ignore.

"Did you say," he said in that dry, sarcastic voice, which she had begun to recognise, "that you do not allow your admirers to pay for your gowns? I cannot believe the one you were wearing last night and the one this morning came out of your salary."

Minella lifted her chin, determined not to allow him to bully her.

"If you want the truth," she replied, "I borrowed them to impress you, and tomorrow evening when I get back to London they will be returned."

The Earl laughed and it was a very spontaneous sound.

"Very well, Minella," he said. "You win! I certainly cannot refute such a very ingenious explanation!"

"I accept your apology," Minella replied, "and now can I gallop *Saracen* again? I may never have another opportunity to do so."

She did not wait for the Earl's permission, but touched *Saracen* with her whip.

The great horse sprang forward and the Earl had some difficulty in catching up with her.

CHAPTER FIVE

As MINELLA CHANGED for dinner she thought it had been the most exciting and thrilling day she had ever known.

Not only had her ride with the Earl in the morning been a delight beyond words, but after a very amusing luncheon he had arranged for everybody who wished to go driving.

Connie and Archie were very keen and two very fast Phaetons were brought to the door, each drawn by a perfectly matched pair of horses.

They set off across the Park, then came to some flat dry fields on which the two men raced each other.

Minella was not surprised that the Earl won, but Archie who was also an expert driver put up a very good fight.

It was all so different from anything she had done

before, and she kept thinking how much her father would have enjoyed it, and even, she thought, could have challenged the Earl better than Archie was able to do.

They drove over a great deal of the Estate, and she saw how the Earl kept it in perfect order.

The cottages seemed to gleam with new paint, and everybody who saw him curtsied respectfully or touched their forelock, but they were also smiling.

"I think your people are very fond of you," Minella remarked, and he replied:

"I hope they find me just and generous, which is all that is required of a good Landlord."

Minella shook her head.

"I think they want more than that. People want affection and although we had no money everybody loved my mother. When she died, her grave was covered with a mountain of flowers, most of them only little bunches, but given with love."

She could not help a little tremor in her voice because it always hurt her unbearably to remember how she had lost her mother.

Unexpectedly the Earl asked:

"What did your father do?"

Too late Minella realised she was speaking as herself and had forgotten her part as the young actress.

After a moment she replied:

"He owned some acres of land."

"So he was a farmer," the Earl said, "and I suppose that is why you like the country and enjoy riding."

Minella had no answer to this and after a moment he went on as if he was following his own train of thought:

"Then why have you chosen the stage? I should have thought it was alien to everything you knew in the past."

It took a moment for Minella to find the answer. Then she said:

"I have to earn my living."

"And of course," the Earl finished, "you find the heady quality of applause irresistible."

There was that dry, sarcastic note in his voice, and because it somehow hurt her that he should speak to her like that she said quickly:

"I have never had such a happy time as I am having here at the Castle."

"Is that really true?" the Earl asked.

"Of course it is. Why should I lie to you? It is not only that everything is so luxurious and magnificent, but because you have been so kind to me."

He took his eyes from his horses for a moment to look at her and said:

"That is what I want to be, but we will talk about that later."

She thought with a lift of her heart that he would find her, as Connie had suggested he might, something to do.

Then she remembered he had said he would get her a part in *"The Runaway Girl"* and that she would have to refuse.

As if he knew she was worrying over what he had just said he looked at her again before he said:

"Trust me, Minella," he said, "and for the moment just enjoy yourself."

"I am doing that," Minella answered with a little lilt in her voice, "and I am hoping I shall be able to ride *Saracen* again tomorrow morning."

"Of course," the Earl agreed.

๑๑๛๑๑๛๑๑๛

Now as Rose brought her the second evening-gown from the wardrobe she saw it was a very soft shade of pink, mostly made of tulle.

It was a very young-looking gown despite the fact that it was extremely elaborate and the skirt was ornamented with little bunches of white flowers glittering with diamanté.

"I thinks your gown last night was very pretty, Miss," Rose remarked, "but this one's prettier still! So I've asked the gardeners to send in some white gardenias for your hair."

"How kind of you!" Minella exclaimed.

She was thinking as she spoke that Connie had said to her this morning:

"I noticed you weren't wearing the ospreys that Natty gave you."

Minella felt guilty.

"I thought they were too over-powering," she replied.

"I only suggested them so that you would attract our host's attention," Connie went on, "but you seem to have done that without any difficulty."

Minella wondered why Connie was so insistent that she should please the Earl. Then she told herself it was only because she had to make up for the absence of Katy.

She could see now only too clearly how uncomfortable for the others it would have been if the Earl had nobody to amuse him.

So she felt she must redouble her efforts to keep him laughing and prevent the cynical expression coming into his eyes and the bored note in his voice.

When she was ready she looked at herself in the mirror and thought that she had never imagined she could look so like a Princess in a Fairy-Tale.

Then she gave a little cry.

"What is it, Miss?" Rose asked.

"My friend was quite annoyed with me this morning because I went out riding without any powder on my face or lip-salve. To tell you the truth, I forgot!"

When Minella had come back from riding, she had met Connie on the stairs coming down for luncheon, having not appeared earlier.

"I have had such a wonderful ride, Connie," she cried.

Connie had looked at her face, then answered in a very low voice:

"You have forgotten your powder and paint. You look like a Lady, and you know that is a mistake!"

"I am sorry," Minella said humbly, and hurried to her bedroom before Connie could say any more.

She had put a little powder on her nose and reddened her lips, but now she was aware that having washed her face when she had a bath she looked like herself, and not the least like the other girls.

"Please, Rose, help me," she begged.

"Of course, Miss," Rose answered, "not that I'm very skilled at knowing what you want. But I'll do my best."

She picked up the powder-puff and said:

"Your skin's as good as my Elspeth's and it's a pity to spoil it."

Minella did not answer.

She merely shut her eyes and when Rose powdered her face and put just a touch of rouge on her cheeks she covered her lips with the same salve and looked at her eyes.

"Your eye-lashes are so long, Miss," Rose said, "and quite dark. I should leave them as they are."

Minella licked her finger and took the powder off them and said:

"All right, it is too much trouble, and I do not suppose anyone will look at me anyway, not with the other girls there."

"Ring when you come to bed, Miss," Rose said as she walked towards the door, "I'll be waiting to hear the bell."

"Thank you," Minella replied.

After dinner it was different from what had happened the night before.

Beryl went to the piano which stood in the corner of the Drawing-Room and started to play some of the songs from *"The Runaway Girl"*.

All the rest gathered round singing at the tops of their voices and although Minella did not attempt to join in she thought that *'Oh, Listen to the Band'*, was the gayest tune she had ever heard.

It was obvious everybody had had a great deal to drink at dinner.

The servants had also brought in a silver tray on which there were a number of decanters and several bottles of champagne, each in its own silver ice-cooler emblazoned with the Earl's crest.

After Gertie had danced a solo while the men clapped her, she had fallen down and Minella thought uncomfortably that everybody, including Connie, seemed rather flushed, red-faced and over-noisy.

She gave a little start when she saw Nellie kissing Lord Skelton without apparently being at all embarrassed that everyone could watch her.

Instinctively because she was thinking her mother would not approve, she moved away from the group around the piano.

As she reached the other end of the Drawing-Room where she had sat last night the Earl was beside her.

"Would you like to go to bed?" he asked.

"If you will not think it very rude," she answered, "I am rather tired."

"That comes from getting up so early," he said. "I think it would be a good idea if you do not let the others see you leave."

Minella gave him a grateful little smile.

He took her away from the Salon as he had the night before, through the Ante-Room and into the passage which led back into the Hall.

When they reached the stairs she held out her hand as she had done before.

He took it in his, but he did not kiss it. Instead he looked down into her eyes and said very quietly:

"Go to bed, Minella, I shall not be long."

She smiled at him and ran up the stairs thinking if she had had a long day, so had he, and he was very wise not to stay up as the others had the night before until three o'clock in the morning.

When she reached her own room she was just about to ring the bell when she remembered that Rose had been tired too and what was more she had had the children with her all day.

She thought instead of ringing for her she would go to her room and ask her to undo the back of her gown.

Besides the bell might easily awaken the baby if he was asleep and that would give Rose another sleepless night.

It did not take her long to run down the long passage and when she reached Rose's room she knocked softly.

As there was no answer she opened the door.

There was a candle alight by the bed and she could see Rose was stretched out on it, still wearing her black dress, her cap and apron, but she was fast asleep and beside her in his cradle the baby was asleep too.

Then she heard a little sound and saw that on the other side of the room Elspeth was sitting up in a large cot.

As she saw Minella she pulled herself up by the side of it to say:

"I'se thirsty! I wants a drink!"

Minella moved across the room towards her and picked her up in her arms.

"If you come with me," she whispered, "I will give you a drink, but you must not wake Mummy. She is very tired."

"Mummy 'sleep," Elspeth lisped.

Holding her in her arms, Minella turned towards the door. Then she thought that if Rose awoke to find Elspeth gone she would be worried.

Thinking quickly she pulled the two gardenias from her hair and put them in Elspeth's cot, knowing Rose would understand.

Then she tip-toed across the room, closed the door quietly and carried Elspeth down the passage.

The child was intrigued and excited at doing anything so unusual.

When Minella reached her own room she shut the door into the passage, locked it, and carried Elspeth to her bed.

"Now you are going to sleep with me," she said, "and let Mummy have a good night. See what a big bed I have!"

"Very, very big!" Elspeth agreed.

She sat looking around her with delight and Minella gave her a lace-edged handkerchief to play with which had belonged to her mother.

Elspeth thought it very pretty and smoothed it out in front of her as if it was a tiny table-cloth.

Minella then gave her some water to drink and by the time she had undressed, having some difficulty in un-hooking her gown at the back, Elspeth was very sleepy.

As she got into bed the child moved towards her and laid her head on her shoulder.

"I likes sleeping with 'oo," she said.

"Then go to sleep as I am going to do," Minella an-swered, "and when we wake up it will be morning."

Elspeth gave a little sigh of satisfaction as if that was what she wanted to hear. As Minella blew out the candle she saw that the child's eyes were closed.

She just had time to murmur a few prayers before she too fell asleep.

❦❦❦❦❦❦

It was half-an-hour later that the Earl opened the door of his bedroom which communicated with the *Boudoir* which lay between his room and that in which Minella was sleeping.

There was only a lighted candelabrum on the table in the *Boudoir* and two candles on the mantelshelf, but they revealed an exquisitely furnished Sitting-Room filled with a profusion of hot-house flowers.

The Earl however passed quickly through it to open the door which led into Minella's bedroom.

Minella had no idea the door existed, since it had a long mirror fixed to it which she had assumed was at-tached to the wall.

The Earl opened the door quietly, and was surprised to find the room in darkness.

He thought he had made it quite clear to Minella that he would be coming to bed soon.

He turned back into the *Boudoir* to take a candle from the mantelpiece, and holding it in his hand he entered the bedroom.

As he walked towards the bed he smiled.

He thought that Minella was certainly unexpected in everything she did and said.

He was used to any woman on whom he bestowed his favours to be waiting for him eagerly.

Usually she would be sitting up in bed, draped in chiffon which tantalisingly concealed her nudity, but with an inviting expression in her eyes that was unmistakable.

Just occasionally the lady in question would be reading and appear surprised at his intrusion.

But it was so obvious a wile that he thought it would not have deceived a young boy, let alone a man as experienced as himself.

But this was the first time he had found the room he was visiting in complete darkness, and when he reached the great bed he looked down and saw Minella was asleep, or else pretending to be.

Her eye-lashes were very long, and her fair hair curled riotously over her shoulders.

Then incredibly, although it took him a long moment to be quite certain his eyes were not deceiving him, the Earl saw she was not alone.

Cuddled against her breast was a small child also fair-haired and fast asleep.

Holding the candle high in his hand so that he could see more clearly the Earl stared at them both, then at Minella alone.

He thought as he looked at her how very young and innocent she appeared and yet, he told himself, it must be an act.

Last night he had thought she was the most brilliant

actress he had ever known in portraying a very young girl taking part in a somewhat riotous house-party for the first time.

Now he knew as he had watched and listened to her all day, that he had not found a single flaw in her performance.

He asked himself now if she was really sleeping, or craftily attempting to intrigue him.

But after a few minutes he could not believe any actress could have faked the rhythmic rise and fall of her breasts, which came from complete unconsciousness, or let her long fingers lie so completely relaxed on the lace-edged linen sheet.

There was a smile on the Earl's lips as he looked down at her that was neither cynical nor mocking.

Then quietly, as quietly as he had come, he walked back to the communicating door, carrying the candle, and passing into the *Boudoir* shut it behind him.

⁕⁕⁕

Minella was awoken by Elspeth asking:

"Where's Mummy?"

"If we ring the bell Mummy will come," she answered, "if it is not too early."

She got out of bed to pull back the curtains, then looked at the very pretty French ormolu clock which stood on the mantelpiece.

It was half-past-seven and she knew both she and Elspeth had had a good night.

"I've lost my hankie," Elspeth was saying, remembering her plaything of the night before.

She was diving about the bed looking for it as Minella rang the bell.

Rose arrived full of apologies, but Minella would not listen to them.

"I only hope you slept as well as we did, Rose!"

"Like a log, Miss, and that's the truth! I've made up

100

now for all the nights young Simon's kept me awake. It was ever so kind of you—it was really!"

She took Elspeth back to her own room, then came back to help Minella finish dressing.

She put on her riding-habit and although she took some time to make herself look as neat as she had the day before, she was still the first arrival in the Breakfast-Room and it was three or four minutes later before the Earl appeared.

"I have beaten you this morning!" Minella exclaimed.

"I hope you had a good night," the Earl replied.

"As Rose said when I asked her: 'I 'slept like a log'!"

There was an expression in his eyes she did not quite understand, but she was intent only in reaching the horses as quickly as possible.

Only as they finished breakfast and turned to walk towards the door did the Earl say:

"When we come back from riding, Minella, I want to talk to you alone."

"Yes, if you wish," she replied. "Where shall I meet you?"

"In my private Study," the Earl replied. "I will tell one of the footmen to bring you to me."

She wondered what he wanted to say to her that seemed so important, but *Saracen* was waiting for her outside.

It was two hours later when she was taking off her riding-habit that she wondered if the Earl had deliberately cut short their ride so that he could talk to her without the rest of the party being aware of it.

She rang for Rose and once again learnt that it was after three o'clock before anybody got to bed.

"There will be nobody down before luncheon, you can be sure of that, Miss," Rose said. "I always says that them as miss the morning miss the best part of the day."

"I agree with you," Minella said, "and this morning has been especially wonderful for me because I was riding the most magnificent horse I have ever ridden in my whole life."

She did not add: "or am ever likely to ride again," which was a depressing thought.

Then she told herself excitedly there was still a lot of the day left before they were to return to London.

The gown Natty had chosen for her was again rather elaborate but it was a very soft blue which was the perfect frame for her fair hair and white skin.

She was, however, in such a hurry to reach the Earl that she did not bother even to look in the mirror.

Rose released her hair from the many hairpins she had put in it, and as soon as she was free, she hurried towards the door and actually ran down the corridor to the top of the stairs.

A footman was waiting for her in the Hall and as she reached him he said:

"Will you come this way, Miss?"

He took her down a corridor where she had not been before.

He opened the door and Minella saw the Earl waiting for her in what was a very comfortable and at the same time, impressive Study.

It had pictures of horses by Wootton, and Sartorius Stubbs on the walls, and in front of the fireplace the sofa and chairs were upholstered in red leather.

But Minella had eyes only for the Earl, and she realised he too had changed.

Although he looked very smart and impressive, she thought she liked him best in his riding breeches.

"You have been very quick, Minella," he said. "Most women take hours, but I expect your work on the stage has taught you, if nothing else, how to change swiftly."

Minella smiled at him but did not reply.

She merely walked towards the marble mantelpiece and held out her hands to the fire where the flames were leaping high above the logs.

The Earl watched her. Then he said:

"Sit down, Minella, I have something important to say to you."

She obeyed him and looked at him tentatively, wondering why he sounded so serious.

He stood with his back to the fire. Then he said:

"What I am going to tell you is so completely in confidence that I am going to ask you to give me your most sacred promise that you will never repeat it to anybody."

"Yes . . . of course I . . . promise," Minella replied.

"By everything you hold holy? I have the feeling that you say your prayers."

"Of course I do . . . every night and every morning."

The Earl gave a faint smile as if that was what he expected. Then he began and she thought although it seemed incredible, that he was nervous:

"Nearly two years ago I was married."

Minella looked at him in surprise, since Connie had never mentioned that the Earl had a wife.

"As it happens," the Earl continued, "she was very like you."

"Like me?"

"She was fair, she had very much the same coloured eyes, although I am not trying to flatter you when I tell you that you are actually far more beautiful than she was."

"Thank you," Minella said quietly.

"It was a hasty marriage," the Earl went on, "and looking back I realise I was not only pressurised into it by my mother, who had wanted me to get married for a very long time, but also by my wife's father, who was a very distinguished retired Ambassador."

There was a pause. Then the Earl said almost as if he was seeing a picture in front of his eyes:

"It all happened in the South of France where my mother lives in a Villa near Nice because the English climate does not suit her, and my wife's father has a Villa near her. They were great friends and they concocted a scheme between them that I should marry the Ambassador's daughter, Olive."

Suddenly the Earl's voice changed as he said harshly:

"It was a trap, and I walked into it like a greenhorn!"

"A trap?" Minella questioned. "But, how?"

"I should have been suspicious," he continued, as if Minella had not spoken, "when they made every possible pretext for us to be married immediately in Nice, and Olive did not appear to want a grand wedding with brides-maids, and all her English friends present."

'Perhaps she felt shy of a large ceremony,' Minella thought.

But she did not speak and the Earl's voice sounded as if it had the sharpness of steel as he said:

"A week after we were married my wife told me that she was having a baby and ran away with an Italian whom she had loved for two years but her father had forbidden her to see him."

"Oh . . . no!" Minella breathed.

"You can imagine what I felt," the Earl said bitterly, "but I was determined that nobody should be aware of my humiliation in being caught by what is one of the oldest tricks in the book!"

Minella did not understand what this meant.

At the same time, she felt desperately sorry for the Earl, knowing how much his wife's behaviour must have hurt his pride.

"What did you do?" she asked gently.

"I came back to England determined that nobody should pity me, nobody should laugh at me behind my back."

His voice became cynical as he finished:

"They were not likely to do so to my face."

"No, of course not, but did nobody know you had been married?"

"Of course they knew!" the Earl said impatiently as if she had asked a stupid question. "The Ambassador announced it not only to all the English newspapers, but also the French. When I returned here I found piles of congratulatory letters, and of course, a large number of wedding-presents."

"It must have been . . . terrible for you!" Minella said softly.

"What I have just told you," the Earl said, "is known only to my mother and to my wife's father."

"I . . . I do not understand."

"I have told my friends," the Earl went on, "that my wife has to be with her father, who is in ill health, in the South of France. Whenever I go away from here or from my house in London, I say that I am visiting her and that I expect her to return to England as soon as her father either recovers or dies."

"And they believe you?"

The Earl's lips twisted in a mocking smile.

"There are few people brave enough to call me a liar!"

"But . . . where is your . . . wife now?"

"With her lover in Italy," the Earl replied, "from where she wrote begging me to divorce her."

Minella looked at him wide-eyed.

"You refused to do so?"

"Of course! Why should I be the victim of a scandal? Why should I allow the whole sordid story to be known not only to my friends and enemies, and I have a number of both, but also to any of the *hoi polloi* who purchase a daily newspaper?"

"I do see that that could be very . . . humiliating," Minella said "but it does mean that you cannot marry again, and have a . . . son to inherit this . . . wonderful Castle."

"I am aware of that," the Earl said sharply as if he resented what she had said.

"I am . . . sorry."

"This is where you come into the story."

"Me?"

"I was invited two days ago before I left London to represent Her Majesty Queen Victoria in Cairo when

105

General Kitchener arrives there on October 6th, after his great victory in the Sudan."

"You mean the Battle of Omdurman?"

"I see you read the newspapers!" the Earl replied. "Yes, as you are aware, he is the hero of the hour. He is to be fêted in Egypt and when he returns to England I am told privately he is to receive an Earldom."

"Oh, I am glad!" Minella exclaimed. "I thought the way he fought the Dervishes was absolutely splendid, and now he has avenged the death of General Gordon."

The Earl raised his eye-brows as if he was surprised that she knew so much before he said:

"Her Majestry has asked particularly that I should attend various official dinners and parties given by the Khedive of Egypt for General Kitchener, and I should be accompanied by my wife."

Minella drew in her breath.

"I do see that makes it very . . . awkward for you. What will you . . . do?"

The Earl, who had been looking across the Study, now turned to look at her.

"I hoped that as you are looking for employment you will allow me to employ you in that capacity."

"I . . . I do not . . . understand."

"It is quite simple," he said. "You look enough like my wife even for those who have seen photographs of her to ask no questions. As I have already told you, you are a brilliant actress, and your performance since you came here has been faultless."

"M . . . my . . . performance?"

There was a faint smile on the Earl's lips as he said:

"I can only describe it by saying you might be a member of an aristocratic family in the way you speak, the way you behave, and when your face is natural, as it is when you are riding."

Minella drew in her breath.

"But that is very . . . different from playing the . . . part of your wife."

"I will see that you make no mistakes," the Earl said.

106

"It will only be a question of perhaps three days in Egypt, and of course meeting the Officers on the battle-ship in which we will be travelling."

"A battleship?"

"That is how we will be travelling to Egypt. I do not know yet if General Kitchener will be returning in her."

"A . . . battleship!" Minella said beneath her breath.

It was something she had always wanted to see, and once again she had to rely on her father's description of the ships in which he had travelled to various parts of the world.

"I am sure," the Earl continued, "that you would wish to be businesslike about this. If you will do what I am asking you to do, Minella, I am prepared to give you £500, which I am sure will tide you over until you find the employment you tell me you are seeking."

"It is too . . . much!" Minella said quickly.

The Earl laughed.

"This is the first time I have ever heard a woman say that what I am offering her is too much!"

"But it is! After all, it will not take very long . . ."

She paused and added:

"But of course I should have to buy some clothes to wear."

"I have thought of that already," the Earl replied, "and there is no time. In fact, when my party leaves after luncheon today, I shall be taking a train to South-ampton."

He looked at her and added:

"And I want you to come with me."

"But . . . what am I to . . . wear?"

"We have already established that my sister's clothes fit you, and as it happens, she has a great number of them here."

"But what will she say if she knows I have . . . bor-rowed them?"

"I am sure she will be delighted to help me," the Earl replied, "and as she has gone out to Madras in India, where it is very hot, for at least a year, I am quite certain all the clothes which she has left behind will be completely out of date by the time she returns."

The sarcastic way he spoke made Minella give a little laugh, and he added:

"And then, of course, like every other women, she will have 'nothing to wear'!"

"That is, in fact, true in my . . . case!"

"Then I am certain you will find upstairs there is a whole wardrobe waiting for you."

Minella clasped her hands together.

"It all sounds very exciting, but at the same time . . . very frightening. Suppose I . . . let you down?"

"I think that is very unlikely," the Earl said.

"Perhaps . . . Connie or . . . Gertie . . . could do it better than I can."

The Earl looked at her as if he thought she could not be serious. Then he said, just as her father had done:

"The Connies of this world are not like you, Minella, and they certainly would not 'pass muster' as the Countess of Wynterborne!"

Minella rose to her feet and walked to the window.

She looked out at the Park where the leaves on the trees were already beginning to turn brown. She had already noticed this morning that there was a little nip in the air which meant Autumn had begun.

She was really wondering whether she should do what the Earl asked, or if her mother would advise her to refuse, however tempting it might be.

£500! It would keep her for ages.

And to travel to Egypt in a battleship! How could she resist anything so inviting, so exciting?

Then, almost as if he was standing beside her, she could see her father looking exceedingly handsome, and at the same time rather raffish with his eyes twinkling, his usual irresistible smile on his lips.

"Never funk a fence," he was saying as he had said so often when teaching her to ride.

She turned round.

"I will . . . do it," she said, "but you must promise

that if I commit any terrible *faux pas* and make you . . .
ashamed of me . . . you will not be very . . . very angry."

"I promise you," the Earl answered, "that I shall
merely be very, very grateful."

Their eyes met, and Minella felt her heart beating
excitedly in her breast. She told herself it was because of
what she had agreed to do.

Then she said:

"What am I to say to Connie?"

"I have thought of that, too," the Earl said. "I will tell
her that instead of your returning to London, I am taking you to stay with my mother at her Villa in the South
of France as she is looking for a young companion."

"That is very clever!" Minella exclaimed. "Do you
think Connie will believe it?"

"I will make sure she does," the Earl said confidently,
"so now just enjoy yourself until the others leave us."

As if he anticipated the question which trembled on
Minella's lips, he said:

"I will see Mrs. Harlow and tell her to pack everything of my sister's that she thinks you will need, and as
soon as the others have gone you can change out of that
very attractive but over-ornamented gown you are wearing into something rather more lady-like."

"I am afraid all my gowns will have to go back with
Connie. They belong to the Gaiety!"

The Earl laughed.

"So that is where you borrowed them from!"

"Yes . . . of course."

"I suppose I was being very obtuse," he said, "but as
they become you so well, I thought they must be of your
own choosing."

"I would never aspire to anything so glamorous!"

" 'Spectacular' is the word for them," the Earl said.
"They are perhaps correct for a Gaiety Girl, if that is
what you want to be in the future, but a definite *faux pas*
as you put it, for my wife!"

Minella laughed.

"I have been feeling like a Fairy Princess, but now I must go back to being just ordinary 'me'."

As she spoke she realised that once again she had been thinking of herself as her father's daughter, and not the aspiring, unknown actress who had been on tour.

She thought perhaps the Earl did not notice and said quickly:

"As it is getting near luncheontime perhaps we should join the others, or Connie will ask me what you were talking to me about."

"Yes, of course," the Earl agreed. "And after luncheon you had better arrange for Mrs. Harlow to give you something of my sister's to wear while she packs up what you have on."

Because he was thinking out every detail, Minella was not as frightened as she might otherwise have been.

Only when she went up to her room after a rather noisy luncheon at which everybody laughed a lot, did she feel as if there were a thousand butterflies fluttering in her breast, because she was setting off on a wild adventure which might end in disaster.

Then Connie came bursting into the bedroom to say:

"The Earl has just told me that he thinks he has found a job for you. It sounds very respectable and exactly what you should have!"

"Perhaps his mother will not . . . want me."

As Minella spoke it occurred to her that once the trip to Egypt was over she would have to go back to Connie in London and ask for her help once again.

It would therefore be a mistake to sound too confident of being employed for a long time.

"I must say it sounds a bit dull," Connie said. "Anyhow, give it a try. If you do not like it, you can always find something else. As I told you, our host can help you better than anybody else."

"I realise I am . . . very lucky," Minella said in a soft voice, "and thank you, Connie, for being so . . . kind as to bring me . . . here. It has been the most . . . exciting thing that has ever . . . happened to me!"

There was silence for a moment. Then Connie said:

"I am glad you have enjoyed it, but you have not been—upset in any way?"

As she spoke Minella thought she looked searchingly at her as if she suspected she was hiding something.

"No, of course not," she answered. "What could have upset me?"

"You went to bed very early again last night," Connie remarked, "and the Earl did not stay up late either."

She spoke a little awkwardly and at the same time there was a note in her voice that Minella did not understand.

"I was tired," she said, "and I think he was too. We rode all the morning, and I was downstairs at eight o'clock."

Connie looked round the beautiful bedroom. Then she said:

"You were not—disturbed in the night?"

"No, not once," Minella said, "even though I had Rose's little daughter sleeping with me."

Connie stared at her incredulously.

"You had what?"

"Rose . . . the maid who has been looking after me . . . is having a bad time with her baby son because he is teething, so I had her elder child who is three to sleep with me. She was very sweet, and we neither of us moved until seven o'clock this morning!"

Connie still stared at her as if she could hardly credit what she was hearing. Then she walked to the window to look out before she said:

"I suppose to the pure—all things are pure! I remember how Papa made you and me translate that into Latin and I found it very difficult!"

Minella did not understand, and she said:

"What will you do, Connie, if your father and mother ever find out you are on the stage?"

"What can *they* do?" Connie parried. "It would upset

111

them, but on Papa's stipend he could hardly cut me off with the proverbial shilling!"

"No, of course not, but . . ."

"There are no 'buts'," Connie interrupted. "I am enjoying every moment of it. I am doing what I want to do and I shall always be grateful to your father for giving me the introduction to George Edwardes."

"And now you have helped me, as you promised you would help Papa," Minella said in a soft voice.

"I hope I have," Connie said. "And I hope very much that, wherever he is, he thinks I have done the—right thing."

There was no mistaking the little sob in her voice and Minella said:

"I am sure he does, and do not worry, Connie. I can look after myself."

Connie laughed and there were tears in the sound.

"Like Hell you can!" she said. "But perhaps you will be all right—with your father looking after you."

CHAPTER SIX

*A*s MINELLA SAT in the train taking them to Southampton she thought that once again she was starting off on an exciting adventure she had never expected to have.

Ever since the Earl had told her that she was to go with him to Cairo, she felt she must be living in a dream and nothing that was happening could really be true.

When she went upstairs to see Mrs. Harlow she had been surprised at how affable and helpful she was.

She thought ever since she arrived at the Castle that Mrs. Harlow had looked with an expression that was not far from contempt at her and Connie and the other girls.

Now when Minella found her in her bedroom she was completely different.

"His Lordship tells me he's taking you to his mother's, Miss," she said. "I know you'll enjoy meeting Her Ladyship. We all loved her when she were here."

"You must miss her now that she has to live in the South of France," Minella said.

"We do indeed," Mrs. Harlow agreed. "Now you're to have Lady Sybil's clothes, and Rose and the other maids are already bringing them downstairs."

"I do hope she will not mind lending them to me," Minella said in a worried voice.

"I'm sure she'll be delighted, Miss! And they'll suit you far better than those gaudy gowns you've been wearing."

As she spoke Mrs. Harlow looked disparagingly at Minella's gown which she was about to take off. Then she added:

"It was ever so kind of you, Miss, to have little Elspeth to sleep with you last night. It gave Rose a proper rest, and that's what she badly needed. I could hardly believe my ears this morning when she told me how charitable you've been!"

"It was no trouble," Minella replied, "and we both slept soundly."

She felt there was a somewhat questioning look in Mrs. Harlow's eyes. At the same time she was so affable that Minella had no wish for her to be anything else.

The Earl's sister, who Minella learnt was married to the new Governor of Madras, had bought all her clothes from the most expensive shops in Bond Street.

They were, Minella knew, exactly what her mother

113

would have chosen and in the soft pastel shades that suited her.

"I think," she said a little hesitatingly, "that Lady Sybil must have the . . . same colouring as I have."

"She's not quite so fair, Miss," Mrs. Harlow replied, "but her skin's clear and white. Her clothes are very smart and up-to-date. At the same time they're 'lady-like', if you knows what I mean."

Minella repressed a desire to laugh because she knew exactly what Mrs. Harlow meant.

But she thought it would be a mistake to say so, and she was only grateful for the extremely elegant gowns which Rose was hastily packing into large, expensive-looking trunks.

A few minutes later Minella found herself wearing a very pretty travelling-gown in a soft blue crepe with a cape to wear over it edged with satin of the same colour.

"You may be cold at sea," Mrs. Harlow was saying, "and I've put in some much heavier cloaks and also a waist-length fur jacket which I am sure will come in useful."

Minella wanted to protest that it was too much.

Then she thought it would be a mistake to take too little in case the Earl was ashamed of her appearance.

"There's one blessing," Mrs. Harlow was saying, "you'll not need to alter the way you do your hair, Miss. We've all admired it because it looks so natural. I've never cared for all those fluffs and curls myself, even though it's the fashion amongst the gentry as well as the —actresses."

The way she spoke the last word made Minella again want to laugh, but instead she said:

"They look very lovely on the stage."

"And that's where they should stay!" Mrs. Harlow snapped.

Then as if she thought she had been rude she quickly began to talk about something else.

When Minella ran downstairs to say goodbye to

Connie, Gertie and Nellie looked at her in a way she did not understand.

"You certainly lost no time in picking the biggest plum off the top of the cake!" Nellie said as she kissed her goodbye. "I think you've been very clever!"

Minella thought she was referring to her journey to the South of France and replied:

"I have always longed to see the Mediterranean."

"I only hope *it* isn't disappointing," Gertie said spitefully.

Then Connie interposed quickly:

"We all wish you the best of luck, Minella dear, and I am sure the Countess will find you are exactly what she needs. His Lordship says she is finding it difficult to read, and you have a beautiful voice. My father always said so."

"I will try to remember how he taught me to pronounce all the words which neither of us could spell!" Minella laughed.

Then the party was driving away in two Broughams and waving out of the windows until they were a long way down the drive.

The Earl looked at Minella and said:

"Now we have to hurry. The carriage will be round for us in a quarter-of-an-hour."

Minella gave a little cry and ran as quickly as she could upstairs.

She found however when she reached her bedroom that there was really nothing to do, because Mrs. Harlow and Rose had finished packing and three big trunks were just waiting to be strapped up by the footmen.

There were two hat-boxes and a hand-bag for Minella to carry, besides a pair of gloves which she was quite certain had cost far more than she would have spent on food in a week.

She was also fortunately able to wear Lady Sybil's shoes although like the hunting-boots they were a little on the big side.

But at least they were comfortable and Minella thought she would have been in misery if they had pinched her feet and made it difficult to walk in them.

Finally having put on a very pretty hat trimmed with quills and the cape that matched her gown, she picked up the hand-bag and said goodbye to Mrs. Harlow, then to Rose.

"Kiss Elspeth for me," she said, "and if I get a chance I will bring her back a French doll. I am sure she would like that."

"That's very kind of you, Miss," Rose said, "and I'll be praying that you gets the post with Her Ladyship."

Minella felt a little guilty that Rose's prayers were to be directed towards an end she was not actually seeking.

Then she thought that in the difficult task which lay ahead of her of pretending to be the Earl's wife she would need everybody's prayers, so she replied:

"Thank you, Rose, and please pray very hard that I will not make too many mistakes."

The Earl was waiting for her in the Hall and she knew as she appeared that he approved of how she looked, although he did not say anything.

They drove to the Halt where the train would stop specially for the Castle if the signal was up.

There was a servant waiting for them at the Halt, and hearing what the Earl said to him Minella realised he was a valet and had just come from London by train.

The train for Southampton came puffing in slowly and Minella found that there was a reserved compartment for the Earl in a First Class coach and one for his valet in the Second Class.

The luggage was all piled into the Guard's-Van, the Guard waved his flag and they were off.

Sitting opposite the Earl Minella looked at him with shining eyes and said:

"This is very, very exciting!"

He smiled at the enthusiasm in her voice.

"At least it will be interesting," he said, "and I am

sure you are looking forward to meeting General Kitchener."

"I have read everything in the newspapers about his
victories," Minella replied, "but apart from being a brilliant General, he sounds a somewhat strange and reserved man."

"He is," the Earl answered. "At the same time, I am
told that when he held a Service in Khartoum in General Gordon's memory, tears coursed down his cheeks."

Minella looked surprised.

"It is difficult to think of a man like that crying."

"I assure you it is something even men do when they
are deeply moved," the Earl replied.

Minella gave a little sigh.

"I suppose I am very ignorant about men," she said,
"because I have met so very few of them in my life."

She spoke without thinking, and only when she saw
the Earl looking at her somewhat cynically did she remember that she was supposed to have been touring
with a Theatrical Company.

As if he thought that once again she was acting for his
benefit, he said dryly:

"You have told me so little about yourself, not even
the name of the Play in which you were performing in
Birmingham."

Minella thought she could not bear to go on lying.
Besides, she was quite certain she would make so many
mistakes that the Earl would become suspicious.

After a pause she said:

"I think it would be a mistake, now that I am pretending to be your . . . wife, to think back to what I have
done . . . previously. I have always been told to . . .
think myself into . . . a new part, and that is what I am
. . . trying to do."

"A very commendable idea!"

The Earl spoke in his most sarcastic voice, and she felt
uncomfortably that he did not believe that was the real
reason for her being evasive.

However as they journeyed on they talked about a

great number of subjects, that had nothing to do with the stage.

They talked of the Earl's horses, of his hereditary duties at the Palace, and of places to which he had travelled abroad, all of which Minella found exceedingly interesting.

Just as she had persuaded her father to tell her of the places where he had been, and the people he had met, so she persuaded the Earl to talk about himself.

He had, she discovered, only very recently returned from India where he had stayed with his sister in Madras.

He described to her the Temples, the tremendous heat, and the importance of his brother-in-law, whose position in India was second only to that of the Viceroy.

"I would love to go to India," Minella said dreamily, "and I have tried to study the Hindu and the Buddhist religions. Although I found them fascinating, it is not the same as actually seeing their Temples and talking to the people."

"Surely that is a very strange thing to interest you?" The Earl remarked.

"Why?" she asked. "In England we are Christians, but other nations all over the world have different beliefs, which make them try to be better and finer people, and that is what matters more than dogma."

She spoke as she might have spoken to her mother, who was always interested in such things.

Because she was looking out of the window at that moment, she did not see the look almost of incredulity in the Earl's eyes.

The train was one of the new type which had a corridor and when it was time for luncheon the Earl's valet carried in a large hamper which had been brought from the Castle.

As he set it down the Earl said to Minella:

"I do not think you have met Hayes who has only been with me a few months."

Minella smiled at the valet who bowed and the Earl said to him:

"As Her Ladyship is not bringing a lady's-maid with her, Hayes, I hope you will look after her as you look after me."

"It will be a privilege, M'Lord," Hayes replied.

He set up a little table between them and served them both what Minella thought was a most delicious meal.

There was also champagne to drink, although the Earl remembered that she preferred lemonade, so she only had half a glass, more to please him than anything else.

When everything had been cleared away Minella said:

"I suppose Hayes believes I really am your . . . wife?"

"That is what I intended," the Earl replied. "And as he had no chance to talk to anyone from the Castle, there is no reason for him to query what I have told him."

"No, of course not," Minella agreed.

Minella was quite tired when they were piped aboard a large battleship that was waiting for them at one of the quays in the harbour.

They were greeted by the Captain and introduced to a number of the Senior Officers.

Then he said:

"As I am anxious, My Lord, to set to sea immediately, I am sure you and Her Ladyship would like to see your quarters."

"Thank you, Captain," the Earl replied. "We are in fact both very tired, and look forward to a good night before we encounter the turmoils of the Bay of Biscay."

The Captain laughed.

"The weather has been calm these past few days, and we are hoping it will not be too unpleasant an experience."

He led the way below saying as he did so:

"I hope you will be comfortable, My Lord. I have given you my own cabin, but the ship is somewhat overcrowded as we are taking out with us replacements for the officers and men who were killed at Omdurman, and also a number of extra troops which makes us think General Kitchener has some further campaign in mind."

"I hope not!" Minella exclaimed.

Yet she thought the two men were talking so enthusiastically of General Kitchener's triumphs that they had not heard her.

They had moved right to the stern of the ship when the Captain opened a door.

The accommodation he had given up for them consisted of a bedroom, which contained, what Minella recognised from her father's description, the traditional Captain's large box four-poster, although some of the latest ships were being converted to bunks.

Opening out of it was a bathroom which Minella considered a great luxury.

On the other side was a Sitting-Room in which was a long table and three armchairs fixed to the floor to prevent them from sliding about with the movement of the ship.

While they had been talking to the other officers, their trunks had been carried down below and the Earl's valet was already unstrapping one which Mrs. Harlow had told Minella contained the things she would want for the night.

"If there is anything you need, My Lord," the Captain was saying, "please ask your valet to let one of the stewards know and it will be brought to you at once."

"Thank you, Captain," the Earl replied, "but I am sure we shall have everything and thank you once again for giving up your own accommodation for us."

"It is a pleasure!" the Captain replied with a look of unmistakable admiration at Minella.

As soon as he had left, Minella ran excitedly to a port-hole to look out to sea.

"I wish we could go up on the bridge and watch the ship going out of harbour."

"I am sure they will let you do that tomorrow," the Earl replied, "but tonight you might be rather in the way."

"It is just exactly what I thought a ship would be," Minella cried. "Papa told me that the Captain's quarters were always very luxurious and panelled as this one is, with curtains over the portholes and pictures on the wall."

They were actually rather badly painted pictures of battleships, but as they seemed so appropriate she enjoyed looking at them.

There was also a bookcase in which she saw there were a number of books about ships, and she hoped there would be time to read quite a lot of them before they reached Cairo.

There was a knock on the door and a steward entered with a bottle of wine in an ice-cooler and also a pot of coffee.

"They are very kind," Minella said when he put it down on the table, "although I suppose I should not drink coffee at night in case it keeps me awake."

"I think nothing could do that!" the Earl replied. "The last two nights at the Castle you slept very soundly."

Minella laughed.

"You must have thought I was very rude going to bed so early," she said, "but as I always get up so early, I am tired soon after ten o'clock. I suppose it has become a habit for me to be ready to go to sleep at what Connie would think a ridiculously early hour."

As she finished speaking she realised once again that she had made a mistake.

If she had been on tour she would have had to stay up a great deal later than ten o'clock.

She was afraid the Earl had not missed what she said, but he made no comment and merely poured her out some coffee while he himself had a glass of wine.

While they were sitting at the table drinking, the valet came in to say:

"I've put everything ready, M'Lord. If there's anything else you want please send someone to fetch me."

"I will do that, Hayes," the Earl replied. "Goodnight!"

"Goodnight, M'Lord! Goodnight, M'Lady!"

The valet left the cabin, and Minella having finished her coffee walked into the bedroom next door taking off her hat and cape as she did so.

She put them down on the chair and looked for a cupboard, when suddenly she stopped dead.

Hayes had laid out her nightgown on one side of the bed, and she saw that on the other side on a chair was the Earl's robe, slippers and nightshirt.

For a moment she could not believe it.

Then she turned and ran back to the Sitting-Room.

"There has . . . been some . . . mistake," she said.

The Earl, who was standing, put down his empty wine glass on the tray beside the cup she had used.

"A mistake?" he asked.

"Where . . . is your bedroom?"

There was silence for a moment. Then the Earl replied:

"I think, Minella, this is the moment when you stop acting the innocent maiden!"

"I . . . I do not . . . understand!"

"It has been a brilliant performance, as I have already told you, and it would deceive anybody who was not as experienced as I am."

"I do not know . . . what you are . . . saying."

"Then let me put it a little more clearly," the Earl said. "I find you very attractive, and I see no reason why we should not enjoy our voyage together to Cairo as what we are supposed to be—man and wife!"

Minella stared at him, her eyes seeming to fill the whole of her face, and for a moment it was impossible to breathe.

Then in a voice that was hardly audible she said:

"D . . . do you . . . mean . . . ?"

"I mean," the Earl said, "that I will look after you

when we return to England. I will provide you with a
house in either St. John's Wood or—if you prefer, Chelsea—a carriage and I think, Minella, we will be very
happy together!"

Minella drew in her breath.

"Are you . . . asking me . . . to be your . . . mistress?"

She was not absolutely certain what this entailed.

At the same time she had read about the mistresses of
Charles II and the French Kings, and vaguely she knew
it was something that in this day and age was frowned
upon, not mentioned by Ladies, even if they knew of it.

The Earl smiled.

"I am asking you to be with me, Minella, and let me
make love to you. If you really want to have a part at the
Gaiety, I promise you will see it is a good one for which
you are well paid."

Minella gave a little cry of horror. Then she said:

"I cannot . . . do any of those . . . things . . . of
course not!"

"Why not?" the Earl asked. "Do you find me so repul-
sive?"

"No . . . no . . . it is not that . . . it is just that I
was only . . . pretending to be an actress because Connie . . . wanted me to make up . . . the numbers at
. . . your party."

"And Connie was quite sure that you would attract
me," the Earl said cynically, "which you have! I want
you, Minella, so stop fighting against something which
we shall both find very delightful."

He moved towards her as he spoke and Minella said
frantically:

"No, no! Connie . . . did not . . . mean that!"

"I am quite certain Connie did!" the Earl replied. "After all, as you well know, Connie is living with Connington, and she has had a number of other lovers, including Charlie until he preferred Nellie, and Roy
Heywood!"

For a moment Minella was absolutely still. Then she cried furiously:

"How dare you . . . say such evil . . . wicked . . . things about . . . Connie! Connie is a good . . . girl. Her father is a Parson . . . and although Papa . . . helped Connie, as he helped everyone, he would . . . never have . . . hurt her . . . Never! Never! Never!"

She spoke so violently that her voice seemed to ring out around the cabin.

Then as she faced the Earl, her eyes flashing with anger, she realised what she had said.

Because she was so shocked and horrified at his insinuations, the tears suddenly blinded her eyes and ran down her cheeks.

She turned away and put her hands over her eyes.

"Are you telling me," the Earl asked in a strange voice, "that you are Roy Heywood's daughter?"

Because she was crying Minella could not answer and he went nearer to her.

"Do not cry, Minella," he said, "I want you to tell me the truth."

"How . . . could you say such . . . terrible and wicked things . . . about Connie . . . and Papa . . ." Minella sobbed.

She felt the Earl's arms go round her and because she was so distraught they were somehow comforting. She put her face against his shoulder and went on crying.

"Connie . . . is good! I . . . I know she is good!" she murmured as if to convince herself. "She . . . admired Papa . . . even when we were very young and . . . doing lessons together . . . but that was all . . ."

"I do not want you to upset yourself," the Earl said, "and of course I believe you, if you tell me that is the truth."

Minella lifted her face wet with tears up to his.

"You . . . do believe me?"

Then she was very conscious of him looking down at her and the expression on his face was different from anything it had been before.

Because she was suddenly aware that the Earl had his arms around her, and his face was very close to hers, she tried to move away, but he would not let her go.

"I suppose you know," he said still in that quiet, strange voice she did not recognise, "that you have tortured me unbearably because I have fallen in love with you."

"You . . . love me?"

The words were hardly above a whisper.

"I love you!" the Earl repeated.

Then he drew her closer and his lips were on hers.

Just for the passing of a second Minella thought she should struggle, then as the Earl's mouth held her captive she knew that this was what, without realising it, she had longed and yearned for.

It was part of the beauty of the fairy-tale wonder that she had found at the Castle, part of her dreams and of everything in which she believed.

The Earl's kiss was at first, very gentle, almost tender. Then as he felt the softness and innocence of Minella's lips he became more possessive, more demanding.

She felt as if he had captured her heart and drew it from her body to make it his.

It was as if the sunshine moved through her and covered everything with gold, enveloping them both with a light that was so dazzling it came from their souls, and yet was part of the Divine.

It was so glorious, so wonderful, everything she had ever imagined a kiss might be with the man she loved, that she knew that if she died at this moment she would have touched perfection.

He opened for her the Paradise she had always known was there for those in love, as her father and mother had loved each other.

Only when the Earl raised his head did she gasp in a rapturous little voice that he could hardly hear:

"I love you . . . I . . . love . . . you! But I did not know . . . it until you . . . kissed me!"

"And I love you!" the Earl said. "I have loved you, my

125

darling, since the very first moment you came into the room and I thought I had never seen anybody so exquisite, so perfect in every way."

"Do you . . . really love . . . me?"

"I love you more than I can begin to tell you."

Then he was kissing her again, kissing her passionately, fiercely as if he was afraid of losing her.

She was not afraid.

She only knew that because in some ways he resembled her father he was the man who had always been in her dreams, the man whom she had prayed that one day she might find.

Then they both realised the engines were pulsating beneath them, and the ship was moving out of the harbour and down Southampton Water towards the sea.

Still keeping his arms round her the Earl sat down in one of the armchairs and pulled Minella down beside him.

There was only just room for the two of them, but the chair was large and he held her closely as if he would never let her go.

Then he looked at her for a long time before he said:

"How could you do anything so outrageous, so dangerous, as to pretend to be an actress?"

"I went to Connie for help . . . because I had to find . . . employment of some sort," Minella said.

She thought the Earl looked puzzled and asked:

"You know Papa is . . . dead?"

"I was told it in my Club, although there was nothing in the newspapers."

"I suppose it was wrong of me not to put it in 'The Times' or the 'Morning Post'," Minella said, "but . . . I had no . . . money."

"No money?"

"Papa left a great many . . . debts and there are still . . . still some to be paid."

"But why did you go to Connie?"

"Connie did not know that Papa was dead," Minella explained, "but she had written a letter to him thanking him for getting her into the Gaiety, and saying that one day she hoped to repay him for his kindness."

She did not notice the expression of understanding in the Earl's eyes as she went on:

"The only alternative was to go to . . . live with my aunt . . . Lady Banton in Bath, who is very old and disagreeable, and I knew she would . . . make me miserable."

"So you came straight from the country to London!" the Earl said as if he must convince himself she had not done anything else.

"I arrived on Friday," Minella said, "and while I was talking to Connie . . . Gertie and Nellie arrived to say that Katy was too ill to come to your party."

"So that is how it happened!"

"It was they who suggested I should take Katy's place."

"A crazy idea!" the Earl exclaimed.

"I do not know why you say that," Minella replied. "Connie said I must let no one know I was Papa's daughter as it was wrong, because I was a Lady, to be mixed up with Gaiety Girls. But I knew the Castle would be just like the ones Papa used to stay in, and I longed to see it."

"Your father has stayed with me," the Earl replied, "and he was one of the nicest and most amusing guests I have ever had!"

"Thank you for saying that," Minella answered, "and so you can understand that I think . . . perhaps Papa is . . . looking after me in . . . bringing me to you."

She spoke a little shyly and the Earl pulled her close to him and kissed her forehead.

"I am sure he is," he said. "At the same time, it was a risk which I am sure your mother would not have let you take."

Minella gave a little laugh.

"That is exactly what I thought myself. But when you asked me to accompany you to Cairo I felt I heard Papa say: 'Never funk your fences!' "

Then as if she remembered how this had all started Minella said in a small voice:

"I love you . . . but I know Mama would not . . . approve of my doing what you have . . . suggested."

"Of course not!" the Earl said firmly. "My precious, I have a question to ask you."

As he spoke he put his fingers under her chin and lifted her face up to his.

He looked at her searchingly before he said:

"If I divorce my wife, as she has asked me to do, will you marry me?"

There was a sudden light in Minella's eyes, and a radiance that transformed her face which told the Earl without words what the answer was.

Then she said hesitatingly:

"You are . . . quite certain you really . . . want me as your wife . . . and not as . . . what you suggested . . . just now?"

"If I suggested that, it was entirely your own fault," the Earl said. "As I have already said, I loved you the moment I saw you, and every moment we have been together I have fallen more and more in love. But, my darling, I did not think it was possible for me to marry an actress, and also you are intelligent enough to realise I was desperately afraid of making a second mistake."

"Perhaps it would be a . . . mistake to . . . marry me."

The Earl smiled.

"I have been fighting against my love for you," he said, "fighting too against every instinct in my body which told me you were pure and innocent, and everything that you pretended not to be."

"And . . . now?"

"Now I know that you are what I have been seeking all my life, only to be disillusioned, hurt and treacherously deceived."

His voice was suddenly hard, and there was an expression in his eyes which made Minella say:

"Oh, please . . . do not feel like that . . . I swear to

128

you that I will . . . never deceive you or hurt you! In fact . . . I want to . . . protect you."

The Earl smiled and his lips were very near to hers as he said:

"I thought that was what I was going to do!"

"Perhaps love makes everybody want to . . . protect the person one loves from anything that might . . . hurt them, either physically . . . or spiritually."

"God, how I love you!"

Then he was kissing her again, kissing her passionately until she felt as if she could no longer think. She only knew that the light that came from them both was blinding.

They were already, she knew, so much a part of each other that nothing, not even the sacrament of marriage, could make them closer.

It was a long time later that the Earl said:

"My darling, you are tired and you must go to bed."

She looked at him enquiringly and he said:

"You know I would not do anything to upset you, and although it will be very hard, we will wait until I am free and we can be married before I make love to you as I want to do."

Minella gave a little sigh of happiness and as she hid her head against his neck the Earl said as if he was thinking things out for himself:

"It will be very embarrassing if I have to ask the Captain for another cabin when he has already told us that the ship is full. I can sleep quite comfortably here in the chair, and in the morning I will come into your room before Hayes calls us."

Minella looked at the chairs and realised they could not even be pushed together so that he could stretch out his legs.

Then she said hesitatingly:

"I have an idea . . . but it might . . . shock you."

The Earl smiled.

"I do not think anything you could say, my darling, would shock me. I am listening."

129

"Well . . . Papa told me once about a strange custom they have in Sweden called 'Bundling' where engaged couples, because it is so cold, are allowed to get into bed together to talk . . . but they are not allowed to . . . touch each other."

"Are you suggesting that is what we should do?"

"Supposing," Minella said again hesitatingly, "I get into bed . . . and you lie on top of the bedclothes with an eiderdown . . . if there is one, and other blankets to keep you warm?"

She stopped and blushed.

"Perhaps," she said in a hesitating little voice, "you will . . . think it . . . immodest of me to suggest such a thing . . . but I do not want you to be . . . uncomfortable."

"I adore you," the Earl said quietly, "and I love you all the more for being so practical and for thinking of me."

Because she was looking at him appealingly, searching his face for a sign of disapproval, his lips found hers and he kissed her until once again it was impossible to think of anything but the sensations he aroused in her.

Then he drew her to her feet and said:

"Go along, I want to stay here all night kissing you, but I do not want you to look anything but exquisitely beautiful tomorrow, so that every man in the ship will be envious of me."

"I have never been with so many men before!"

They were walking towards the Sitting-Room door as she spoke and the Earl stopped and put his arms around her again.

"I warn you," he said, "I shall be wildly, frantically jealous, and if you so much as look at another man I will not let you leave the cabin until we reach Egypt. Then I shall take you home and lock you up in one of the dungeons of the Castle until we can be married!"

Minella laughed, and it was a very happy sound.

"You need not worry," she said. "I did not believe there was a man in the world as attractive as Papa until I met you, and now I know that no one could be so wonderful as you are . . . or so . . . exciting."

She hesitated over the last word and he saw the flush on her cheeks and thought it was the most wonderful thing he had ever seen.

Resolutely he took her into the bedroom and looking at the bed saw that it was very wide and comfortable and it would be possible for two people to lie side by side with a large space between them.

There was an eiderdown, as Minella had thought, and because Hayes knew his duty to provide him with every comfort there were two extra fluffy white blankets rolled up neatly on one of the built-in chests that surrounded the wall.

Minella looked at them at the same time as he did and gave a little laugh.

"I can see I was right!" she said.

"I realise I am going to have a very comfortable night," the Earl replied, and kissed her again.

He then picked up his night-clothes from where Hayes had left them and walked towards the Sitting-Room.

"Call me when you are in bed," he said. "Do you want me to undo your gown?"

"I . . . I can manage," Minella answered.

She stood looking at him as he walked towards the door and when he reached it she said:

"Promise me you are . . . not shocked . . . perhaps you would think it better if I slept in the Sitting-Room because I am . . . much smaller than you are . . . and I could . . . curl up in a chair."

The Earl held out his arms and she ran towards him.

"We will try out your plan tonight," he said as he held her very close, "and tomorrow night if you want anything different you have only to ask me. At the same time, my precious, I want you to trust me."

"Of course I do!" Minella replied.

She sounded as if she was surprised, and the Earl knew she did not really understand what he was saying.

As he went into the Sitting-Room and shut the door he thought that no man could have been more fortunate or more blessed than he was.

He did not believe that in the Social World in which he moved, and certainly not amongst the Gaiety Girls who amused him, he would find anyone so pure and innocent as he realised Minella was, and at the same time so intelligent and so interesting.

He had been bewildered and bemused by almost everything she had said to him during the weekend at the Castle, and it had seemed incredible that anybody so intelligent and so well-read should want to go on the stage.

The Gaiety Girls like Gertie and Nellie were beautiful and alluring, but the majority of them were certainly not stimulating to a man of intelligence.

Never in his whole life had he conversed with any woman, whatever her social standing, on the subjects he had covered with Minella.

Now as he walked to the porthole to look out on the distant shores as the ship moved down Southampton Water, he thought that his life would be enriched by her, and she would open new horizons to him that he had not been aware of before.

It seemed extraordinary that considering she was so young, he should be aware of her intellectual potentialities.

But he knew they were there, just as he knew that no woman had ever attracted him before in the same way as she did.

He desired her—of course he did—and her beauty astonished him.

At the same time, there was something not only physically alluring about her, but an innate spirituality which he now recognised was a purity not only of body but of mind which he had never found and thought was only part of his ideals.

"I love her!" he told himself and wondered frantically how long it would be before he could marry her.

He was undressed and wearing his silk robe which reached to the ground when he heard Minella calling.

He went in and saw she had extinguished all the lights except for one which stood by the bedside, and she was lying back against the pillows, her fair hair falling over her shoulders as he had seen her when he went to her bedroom last night.

He knew he must never tell her what he had intended, and what she in her innocence had never anticipated.

He had known then, although he dared not face it, that what he wanted was to have her as his wife and to see her holding his child against her breast as she had held Elspeth.

He walked towards the bed and realised that Minella was shy. Her eyes could not meet his and the colour had risen in her cheeks.

"I . . . I have put a . . . bolster down the . . . middle of the bed," she said, "just like . . . Papa told me they do in . . . Sweden . . . I thought it might make it more . . . comfortable for you."

There was a faint smile on the Earl's lips, but he did not say anything.

He merely sat down beside the bed facing Minella and took her hand in his.

"You know I love you, my lovely one, and one day I will be able to make you mine completely. It will not only be wonderful for us both, but something holy and sacred which we will remember all our lives."

He spoke very solemnly and Minella's fingers tightened on his.

"I . . . I am . . . afraid," she said, "I am . . . very ignorant about what . . . making love means . . . because Mama . . . never told me . . . but I know that . . . if it is like . . . kissing you . . . then it will be the most . . . glorious and perfect thing . . . ever given to us . . . by God."

"That is what it will be," the Earl said. "And now,

goodnight, my dearest, and promise you will dream of me."

Minella gave a little laugh.

"I think it would be impossible not to!"

He kissed her hand, then walked around the bed taking the light with him.

He lay on top of the blankets and he could feel the bolster that Minella had put between them, and he covered himself with half the eiderdown, then put another blanket over it.

"You will be warm enough?" Minella asked anxiously.

The Earl had not taken off his robe and he replied:

"You are not to worry about me, and I can assure you that when I was in the Army I very often slept on the ground, which I am ready to do tomorrow night, if you make me move to the other cabin."

"I love having you here," Minella said. "I feel . . . safe and no longer nervous of doing the wrong thing and making you angry with me."

"I will never be that," the Earl replied.

"Nellie said she thought you were a . . . frightening person and so did I . . . when I first . . . met you . . ."

"And now?" the Earl asked in the darkness.

"I think you are . . . very . . . very wonderful! I am going to say a long prayer of thankfulness . . . because you . . . love me."

"Then you must go to sleep," the Earl said quietly. "Goodnight, my precious."

"Goodnight," Minella said.

She began her prayers, but she was very tired and she fell asleep before she had finished.

The Earl lay awake for a long time listening to her gentle breathing.

He was thinking that although he did not deserve it, he had somehow, by the mercy of God, reached the threshold of Heaven.

CHAPTER SEVEN

❦

WHEN THEY REACHED the Bay of Biscay the ship began to pitch and toss, and Minella was very glad that she had the Earl beside her at night.

She noticed that he never touched her once she was in bed except to kiss her hand goodnight.

Although she did not understand, she thought it was the special way he had of showing her that he loved her and also revered her as his future wife.

At the same time, because she loved him more every moment they were together, she wanted his kisses.

As soon as they were alone in their Sitting-Room she would melt into his arms and feel once again that he carried her up into a special Heaven which she had never known existed.

Now the ship began to make some very strange movements and she could feel the whole hull shudder as it ran into heavy seas. Fortunately she did not feel sick, but she was frightened.

The sea had been smooth as they cruised down the Channel, but she had been aware this evening while they were dining with the Captain and some of the other officers that the wind was growing stronger.

"Are you a good sailor, M'Lady?" the Captain had asked.

"I hope so," Minella replied, "but certainly, this is the first time I have been at sea."

"Then we must do our very best that you should not have unpleasant memories of being aboard," the Captain smiled.

When dinner was over and Minella and the Earl had sat for a while in the Officers' Mess, they had said good-night and retired to their own quarters.

For the first time Minella found it was difficult to walk and slipped her arm through the Earl's so that he could support her.

Once they were in the privacy of their own Sitting-Room he pulled her down beside him in a chair and kissed her until she forgot the sea and everything except how wonderful he was.

After they were in bed, Minella was aware that the movement was getting worse, and after rolling from side to side, the ship was now pitching and tossing.

Quite suddenly she felt frightened and putting out her hand towards the Earl she said:

"You do not . . . think we shall . . . 'turn turtle' and go to the . . . bottom?"

She thought he was awake although she was not sure, and instantly her hand was in his, and she knew that he turned towards her as he replied:

"We are quite safe, my precious. These ships are made to stand up to far worse seas than this!"

"I cannot . . . help feeling rather . . . frightened!"

"I can understand that," he said, "but we are in good hands, and I am quite certain that when we do die it will not be from drowning."

Minella did not take her hand away and very gently he reached out and put his arm around her shoulders.

"I am so glad you are here," she said in a whisper, "otherwise I think I should just . . . cover my head with the . . . blankets and say my . . . prayers."

"Instead of which we will talk about ourselves," the Earl said, "which will give you something else to think about."

"It is difficult to think of . . . anything but . . . you."

"That is what I want you to say," he replied. "Now let me tell you of my plans."

The way he spoke made her ask somewhat apprehensively:

"What . . . are they?"

At the same time she was no longer frightened because his arm was around her, and although he had not kissed her she knew his face was very near to hers.

"I have told the Captain," the Earl began, "that I have an important message for our Ambassador in Italy from Her Majesty the Queen. He did not intend that we should stop in Naples, but he has now agreed to put into the harbour just long enough for me to carry out my mission."

Minella was listening intently, but she did not quite understand until the Earl said:

"What I really intend to do is to see my wife and ask her to give me the evidence I will require to start divorce proceedings immediately we return home."

"Does that mean there will be reports in the newspapers?" Minella asked.

He sighed.

"I am afraid so, and of course I am nervous of what the papers will say. Above all you must not be involved in any way and that means we shall have to live apart from each other."

Minella gave a little cry.

"Oh . . . no . . . I cannot . . . bear it!"

"There is nothing else we can do," the Earl said quietly, "and I am wondering whether it would be best for you to go to your aunt's, or if not, I could leave you with my mother on the way back from Cairo."

Minella did not speak and as if he was following his own train of thought he said:

"It will be some months before proceedings can begin, and by that time the people who have seen us together in Cairo may not think it so strange that we have quarrelled and parted."

There was a harsh note in his voice as he said:

"I cannot tell you how much I loathe and detest the idea of anybody believing you would behave in the despicable way my real wife has done."

He paused to add more quickly:

"But for the moment, there is nothing else we can do but take every precaution by keeping out of the public eye. I shall of course employ the best Lawyers obtainable."

There was silence. Then Minella said in a very small voice:

"Perhaps because you . . . hate it so . . . much it would be . . . best if I did not . . . marry you."

The Earl's arms tightened around her.

"Do you really think I could lose you now?" he asked. "Every minute we are together, my darling, I fall more and more in love and I have never known such happiness until I found you."

"Is that . . . true?"

"I think now that we know each other so well that you would be aware if I was lying."

"As you would . . . know if I . . . was."

"You will never deceive me again," the Earl said. "Actually I was not really deceived, only bewildered that while you told me one thing, my instinct told me something very different."

"Did you really believe I was . . . fast and . . . immoral like Nellie and . . . Gertie?"

The Earl realised that she had deliberately omitted Connie's name and he said quietly:

"You told me that you intended to 'think' yourself into the part, and while at the moment you are playing the role of my wife, it is something you will be, in reality, as soon as the law allows it."

His arms tightened round her as he added:

"As the Countess of Wynterborne you will know nothing about Gaiety Girls except what you have seen from the Stalls!"

Minella gave a little laugh. Then she said:

"I thought the Show was the most beautiful

experience I had ever had. The music was so lovely, and so were all the girls performing in it."

"What you will always remember is what you saw from the front of the stage," the Earl said firmly, "and not what you have heard and seen behind it."

"I will do that . . . if you want . . . me to," Minella replied simply.

"I adore you!" he said. "And now, my darling, I think you should try to go to sleep. I hope the sea will have abated in the morning, but if you are frightened, I am here."

"It is so . . . marvellous to . . . feel your arm . . . around me," Minella whispered, "perhaps I might . . . pretend to be frightened."

The Earl laughed. Then he said:

"I shall know when you are acting, so go to sleep. I promise that you are quite safe."

With an effort Minella turned away from him and shut her eyes.

But she was thinking as she did so how much he would hate the scandal and inevitable gossip in a divorce, and wondered what she could possibly do to prevent it hurting him.

"Perhaps I ought to . . . leave him," she told herself.

Then she sent up a prayer to her father saying:

"Help me, Papa! Help me to do what is right. You know his world so much better than I do, and I could not bear that he should find his position at Court damaged or be sneered at by his friends."

She was still praying when she fell asleep . . .

❧❧❧❧❧❧

The next morning the worry was still in Minella's mind and even the beauty of the Mediterranean when they reached it did not dispel the little shadow over her happiness.

The evening before they were to reach Naples they

139

dined alone in their cabin and when the steward had withdrawn Minella said to the Earl:

"I . . . want to talk . . . to you."

There was a serious note in her voice that made him look at her sharply and she said:

"Come and sit down comfortably."

He did as she asked, sitting in one of the big arm-chairs and putting out his arms to her, but she shook her head and instead sat down on the rug at his feet.

Her gown which was a very pale shade of blue billowed out over the floor and her white neck and shoulders were framed by the soft chiffon which formed the décolletage.

The Earl thought that with her fair hair and her child-like expression of trust she looked like a small angel peeping through a summer sky.

Now he knew her better he was aware that he had never known a woman whose eyes mirrored her feelings more clearly or who could express herself in words which sounded like poetry.

It was true, as he had said to Minella, that he was falling in love with her more every minute they were together.

He knew that unexpectedly he had found what all men seek, perfect love and a woman who was also the complement of himself.

While he was blasé, cynical and in the past ready to mock at anything that was sentimental or even sacred, Minella's instinct for what was good had made her walk innocently and safely through the dangers that she encountered in going to London and to Connie for help.

The Earl did not underestimate what might have happened to her, and yet he knew that it was Minella's innocence and purity which had protected her far more effectively than anything else could have done.

He told himself now that whatever the cost to himself he would in the future protect her from anything that might hurt or spoil her, and he knew that once his affairs were settled they would be blissfully happy together.

The only difficulty lay in the length of time the divorce would take and the consequences which would undoubtedly for a little while at any rate, damage his position at Court, and distress the family of which he was the head.

Then as he was aware that Minella sitting at his feet was looking at him pleadingly, he asked:

"What is it, my precious?"

"I am thinking about . . . tomorrow."

For a moment the Earl's eyes darkened as he thought how much he disliked the idea of seeing his wife again.

He would also encounter the man who had undoubtedly plotted with her to go through the marriage arranged by her father so that he would be responsible for the child she was carrying.

The Earl had not mentioned it to Minella as he realised she would not understand, but if the child which had been born to his wife was a boy, it was legally his and would in time be the heir to his title.

Because the whole idea disgusted him and made him angry, he had deliberately not enquired when it was born or what sex it was.

He had ignored the letters his wife had sent him, begging for the unborn child's sake that he would grant her a divorce.

He had, however, because he had no wish to lower himself to the level of his wife and her lover, continued the allowance that he had given Olive when they were married.

It was quite a considerable sum, which his bank transferred to Naples every quarter.

But it had not really been a generous gesture, merely a way, he admitted to himself, of preventing anybody being aware that he had been deserted a week after his marriage.

Now in a voice that Minella had not heard since they declared their love for each other he said bitterly:

"I have no wish to think about tomorrow, but it is something which cannot be avoided."

"I . . . I know that," Minella said, "and . . . because I love you . . . I have had an idea."

"What is it?"

She did not touch him, but he was aware that she was trembling and the colour rose in her cheeks as she said in a voice he could hardly hear:

"When we first . . . came aboard you . . . made a suggestion to me which I . . . refused."

"You know I only suggested it because although I loved you I had no idea then that you were both your father's daughter and also everything I ever looked for and wanted in my wife."

"I love you for . . . saying that," Minella said, "but because I know it will . . . hurt you to have a divorce . . . and because you will . . . hate it so much . . . I am ready now . . . to accept your . . . s . . . suggestion."

Because it was difficult to say she stumbled over the words, and as if she was too shy to look at him she put her cheek against his knee.

For a moment the Earl was still. Then he said very quietly:

"Now I know, my darling, that you love me as much as I love you, and I shall always remember what you have said, and treasure it in my heart."

He put out his arms and lifted her onto the chair beside him and held her very close.

"But my answer, my precious one, is 'no'!"

"B . . . but . . . why?"

"Because," he said quietly, "while I worship you for what you have said to me, I do not want you hidden secretly away in a house in St. John's Wood or Chelsea, as I very stupidly thought possible, but with me as my wife."

He kissed her hair before he went on:

"You will be the chatelaine of the Castle and all my

other houses, and be with me every day, and in my arms every night."

The way he spoke was so moving that Minella felt the tears come into her eyes.

"I am trying to . . . help you," she whispered.

"I know that," the Earl answered, "but what you are offering is not enough. I want you completely and absolutely. Mine, not only from the top of your head to the soles of your pretty little feet, but with every breath you draw, with every thought you think. You are mine, Minella, and I cannot live without you."

Then he was kissing her, kissing her fiercely, demandingly, possessively and it was impossible to say any more.

At the same time, when they went ashore at Naples Minella was apprehensive, because she knew that the Earl was already upset, and she was afraid of what might happen after he had seen his wife.

At any other time she would have been thrilled at her first glimpse of Naples rising above the harbour with the sunshine glittering on the roofs and spires, and the colour that seemed to be everywhere.

There was too, the 'shimmering light' that she had read was very characteristic of Italy.

Because there had been guide-books in the bookcase she had also read the history of Naples, and she only wished they could stay longer and visit Pompeii.

She could see Mount Vesuvius silhouetted against the sky, but nothing was of any importance except the ordeal which the Earl faced from which she felt helplessly she was powerless to save him.

There was a carriage drawn by two horses waiting for them on the quay.

They were rowed ashore in the ship's launch with the sailors looking very smart with white covers on their caps which they had assumed as soon as they reached the sunshine.

Although she was unlikely to see anybody, Minella had chosen because she wanted to please the Earl, one of the many gowns from her trunks which was a very pretty summer one of spring green.

It was trimmed with white lace and had a wide-brimmed hat which was encircled by a wreath of white roses.

She looked very young and very spring-like, but although the Earl's eyes rested lovingly on her she felt there was a shadow in them, and she wanted to put her arms around him to protect him.

As the carriage drove through the narrow streets where the washing seemed to be hanging from every balcony and there were even washing-lines stretching across the street itself, several storeys up, the Earl did not speak.

Although Minella wanted to exclaim excitedly at everything she saw, she felt it would be inappropriate.

They drove until they reached the high part of the town, then stopped outside a house that was very picturesque.

It was, Minella thought, exactly the sort of place where an artist would choose to have a Studio.

For a moment the Earl did not move and Minella slipped her hand into his and said softly:

"God go with you, my darling!"

She felt the quick pressure of his fingers.

Then almost as if he went into battle he squared his shoulders and stepped from the carriage.

He told the coachman to wait, and because the sun was hot Minella opened the white sunshade she had brought with her and held it over her head.

She wondered if perhaps, after all their wild anticipation of what would happen, the Earl's wife might be away or might even refuse to see him.

Then as she saw the door, which was up a long flight of stone steps, open and the Earl walk inside the house, she knew that one hurdle at any rate was crossed.

Now there was nothing she could do but pray as she had prayed before that there might be no difficulties in getting a divorce and that as the Earl's wife lived in Italy the English public might perhaps, be kept in ignorance.

"Please . . . God . . . please . . ." she prayed.

Then as if she thought only her father could help her she was talking again to him.

"You understand even better than I do, Papa, how much he will suffer if every detail of his marriage is reported in the newspapers. But I love him, and I know we can be happy as you and Mama were happy together . . . so . . . please . . . please . . . make things come right . . . and quickly!"

Because Minella was so innocent, she did not at all understand how difficult it was for the Earl to lie beside her every night and not touch her.

At the same time, she was women enough to be aware that she excited him when he kissed her.

Once or twice during the night, after the sea was again calm and he knew she was not afraid, he would leave the bedroom and go into the Sitting-Room.

She did not say anything or ask the next day why he had done so.

But instinctively she felt it was because he wanted to be closer to her, to kiss her, but he was controlling his desires because of some rule of behaviour he had made for himself.

"He is so magnificent, so wonderful!" Minella murmured. "I want to be his wife and to give him . . . children who will . . . love the Castle as much as he . . . does."

She seemed to have waited for almost an eternity before at last the door of the house opened and the Earl came out.

He came alone, and there appeared to be nobody to see him off as he walked down the steps and climbed into the carriage beside her.

"To the British Consulate!" he told the coachman.

As the horses moved off Minella found herself holding her breath.

Her eyes were frightened as she looked at the Earl,

afraid of what she would read in his face even before he spoke.

Then he smiled faintly and she felt as if the sun was peeping through the clouds.

"It is . . . all right?"

Her voice trembled and it did not sound like her own.

He took her hand in his and held it so tightly that his fingers hurt her.

"I cannot believe it is true!"

"What . . . is?"

"My wife died over a year ago and the child she was carrying was born dead."

Minella stared at him.

"They . . . did not . . . let you know?"

"The man for whom she left me, is a despicable character and wanted to go on receiving her allowance."

"Then . . . you have been . . . free a long time!"

"For well over a year!" the Earl replied.

As if the full implication of what it meant swept over him he turned for the first time to look at Minella as he said:

"And now, my darling, we can be married!"

"Are you . . . sure? Are you . . . really sure?"

"Very sure!" the Earl said. "And it is something I am not going to delay for one moment."

"We are to be married at the British Consulate?"

He shook his head.

"No, that would be a mistake because it would then be known that you have travelled with me here, without actually being my wife."

"Then . . . what are we going to . . . do?"

"I have just been thinking it out," the Earl said, "and I have a plan of which I hope you will approve."

Minella put her hand over his.

"Are you really . . . saying we can be . . . married?"

"We are going to be married," he said, "and, my darling, I think your prayers have made everything I have longed for, but believed impossible, come true."

"Tell me . . . tell me quickly what you are . . . planning."

The Earl drew in his breath before he said:

"We are making a courtesy call at the British Consulate, and when we return to the ship I shall inform the Captain that while I was there I received some very disturbing news from England."

"And what will you tell him?" Minella asked anxiously.

"I shall say that I have learnt that my marriage, which took place eighteen months ago by Special Licence in the Protestant Church in Nice, was not in the opinion of the Archbishop of Canterbury completely legal, because the Parson who performed it was not a reputable member of the Church."

Minella stared at him wide-eyed, and he went on as if he was still working it out for himself:

"Therefore, swearing the Captain to secrecy and explaining that I have no wish for such a situation to be made public, I shall ask him to marry us at sea."

"At . . . sea?" Minella repeated faintly.

"It is, as I expect you are aware, completely legal for a ship's Captain to marry at sea anyone on board who asks him to do so, and when he performs the ceremony you will be my wife!"

Minella gave a little cry. Then because she could not help it, the tears were running down her cheeks.

"My . . . prayers are . . . answered!" she said brokenly, "and I am sure Papa . . . as well as God . . . listened to me when I asked that there should be no . . . publicity to upset you and that you would not . . . suffer the stigma of a . . . divorce."

"How could your prayers not be heard?" the Earl asked.

Then as Minella hastily wiped her tears away she saw the Union Jack as the horses drove in through the gates of the British Consulate.

Later that night, as Minella lay in bed with only one light beside her, the Earl came into the room as he had every previous night they had been at sea.

He walked as he had before to her side of the bed and sat down facing her, taking her hand in his.

As she looked at him she thought that no man could look more happy, and at the same time so overwhelmingly handsome and masculine.

Because she knew that tonight everything was different she felt herself blush and it was hard to meet his eyes.

She had felt shy after they had returned to the ship and the Earl had left her alone in the cabin, when he went to talk to the Captain.

He was away for some time but Minella found it impossible to sit down and wait quietly.

Instead she moved restlessly about the cabin aware that the ship had already started to move out of port as soon as they returned, and they were once again on their way to Egypt.

She had changed from the dress she had worn to go ashore with the Earl into a very lovely gown that she was sure must have been one of Lady Sybil's best.

It was made of chiffon and there was frill upon frill cascading like little waves around her feet while the bodice fitted very tightly into a tiny waist.

It was a white gown which she thought appropriate.

At the same time there were touches of colour in the pink sash, and the Earl had bought her two huge baskets of flowers in Naples on their way back to the ship, one of pink roses that were still in bud, and the other of star-shaped orchids.

"You were wearing orchids the first time I saw you," he said, "and I thought they shone like stars in your hair and you yourself glowed with a spiritual light that I had never seen before."

Because she thought it would please him, Minella held a bunch of the orchids in her hand and had pinned some of the pink roses to the waist of her gown.

When the Earl came into the cabin with the Captain there was an expression in his eyes that told her how much he loved her.

She did not realise that her own face was radiant with a happiness that seemed to pulsate through her like the music of angels.

The Captain shut the door behind him and said:

"His Lordship has explained to me, My Lady, your predicament, and of course it is quite easy for me to put right anything that was legally wrong with your marriage."

"Thank you . . . it is very . . . kind of you, Captain," Minella managed to answer.

"May I say it is an honour and a privilege," he replied, "and you can trust me never to speak of it, unless it ever became necessary from a legal point of view."

"My wife wants to thank you as I do, Captain, for coming to our rescue," the Earl said, "because you will understand that we were most upset at the information I received at the British Consulate."

"Of course, I understand," the Captain replied, "and now, if you will both stand in front of me, I will make sure that you are properly joined together for life."

He opened the Prayer-Book he held in his hands as he spoke and began the Marriage Service.

The Earl held Minella's hand as they made their responses, and as he put her wedding-ring back on her finger she felt as if the whole host of Heaven was singing a special *Hallelujah*.

She was also sure that her father was beside her, giving her away as he would have done had he been alive.

She was as vividly conscious of him as she was of the Earl, and she knew that whatever troubles or difficulties lay ahead of them, he would always be there to help and protect her.

As the short Service ended, the Captain said:

"By the Power invested in me as Captain of '*H.M.S. Victorious*' by Her Majesty Queen Victoria, I pronounce that you be man and wife together, and may God bless your union."

There was a little silence as he closed his Prayer-Book. Then the Earl said very quietly:

"Thank you. My wife and I are extremely grateful."

"I think, My Lord," the Captain said, "this calls for a celebration! I have already ordered a bottle of the best champagne we can manage aboard to be put on ice!"

It was brought to the cabin and the Captain drank their health, then left them alone.

Only when the door closed behind them did the Earl hold out his arms and Minella flung herself against him.

"We are married!" she cried. "We are really . . . married!"

"We will have a thousand other Services, if you want them," the Earl said, "but all that matters is that you are now legally my wife, and nobody can take you from me."

The Earl's voice had a note of elation in it as he went on:

"There are no more difficulties to face."

"What will you tell . . . everyone at home?" Minella asked.

"Leave that to me," the Earl replied. "I have it all planned out. I shall let the Newspapers be aware my wife died a long time ago, then after we return from a long—very long honeymoon we will announce our marriage."

Then before Minella could speak he was kissing her passionately insistently.

At the same time, because she knew that he was as moved as she was, there was something reverent and sacred in his kiss which told her how much she meant to him . . .

But now, after all they had been through together, she felt shy.

As if he understood the Earl said:

"I could sit here all night just looking at you because you are so beautiful, and telling you how much I love you. But, darling, I want you closer without that bolster between us! Whoever invented 'Bundling' ought to be shot!"

Because it was not what she expected him to say, Minella laughed, and the Earl took off his robe and got into bed beside her.

He pulled her into his arms but did not kiss her, only held her very close, before he said:

"I will be very gentle, my darling. You are not afraid of me?"

Minella had her face against his shoulder and whispered:

"I am so . . . ignorant . . . I am afraid of doing something . . . wrong."

The Earl held her very close and there was an expression in his eyes no woman had ever seen.

"My darling, my wonderful little love," he said, "nothing you do is anything but right and perfect, but I could not bear it if I did anything which made you stop loving me."

Minella lifted her face to his.

"That would be impossible, and I love you until I feel as if we have . . . fought a tremendous battle . . . side by side, or perhaps dived dangerously down into the very depths of the sea . . . but emerged triumphant!"

"That is what we have done," the Earl agreed, "but how could I ever have guessed or hoped that fate would be so kind to us?"

He did not wait for Minella to answer, his lips were on hers.

As she felt him draw her closer and closer she knew that whether it was fate or God, or her father and mother who had smoothed their path and swept away the obstacles, they would both of them, show their thankfulness by giving some of their happiness to other people.

It was what her father had always done with his laughter and his kindness.

She was sure it was something she and the Earl must do in the future, not only by being happy themselves, but by making other people feel the same.

Then it was impossible to think while he was kissing her but only to feel the wild sensations of excitement surging through her.

As his lips were on hers and his hands touched her body Minella heard again the music of angels and felt a light illuminating them both that came from their hearts and souls.

"I love you . . . I love you!" she wanted to say.

Instead she was carried away on the ecstasy of love into the Heaven to which the Earl had taken her before, only now it was even more rapturous, more perfect, and also gloriously divine.

It was a love which consumed them both like a burning fire, leaping higher and higher until they were no longer human but one with the gods.

"I love you!" the Earl was saying hoarsely. "My darling, precious, perfect little wife, I love you!"

"I . . . adore you!" Minella whispered. "Show me how to . . . love you as you . . . want to be loved and make me your . . . real wife now and . . . for always!"

Then there was only the music of the angels and the blinding light of eternal love.

Love in the Moon

Author's Note

When I visited the Dordogne area this year (1980) I thought it beautiful, and I also enjoyed passing through the prolific and famous vineyards round Bordeaux. The depression, as I related in this story, started in the early 1860s when phylloxera was introduced into France by infected stock from America.

By the time the nature of the disease was fully understood, the pest had spread so rapidly that little could be done to check it.

In Périgord the worst of the ravages occurred in the late 1870s and by 1892 the area devoted to vines was only a fifth of what it had been twenty years earlier.

But, though the population is still less than it should be, crops are now well established. Strawberries are sent daily during the season by lorry to Paris; Dordogne is the leading department in France for the production of walnuts; tobacco is often the peasant farmers' best source of cash.

A dozen papermills employ fifteen hundred workers, while the industries concerned with trees, fruit, and pedigree bulls employ many others.

But tourism beats them all, and the fascination of "a corner of the moon" lies in the battle cry of a Périgordin made a thousand years ago.

"A stone for the wicked, a loving heart for one's friends, a sword for the enemy—if you can find all three, you are a Périgordin."

CHAPTER ONE

❧

1878

THE EARL OF LANGSTONE helped himself to another lamb cutlet from a large silver dish as the door of the Dining-Room opened and his sister came in.

She was dressed in a riding-habit, and he looked up from the breakfast-table with a smile to say:

"You are late, and I suppose the excuse is the usual one, that your horse kept you."

"Of course he did!" Lady Canéda Lang replied. "Who else would be so alluring at this hour of the morning?"

Her brother laughed.

"That is for you to say. What happened with Warrington last night?"

Canéda did not reply as she helped herself to bacon and eggs from a side-table. Then as she sat down opposite her brother she said:

"I think, Harry, you will have to speak to him. He is becoming a nuisance. He made me go with him into the Conservatory and kept me there practically by force!"

"It would save a lot of trouble if you would accept him," the Earl replied.

His sister made a derisive sound.

"I have no intention of marrying Lord Warrington or any other of those half-wits who have proposed to me these last two months. I keep remembering they would

157

not be so keen if you had not come into a title and a very large fortune."

The Earl laughed.

"A cynic at nineteen!" he teased. "My dear Canéda, you are a very pretty girl, and it is not surprising that men throw their hearts at your feet, especially when you are well gowned."

Canéda's eyes softened.

"That I owe to you, Harry, and there is not a moment of the day when I do not enjoy feeling like a Princess in a fairy-tale and remember that my wardrobe is full of other gowns just as delectable."

"I have the idea," her brother answered, "that you are fishing for compliments, but I am sure you know without my telling you that fine feathers make fine birds."

"That is true," Canéda replied, "but, Harry, it is exciting, is it not, to be rich, to be living here, having all those wonderful, wonderful horses you have bought me to ride, as well as Ariel?"

"What have you been teaching him this morning?" the Earl enquired.

"I have two new tricks for you to see as soon as you have the time. You never believe me, but I swear he understands every word I say to him! However many gorgeous horses fill your stable, there will never be one as marvellous as Ariel!"

The Earl did not argue.

He knew what his sister felt about the horse she had had since it was a foal, and which when they were poor she had looked after herself.

It had been an extravagance for her to have a horse of her own in addition to those shared between father and son.

Canéda had always been crazy about horses ever since she was a child, and the Earl had to admit that Ariel was, as a result of her teaching, a very remarkable horse indeed.

But it was with almost the same enthusiasm as his

sister showed, and with a sense of great satisfaction, that he thought of the stables at Langstone Park, which were now filled to capacity.

He had plans being drawn up for extending the buildings to accommodate more horses, which he had every intention of buying in the near future.

It was only nine months ago that Harry Lang had awakened one morning to find incredibly and with a distinct sense of shock that he had become an Earl.

There had been three lives between him, the only son of a younger son, and the title and Estates of the Earls of Langstone. His father had been killed in a hunting accident two years earlier, and now a storm in the Irish Sea had caused the death of his uncle and his two sons as they were returning to England from the Emerald Isle.

Because Harry's father had never got on with his elder brother and it was up to the head of the family to finance the other members of it, they had been extremely poor.

But they had also, Canéda often thought, been much happier in their small Manor House in an equally small village than their relations who lived in grandeur in the family mansion and apparently had a huge fortune to play with.

The Earl's two sons, both of whom were older than Harry, enjoyed themselves so much amongst the gaieties and frivolities of London that they had both, despite insistent pressure from their parents and other relations, refused to marry.

One pursued social beauties who were inevitably already married; the other preferred the exceedingly attractive actresses who were to be found on stage at Drury Lane and the Gaiety Theatre, which was already becoming famous for its lovely women.

In consequence, they were both nearly thirty and unmarried, so that Harry at twenty-four stepped into their inheritance and became the ninth Earl.

To Canéda it was as if fate had waved a magic wand over them, so that while sitting like Cinderella among the ashes she was suddenly transplanted in a "pumpkin" carriage to a Prince's Palace.

Langstone Park, which she had visited only a few times in her life, certainly justified that description.

Enormous, in the grandiose style of Blenheim Palace and Castle Howard and built by the same architect, Vanbrugh, it looked breathtaking as they drove down the drive.

Although Harry said very little, she had known by the pulse throbbing at the side of his cheek that he was as thrilled as she was.

First of all, there had been the Funeral of the late Earl and his two sons, when the great house had been filled with relatives from all over England, who had flocked there not only to pay their respects to the dead but also to inspect critically and a little apprehensively his inheritance.

Because Gerald Lang had paid little attention to his relatives and they to him in the past twenty-five years, it was obvious that they were all wondering what the new head of the family would be like and if Harry would live up to its traditions.

It would have been impossible, Canéda had thought as she watched their sideways glances at her brother, for them not to be impressed by his appearance.

He was tall, broad-shouldered, fair, and handsome in the Lang tradition.

In fact, it was difficult to imagine that he was not entirely English although his mother had been French.

Canéda, on the other hand, resembled the exquisite Clémentine de Bantôme, whom Gerald Lang had seen when he was exploring France, and he had instantly determined that she should be his wife.

It was not only the Langs who thought it an undoubted mistake for one of their family to marry a foreigner, but also the de Bantômes, who were furious that an impecunious and to them unimportant Englishman should persuade Clémentine to run away with him on the eve of her marriage to another man.

The *Comtes* de Bantôme had always given themselves great airs.

Their Estate in the Périgord region of France on the banks of the Dordogne had been theirs for centuries and they were also rich and powerful.

Therefore, like all French aristocrats, they were determined that the noble strain in their blood should be matched by the nobility of those who sought their children's hands in marriage.

Clémentine had been betrothed to the *Duc* de Saumac, a man very much older than she was.

In running away with her, Gerald Lang had offended not only the de Bantômes but the *Duc*, who was equally as powerful in the Loire Valley, where his Estate was situated.

It was an insult that was translated into a vendetta against Gerald Lang, and it had its repercussions in various ways.

The first thing Gerald found after he married Clémentine was that it was impossible for him to visit France without being arrested on some trumped-up charge or another.

At first he could hardly believe that it was not just chance that he, an ordinary tourist, was being continually taken to the nearest *Gendarmerie* for questioning.

He soon discovered who was behind it, and it became such a persecution that he knew it was impossible for either himself or his wife ever to stay in Paris again.

He also suffered insults and hostility in London, where the French Ambassador had obviously had instructions from the *Duc* to stir up trouble.

It was therefore fortunate that Gerald Lang had no wish to shine socially and was perfectly content to settle down in the country with his wife, his children, and, when he could afford them, his horses.

Fortunately, as he was such an outstanding rider, he more often rode other people's horses than his own.

Neighbouring Squires liked the Langs and often lent

both father and son their horses to ride in races, steeple-chases, Point-to-Points, and hunting.

Because she was so attractive they would also gladly have mounted Canéda, but she had been content for the last three years with her own horse, which she loved more than anything else in the whole world.

For Harry to become the owner of what was even before he added to it a first-class stable, and to know that he would have every facility for racing his own horses, was a joy beyond words.

The brother and sister had become an instant success when they opened Langstone House in Grosvenor Square.

They had paid a perfunctory gesture in respect of mourning their uncle and had appeared in London in the sixth month to take the Social World by storm.

Harry's looks and charm in addition to his title and wealth threw every door open to him, and Canéda had a very different type of success but one that was no less gratifying.

If Harry looked like his English forebears, Canéda was like her mother.

She was small, her dark hair had mysterious blue lights in it, and her oval face was dominated by two huge eyes outlined by long dark eye-lashes.

But there the French resemblance ended, and Canéda's eyes were the same blue as her brother's, making her already lovely face even more arresting because the combination was so unusual.

She was beautiful enough to make any man who looked at her want to look again, and once his eyes were caught by her blue ones he became her captive and there was no escape.

"It cannot be true, Harry!" Canéda said breathlessly a few weeks after they had been in London. "I have had no less than three proposals of marriage tonight!"

"I am not surprised," Harry replied.

He had been aware during the Ball which they had both attended that his sister shone like a star amongst the other rather gauche, tongue-tied, shy young women of the same age.

Even compared with the dazzling, sophisticated older women she seemed to have a quality which was missing in them and which, even though she was his sister, Harry thought had something irresistible about it.

It was perhaps her vivacity, the way her eyes shone and her lips curved in a smile, that made her appear more alive than anybody he had ever met.

Because brother and sister were so close to each other and because all through their childhood they had had a companionship that was unusually intimate, Harry felt very protective about Canéda and was determined that no-one should rush her into marriage.

Elderly aunts who had constituted themselves Canéda's Chaperones were already pressing him to make her accept one of the very advantageous offers she had received.

"Lord Warrington is exceedingly rich," they said, "and his house in Huntingdonshire is almost as fine as Langstone Park."

Harry had not been responsive, and they had gone on almost angrily:

"We are told that Canéda rejected the Earl of Headingly without even listening to what he had to say! How can she be so foolish?"

Harry, who had his own opinion about the Earl of Headingly, had not been very impressed.

"Canéda can marry whom and when she wants," he said, "and the longer she takes about it, the better I shall be pleased, as I like to have her with me."

"You have no right to spoil her chances," his aunts protested, but Harry had only laughed.

He knew what his sister felt about marriage, and he could understand how the men who pursued her must feel frustrated at her refusals to take them seriously.

He was also aware that Lord Warrington in particular was growing more and more desperate.

But before he could say any more, the Butler came

into the room carrying the morning's post on a silver salver.

There were three letters on it which he offered to Harry, saying:

"Mr. Barnet's compliments, M'Lord, and as he thought these would be private communications he didn't open them."

"Thank you, Dawson."

Harry picked up the letters and opened the first one casually.

As he did so, he realised that the others were from two attractive ladies to whom he was paying court.

He had thought they would notice that he had not called on them for several days, and he realised with a twinkle in his eye that he now had proof of it.

It was only as he drew the letter he was opening from its envelope that he realised that it came from France.

Then he saw to his astonishment that beneath an impressive crest which was surmounted by a coronet was an address which read: *Château de Bantôme*.

Canéda had risen from the table to help herself to some freshly picked mushrooms from the country, cooked in cream.

It was only after she had turned round that she saw the surprise on her brother's face and realised that he was reading a letter with, for him, unusual concentration.

He finished it, and as she sat down at the table he flung the letter across to her, saying:

"If that does not make you laugh, nothing will."

"Who is it from?" Canéda enquired.

"You will not believe it," Harry replied, "but it is from Mama's relations! How dare they, after all these years, write to me just because I have come into a title? It makes me want to spit!"

He spoke so derisively that Canéda laughed.

At the same time she picked up the letter from the table and read it with interest.

It was written in French, which, because she was bilingual, she had no need to have translated into English.

In a firm, authoritative hand someone had transcribed:

Château de Bantôme

My Dear Grandson:

It is with great pleasure that your Grandfather and I have learnt that You have inherited the Earldom of Langstone and are now the head of such a distinguished Family.

We think it is in the interests of both our families that the silence between Us should end, and that you should become acquainted not only with your older Relatives like your Grandfather and Myself, but also with your young cousins, Hélène and Armand, who are very anxious to visit England.

It is time for Hélène, who is eighteen, to make her curtsey to Her Majesty the Queen, and for Armand to attend a levée held by the Prince of Wales. But of course, it would be much more pleasant for them if They had your support.

But first Your Grandfather and I would like to extend to you an invitation to visit Us here to meet the surviving members of the great, historic family of Bantôme, to which You belong.

We would of course be delighted if Your Sister could accompany You, and We will do everything in our power to make Your visit as pleasant as possible.

I remain, in anticipation of a favourable reply,

Your Grandmother, whom unfortunately You have never met,

Eugenie de Bantôme

As she finished reading the letter Canéda gave a little gasp.

"You are right, Harry. It is unbelievable!" she said. "After ignoring Mama as if she had been swept off the face of the earth, how dare our Grandmother write such a letter! I have never heard such cheek!"

"I agree it is a damned impertinence on their part!" Harry exclaimed.

"Mama told me once," Canéda said in a low voice, "that when you were born she wrote to her mother telling her that she had a son, because she thought it would please her."

"I can guess what happened," Harry answered. "There was no reply."

"Worse than that, the letter was returned unopened."

"That is what I might have expected. So how dare they write to us now, just because our circumstances have changed? I suppose if Papa had been an Earl when he eloped with Mama, they might have forgiven her for chucking the *Duc*."

"I hate them!" Canéda cried. "Sometimes when Mama used to talk to me about her childhood, I knew how home-sick she was and how much she longed to see not only her friends again but also the Dordogne."

"I know," Harry agreed. "She loved it."

"She used to talk of the river and the Castles which gave it, she said, a fairy-like appearance. She used to make it sound so romantic that I longed to see it. But because Papa was barred from France, I never thought I would ever have the chance."

"It was the damned *Duc*'s fault," Harry said. "When Papa, who had visited France ever since he had been a small boy, found that he was no longer able to go there, it hurt him."

Canéda sighed.

"They certainly paid the price for running away with each other, but I do not think they ever regretted it."

"No, of course not," Harry agreed. "I have never seen two people as happy as Papa and Mama, and I only hope when I get married I shall be half as happy."

"That is exactly what I think too," Canéda said, "so you will understand that, whatever Aunt Anne says, I cannot marry Lord Warrington or any of those other stupid young men who have nothing better to do than to try to steal a kiss!"

Harry laughed.

"You ought to feel flattered!"

"Well, I do not!" Canéda said. "When I do marry, I want a very different kind of man from any of those I have met so far."

"Let me know when you find him," Harry said. "I do not mind telling you that the aunts are complaining that you are getting yourself talked about, and it is something of which they most ardently disapprove."

Canéda shrugged her shoulders in a gesture that was indisputably French.

"I cannot help it if men fall in love with me," she said, "and I knew Aunt Anne was furious last night because I had been so long in the Conservatory. But, short of screaming for help, I do not know how I could have got away from Lord Warrington any more quickly than I eventually managed to do."

"Shall I tell him to behave himself?" Harry asked.

"I do not believe it would do any good," Canéda replied. "The only thing is that I find it such a bore having him follow me round like a dog. Perhaps we could get away from London and him."

"What are you suggesting?" Harry asked. "That we should go to Langstone Park, or even to France?"

Canéda did not reply and he said:

"That is certainly one place in which I will never set foot, except that I would just like to tell my grandmother and grandfather and all the other de Bantômes exactly what I think of them!"

He made an exclamation of anger and went on:

"How dare they treat Mama as they did, cutting her off as if she were a leper! As for the *Duc*, however much he felt insulted, he had no right to try to ostracise Papa in Paris and London. I wish I could give him a taste of his own medicine."

"I expect he is dead by now," Canéda replied. "He was much older than Mama, and he wished to marry her because his wife was dead and he wanted a young woman to give him more children."

"That is the sort of reason one would expect," Harry said scornfully. "If his son, or whoever has inherited the title, ever comes to England I will take my revenge and make it a pretty sharp one."

Canéda did not answer. She stared at the letter as if she was reading it again.

Suddenly she exclaimed:

"Harry, I have an idea!"

"What is it?"

"I think I might accept this invitation to go to France."

"Are you mad?" he asked. "Why on earth should you want to do that after the way they behaved to Mama?"

"It is because they behaved to Mama the way they did that, like you, I want to teach them a lesson," Canéda replied.

"I do not understand. What are you intending to do?" Harry asked.

"There is something I heard someone say at a party last week," Canéda said. "I did not pay much attention at the time, and I must find out more about it, but I have a feeling that those who live in the Dordogne region of France are suffering financial losses."

Harry stared at her.

"Are you saying that the *Comtes* de Bantôme may have lost their money?"

"I do not know," Canéda answered. "Now that they know you are so rich, it would explain—would it not?— why they are trying to patch up the differences between us. And perhaps they want Cousin Hélène to marry an Englishman."

"I do not believe it! It is too far-fetched!" Harry said. "But if that is what they want, then you should certainly refuse to help them."

"I am not going to help them, stupid!" Canéda replied. "If I go to Bantôme I shall go not as an ordinary lady-like member of the family but as Lady Canéda, very

rich and grand, and when I have made them thor-
oughly envious, I will make it very clear that we would
not lift a little finger to help them."

"It sounds quite an idea, if you can be certain they
have fallen on hard times," Harry agreed. "From all
Mama used to tell me, they were rich and powerful and,
with their vineyards, sitting on banks of gold."

"Yes, I know," Canéda said, "but supposing the vineyards became not so productive? What would happen
then?"

"Your guess is as good as mine," Harry replied, "but
if you take my advice, you will stay at home. Not even to
avoid Warrington would I make the trip to France."

"It is no hardship," Canéda said in a dreamy voice. "I
have always longed to see the country to which Mama
belonged and with which half of my blood has an undeniable affinity."

Harry did not reply and she went on:

"I read every book about France that ever comes my
way, and all I can tell you is that, while I long to see
Paris, I want more than anything else in the world to
visit the parts of France that Mama described to me: the
Dordogne, of course, which was her own country, and
the Loire Valley, where she would have lived if she had
married the *Duc*."

"She used to talk about him sometimes," Harry said,
"and about his great *Châteaux,* and how wonderful the
others were—Chenonceaux, Chambord, Chaumont,
and of course Saumac, where she would have lived with
all the grandeur of a *Duchesse*."

"Let us go there," Canéda begged suddenly. "We can
feast our eyes on what we have always wanted to see,
and at the same time wreak our vengeance on the de
Bantômes, and if possible the *Duc* de Saumac as well."

"And leave all this?" Harry asked. "You must be rav-
ing! Do you think at the moment I would really leave
Langstone and all the fun I am having in London?"

Canéda smiled.

"I grant you she is very alluring."

169

Harry grinned.

"That is what I find, and I assure you there are several men only too ready to step into my shoes."

"Then I might, I just might, go to France alone," Canéda said reflectively.

"You will do nothing of the sort!" her brother replied sharply. "You know as well as I do that you have to be chaperoned."

"I was not suggesting that," Canéda answered. "I meant if you would not come with me, I know exactly who would accompany me, if I asked her to do so."

"Who?"

"*Madame* de Goucourt!"

There was silence for a moment. Then Harry said:

"I do not doubt that she would go anywhere if we were paying for her. But quite frankly, Canéda, I think this is a mad idea! Let us tear up the letter and leave them wondering if we have ever received it, or keep them on tenterhooks for a little while at any rate."

He paused to add:

"If those damned cousins come here, I swear I will do everything I can to make their visit a fiasco."

"I doubt if you will succeed," Canéda said. "My way is far cleverer and very subtle, and it would be the direct answer to the way they treated Mama after she left them. She even had a little money of her own, but her father arranged through his Lawyers that she could not have it unless she lived in France. It was an illegal enactment, but Papa could not afford the legal fees to fight it."

"So they literally stole Mama's money from her and kept it all these years! I agree with you, they are despicable," Harry said. "But what is the point of torturing yourself by going to meet them?"

"I want revenge as much as you do, if not more," Canéda said, "and I am just wondering how I can revenge myself on the *Duc*. He is dead, but I suppose his son, if he had one, will have inherited his position.

Perhaps I could make him miserable in one way or another."

"You had much better enjoy yourself in England."

"If I go, I will not be gone for long," Canéda replied. "May I use your yacht?"

Harry threw out his hands in what was a slightly un-English gesture.

"I have not seen it yet, but of course it is yours to command."

"Thank you, dearest. I hope it is very large. I shall be taking carriage-horses with me, out-riders, and of course Ariel."

"Oh, for Heaven's sake!" Harry exclaimed. "The whole idea is crazy, and I warn you, you are not setting foot outside this house without being properly chaperoned. So if *Madame* de Goucourt says 'No'—no it is!"

"But *Madame* de Goucourt will say 'Yes,'" Canéda replied. "I am going to get in touch with her this morning. She lives in a small, uncomfortable little house in an unfashionable part of London, now that the glorious days when her husband was the French Ambassador have ended."

"She knew Mama and loved her," Harry said, "so I trust her to look after you."

Canéda did not contradict him, but in the depths of her blue eyes there was a glint of mischief which her brother did not see.

⸙⸙⸙

Madame de Goucourt's house was, as Canéda had said, small and slightly shabby in a narrow street off a fashionable Square.

The Frenchwoman had been much younger than her husband the Ambassador. She was now only just fifty, and she resented the fate which had swept her from her importance as a member of the Diplomatic Corps into virtual obscurity.

However, her daughter had married an Englishman

171

and her younger son was still finishing his education at Oxford, so, because she wanted to be near them, she had stayed in England rather than return to her native land.

She had known Clémentine de Bantôme ever since they were children and she had always been deeply sympathetic over the way she had been treated.

"It is not as if your husband is not of noble birth," she would say indignantly. "He belongs to a very distinguished English family, and although he has no money, I can understand that he is, *ma chérie*, a man from whom, having once given him your heart, you could not take it back."

"That is true," Clémentine Lang had said with a smile. "I love Gerald, and I am the happiest woman in the whole world. But sometimes, just sometimes, Yvonne, I long to hear French voices, to eat French food, and to see the river, blue as the sky above it, winding its way through the vineyards and the deep gorges which as a child I was certain contained prehistoric animals!"

Madame de Goucourt had laughed.

"I understand how you feel," she had said, "but you have your husband and those two adorable children."

"You do not suppose I have ever regretted running away, do you?" Clémentine had enquired. "It was the luckiest and most marvellous day of my life! But I can never forgive the *Duc* de Saumac for what he did to Gerald."

"That I can understand," *Madame* de Goucourt had said. "It was cruel and wicked, but then he was a very strange man."

It seemed now to *Madame* that the years rolled back and it was not Canéda sitting in her small Sitting-Room, asking her questions, but Clémentine.

"Tell me about the *Duc* de Saumac, *Madame*," Canéda asked.

"*Mon Dieu!* What makes you think of him, my little one? I thought you had come here to tell me about your successes in the *Beau Monde*. Everyone is talking about you and how beautiful, intelligent, and charming you are, and as for Harry, all the ladies are wild about him."

"I know that," Canéda answered, "and it is very exciting for both of us after having lived so quietly for so long. But please, *Madame*, answer my question about the *Duc* de Saumac."

"What is there to tell you?"

"Tell me about the old one . . . the one who was so cruel to Papa."

"Oh, he is dead, and I daresay he is not mourned by many people. As I expect you know, he wanted to marry your mother because, having only one son by his wife who was ill for many, many years, he wanted when he was nearly sixty to start a new family, just in case anything should happen to his heir."

"And did anything happen to him?" Canéda enquired.

"No. He is now the *Duc* de Saumac, and let me see— he must be at least thirty-two or thirty-three years old."

"And in good health, I suppose," Canéda said a little bitterly.

"*He* is," *Madame* de Goucourt replied.

"Why should you say it like that?" Canéda enquired.

"Because in a way it is very sad. His wife went mad soon after he was married. He was very young and in fact had just come of age."

"She went mad?" Canéda repeated to herself, and there was just a note of satisfaction in her voice.

"It was, of course, hidden away as it always is in France," *Madame* de Goucourt said, "but the old *Duc* must have been very bitter when he realised that there was no likelihood of his daughter-in-law producing any children, not even one, as he had managed to have himself."

"Well, I am delighted he was upset!" Canéda said.

"I believe the present *Duc* is a strange man," *Madame* de Goucourt continued, as if she spoke to herself.

"In what way?" Canéda enquired.

173

"Well, apparently he is very upset and sensitive about his wife's condition, and he withdrew from Society to live all the time at his Castle on the Loire. He runs a Riding-School there in which he trains horses for the Cavalry Regiments and of course for his own pleasure."

"A Riding-School!" Canéda exclaimed.

"He is, I believe, quite famous by now in that part of France," *Madame* de Goucourt said. "General Bourgueil when I last saw him was talking about it and saying what excellent horses his officers were able to obtain from the de Saumac School."

Canéda was silent for a moment. Then she drew from her bag the letter that Harry had received from the *Château* de Bantôme and gave it to *Madame* de Goucourt.

"Read this," she said.

Madame de Goucourt took it from her and, holding up a very elegant lorgnette, read it carefully.

When she finished she gave a little cry.

"This is extraordinary! Quite extraordinary!" she exclaimed. "Was not your brother surprised to receive it?"

"He was indeed," Canéda replied, "and so was I!"

Then, as if she could not contain herself any longer, she said angrily:

"How dare they write to us just because Harry has inherited the title and is now of some importance! Why did they not ask us to stay when Mama was alive? You know she was never a person to bear a grudge. She would have forgiven them, and it would have made her so happy."

There was just a little throb in Canéda's voice about her mother having been exiled from her kith and kin for so long.

"It is impossible to undo the past, *ma chérie*," she said softly. "But if you can patch up the feud, you could perhaps make these people happy before they die."

"Make *them* happy?" Canéda cried. "I hate them and Harry hates them too! But I have an idea how I might make them really penitent and really ashamed of the way they behaved."

Madame de Goucourt put down her lorgnette and looked at Canéda in surprise.

"What are you saying?" she asked. "What are you suggesting?"

"First of all," Canéda answered, "I want you to tell me why, at this particular moment, apart from the fact that Harry is now important in England, they should have written to us."

There was a moment's hesitation and Canéda said insistently:

"I want the truth, *Madame*. I feel there is something behind it and I want to know what it is."

"Of course, I cannot be certain," *Madame* said slowly after a moment, "but there have been reports of trouble in the Dordogne."

"What sort of trouble?"

"First of all, their harvests have been bad and my friends tell me that locally grown wheat cannot compete with cheaper American wheat which is imported and has depressed the prices of the French."

She paused, and Canéda, watching the expression on her face, asked:

"And what else?"

For a moment she thought *Madame* de Goucourt would not tell her. Then she said:

"I have heard, although it is only a rumour, that phylloxera has affected a great number of vines in the region."

"Phylloxera!" Canéda exclaimed.

She would not have been her mother's daughter if she had not known something about the wine-growing which had been so essentially a part of Clémentine de Bantôme's youth and which was so important to France.

Gerald Lang had always appreciated French wines and he had taught his children to recognise the good ones, while their mother had explained how the greatest wines of France came from the Dordogne region.

Phylloxera was, as Canéda knew, the greatest disaster

that could occur to any vineyard, and the insect itself was dreaded as other countries dreaded the plague.

Phylloxera had been introduced into France by infected stock from America in the early 1860s.

Clémentine Lang had read about it in the newspapers, and it had not been difficult for her family to understand how tragic she thought it was.

It was the French newspapers which their mother occasionally received from English friends who visited France, or from French friends like *Madame* de Goucourt, who knew how much she treasured them, which told her what was happening.

With phylloxera the vines lost their leaves and died, and it was a little while before it was discovered that the phylloxera aphid had affected the roots of the vine.

What was frightening was that by the time the dead vines were dug up and inspected, the insects had moved on to other plants which, above ground, appeared to be unaffected and which the vine-growers therefore were loath to uproot.

"It is very, very dangerous for the vineyards," her mother had said after she had read aloud what was in the newspaper.

"What does it matter to us, who are not even allowed to look at the vines?" her husband had asked bitterly. "Although, thank God, there still seems to be a great deal of good Burgundy and claret in England!"

Clémentine had therefore said nothing more, but Canéda, because she was so close to her mother, realised that she was worrying, and she thought it pathetic that after all these years of being exiled by her family, she still worried over their possessions, especially the vineyards on which their fortune was based.

Privately she had thought in her heart that it would teach them a lesson if they suddenly became poor like her father and mother, and now from what *Madame* de Goucourt had said, she thought that was exactly what had happened.

"What you are saying," she said aloud, "is that the

stuck-up *Comte* de Bantôme, my grandfather, needs Harry's and my help to launch his grandchildren into the Social World. And what of the help they gave us when we needed it?"

"I can understand that you feel bitter, Canéda," *Madame* de Goucourt said softly, "and I knew how much your mother minded, even when she was so happy, that she was isolated from her own people. We French are very close to one another, and the family means a great deal to us."

She paused before she went on:

"Although your mother was the happiest woman I have ever known in my life, I think sometimes she longed with one part of her for the closeness of her parents, her brothers, her sisters, and of course their children, some of whom will be about the same age as yourself."

She paused again.

"The de Bantômes are a very large family, and I think you would enjoy knowing them, and they you."

"They are not going to know me, except as an avenging angel," Canéda answered, "and because that is what I intend to be, I want your help, *Madame*."

"My help?" *Madame* de Goucourt asked in astonishment.

"It is quite simple," Canéda replied. "I want you to come with me to France."

She saw a sudden light come into the Frenchwoman's eyes which told her that the invitation would not be refused.

Then she added:

"I intend, *Madame,* to teach a lesson not only to the de Bantômes but, if it is possible, to the *Duc* de Saumac as well, and it will be one he will never forget!"

CHAPTER TWO

WITH ITS WHITE SAILS billowing out in the wind, the *Sea-Gull* nosed its way slowly into the port of St. Nazaire.

Canéda had been on deck since dawn as they sailed past Belle Ile and entered the harbour.

She was so excited that she had found it almost impossible to sleep since she had left Folkestone. It was there that the late Earl's yacht had been moored in order always to be ready to carry its owner across the Channel anytime he wished to go.

She was certain that Harry would soon avail himself of this new toy, but there were so many other distractions among his possessions that he had been quite content for Canéda to see and use the *Sea-Gull* first.

The *Sea-Gull* had been commissioned by their uncle only three years before he died, and therefore it was of the most up-to-date design. To Canéda's delight, there was plenty of room to carry quite a number of horses besides a travelling-chariot.

She had been a little apprehensive lest the sea should be rough and the horses upset, especially Ariel, but Ben, who was in charge, had been very reassuring.

"Now ye leave it to me, Miss Canéda—I means M'Lady!" he said. "Th' horses'll be all right—I'll see t' that."

Canéda knew he meant what he said, and there was

no doubt that Ben was a wizard not only in training the horses but in looking after them.

When Canéda was fourteen she had rushed into her father's Study to tell him that there was news of a Circus coming to the small market-town which was only two miles from where they lived.

"We must see it, Papa! You must take me to the Circus!" Canéda had cried.

"I hate to see wild animals in captivity," Gerald Lang had replied.

"It is not the wild animals I want to see," Canéda answered, "but a poster hanging up in the village says there is a performing horse that will obey every command she is given, which makes her the cleverest animal in the world."

Gerald Lang had looked skeptical, but because Canéda was so insistent he promised to take her to the Circus.

He knew exactly the tumbledown show it would be, consisting of a few mangy old horses, some clowns who were not very funny, a Ringmaster who doubtless owned the Circus and drank away his financial troubles, and, if they were fortunate, a couple of acrobats.

But he was well aware that for Canéda, living very quietly in the country and especially with Harry away at School, it would be a delight that would rival Ashley's Circus in London.

Clémentine Lang had said she was too busy in the house to accompany them, and father and daughter had set off.

They travelled in the old-fashioned gig which Gerald Lang drove with an expertise and a flourish that made Canéda aware that he should have had an up-to-date chaise with two or even four superlative horses.

The gig had been the only form of transport they could afford, but as far as she was concerned she was so happy to be with her father that nothing else mattered.

They reached the small town and Gerald Lang saw that there was the usual collection of farmers' wives selling their wares in the market-place, with the towns-folk taking a long time to make up their minds whether they should buy an old hen suitable for boiling or a more expensive fat chicken to roast.

There were turnips, beets, and cabbages brought in from the countryside, pats of golden butter, honey-combe, and inevitably rabbits and hares that had been trapped or snared, regardless of what time of year it was.

Canéda was not interested in the market which stood in the centre of the town.

She was waiting breathlessly for her father to drive to where, in the field that sloped down to the river, the Circus had been erected.

There was a big tent which let in the rain in bad weather and there was a sawdust ring with rows of rickety seats round it.

They had gone for too many months without repair and at any unexpected moment were likely to precipitate to the ground those who sat on them.

There was a Band playing, and to Canéda the Ring-master, in his red coat, top-hat, and cracking his long whip, was very impressive as he introduced his performers to an audience that consisted mostly of gaping children, a few farm-hands, and some giggling girls.

The first turn was quite ordinary, at least to Gerald Lang, and consisted of four grey horses with feathers on their bridles and ballerinas perched precariously on their backs.

He thought the horses looked as old as their riders, and there was certainly not much skill in raising a leg above a frilly ballet-skirt while holding on tightly to the front of the saddle.

But Canéda's small face was rapt with enjoyment and Gerald Lang said nothing but watched his daughter rather than the performers.

The clowns made her laugh, and there was an acrobatic turn which made her hold her breath.

Then the Ringmaster announced:

"Now, ladies and gentlemen, you'll see the most sensational, the most intelligent, the most unusual horse in the world. Her name is Juno and she understands every word that is said to her. She also can dance in a manner that no other horse has been able to do in all my long experience of them."

There was applause from the crowd as Juno came into the ring.

She was black with a white star on her nose, and Gerald Lang saw that she had once undoubtedly been a very fine mare but was now getting old.

Riding her was a small jockey with an ugly, impudent face, a disarming grin, and twinkling eyes. He made her perform as if she were a musical instrument in the hands of a master of the art.

Juno waltzed in time to the Band, then she danced the polka, which had just become fashionable. She walked on her hind legs, and answered questions by shaking or nodding her head.

Finally, when jumps had been erected round the ring, Juno sailed over them in a style that made Canéda clap her hands wildly at such a brilliant performance.

The enthusiastic applause of everyone in the big tent made her rider decide that she should take the jumps once again, and now with a roll of the drums she started off, taking each fence in a way which made her seem almost to fly through the air.

Quite suddenly when she reached the last fence of all she rose off the ground, seemed to stagger, and the next moment, almost before anyone could realise what was happening, she crashed down on the other side of the fence in a crumpled heap.

There was a scream from the women in the audience, a groan from the men, and Canéda clutched at her father's hand.

"What is happening, Papa?"

"Her heart, I should imagine," Gerald Lang replied.

"Oh, she cannot die!" Canéda cried. "Please, Papa,

see if there is anything you can do. I could not bear that beautiful horse to die in such a manner."

Because Gerald Lang knew only too well what his daughter was feeling, they went round to the back of the tent as Juno was dragged out of the ring and the clowns went on to take the audience's mind off the tragedy.

There were a few grooms with the small man who had been riding her when Gerald Lang and Canéda reached them, but it was obvious at first glance that there was nothing anyone could do for the mare.

Juno was dead, because her heart, as Gerald Lang had rightly suspected, had given out.

Canéda crouched down beside the mare, and as she did so she saw that the small jockey who had been riding her in his gaudy theatrical costume was now kneeling on the other side.

He was crying unashamedly, tears running down his ugly, lined face, and his despair was in itself very moving.

"I am sorry," Canéda said softly.

"She were a wonderful 'orse!"

"Have you been with her long?" Canéda enquired.

"For ten years, Miss," he replied. "I started to train 'er with 'er first master, and when 'e dies 'e gives 'er to me. She were mine, me very own."

"I know what you must be feeling," Canéda said softly, "and there is nothing I can say, except that I am so very sorry for you."

She could understand that he was desolate over losing such a magnificent horse and one who was so clever.

"I've got some'at to show ye, Miss, if ye'd come with I," the man said.

"Yes, of course," Canéda agreed.

He rose to his feet, and as she rose too, she found her father standing beside her.

"He has something to show us, Papa," she said, slipping her hand into his.

Gerald Lang nodded but did not speak. With his daughter he followed the jockey with his red-and-gold-braided coat until they came to a battered tent where all the horses that worked for the Circus were housed.

The greys were already back tethered to posts, but still wearing their feathers on the fronts of their bridles as they would be wanted in the finale. But there was one end of the tent shut off from the rest, which appeared at first to be empty until, as the jockey walked into it, Canéda saw something moving.

It was then that she was aware of what he had brought her to see. It was a foal of about six or seven weeks old, and already it showed the good breeding of its mother.

As Canéda stroked its neck it nuzzled its black nose against her, and she heard her father say:

"What are you going to do now?"

"I don't know, Sir, an' that's the truth," the little man answered. "Juno were me living, so to speak, and it'll be a year or two afore I can do anythin' with Ariel, and that'll be too soon for most Circuses to be interested in 'im."

There was something both helpless and hopeless in the way he spoke, and Canéda suddenly knew what she wanted.

She rose, moved closer to her father, and, putting her hand on his arm, looked up at him with pleading eyes.

"Please . . . Papa."

She knew even as she spoke that he was thinking they could not afford it, and yet because she knew instinctively that it was not only what she wanted but what would please him too, she said again:

"Please . . ."

Gerald Lang was well aware that the old groom who had looked after his horses ever since he had been married was past working and should have been retired ages ago.

He had, however, been afraid of what a younger man might cost him, and he had already discussed with his wife how they could not afford to pension off the old groom and pay someone to take his place.

But he could not bear to refuse his daughter, and he knew how much the foal could mean to her when she had few amusements and little companionship when Harry was away at School.

"Supposing for the time being," he said to the small man beside him, who still had tears on his cheeks, "you and Ariel come and stay in my stables. That will give you time to get over the death of Juno and think about your future."

"D'you mean that, Sir?"

"I mean it, and we will be expecting you later tonight, or tomorrow morning."

The expression of gratitude and relief on the little man's face was pathetic.

"Me name's Ben, Sir, an' your kindness be some'at I'll ne'er forget."

Only when they had left the Circus, after giving Ben directions to the Manor, did Canéda say nervously:

"You do think he will come? Supposing he wants to stay with the Circus?"

"I have a feeling he will come," her father answered.

"I feel the same. I will look after Ariel and leave Ben plenty of time to see to your horses."

"Of course," her father replied. "That is part of the bargain."

Canéda put her cheek against his arm.

"Thank you, thank you," she said. "How can I ever thank you enough for being so kind?"

"I am just wondering what your mother will say," Gerald Lang replied a little ruefully.

Clémentine had understood.

She could never bear to see people suffering, and when Canéda told her how Ben had cried, she had known it would have been impossible for her husband and daughter to walk away without trying to help.

Ben had arrived with Ariel, and without his theatrical clothes he had seemed strange and insignificant.

He may have been small, but the Langs found that he

was immensely strong. He never seemed to tire and he never appeared to stop working.

Gerald Lang had never had his horses groomed better or looked after in a manner which could not have been improved on even in the finest stables in England.

What was more, from the very first Ben seemed to settle down and make the place his home almost as if he had been born there.

And as for Ariel, words would fail Canéda every time she thought of him.

He grew prodigiously in the first year, changing from a small foal into a beautiful creature who looked as if he had stepped straight out of mythology.

He had beautiful lines, a fine head, and a coat which shone as if it were made of polished ebony.

He grew and grew, and by the time he was two years old, one of the sights of the countryside was that of Canéda, looking very small but very lovely, riding an enormous black stallion that appeared too spirited for her to handle.

But from the moment Canéda and Ben came together they started to teach Ariel the same tricks that had made his mother, Juno, so extraordinary, and a great many more.

Ariel would obey both Canéda and Ben, and they would vie with each other in thinking up new things for him to do, teaching him not by threats or through fear but with love.

Sometimes Canéda felt as if Ariel thought up his own tricks and was ready to perform them almost before she had been able to explain to him what she wanted.

"He understands, he really understands!" she would say to Ben, who would scratch his head and say:

"Animals, Miss Canéda, can be a sight cleverer than most folk, especially 'orses like Ariel and Juno."

The little man had loved Juno, and Canéda suspected that he sometimes cried at night because he missed her so.

She often felt a little guilty because she had the feeling

that Ariel preferred her to Ben and he might feel that she had taken Ariel away from him.

But Ben put her right on this. One day she said to him:

"You are happy here, Ben? You would never leave us, would you?"

There was a touch of anxiety in her voice because she felt afraid that Ben might want to go roaming again, and it would break her heart to lose Ariel.

But Ben had nodded his head.

"I be happy, Miss Canéda, 'cos yer father, yer mother, and ye treats I as one of th' family. Ye've made this a home for I as you have for Ariel, an' that's all any man could ask."

When Canéda had told her mother what Ben had said, she had answered:

"Ben is a dear little man, and he is good. No-one could have the control over a horse that he has and not be a good man. Animals, especially horses, sense better than we can what a man is like in his soul."

It was Ben who had chosen which horses, which grooms, and which out-riders should accompany Canéda on her trip to France.

Harry, who also looked on Ben as one of the family, had taken him aside to say:

"You will look after Her Ladyship and see that she does not get into any trouble?"

"I'll do that, M'Lord," Ben promised.

"I do not approve of her going off on this wild-goose chase," Harry went on, "but she has set her heart on it, and so I have agreed. But if anything goes wrong, you are to bring her home immediately. Do you understand, Ben?"

"I understands, M'Lord," Ben replied, "and 'Er Ladyship won't come to no harm if I can 'elp it."

"I trust you, Ben," Harry said, putting his hand on the little man's shoulder.

The yacht with the wind in her sails was moving slowly but surely into the harbour as Ben came up to join Canéda.

"We have made it, Ben," Canéda said, a note of satisfaction in her voice.

"Yus, I knows, M'Lady. What now?"

"When we have got the horses off and the carriage ready, we will set off for Nantes, where we will stay the night."

"Very good, M'Lady."

"We will be riding, if not today," Canéda replied, "certainly tomorrow."

She smiled as she spoke and Ben smiled back.

"It's just what Ariel be a-waiting for, M'Lady, a good gallop. 'T'll take the stiffness out of 'is legs."

"He is all right?" Canéda asked quickly.

"Right as rain, M'Lady, so don't ye worry about 'im. A little hardship never hurt a 'orse as long as 'e ain't frightened."

Canéda knew that none of the horses on the yacht had been frightened by the roughness of the sea, simply because Ben had been with them, calming them.

She was quite certain that he had stayed with them all night, sleeping below so that he was there ready to soothe them at the slightest whimper.

She thought once again how lucky she was to have Ben, and as if he knew what she was thinking, he said:

"Now don't ye worry, M'Lady, everything's fine, an' there's nothing for ye to do but enjoy yerself."

Canéda was only too willing to obey.

France, as she drove along beside *Madame* de Goucourt, was exactly as she had thought it would be.

The wide open countryside, the green banks of the Loire, and rising ahead of them the towers and spires of Nantes.

They stayed the night at an ancient Inn where the

beds were made of the softest goose-feathers and the food was gastronomic.

The Proprietor and his buxom wife were obviously extremely impressed by the elegance of their guests and their large entourage.

It was only when *Madame* de Goucourt and Canéda had finished dining in the comfortable private room and the Landlord had bowed his way out that *Madame* said:

"Well, *ma chérie,* you are in France, but you have still not told me why we have disembarked at St. Nazaire rather than Bordeaux. As you are well aware, at this moment we should be staying somewhere beside the Dordogne rather than the Loire."

Canéda gave a little smile which told *Madame* de Goucourt without words that she was plotting something.

"Now, Canéda, I have been given strict instructions by Harry to look after you," she said. "You know as well as I do that he expected us to stay just for a short time with your grandparents, then return home. Therefore, I ask you again—why are we here?"

"I have a plan, *Madame,* but I do not wish to talk about it in case it does not come off. All I can do is beg you not to ask me too many questions. Let me play my cards my own way."

Madame de Goucourt laughed.

"I am well aware that you are up to something, Canéda," she said, "but because I am so grateful to you for bringing me back to my beloved country and for spoiling me by giving me such elegant gowns in which to dazzle my friends and relatives when I meet them, I cannot command but only beg you not to do anything outrageous."

Canéda tilted her head a little to one side.

"It depends what you call outrageous, *Madame,*" she replied. "Shall I say I am taking justice into my own hands, rather than waiting for it to work by chance?"

"Oh, Canéda, Canéda!" *Madame* de Goucourt cried.

"You make me very apprehensive. But because I am tired, I intend to take a soothing tisane and retire to bed, hoping that tomorrow I shall not be in a terrible state of anxiety and worry."

"You will be neither, *Madame,*" Canéda said reassuringly. "And you did say you had some friends who live near Angers."

"Yes, indeed," *Madame* de Goucourt replied, "some old friends whom it will give me great happiness to see again. They are not very rich or fashionable, you understand, and therefore you might find them rather dull, but I could not come to this part of France without seeing them."

"That is what I thought," Canéda said with satisfaction, "and I promise you that you shall have plenty of time with your friends, while I shall be with mine."

It was only the next day when they were driving along the side of the Loire through the most beautiful country towards Angers that *Madame* de Goucourt said:

"Do you realise, Canéda, that you have not told me the name of the friends you intend to visit?"

"I do not think you would know them," Canéda replied, "and I want, *Madame,* to ask you a favour."

"But of course," *Madame* de Goucourt replied.

"Do not tell your friends too much about me," Canéda said. "It will only make them curious, and for the moment I do not want anyone in this part of the world to know who I am."

Madame de Goucourt looked at her in utter astonishment.

"Are you telling me that I am not to say I am accompanied by Lady Canéda Lang?"

"Please, I beg you not to mention my name," Canéda pleaded. "If you need to make any explanation for the carriage and the horses, you could say that you have been loaned them by a rich English nobleman. After all, no-one would be surprised at that, and they will naturally assume that it is a *Beau* who has been so generous."

Madame de Goucourt laughed.

"You are frightening me! You are up to some monkey-tricks which will make your brother very angry with me, and you will not be the only one to be in disgrace."

"Just trust me," Canéda begged.

Although *Madame* de Goucourt pleaded with her, she refused to be drawn into a discussion or explanation as to what her plans for the future might be.

As *Madame's* friends were in straitened circumstances, Canéda refused to consider staying with them.

Instead they passed through Angers and found a delightful Inn a few miles outside the town, situated on the north bank of the Loire.

Here too the Proprietor was exceedingly impressed by his visitors, and although Canéda privately thought the food was not as good as that which they had enjoyed the first night, the whole staff of the Inn tried to please and it was impossible to find fault.

Only after they had settled into their bedrooms and finished a meal in a private Sitting-Room did Canéda say to the Landlord:

"I wish to see my Head Groom before I retire to bed. Would you be kind enough to send for him?"

"Of course, *Madame,*" the Inn-Keeper replied.

Madame de Goucourt rose to her feet from the comfortable chair in which she had been sitting.

"If you are going to talk horses, I shall retire to bed," she said. "Gossip about people I always enjoy, but I cannot acclimatise myself to a long and intensive conversation over the well-being of a horse."

Canéda laughed.

"Go to bed, *Madame,* and have your beauty-sleep. Your friends must not think that Britain has aged you since you last met, which would definitely be an aspersion on our poor country."

"As it is at least six years since I have seen them, *mon amie,*" *Madame* replied, "they will doubtless notice there are new lines round my eyes, and I am definitely stouter than I was when I was last here."

"Rubbish!" Canéda replied. "You look lovely and you

know it! After all, *Madame,* Mama always told me that while your husband was the *Doyen* of the Diplomatic Corps, you were undoubtedly the *Belle* of it!"

"You flatter me, child!" *Madame* de Goucourt said with satisfaction.

She kissed Canéda affectionately and went upstairs, leaving her alone in the small private room.

Canéda had not long to wait before there was a knock and Ben came in.

He was looking exceedingly smart in his well-cut Langstone livery with its crested silver buttons and waist-coat of blue and yellow stripes.

The out-riders wore powdered wigs, but Ben had a high cockaded top-hat which he wore impudently on the side of his dark hair, which was just beginning to turn grey.

He was holding it now in his hand, and he put it down on a chair near the door and stood waiting for Canéda's instructions.

"Are the horses all right, Ben?"

"Th' stables be satisfactory, M'Lady. I gets the lads to muck 'em out an' put down fresh straw. The 'orses'll have a good night, as we all will."

"While we are here there is something I want you to do for me, Ben."

The way Canéda spoke made the little man's eyes alert, as if he already knew that what she had to say was important.

"About two miles away on the other side of the river," Canéda began, "there is the *Château* de Saumac. It is what you and I would term a Castle. I have always been told that as it stands on a hill, you can see it from miles away, silhouetted against the sky-line."

Ben was listening and Canéda went on:

"The *Duc* de Saumac has a Riding-School in the small town beneath the *Château.* I have learnt there are some fine buildings attached to it where the Cavalry officers stay when they bring their horses for schooling."

Ben nodded but did not speak, and Canéda continued:

"I was told in Nantes that there is a wall surrounding the outside grounds where the horses exercise, but this I want you to ascertain. Also, find out everything you can about when the *Duc* is in the School, how much time he spends there supervising the jumping, and how we can approach him."

"I understands, M'Lady."

"What is important is that no-one must know who you are."

"Ye mean that I'm not in yer employment, M'Lady?"

"I mean that you are to be just an interested stranger, and on no account must you mention my name. Moreover, and this must be remembered, Ben, none of my men are to talk about me to anybody."

She paused for a moment to let this sink in. Then she said:

"If anyone asks, you are employed by *Madame* de Goucourt. You are her servant and at her command. Is that understood?"

"Yus, M'Lady."

"You have told me that you understand French, since you went to France with the Circus."

"That be true."

"I will tell you what I intend to do once you have the information for me. But remember, we are definitely English and not French in any way."

"That makes it easier for I, M'Lady."

It was obvious to Canéda that Ben was beginning to sense they were to be involved in an adventure.

She had often wondered if after the roving life he had lived with the Circus, going from place to place, having different problems and new difficulties day after day, he was not now sometimes a little bored.

Life in their Manor home had been very quiet, with too few horses to look after and nothing more exciting happening than to attend the nearest Hunt-meeting or accompany her father to the local Point-to-Point.

Ben had certainly welcomed the change in their circumstances and had been thrilled and overwhelmed, as they all were, by the stables at Langstone, the horses Harry had inherited, and the new ones he immediately began to buy.

Although Ben said nothing, Canéda thought that what she was planning now would be an escapade after his own heart.

She knew he had already half-guessed what she intended, from the instructions she had given him before they left England as to what he was to bring with him.

"How soon can you get me the information I require?" Canéda enquired.

"I'll get over t' Saumac at th' first light o' dawn, M'Lady. By the time ye're having yer breakfast, I should be able to tell ye what ye wants to know."

"That is what I hoped you would say."

"Leave it t' me, M'Lady. I'll see that th' lads keep their mouths shut. They're a good lot and'll do what I tells 'em."

"I know that," Canéda replied, "and thank you, Ben. What I am planning I could not do with anyone else but you."

She liked his smile as his lips parted. Then he said:

"I be a-betting, M'Lady, ye've not told 'Is Lordship what's in the air."

"Certainly not!" Canéda replied. "What the mind does not know, the heart does not grieve over. His Lordship thinks I am on the way to Bordeaux."

"We'll be going there, M'Lady?"

"Later," Canéda replied. "But the first thing is the assault on the *Château* de Saumac."

She spoke the last words almost beneath her breath, but she thought that Ben had heard them, judging by the way he grinned before he bade her good-night.

When she was alone she drew a deep breath and told herself that everything was going well.

She had reached Angers and she would reach the *Château* de Saumac. The only difficulty was how to bring herself to the notice of the *Duc* and take the shortest time possible in achieving her revenge on him.

What *Madame* de Goucourt had told her about him made it seem less easy than it had when the idea had first come to her.

A recluse, a man embittered by the madness of his wife, was rather different from the ardent, eager admirers like Lord Warrington whom she had left behind in England.

Then she told herself there was one link that was more important than anything else—their love of horses.

No man could build a Riding-School and devote, from all she had heard, all his waking hours to horses without loving them.

At the same time, looking at the flaws in her plan, Canéda told herself that she knew very little about Frenchmen.

She might be half-French, but the men she had met since leaving School had all been English, and mostly, Canéda thought, very traditionally English at that.

What she wanted to know was how to arouse a Frenchman's interest in her.

If books were to be believed, Frenchmen were always ready to pursue a pretty woman and, if possible, to seduce her.

Canéda was not quite certain what this entailed, but she had read some of the ardent, passionate poems that had been amongst her mother's books.

She had also read a number of the French novels that French friends like *Madame* de Goucourt often loaned or gave to Clémentine Lang because they thought she should be *au fait* with what was being discussed in the Salons of Paris.

"Love to a Frenchman is very important," her mother had said once. "He thinks about beautiful women, he dreams about them, while the Englishman of the same age is concerned mainly with sport and of course with horses."

"Papa loves you, Mama," Canéda had said.

Her mother had laughed.

"Yes, darling, that is true, but I sometimes feel I am being beaten to the winning-post by a horse!"

Her father had heard what she had said as he came into the room. He put his arms round her and turned her face up to his.

"Do you want me to show you that you mean more to me by promising that I will never ride again?" he asked.

"No, of course not!" his wife cried. "Just tell me that I come first in your heart, and that your four-legged loves are left well behind!"

"When you are running they do not even leave the starting-point," Gerald Lang replied.

He kissed his wife, and when he released her, Canéda had seen the flush on her mother's cheeks and the light in her eyes, and had known how happy she was.

But that had taught her very little about Frenchmen.

Then she tried to reassure herself that at least it would be a sporting effort.

She went to bed, but although it was exceedingly comfortable and she was tired, she found it difficult not to go over and over every detail of her plan once again.

She had been turning it over in her mind ever since she had decided to come to France, but she had known it would be a great mistake to say too much to Harry or even to *Madame* de Goucourt until it was too late for them to try to stop her.

Now she was actually here, two miles from the de Saumac *Château*, and she lay in the darkness wondering what the *Duc* was like.

"If the *Château* is barricaded against me," she told herself, "it will be in keeping with his father's nasty, vindictive character."

She felt blazing within her almost like an avenging fire the anger she had always felt when she thought about the way the *Duc* had behaved.

"I have to make him suffer," she murmured, "and

however much he does suffer, it cannot make up for all that Papa suffered for over twenty years."

She fell asleep just before dawn, and when the first of the sun's rays threw a golden light on the slow-moving Loire, Ben, on one of the least noticeable horses they had brought with them, rode along the side of the river to where he had learnt there was a bridge.

He arrived in Saumac just as the housewives were opening their doors and windows and the streets sprang into activity with the merchants, the vendors, and the sweepers starting the day.

Saumac was a small place with pretty gabled houses and an ancient Church overshadowed by the huge *Château* soaring above it. The pointed, turreted towers were silhouetted against the sky, as Canéda had said they would be.

It had been a fortress from which many battles had been fought at the end of the Sixteenth Century.

Now it looked more beautiful than formidable, and with the morning sunshine glinting on the long windows which had replaced the arrow-slits of the original building, it had an elegance that was very different from what had been its war-like importance.

However, Ben's instructions did not concern the *Château*.

He found the Riding-School without difficulty. The buildings of which Canéda had spoken were an example of fine Eighteenth-Century architecture and so were the stables attached to them.

Surrounding them was a high wall built in a square and with only one gate, which was of wood ornamented with heavy iron hinges and a very formidable-looking lock.

Ben engaged in conversation the first passerby who seemed friendly.

"What's in there?" he enquired in his bad but understandable French.

"A School for horses," was the answer.

"Sounds interesting," Ben remarked. "I'd like to see it."

The man to whom he was speaking shook his head.

"Ye can't do that."

"Why not?"

"Monsieur le Duc will not allow anyone in except those concerned with horses."

"No spectators?"

"Not often."

"B'ain't ye curious to see what goes on?"

"Horses don't interest me, *Monsieur,*" was the reply, "only women!"

They both laughed, then Ben looked serious.

He rode several times round the huge square. Finally he found a tree which he could climb without difficulty, and when he descended and mounted his horse again, he rode back the way he had come with a smile on his lips.

He had discovered what Canéda wanted to know.

CHAPTER THREE

THE SUN WAS REFLECTED in the wide river, and there was the freshness of the morning in the scent which came from the blossoming shrubs which bordered the road along which Canéda and Ben were riding.

She had crept out from the Hotel while *Madame* de Goucourt was still asleep, knowing that she would have been horrified at her appearance.

She had in fact spent a great deal of thought on choosing her habit, which was certainly not one that a Lady of Quality would have worn in Rotten Row.

In fact it would have been too *outré* and extreme even for the Pretty Horse-Breakers who met at the Achilles Statue to show off their mounts and themselves.

If Canéda had wished to be spectacular, she had certainly succeeded.

After changing her mind several times she had finally chosen a habit made of heavy silk, camelia-pink in colour.

It was frogged with white braid and ornamented with large pearl buttons.

The gauze veil which floated behind her was also pink, and the only other colour to complete the ensemble were the toes of her highly polished dark riding-boots, which peeped from beneath her skirts, and her own dark hair.

That she looked lovely went without saying, but she also looked very theatrical.

She accentuated this impression by reddening her lips with a different salve from what she used sparingly on other occasions.

Her skin was so dazzlingly white that it did not really need the film of powder she had applied to it.

On Ariel's back she certainly looked striking, and it was fortunate that it was so early in the morning, otherwise she might easily have attracted a crowd.

She was complemented by Ben, who on her instructions was wearing the lavishly gold-braided red coat he had worn in the Circus.

His new cockaded hat set at an angle on his head needed no embellishment, his white breeches were smartly cut, and his white gloves had been expensive.

He and Canéda had discussed at some length what horse he should ride, for they had nothing with them to equal the appearance of Ariel.

Harry had recently purchased a black stallion with a white nose and four white fetlocks.

He had christened it "Black Boy," and Canéda thought the horse added to their theatrical appearance.

They rode quickly and in silence.

Canéda, going over in her mind all that Ben had told her of the Riding-School, was determined that she would not make a mistake in anything she did, for she knew that everything depended on there not being a snag at the last moment.

Because she was apprehensive she could not help thinking that perhaps the *Duc* would decide not tó attend the School this particular morning—or that when she did appear, he would order her abruptly from the grounds.

Then she told herself that if she could command the attention, admiration, and adoration of so many Englishmen, one Frenchman could not be so very different.

They crossed the bridge over the River Loire and Canéda looked ahead of them to where the *Château* de Saumac stood like a sentinel above the small town.

She thought there must be a magnificent panoramic view from its windows over the river and the valley, and she wondered if she would ever see it.

Then she told herself that this was the moment when she must have complete and absolute confidence in herself and in the knowledge that what she was doing was right and just.

When they had crossed the bridge she let Ben go ahead to lead her straight to the Riding-School.

They twisted their way through some small, attractive streets with old gabled houses.

Then suddenly, as she had expected, Canéda saw the high wall that Ben had described to her and at the far end the large, attractive buildings that had been built to house the Cavalry officers.

Now was the moment when they must not waste time, for though there were only a few people moving about the streets, they stared at them in astonishment.

The last thing Canéda wanted was to collect a crowd who would perhaps get in the way.

Ben drew his horse to a standstill beneath a chestnut tree that was just coming into flower, and Canéda guessed it was the one from which he had observed the School yesterday.

He tied his reins to an adjacent railing, and with the expertise of a Circus performer climbed agilely up the tree without marking his clothes or making it seem any more difficult than taking an ordinary walk.

There was a moment when Canéda held her breath in case, as she feared, the *Duc* was not there.

Then Ben smiled and nodded his head, and she instantly moved Ariel back some distance from the wall and waited for Ben to give her the signal they had arranged.

As she felt a little nervous and was frightened that it might communicate itself to Ariel, she bent forward to pat his neck with her gloved hand.

"Steady, boy! I am relying on you!" she said softly, and Ariel twitched his ears as if he understood what she was saying to him.

Then as she heard Ben give a low whistle she rode forward.

The wall was high, but Ariel cleared it with several inches to spare, tucking his legs under him in the way Ben and Canéda had taught him to do over the jumps at Langstone.

He landed on the other side of the wall on sandy ground, and Canéda, looking ahead, saw as she had expected a man standing in the centre of the School, astride what she knew was an exceptionally fine grey.

There was no time, however, to do more than recognise him from Ben's description, for at the word of command, Ariel rose up on his hind legs and moved quite a way towards the *Duc* before he was back on four.

Then he waltzed round and round as Canéda had taught him to do.

It was the dance his mother had performed in the Circus and he reversed as she had done.

By now they were within ten feet of the *Duc* and Canéda pulled Ariel to a standstill. At her quietly whispered order he put out his front legs and bowed his head, while Canéda, sitting bolt upright in the saddle, raised her jewel-handled whip in salute.

Now as she looked directly at the *Duc,* she saw that he was not in the least what she had expected.

She had thought he would be small, but he was large, with square shoulders. He was dark, but not overwhelmingly so, and she had the idea that his eyes were grey.

She had expected him to look grim and perhaps, because everyone had said he was so reserved, secretive.

Instead he looked raffish, and in fact there was almost a devil-may-care expression on his very handsome face, as if he defied the world and was derisive of anything it could offer him.

Ariel rose to his feet, and now Canéda and the *Duc* were facing each other and for a moment there was silence.

Then the other riders who had drawn in their mounts to watch Canéda burst into applause and she had no time to notice any more.

They clapped enthusiastically, and until they were finished there was no chance of either Canéda or the *Duc* speaking.

As if she took the appreciation as her due, Canéda smiled at them, bowing her head gracefully in first one direction, then the other.

Then her eyes came back to the *Duc* and she looked at him questioningly as if she wondered why he did not applaud what he must admit was an outstanding performance.

"Who are you?" he demanded.

"Bonjour, Monsieur le Duc," Canéda replied. "I am delighted to make your acquaintance."

"In a somewhat unusual manner!" he remarked drily.

"I may be wrong," Canéda replied, "but I rather doubted if your awe-inspiring gates would open for me, and I was so very anxious to meet you."

Her voice softened on the last words and she deliberately made her blue eyes seem flirtatious and inviting as she looked at him, then fluttered her dark eye-lashes.

"I asked you a question," the *Duc* said. "Who are you?"

"My name is Canéda."

There was a pause before he enquired:

"Is that all?"

"It is the name under which I perform."

For the first time there was a faint smile on his lips.

"So you belong to the Circus."

"A very superior one."

"That, of course, I would not doubt."

Again there was a pause before the *Duc* said:

"Well, *Mademoiselle*, now that you are here in a somewhat unconventional manner, what can I do for you?"

"That is what I hoped you would ask me, *Monsieur*. I want to know if there is anything you can teach me, anything that my horses do not know already."

She accentuated the plural, and as she realised that the *Duc* had noticed it, she said:

"Perhaps you will allow my groom to join me. He has another horse I would like you to see, although he is not in the same class as Ariel."

"That is the name of your magnificent stallion?"

"Yes, I pronounce it in the English way."

Canéda smiled.

She felt with a little sense of triumph that the conversation was going exactly as she wished it to do.

"Perhaps I should explain, *Monsieur*, that when I am in England I am English, and in France I am French."

She thought he was puzzled, and she explained:

"My mother was French, my father . . . so I have always been told . . . was English."

Again at the frankness of her words she saw a faint smile on the *Duc*'s lips.

He had a hard mouth, she thought, it might even be a cruel one, but it was belied by the expression in his eyes, which made her think he was what the mediaeval Knights must have looked like who warred so ferociously over France in previous centuries.

He lifted his hand and one of the men in uniform rode to his side.

"Have the gates opened for *Mademoiselle*'s groom to join her," the *Duc* ordered.

The officer saluted and rode towards the gateway.

The *Duc* turned his face again towards Canéda.

"We appear to have something in common besides horse-flesh," he said. "You say you are half-French and half-English, and I am the same. Except my mother was English and my father French."

Canéda was both startled and intrigued.

Not even *Madame* de Goucourt had told her that the *Duc* had English blood in him, but it would certainly account for his height, the breadth of his shoulders, and the fact that despite his dark hair he did not look as conventionally French as she had expected.

"Your French is certainly exceptional," the *Duc* went on, "and I am not certain I am prepared to compare my English with it."

"If we are obliged to speak English, *Monsieur*," Canéda replied, "Ariel shall be the judge of how intelligible you are."

She spoke so provocatively and with such a look of mischief in her eyes that the *Duc* made a little sound that might almost have been termed a laugh.

She was quite sure he did not laugh often, and she felt that, if nothing else, this was a point in her favour.

Then she saw Ben come through the gates and ride towards her, and she knew that the officers in the School watched him and that his theatrical appearance undoubtedly amused them.

He looked very small on Black Boy's back. At the same time, he rode conventionally until he was halfway between the gates and the *Duc*.

Then he stood up in the saddle, holding on only to the reins, while Black Boy carried him until they reached Canéda and were facing the *Duc*.

As the horse came to a standstill, Ben swept off his top-hat and made a deep bow, then sat down in the saddle again.

The *Duc*, however, was looking at Black Boy rather than at Ben, and Canéda was sure it was deliberate.

"A fine animal," he said at length. "Can he do the same tricks as yours?"

"He is young and still a learner, as I wish to be, *Monsieur le Duc*."

"It is doubtful if there is much we can teach you," the *Duc* replied, "and as you have already given such an instructive performance, perhaps it would be unfair to ask for an encore."

Canéda gave him a dazzling smile.

"It would be a pleasure, *Monsieur*, if that is what you want."

"I feel that my officers would be very disappointed if, having aroused their interest and curiosity with an *aperitif*, you denied them the rest of the meal."

Canéda gave a laugh that seemed to ring out infectiously.

"We will give a performance, *Monsieur*, but I shall expect payment in kind."

"Of course, *Mademoiselle*," the *Duc* agreed.

Again he summoned an officer to his side, and as he saluted respectfully, Canéda was aware that the young man was looking at her rather than at the *Duc*.

"*Mademoiselle* Canéda has most graciously said she will show us what her horse can do, and I have promised in return that we will show her what we have achieved after two months of hard training."

There was a bite in the last words as if the *Duc* challenged the Cavalrymen not to let him down, and Canéda was sure he was a stern taskmaster and that the young officers would be afraid of him.

However, at the moment she was concerned with

looking at the jumps which were arranged in a circle round the centre of the ground on which they were standing.

They were almost as high as the wall which Ariel had just cleared, and were arranged in a manner which made it sometimes difficult for a horse to take the second jump as easily as he took the first.

There was also an imitation wall made of loose bricks which would be easy to dislodge at a touch.

Canéda glanced at Ben and knew he was thinking that there was nothing that need make Ariel or Black Boy the least apprehensive.

The ground was cleared and the Cavalrymen arranged themselves on either side.

She smiled at the *Duc*.

"I hope, *Monsieur,* that you will not be disappointed."

"I am quite certain, *Mademoiselle,* that would be impossible," the *Duc* replied.

His voice held a slightly dry note which did not make his words sound like a compliment, and *Canéda* told herself that she would have to fight to get what she wanted, which in a way made it even more exhilarating.

She had only to look at the young officers watching her to know that she would see in their eyes the admiration which could so easily be heightened by a glance or a provocative little twist of her lips.

But with the *Duc* she was not certain.

She had surprised him. He had so far fallen in with her plans, but it might be difficult to extract any more from him.

However, for the moment she was concerned only with giving a performance which would make him admire her horses if not herself.

There was no need for her to touch Ariel with her whip. She had only to speak to him in a voice he had always obeyed.

Then he was off, sailing over the jumps disdainfully and treating the wall with contempt.

They went round twice, then Canéda drew him up in the centre while Ben rode off on Black Boy.

Black Boy was a good jumper, but there was nothing particularly original about that.

It was Ben whom they watched.

He did the Cossack trick of travelling between the jumps at the side of his horse rather than in the saddle.

He stood up as he had when he arrived, but this time without holding on to the reins, and he vaulted to the ground and back onto Black Boy without making him slow his pace.

In fact, he did a dozen tricks that he had done in the Circus, but Canéda knew it was all the more remarkable because he had only been training Black Boy for the last nine months.

When finally he finished the course and trotted away, there was a grin on his face that told her he was as pleased as she was that it had gone so well.

Then Canéda made Ariel dance again. He waltzed and polkaed as Juno used to do, and, because there was no Band, Canéda hummed to him.

There were many other small tricks he could do which Canéda knew would impress the *Duc,* as only a really good horseman would know how difficult they were to teach and the patience that was required to bring them to the perfection that Ariel showed.

Finally both Ariel and Black Boy went down on their knees and put their heads down on the ground, with their riders still sitting in the saddle.

It was then that the applause broke out, and this time it was accompanied by cheers and "Bravos" that seemed to echo round the Riding-School.

As the horses rose to their feet, the *Duc* rode up to them.

"Thank you, *Mademoiselle!*" he said. "There is no need for me to tell you how magnificent your performance was, or how much it has been appreciated by me and the officers of the Cavalry Corps."

Canéda bowed, and he continued:

"You have offered us a challenge, and now if you will stand at the saluting-base, we will see what we can offer you."

Canéda smiled at him, and they rode side by side to the saluting-base while Ben followed to stand behind them.

As if she had inspired the Cavalry officers, they took their horses over the jumps in record time, first one man completing the course, then two together, and finally three.

It was impressive, and Canéda clapped her hands.

"You have trained them well, *Monsieur*."

"I am glad you did not visit us two months earlier, *Mademoiselle*," the *Duc* replied drily.

Then the riders not only completed the course as quickly as they could, but dismounted, changed horses, and went round again.

The best rider was incredibly quick, and Canéda decided this was certainly something she would try out with Harry and his friends at Langstone Park.

She thought it would be a change from steeple-chasing, and was deciding what prize they would offer to the winner, when the *Duc* interrupted her thoughts.

The race had just finished and he said:

"I would now like to show you, *Mademoiselle*, what the horse I am riding can do. He is one of the best in my stables, and while he has no tricks to compare with Ariel's, I think you will agree that he is an excellent jumper."

He did not wait for Canéda's answer but started off over the jumps, and there was no doubt that the horse he was riding was very superior to those they had watched before.

He could easily have jumped fences several feet higher than those that were erected in the School, and he had a style that Canéda recognised as exceptional.

When the *Duc* came back to her she said enthusiastically:

"That was wonderful, *Monsieur*, really wonderful! I

would love to ride such a remarkable animal and feel as if I could jump over the moon!"

There was a little pause while she knew the *Duc* turned the idea over in his mind. Then he said:

"I should be delighted, *Mademoiselle,* for you to do so, but I think, as it is now luncheon-time, we should allow the horses to take a well-earned rest before the afternoon's programme."

Then he added:

"I should be honoured if you would give me the pleasure of having luncheon with me."

"I should be delighted, *Monsieur,* to accept your invitation," Canéda replied.

She felt a sudden surge of excitement, knowing that her hopes had materialised and her plan was working out. Whatever happened now, at least she had not failed ignominiously at the outset.

Then Canéda was riding beside the *Duc,* with Ben following, out of the Riding-School and through several narrow streets before they reached the steep incline that led up the hill towards the *Château.*

The hill was steeper than Canéda, looking up at it from below, had expected, and as they reached the top she saw the moat which surrounded the Castle.

There was a bridge over it which had once been a drawbridge in time of siege but which now led them into a large courtyard in the centre of the *Château.*

Grooms came to take their horses and to look after Ben, while the *Duc* led Canéda through a large doorway embellished with the de Saumac coat-of-arms in stone. They climbed a stone staircase up to a large Salon with high, narrow windows looking out over the Loire Valley.

Without speaking, Canéda moved towards the nearest one and saw, as she expected, a view that was so breathtaking that she was for the moment speechless.

The Loire Valley lay in front of her, the river winding through the flat green fields which swept away towards the misty horizon, with many spires and castellated roofs peeping above the tops of the trees.

It was so lovely in the golden sunshine that she exclaimed:

"Now I feel as I have always wanted to do, that I am standing on 'the corner of the moon'!"

The *Duc* smiled.

"Shakespeare!" he said. "And—I think—Macbeth!"

"You are well read, *Monsieur*."

"I like to think so," he replied, "but I did not expect . . ."

He stopped, and Canéda realised that he was suddenly aware of what he had been about to say and that it would have been rude to suggest that a woman from the Circus, whether she was English or French, would not have read Shakespeare.

She made no comment and he quickly pointed out the roof of a *Château* in the distance.

"I expect you would like to wash before we eat," he suggested, "and take off your hat. I would like to see your hair."

His tone was different from the way he had spoken before, and for a moment Canéda was surprised.

Then she remembered that she was not a Lady who would resent such familiarity, but a Circus performer, and doubtless in the *Duc*'s estimation she was a woman who was not particularly concerned over her morality or anybody else's.

With an effort she swept the surprise from her eyes and replied:

"Thank you. I am flattered, *Monsieur*."

Outside the Salon, a maid-servant was waiting to take her to a large, beautifully furnished bedroom on the same floor.

It was so impressive and so exquisitely decorated that Canéda guessed it was one of the State-Rooms and wondered if it had been used by the famous *Duchesses* de Saumac.

She wanted to ask the maid if her supposition was correct, then thought it would be a mistake.

At the same time, she was exceedingly intrigued that the *Duc*'s mother had been English.

She wondered whether *Madame* de Goucourt had known this, but she supposed that because the *Duchesse* had been ill for years she had not become well known in the Social World of the time.

Then there was the *Duc*'s wife.

Had he loved her? Had he found her attractive, Canéda wondered, before she went mad?

Perhaps she had slept in this room and looking out the window had not found the panoramic view attractive or felt as if she stood upon a corner of the moon, but instead had felt she was in a prison, cut off from all human contact with those far away below her.

As she washed her hands and took off her elegant riding-hat to tidy her hair, Canéda felt that her imagination was running away with her, as her Nanny would have said.

This was all so exciting, and yet in a way it was frightening, because she was doing what she had no right to do, and Harry would have considered it reprehensible.

She had never had luncheon or dined alone with a man before, as since she had arrived in London she had always been strictly chaperoned by one of the Lang aunts, and she thought that, if nothing else, this would be an experience in itself.

Then she remembered that she had a serious task ahead of her, and that was to intrigue, captivate, and fascinate the *Duc*.

She looked at her reflection in the mirror.

Canéda would have been very foolish if she had not been aware that she was very lovely, with her straight, classical features.

Her sparkling blue eyes and a mischievous twist to her red lips constituted a snare for any man, unless he had locked away his heart behind steel doors, where no-one could reach it.

"Is that what happened to the *Duc* after his wife went mad?" Canéda asked herself.

Had he, in consequence, almost a dislike of women? She was somehow sure that was not true.

There was something about him, autocratic though he might seem, which told her that he was very masculine!

There was a smile on Canéda's lips as, having thanked the maid-servant, she walked back towards the Salon.

She knew her riding-habit did not make her look out-of-place, because it was of silk and was fashioned more like a gown than a habit.

It fastened down the back and had a collar that was low round her neck, with a soft bow in the front above the large pearl buttons, and white braid.

The *Duc* was waiting for her, standing in front of a large mediaeval fireplace.

He did not move as she entered the Salon, but watched her walk towards him in the same way, Canéda thought, as he had watched the horses take their fences.

As he did so, she had the feeling that he was trying to be critical, and although she thought it was an impertinence, it was still a move in the right direction.

He waited until she was beside him before he said:

"You walk with a grace that is surprising."

"Why surprising?" Canéda enquired.

"Because most women who ride as well as you do not dance as well as they sit a horse, but I would not mind waging a large sum that you are a remarkable dancer."

"I think I should allow you to judge that for yourself," Canéda answered.

"But of course, that is what I am hoping you will do," the *Duc* replied.

A servant approached with glasses of wine.

"This is from my own vineyards, and I hope it will please you," the *Duc* said.

The wine was cool and delicious, and because

211

instantly her mind went to the vineyards belonging to her grandparents, Canéda said:

"The vines here are in good heart?"

"I have no complaints," the *Duc* replied.

"I had heard, and it must have been from someone in Angers, that there is an outbreak of phylloxera in the Dordogne region."

"It is very serious," the *Duc* said quietly, "and we can only pray that in the North we shall remain immune."

Canéda did not pursue the subject—she had found out what she wanted to know.

Then as they went into luncheon in a room almost as large as the Salon and again with long narrow windows looking both North and East, she set out to amuse the *Duc*.

She told him of the race-meetings she had been to in England, of the horses that were for sale in Tattersall's Sale-Rooms, and of the successes on the Turf gained by members of the Jockey Club.

She drew freely on her imagination and also remembered many amusing things that Harry had told her of the race-meetings which she had not attended personally but at which he had been present.

The *Duc* laughed several times, and a sideways glance from one of the flunkeys told her that it was a sound they did not often hear in the *Château*.

Finally, when after a delectable meal the coffee had been poured out and Canéda at the *Duc*'s insistence had accepted a small glass of liqueur made from strawberries, the servants withdrew and she said:

"Now it is only fair for you to tell me about yourself."

"What do you want to know about me?" he parried. "And what induced you to come here and indeed approach me in such an unusual manner?"

"It is quite simple," Canéda replied. "I wanted to see your Riding-School, and I was quite certain you would have a notice on the gate saying: *'Women Keep Out!'* "

The *Duc* smiled.

"But you entered in a somewhat unconventional

manner. I suppose you realise it was a dangerous thing to do?"

"Why? Ariel made light of it."

"You might not have landed on the sand, and there might have been something in the way. It is a risk you must never take again."

"It is a risk I have no wish to take, if the gate is open to me."

"There is no need for me to tell you that you may ride in the School whenever you wish, but not during the hours when the officers are having their lessons."

Canéda raised her eye-brows, and he said:

"You must be well aware, *Mademoiselle,* that you would be, to put it mildly, a distraction."

Canéda gave a little laugh.

"I am not certain whether you are flattering me or insulting me, *Monsieur,* but let me promise you I will not interfere with your lessons for long. I am only passing through this part of the country."

"To where?"

She made a vague little gesture with her hands.

"I am not quite certain. Shall I say I am exploring France?"

"You sound as if this is the first time you have been here."

"It is!"

"And yet your mother was French?"

"We lived in England, and she was very poor."

This was at least the truth, and Canéda was determined to lie as little as possible, which was why she had not given herself a false name.

She remembered her father saying to her a long time ago:

"If one is going to lie, one should tell a really good one, and as near the truth as possible."

Her mother had given a cry of protest.

"Really, Gerald, how can you say such things to the child? You know as well as I do she should not lie in any circumstances."

"You cannot go through life always telling the truth on every occasion," Canéda's father had replied. "Nothing is more uncomfortable or disagreeable than someone who tells the truth for what he calls 'your own good.' "

"You know that is not what I am talking about," Mrs. Lang had said. "I loathe lies of all sorts, and I want Canéda always to tell the truth and take the consequences."

"You are so good, and I love you for it, my darling, but I think Canéda will find in life that it is sometimes easier to 'trim one's sails to the wind.' "

"You are not to listen, Canéda," her mother admonished her.

At the same time, she had smiled as she spoke and it was not really a rebuke.

Canéda in fact hated lies as her mother hated them, and only when it would be unkind or rude to be too frank did she "trim her sails to the wind."

Now she decided she would be as truthful as possible while masquerading as somebody very different from herself.

She took a sip of her liqueur and realised that the *Duc* was watching her.

There was still not the glint of admiration she had hoped for in his eyes, but at least she held his attention, and she was almost sure that she intrigued him and he wanted to know more about her.

"Who is travelling with you on this trip?" he asked.

"I am with a friend."

She spoke lightly before she realised what he might infer from the remark.

"I am sure he is very charming," he said with a twist of his lips.

"As it happens, it is not a man but a woman. A Frenchwoman who was anxious to return to the country from which she came, to see her relatives and friends, and so we came together."

"And she is with you now?"

"She is not far from here."

There was a little pause. Then the *Duc* said:

"Supposing I invite you to stay with me while you learn what you wish to learn from my horses? Would I have to extend the invitation to her as well?"

Canéda shook her head.

"No. In fact, I am quite certain she would rather be with the people she loves."

"And whom do you love?" the *Duc* enquired.

Canéda was astonished at the question and for a moment she felt she could not have heard him aright.

Then she told herself once again that if he was over-familiar, it was because of the way she was dressed.

"Why should you suspect that I love anybody?" she asked.

"I cannot believe," he replied, "that your horse, magnificent though he is, fills your life to the exclusion of everybody else, and I suppose even Englishmen have eyes in their heads!"

"They have!" Canéda agreed. "But for the moment I am curious about Frenchmen. You see, *Monsieur,* they are not a species one meets very often in England, not in the places where I have been."

That again was true, Canéda thought. There were no Frenchmen living within fifty miles of the village, and the only ones she knew were those who visited her father and mother when they came over from France.

But the visitors were mostly women like *Madame* de Goucourt, whose husband was too occupied and too busy to come to the country.

"There are plenty of Frenchmen at the Riding-School," the *Duc* replied, "and they are, as you have seen, only too eager to make your acquaintance."

"For the moment I am content to talk to you," Canéda said. "Do you live here in this enormous *Château* all by yourself?"

"I am not always alone—but most of the time."

"What do you do . . . read?"

"A great deal."

"But you must feel lonely."

"There is plenty of companionship if I need it."

"Do you mean the officers in the School? You see them in the daytime."

There was a smile on his lips, as if he was aware what Canéda was trying to find out, and he said:

"I am alone only when I wish to be."

The way he looked was more eloquent than words, and it suddenly struck Canéda that of course he had a mistress.

The books she had read had told her that Frenchmen were ardent lovers and that Kings like François I had wandered round the town at night, incognito, in search of attractive women.

And of course Louis the XIV and Louis XV had had innumerable mistresses. She had read about *Madame* de Pompadour and *Madame* de Maintenon and all the others.

But it had never crossed her mind that while the *Duc*'s wife was locked away because she was mad, that would not preclude him from enjoying female companionship.

Perhaps some of her thoughts revealed themselves in her eyes, for the *Duc* asked mockingly:

"Surely you did not expect anything else?"

"I was just being . . . curious about you . . . living here on the . . . corner of the moon, apparently . . . alone."

She did not know why, but it was disconcerting to find that the *Duc* had women to amuse him.

She had somehow expected, from what had been said about him, that he was a monogomist, and that because fate had destroyed his married life, he would no longer be concerned with the female sex.

"Even the moon has adjacent stars twinkling round it," he said.

Of course, Canéda told herself, there would be women in his life.

He was far too attractive as a man, and of course as a

Duc and a rich one, women would flock to him like bees round a honey-pot.

"Of course," she agreed aloud, and thought her voice sounded a little bleak.

For the first time things did not seem to be going so smoothly.

She had somehow expected to walk in, beautiful, sensational, and take him by storm because he was cynical and embittered by the way he had been treated by fate.

It was disconcerting to find that he was obviously well content with his life as it was and was missing none of the comforts that only a woman could give him.

Canéda put down her glass.

"Perhaps we should get back to the Riding-School."

"There is no hurry," the *Duc* replied. "Come and sit in a room where I think we will be more comfortable."

He rose as he spoke, and when they left the Dining-Room they did not return to the Salon where they had been earlier.

Instead the *Duc* took her along a passage and opened a door which led into one of the most intriguing rooms she had ever seen.

It was small and round, and she knew that it must be situated in one of the towers which stood at each of the four corners of the *Château*.

There were windows looking in three directions, and a large, comfortable sofa covered with silk cushions which the *Duc* indicated as a place for Canéda to sit.

Instead she stood at the window, looking out once again on the amazing panorama and the silver river that seemed to grow longer and go farther every time she looked at it.

She stood there for some time, aware without turning her head that the *Duc* was watching her.

"Well?" he asked at length. "Are you still content with the moon, or do you wish to come back to the earth with all its troubles?"

"I have none at the moment."

"Then you are very lucky!"

217

"What are yours?"

She turned from the window to face him as she asked the question.

"I have none except the difficulty of deciding whether you are real or just a figment of my imagination."

"I assure you I am very real."

"And very different from anyone I have ever seen before," the *Duc* finished. "I may be wrong, but I have a feeling that how you appear on the surface may not be quite genuine."

Canéda started.

"Why should you think that?" she asked quickly.

"Shall I say that living up here on what you call the moon, I have grown perceptive about people. I use my instinct rather than my ears."

Without really thinking, because earlier they had been speaking of Shakespeare, Canéda quoted:

" *'Love looks not with the eyes, but with the mind.'* "

Even as she said the words she blushed, knowing that it was a mistake to mention love, but it was too late to retract the words.

"Now the most abused word in the French language appears," the *Duc* remarked. *"L'amour!* I wondered when we would get round to it."

"That is not what I meant, as you are well aware, *Monsieur,*" Canéda said almost crossly. "I was merely quoting from *A Midsummer Night's Dream.*"

"I know that," the *Duc* said, "and I thought perhaps I should have quoted that particular play when you talked about my being alone. Surely you remember— *'One grows, lives and dies in single blessedness'*?"

Canéda thought he was throwing her a challenge, but, because she could not say that his single blessedness was thrust upon him because of his wife's madness, and feeling that the whole conversation was becoming somewhat uncomfortable, she moved from the window to sit down on the sofa.

"I must go soon," she said in a different tone of voice.

"Ben and I have quite a long ride to get back to where we are staying."

"I have already suggested that you might prefer to stay with me," the *Duc* said.

The question: "Unchaperoned?" trembled on Canéda's lips. Then she told herself that he would think her idiotic if she said anything so superfluous.

Of course a woman from the Circus would not expect to be chaperoned.

Then while she thought it would be amusing and a step forward to stay with the *Duc,* she wondered what else he might expect if she did so.

Then she told herself that she was sure she could look after herself.

She knew that for her to stay at the *Château* without *Madame* de Goucourt would make Harry very angry, and certainly it was something of which her mother would not have approved.

But she had wanted the *Duc* to invite her and now he had done so, and it seemed foolish to back off from the very moment when she could give him a short, sharp lesson and then leave him, she hoped, disconsolate without her.

'If I can see him only in the daytime, it will take much longer to get him in the position in which I want him,' Canéda thought to herself, 'which is at my feet, where Lord Warrington and all those other men have been.'

It was as if her thoughts had been discernible in her eyes, because after a moment the *Duc* said:

"I am not in the habit of having my invitations considered so carefully."

"I am trying to make up my mind whether to say 'Yes' or 'No.' "

"That is obvious!" the *Duc* replied. "Most people to whom I extend my hospitality are only too eager to accept it."

"I am glad I am different," Canéda retorted.

"I shall be very disappointed if you are so different that you refuse me."

219

Canéda looked down and her long eye-lashes were dark against her cheeks.

"What I am wondering, *Monsieur,* is what you . . . expect from your . . . guests when you . . . entertain them."

As if he understood what she was trying hesitatingly to say, the *Duc* smiled before he replied:

"Shall I answer that by saying that I expect as much as you are prepared to give? I am not an ogre or a barbarian."

Canéda drew in her breath. Then she said:

"With that assurance, *Monsieur,* I am delighted to accept your invitation."

"Then what we will do," the *Duc* said, "is to send your man back to collect what clothes you need. He can take one of my carriages, and if he leaves soon he can be back in plenty of time for you to look beautiful at dinner."

"I will certainly try," Canéda replied, "but now I want to ride your horse, as you promised me I could."

The *Duc* opened the door and she went back to the bedroom to put on her riding-hat.

As she looked at herself in the mirror, she could not help but feel a little tremor of fear when she thought how angry Harry would be if he had any idea what she was doing.

Then she told herself that what the eye did not see the heart would not grieve over.

He need never know that she had done anything so outrageous, only that she had taken her revenge on the *Duc* as she had intended to do when she had left England.

There was still *Madame* de Goucourt to contend with, and Canéda sat down at a *secretaire* in the corner of the bedroom, and, carefully choosing a plain piece of writing-paper that was not embossed with the name of the *Château,* she wrote a quick note.

She told *Madame* that she had decided to stay the

night with the friend she was visiting and hoped to be back tomorrow.

She finished:

Do not Worry about me, Dear Madame, I am well looked after, and I will return tomorrow. Enjoy Yourself with Your friends, and We will compare Notes later.

My love and gratitude,
Yours affectionately,

Canéda

She sealed the letter, addressed it to *Madame* de Goucourt, and put it in her pocket so that she could give it to Ben without the *Duc* seeing it.

'I am behaving very badly,' she thought as she left the bedroom, knowing that she would return to it later.

Then she thought that at least it was fun, but perhaps that was an inadequate word.

It was intriguing and exciting and splendidly exhilarating to think that her revenge on the *Duc* de Saumac was working out exactly as she had intended.

CHAPTER FOUR

RIDING ROUND THE SCHOOL on the *Duc*'s grey horse, Canéda thought she had never enjoyed herself more.

Although she had ridden constantly with Harry and

they had raced against each other, she had been aware that because he was older than she and was a more experienced rider, he would always be the winner.

But she had with Ariel just beaten all the officers competing against her over a timed course, and now she was attempting to beat the *Duc*.

He had challenged her, saying:

"Up to now I have been the judge. Now I think I should be a participator."

Because she thought it might annoy him and also draw his attention, she had replied:

"But of course, and I would be prepared, if you are faster than I am, to concede victory on one condition."

"What is that?" he enquired.

"That you allow me to ride *Toujour*."

This was the name, she had discovered, of his grey horse, and she had the feeling that he was very confident of winning because *Toujour* in his own way was as exceptional as Ariel.

The *Duc* hesitated before he replied, and she saw the twinkle in his eyes.

"Are you suggesting," he asked, "that I should have an unfair advantage if I rode my own horse?"

"But of course you would!" Canéda replied. "*Toujour* knows the course far better than Ariel, and I am sure that the reason you have not competed before was that you felt it unsporting not to give your competitors a chance."

The *Duc* laughed.

"Very well," he said. "You shall ride *Toujour* and I will choose another mount."

He gave an order to one of the grooms, who brought forward a horse that had not jumped so far.

He was a young chestnut and only to look at him made Canéda aware that he would be very fast.

She was, however, delighted to think that she could ride the *Duc*'s horse, because she knew from the expression on the faces of his officers that never before had anyone other than his owner been allowed to mount him.

Because she was very experienced in handling horses and both Harry and Ben had taught her how to control them, she did not attempt to mount *Toujour* until she had made a great fuss of him.

She patted his neck, stroked his nose, and talked to him in a soft, beguiling voice, and only when she felt that the horse was really aware of her did she move to his side to show that she was ready to be helped into the saddle.

The groom would have done so, but the *Duc* gestured him to one side.

Instead of cupping his hands in the usual way, he stretched out his fingers on each side of her tiny waist and lifted her into the air.

For one moment as he did so their faces were very close together and she thought there was the expression in his grey eyes that she had hoped to see.

Then she was seated in the saddle and the *Duc* with an experienced hand arranged her skirt over her stirrup.

She moved *Toujour* into position, then waited while the *Duc* took out his stop-watch.

"*Bon-chance!*" all the young officers were murmuring.

The *Duc* was very businesslike as he asked:

"Are you ready, *Mademoiselle?*"

"I am ready, *Monsieur.*"

"Then—Go!"

He pressed the button of the stop-watch and there was no need for Canéda to use either her whip or spur on *Toujour*.

He knew exactly what was expected of him and he took the first fence magnificently.

He was a very large horse, higher even than Ariel, and she found it a thrilling experience to ride something so magnificent and as a special privilege accorded only to her.

They went round the course in what she was sure was

record time, and there were cheers and applause from the officers who were watching.

Then as she drew *Toujour* to a standstill in front of the *Duc,* they rushed forward, exclaiming:

"Magnificent! Fantastic! You were sensational, *Mademoiselle!*"

"I had a sensational horse," Canéda replied.

She would have slipped from the saddle, but before she could do so the *Duc* was there to lift her to the ground.

As he did so, she said:

"I admit, *Monsieur,* that *Toujour* is the second most wonderful horse in the world!"

"Both he and I are honoured!" the *Duc* replied formally.

She thought, although she was not sure, that he lifted her down more slowly than he need have done and that his hands lingered for a moment on her waist.

Then he turned to mount the chestnut, and a Senior Officer had the stop-watch in his hand.

Watching him, Canéda knew that he rode better than any other man she had ever seen in her life.

She had felt that no-one could be a better rider than her father, until Harry grew up.

Now, although she hated to admit it, she knew the *Duc* was better than either of them.

There was something about the way he rode that made him seem a part of his horse, and they moved in unison and with a rhythm that was almost like hearing the sound of music.

He did not appear to hurry, but as he reached the last two fences she knew that the officers were tense, and she herself held her breath.

One second—two seconds.

He brought the chestnut to a standstill and the officer holding the stop-watch said:

"You are the winner, *Monsieur le Duc,* by half a second!"

A cheer went up but it was somewhat half-hearted after the applause Canéda had received.

The *Duc* dismounted and walked to her side.

"Are you satisfied?" he asked.

She raised her eye-brows at the strange question.

"That I was not cheating," he explained.

"I did not think you would do so, and anyway I was only teasing. Moreover, though it may surprise you, I am aware that as a woman I am expected to take second place."

"Most women expect to be first in everything," the *Duc* answered.

"Except of course in sport."

She saw by his smile that her reply amused him.

When they returned to the *Château* they duelled with each other in words, and again Canéda found it an amusing experience that she had not known before.

She had always been aware that she had a quick brain and would like to argue and exchange views with a man.

But ever since she had been in London the men had persisted in flattering her, to the exclusion of all other conversation.

Whatever she tried to talk about, the subject always got back to love in one way or another, but now with the *Duc* every word they spoke was more like a rapier thrust.

She had the feeling while she was sparring with him that he was determined to be the victor not only in riding but also because he was a man and she was a woman.

He was so essentially masculine that she found herself vividly conscious of him even when he was silent.

She was sure that he would be very difficult to understand, and she realised how easy it had been for him to build up a reputation of being awe-inspiring and aloof from other people.

The mere fact that he lived alone in his fantastic fortress of a *Château* far above the earth below him, and was not interested in the social life that was so much a part of the Loire Valley, made him a law unto himself.

When they arrived back at the *Château,* Canéda found that Ben had not yet returned with her clothes.

Therefore, she merely took off her hat as she had for luncheon, and, having washed, she joined the *Duc* in the tower Sitting-Room where he told her he would wait for her.

To her surprise, beside the sofa there was a small table on which was a silver tray containing what was obviously an English silver tea-pot and a number of *pâtisseries.*

Canéda gave a little laugh of delight.

"You are very considerate, *Monsieur.*"

"I know the English are at a loss without their cups of tea."

"I am astonished that you should be aware of that," Canéda said, remembering that his mother had died when he was very young.

"Shall I say that I have been taught a number of English customs by one of your countrywomen?"

Canéda knew by the way he spoke that she had been someone close to him, and although she did not know why, she felt a little tug at her heart.

She sat down on the sofa and poured herself out a cup of tea, saying:

"I presume, as you are being very French at the moment, you do not wish to join me."

He was obviously more perceptive even than she had suspected, for he replied:

"Because I suggested I have a *chère amie?* What else do you expect?"

"I expect nothing, *Monsieur.* Why should I?"

"Because like all women," he said cynically, "you like to think of a man with a wife constantly at his side."

"I think you are putting words into my mouth," Canéda said sharply.

"But it is true," he persisted. "I can assure you that I am very happy living in my corner of the moon, although of course you will understand that I occasionally step down from the sky and mix with mere mortals on the earth below."

Canéda knew that he was mocking her, and she resented it because he was making her feel as if she had been rather gauche and foolish.

She set down the tea-pot and said:

"Perhaps I have interrupted your plans and engagements, and the best thing I could do would be to return to my friend."

The *Duc* laughed.

"Now you are definitely trying to punish me for a crime I have not committed, and I reiterate, you are interrupting nothing. If you were not here, I should have dined alone in all my glory!"

"And that would have amused you?"

"The answer actually is 'Yes,' " the *Duc* replied. "I have learnt to be self-sufficient, and when I am alone I have books and a certain amount of work to do."

"What sort of work?"

"I keep a record of the horses that pass through my School and the men who ride them. I am also compiling a Thesis on the schooling of horses."

"That is wonderful!" Canéda exclaimed. "Please, may I have a copy of it?"

"It is not yet finished," the *Duc* replied, "but of course I will send you one if you will give me an address."

"That might be difficult, as I am a wanderer on the face of the earth! It is only chance that I have dropped in on the moon in passing."

He gave her a shrewd glance which told her that he was not deceived by this remark.

"By chance?" he questioned. "I doubt that!"

"Why should you do so?"

"Because your entrance was too well thought out. You must have known that I would be in the School at that particular time, and you must also have known, because you care for your horse, where it was safe to jump the wall."

He was more intuitive than she had expected, and because she did not wish to be drawn into a discussion as to why she was there, Canéda relapsed into silence.

He sat looking at her until he said:

"Tell me about the Circus to which you belong, if in fact it exists."

"Why should you doubt that it does?"

"Because I find it hard to believe, despite your expertise in handling Ariel, that you perform in a Circus or that you have ever mixed with the type of person one finds in them."

"What do you know about Circuses?"

"Quite a lot, as it happens," the *Duc* replied. "A number of them come here every summer because they hope to sell me their horses. It may surprise you, but the chestnut on which I beat you this afternoon was born in a Circus."

"Like Ariel!" Canéda exclaimed.

Then, because she wanted to convince him that she was with a Circus, she told him about Juno and her death and how all she had left behind was Ariel and Ben.

She saw that the *Duc* was interested, and when she had finished he said:

"You are too young and too lovely for such a life. Surely there is something else you could do—like getting married?"

"To one of the clowns?" Canéda asked lightly.

"If marriage is not on your programme," the *Duc* said, "I can only imagine that you have a rich Protector."

He spoke quite casually, but the colour flared into Canéda's cheeks as she said sharply:

"How dare you suggest such a thing! And you are quite wrong."

She was so positive that the *Duc* said:

"I must apologise if I have insulted you, but I cannot believe that a Circus Proprietor, unless he is a very exceptional one, would have provided you with the habit you are wearing now, and which undoubtedly cost at least double the salary an ordinary Circus performer could earn in six months."

Canéda was so surprised that she forgot to be angry, and she stared at him wide-eyed.

"How can you know something like that?"

The *Duc*'s lips twisted and there was no need for explanation.

Because she felt she was fighting a losing battle, Canéda rose from the sofa to walk to the window and look out again at the view.

The sun was beginning to sink on the horizon and the sky above it was a blaze of colour.

She was so absorbed in its beauty that she started when the *Duc* spoke just behind her, because she was not aware that he had risen from his chair.

"Are you still considering whether or not to leave me?" he asked. "I shall almost certainly prevent you from doing so."

"How would you do that?" Canéda enquired.

"I suppose I could always lock you in the dungeons, which are below the level of the moat and are very unpleasant," the *Duc* replied, "but instead I will merely plead with you to keep me company as I want you to."

There was a note now in his voice which Canéda knew she had been waiting to hear, and yet somehow it did not give her the elation she had hoped for. Instead it seemed in some way to vibrate within her and evoke a response she had not expected.

"I still . . . think I would be . . . wise to . . . go."

"Because I have shocked you?"

She raised her chin.

"I did not say you have . . . done that."

"Nevertheless, I think it is what has happened," the *Duc* said.

He drew nearer and stood beside her at the window where he could look at her profile against the grey stone.

She did not move but kept her eyes on the sunset, and after what seemed a long time he said:

"You are very beautiful, and, as dozens of men must

229

have told you, your blue eyes fringed with dark lashes are enchantingly original."

He spoke in the dry way that was habitual to him, and he did not make it sound such a compliment as it would have been from any other man.

Because she was afraid that the conversation had grown too serious and too personal, Canéda said:

"My eyes are English, but my lashes and my hair are French. You can make a choice of which you prefer."

"As a Frenchman I am for the moment intrigued by the English," the *Duc* replied, "so shall we speak that language for a change?"

The last sentence was spoken in English, and Canéda gave a little cry as she exclaimed:

"But that is good!"

"I had an English mother, an English Nanny, and at one time an English Governess," the *Duc* explained.

"They certainly did a good job!"

It was true. The *Duc* had only the very faintest shadow of an accent, but because he was speaking English she felt, although it was ridiculous, that he was not quite so menacing as he had been when he spoke French.

She gave him a mischievous glance as she said:

"Now that you are speaking like an Englishman you must behave like one, and we must start talking about horses instead of ourselves."

"Quite frankly, I only want to talk about you," the *Duc* said. "You intrigue me, and, shall I add, I am very curious."

It was exactly what she had wanted him to be, Canéda thought, and she told herself that she had been very clever.

She turned her face once again to the window.

"I think it would be a mistake to be too prosaic about detail," she said. "You admit this is an enchanted place outside the ordinary, mundane world of human beings. Very well, for the moment we are not human."

"Then what are we?"

Canéda gave him an enchanting smile.

"You, of course, are the Man in the Moon, and I am just a shooting star who has called in."

"A very good description!" the *Duc* approved. "You shine like a star, and you certainly dress like one."

His eyes flickered for a moment over her pink riding-habit, and Canéda was suddenly aware that because she had intended to look theatrical, her bodice was very tight and revealed the curves of her breasts.

Her waist was also accentuated more than she would have considered proper in one of her ordinary habits.

She felt shy and wished that she had relied on her riding to attract his attention rather than on the theatrical effect of her clothes and those in which she had dressed Ben.

Because she was afraid of what the *Duc* was thinking, she said quickly:

"I am sure Ben will be back by now with my luggage, and if possible I would like a bath before dinner."

"Of course," the *Duc* replied. "I am sure that has been arranged, and as I have a great deal to talk to you about, shall we dine early?"

He took his watch from his waist-coat pocket and said:

"I will meet you here in an hour."

"An hour will suit me perfectly," Canéda replied, "and thank you, *Monsieur,* for a very entertaining afternoon."

She would have passed him to leave the room, but he reached out, took her hand in his, and raised it to his lips.

"I must thank you," he said, "for an experience I shall not forget."

She felt his lips on her skin and it gave her a strange sensation.

Many men had kissed her hand, but somehow this was different, and she did not wish to think why.

Instead she moved quickly away from him, and he only just had time to open the door for her.

As she hurried along the passage to go to her bedroom, she had the feeling that she was escaping from something that was frightening yet exciting, and at the same time menacing.

She opened the door of her bedroom and found that the maid was unpacking the things she had listed for Ben to bring back from the Inn.

He could have taken one of the *Duc*'s chaises, but because Canéda was very anxious that no-one at the *Château* should know where she was staying, she had insisted that Ben go on horse-back.

"Can you manage everything I will want?" she had asked.

"Yes, I can, M'Lady," Ben replied.

"Remember, it is very important that the servants should not know where I am staying."

"Ye can trust I, M'Lady."

Canéda had put the list into his hand.

"Remind my maid that the gown I require is the pink one that I told her to pack apart from the others."

"I'll remind her, M'Lady."

"If you see *Madame* de Goucourt, and I hope you will not," Canéda went on, "tell her I shall be back tomorrow and that everything is all right."

"Leave it to I, M'Lady."

Canéda was just about to send him away when she had a sudden thought.

She went close to him and spoke in a very low voice, just in case they should be overheard.

She knew, as he nodded agreement to everything she said, that he would not fail her. Then as he hurried away she had gone back to where the *Duc* was waiting for her with a smile on her lips.

This had been after luncheon, and Ben had had plenty of time to reach the Inn and return.

She wished she could speak to him and find out if everything was all right and *Madame* de Goucourt was not upset at the thought of her staying away.

Then Canéda told herself that there was no reason to worry.

The maid in the bedroom was shaking out the gown that had been packed in such a way that it could be carried on the back of a saddle.

It was pink, but Canéda saw that it was not the gown she had asked for.

When she had left England she had deliberately not taken with her the experienced, older lady's-maid who had been looking after her since Harry had inherited the title and they could afford the best servants.

She was a woman Canéda both liked and trusted, but because she had always been in the "best houses" she was not the type of maid Canéda wanted on this particular journey.

She had therefore insisted on taking with her one of the young housemaids, an honest, hard-working girl who was obviously not over-blessed with brains.

Canéda knew she would do as she was told and not ask too many questions, and that was what she required.

She had said her own lady's-maid could have a holiday, and fortunately she had also discovered that she hated the sea and was seasick at the sight of a wave.

She had therefore packed everything that Canéda needed, giving the younger maid innumerable instructions that she only half-understood, for she was too excited at the prospect of going abroad to worry about anything else.

'It is typical of her stupidity,' Canéda thought, 'that while she has sent me a pink gown, it is not the flamboyant one I chose for this occasion.'

She had bought the pink gown at the same time as she had bought the pink riding-habit with which to attract the *Duc* and make him believe that she was a performer in a Circus.

Instead, what had arrived with Ben was a very expensive, very lovely gown from one of the most exclusive Bond Street dressmakers who prided herself on giving her clients Paris *chic*.

Looking at it as the French maid hung it up in the wardrobe, Canéda wondered what the *Duc* would think of it, and had the uncomfortable feeling it would make him more suspicious than he was already that she was not what she appeared to be.

Then she told herself that what he thought was immaterial.

She was certain he was already becoming enamoured of her, and when she had made sure of it she could disappear as she wished to do, leaving him, she hoped, unhappy and frustrated.

It had seemed such a clever idea when she had planned it all in England and during the voyage, and yet now, even when it was working exactly as she had intended, she felt anxious.

In her imagination the *Duc* had been only a cardboard man without reality and not made of flesh and blood.

He had been just a boy in the story that had started when her mother had run away from his father and married the man to whom she had given her heart. As a result of which his father, the old *Duc,* had sworn to take revenge and had tried to make life intolerable for his rival.

It was the sort of tale, Canéda often thought, that should have been written by a novelist.

And what could have been a better ending than that her father and mother had been so happy?

It was she who had refused to allow the tale to end there.

She had always wanted to avenge herself on the *Duc* who had hurt her father, and on her grandparents who had been so heartless towards her mother.

The opportunity had come with the arrival of her Grandmother's letter, and now a new story was unfolding itself and she was actually here in the "Ogre's Castle."

It remained only for her to carry out the rest of her plan, and the first chapter in her pursuit of revenge would have ended.

Then, on to the next.

As she bathed in water scented with a fragrance distilled from camelias, Canéda continued, to her surprise, to feel apprehensive.

Why she should do so she had no idea, and she told herself that she was not really afraid of being alone in the *Château* with the *Duc*.

He might seem raffish but he was a gentleman, and she could not believe that he would not respect her wishes or that she could not, as she had told herself at the beginning, look after herself.

She had always known that it was only cads and bounders who forced themselves on women who did not want them.

All the men who had approached her, even though they were madly in love, had obeyed her when she had refused to let them kiss her, and although they had pleaded with her on many occasions not to leave them, they had not tried to prevent her from doing so.

The *Duc* would be the same, Canéda thought as she dried herself with a soft towel.

It struck her that perhaps, because she was pretending to be not a Lady but a Circus performer, his attitude might be different.

Then she reassured herself by thinking that she was a woman and as such was able to command the respect of any man, however lowly he might suppose her to be.

At the same time, she found herself thinking that she ought not to have agreed to stay the night.

'Harry would be horrified!' she thought.

And she did not pretend that her father and mother would not have been shocked.

Then she put up her chin.

"The end justifies the means," she told herself.

She was quoting an old Jesuit adage, and the end she was aiming for was that the *Duc* should be humiliated in wanting a woman who eluded him and who vanished from his life after he had expressed a desire for her to stay.

'Perhaps . . . he will . . . ask me to become his . . . mistress,' Canéda thought.

She could not help remembering that he had made it clear that he was not always alone, and she told herself that she had been very foolish.

Of course there would be women in his life, and it was distinctly annoying that one of them had been English.

Canéda wondered what she had been like: fair and blue-eyed, she supposed, as a Frenchman would expect an Englishwoman to be, just as she had expected him to have dark eyes instead of grey ones.

She tried to reassure herself that if, as he had said, he was half-English, he would have an Englishman's code of honour where she was concerned.

He would therefore behave in the same way as Lord Warrington or the other men who had asked her to marry them.

They had begged her and had even threatened to destroy themselves if she would not say "Yes."

But they had never tried to molest her, kiss her against her will, or even touch her if she did not want them to.

'The *Duc* will be the same,' Canéda thought, as she instructed the maid who was waiting on her how to arrange her hair.

When she was dressed she stared into the mirror and with a little frown realised that she looked very different from what she had intended.

The gown she had asked for and her stupid maid had not sent was a bright shade of pink embroidered with sequins and diamanté, over-elaborate even though the fashion at the moment was for heavily decorated evening-gowns.

As she was small, Canéda had thought them too overpowering and had therefore chosen gowns that really had a French *chic* about them because they relied on line rather than decoration.

The one she was wearing now was of soft, almond-blossom pink, and it was almost plain compared to the gowns worn by other débutantes.

Yet because it revealed Canéda's perfect figure and tiny waist, with the front swept back into a bustle at the back, it made her look like a young goddess stepping out of the rising sun to bring life and beauty to a dark world.

Canéda had also bought before she left London some false theatrical jewellery that she intended to wear instead of her real jewels.

In her hurry she had said: "Just pack the necklace, bracelets, and stars that go with the pink gown," and thought her maid would understand.

Instead, she had packed Canéda's real jewellery, and although she thought the *Duc* might look at them questioningly, she wanted to wear them because she knew they complemented the elegance of her gown.

There were three stars to arrange in her hair, besides a small necklace of real pearls which Harry had given her, and a narrow bracelet of diamonds and pearls which they had found in the Langstone collection amongst other jewels which had belonged to the late Countess.

Some of them were magnificent and obviously were family heirlooms.

Harry had put those in the safe, saying that Canéda was too young for them, but of the rest he had said carelessly:

"Wear them until I want them for my wife, and until you have a husband who will give you better ones."

Canéda had thanked him, and because she liked jewellery but had never had any, she had worn the smaller brooches, necklaces, and bracelets, and had enjoyed doing so.

Now as she looked at her reflection she thought she looked much more like a débutante than a Circus performer, and certainly and unmistakably she looked like a Lady.

Then she told herself there was nothing she could do about it except put a little extra lip-salve on her lips.

When she had done so, her mouth seemed in contrast to the rest of her appearance to create a jarring note, so she wiped the salve away and turned from the mirror.

She thanked the maid, then went from the bedroom and walked with a lilt in her step down the passage towards the room in the tower.

However reprehensible, however wrong what she was doing might be, it was still an adventure!

An adventure to be in this magnificent *Château* high above the world, and to dine alone with the most enigmatic and certainly the most interesting man she had ever met.

A servant opened the door and she entered to find that the candles had been lit, although there was still a faint light from the setting sun coming through the uncurtained windows.

The room held an atmosphere of mystery but it was impossible for the moment to think of anything but the *Duc*.

If he had seemed impressive in his plain, well-cut riding-clothes, he looked very different in evening-dress. In fact, there was a magnificence about him and Canéda thought that if she had seen him anywhere in England, he would still have been outstanding and it would have been impossible not to notice him.

She stood still for a moment, just inside the door, looking at him as he stood with his back to the fireplace in which a fire had been lit. Their eyes met and it was impossible to look away.

Almost as if it was an effort, she walked towards him and he said:

"That is how you always ought to look. I know now what was wrong."

"Wrong?" Canéda questioned, even though she knew exactly what he meant.

"The fancy dress," he said. "Effective, undoubtedly eye-catching, but, let me add, quite unnecessary."

Because it was what she had thought herself, Canéda felt for a moment as if she had no answer ready, and inexplicably, for it was something she never was, she felt shy.

The *Duc* took a glass of champagne that was waiting on a side-table and put it into her hand.

"As this is our first dinner together," he said, "I feel I should drink a toast, but it is difficult to find the right words."

"Surely that is unusual for a Frenchman?" Canéda managed to reply.

"I think tonight I am feeling English," the *Duc* said, "and I am trying to express myself sincerely rather than eloquently."

"I am glad you think the English are sincere."

"I would like to believe they are both sincere and truthful," the *Duc* replied.

He looked deeply into her eyes as he spoke, but she looked away from him.

She had the feeling that he was probing, looking down into her very soul, trying to penetrate her facade to find out what she was keeping secret from him.

"It is easy for me to give you a toast," she said, to distract his attention.

She raised her glass.

"To the Man in the Moon, and may he never cease to shine his light on those who need it!"

"Is that what you think I am doing?" the *Duc* asked cynically.

"If you are not, then perhaps it will alert you to your duty," Canéda replied.

She sipped a little of the champagne, then set it down on a small table.

"Do you think Ariel has been stabled all right?" she asked conversationally.

"Are you doubting the hospitality of my stables?" the *Duc* enquired.

"From the outside when I passed them they looked superb," Canéda replied.

"Tomorrow I will show you the inside," the *Duc* said. "I have lately added many modern improvements which I hope will impress you."

"I cannot think they will be better than the stabling we have in England."

"Is your Circus wealthy enough to own stables?"

Canéda realised that she had forgotten she was supposed to be permanently with a Circus and had in fact been thinking of the stables at Langstone Park.

"I have seen quite a number of stables that have nothing to do with the Circus," she replied.

"Their owners perhaps had something to do with you?" the *Duc* remarked.

He was speaking in French and it sounded less direct than it would have done in English.

Nevertheless, Canéda was annoyed.

"If you mean to be unpleasant, *Monsieur*," she said, "then let me inform you, you have succeeded!"

The *Duc* took her hand in his.

"Forgive me," he said. "It was just that I find you extremely tantalising! Who are you? Why are you here? These are the questions I am going to ask you until I get the right answers."

"And when you get the answers, what difference will it make?" Canéda enquired.

"That is what is intriguing me."

"I very much doubt it, but at least it will give you something to think about."

"You have given me that already," he said, "and shall I add to what I have already said, that although you bewilder me, I find you entrancing!"

He raised her hand to his lips as he spoke, and once again as he kissed it she felt a strange sensation within her.

It was almost a relief when dinner was announced and they moved once again to the Dining-Room in which they had had luncheon.

Now the curtains were drawn and the big gold

candelabrum on the table furnished the only light in the room.

It seemed to Canéda as she sat beside the *Duc* that the whole setting accentuated the impression that she was living in a fairy-story.

He certainly did not seem real as he sat back in the huge carved armchair with his coat-of-arms embroidered on the red velvet.

Servants in elaborate livery brought gold dishes of food which was more delicious than anything Canéda had ever eaten before.

The wine and the conversation as dinner progressed made her feel that she was acting on a stage in a play that was so skillfully written that it was difficult to know what would be the end of the Act.

Once again she and the *Duc* were duelling in words, and everything they said seemed to have a *double entendre* which made it impossible for them to speak in anything but French.

Only when dinner was finished and the servants had left the room did Canéda exclaim:

"That was the most delicious meal I have ever had!"

"I hoped you would say it was one of the most interesting."

"That goes without saying! I enjoyed our conversation more than I can possibly tell you."

"And so have I," the *Duc* said. "How can you be so intelligent?"

"I suppose it is because I have been well educated."

"I do not think that is the real reason."

"Then what is?"

"Because you think. Very few women think about anything except themselves."

"Is that your experience?"

"It is most men's, and what I am saying, Canéda, is that you are unique."

He had called her by her Christian name ever since they had started dinner, and Canéda thought it would

241

seem rather foolish and pretentious to insist that he address her as *"Mademoiselle."*

She gave him a slightly mocking smile as she answered:

"I am gratified that you should think so. I enjoy being different."

"That I can well believe, because you *are* different, very different in a way that is difficult to describe."

"You might say the same about yourself. Of course you are different from other men, and you know it! I think, if you are honest, it is a contrived difference as well as one you were born with."

"Are you accusing me of play-acting?"

Canéda shrugged her shoulders.

"If you like the expression. I think we all act in one way or another."

"Some more than others, as you are acting now," the *Duc* insisted.

"I do not understand why you keep saying that."

"Because it is obvious. You are playing your part very skillfully, but you do not deceive me."

"Why should I wish to do so?"

"That is for you to say," he said, "and it is what I want to know."

He was again being perceptive, Canéda thought, and that was dangerous.

"Let us go back to the Sitting-Room," she suggested. "I would like to see what you have written so far about schooling horses. I know it is something that will interest me."

The *Duc* did not reply, but he rose as she did and they walked slowly back to the Sitting-Room.

Now the curtains had been closed, the flames from the fire leapt high over the logs, and it looked cosy and romantic.

A servant shut the door behind them and Canéda walked towards the fire and held out her hands in front of it.

"It still gets a little cold at night," she remarked. "I

like your big log fires. I was always certain it would be cold on the moon."

She turned her head to smile at him and found that he was standing closer to her than she had anticipated, and there was an expression on his face that made her heart leap.

She straightened herself, and he said in a low voice that she could barely hear:

"You are very lovely—unbelievably so!"

"I am glad you . . . think . . . so," she tried to say lightly, but somehow the words seemed almost to stick in her throat.

"I have always believed there was someone like you somewhere in the world," the *Duc* said, "and I must have dreamt of you, because I knew today that I had seen you somewhere before."

Canéda felt herself give a little quiver of fear.

She had often wondered if the old *Duc* had a portrait of her mother, for if he had, that was where the present *Duc* would have seen her face.

She did not reply and he went on:

"What am I to do about you? How long can you stay with me, and when you leave me, what will I feel?"

Because he spoke with a seriousness she had not expected and because what he said was somehow out-of-character, Canéda moved a few steps away from him, saying:

"I told you I was a shooting-star who had just called in while I was passing. Why should we worry about to-morrow?"

"Why indeed, when we have *tonight?*" the *Duc* replied.

He accentuated the last word, and suddenly Canéda was frightened.

He had not moved, but she put up her hands as if he encroached upon her.

"Please," she said, "let us . . . talk about our . . . horses."

"I want to talk about you."

"No . . . please . . . no!"

243

"Why not?"

He moved a little closer to her, and now when she would have retreated, there was a chair behind her and she could not get away.

"If you are going to be tiresome," she said before he could speak, "I shall be sorry I stayed."

"I do not think that is true," the *Duc* said. "When you were talking at dinner I knew you were enjoying yourself, as I was. And now we are alone, and no-one shall interrupt us."

"You . . . frighten me," Canéda said in a small voice.

"Why should I do that?"

"I . . . I do not know . . . but you . . . do. Please . . . please . . ."

There was silence for a moment. Then the *Duc* said:

"Look at me! Look at me, Canéda! I want to see your eyes."

For some reason which she could not explain to herself, Canéda knew she should not look at him.

Again she made a little gesture with her hands. Then he said softly but insistently:

"Look at me!"

It was a command, and like Ariel she could not refuse it.

Because he compelled her to do so, she raised her eyes and looked into his.

For a moment they were both very still. Then it seemed to Canéda as if everything vanished—the room, the candles, the *Château*, the view outside.

There were only two grey eyes and they filled the whole Universe.

Canéda moved, or the *Duc* did; she knew only that with his eyes holding hers, his arms went round her, then his lips held her captive.

Even as he did so, she knew at the back of her mind that this was what she had been wanting and at the same time was what she had been afraid of—yet it made every moment while she had been with him exciting and thrilling.

She had never been kissed before, but it was exactly as she had thought it would be, and she felt as he drew her closer and still closer to him that they became one and indivisible.

Then she became part of the moon itself and there were stars all round them, and there was no world, no problems, no people, only the sky and an ecstasy that enveloped them like a light which came from within themselves, and yet was part of the Divine.

It flashed through Canéda's mind that this was love—love as she had always thought it would be when she found it, but it had always eluded her until now.

It was the love that was so demanding and yet so utterly and completely perfect that she could not fight it and there was no escape.

The *Duc* kissed her until she could no longer think but only feel the wonder of it.

Then as he raised his head Canéda gave a little murmur and hid her face against his neck.

"Now do you understand what I have been trying to say?" he asked very softly.

He was speaking in French, and she thought there was a tremor in his voice but she could not be certain.

It was impossible to answer him; she knew only that she felt pulsating through her body an incredible rapture which seemed to end in her throat.

It was in the beat of her heart and in every breath she drew.

The *Duc* put his hand under her chin and lifted her face up to his.

"There is no need for any questions between us," he said. "You are mine as I knew you were from the very first moment I saw you and thought you had stepped out of my dreams."

His lips were very near to hers as he said again:

"You are mine, Canéda, and I want you! I want you now!"

As he finished speaking his lips were on hers and he was kissing her.

Now there was a fire on his lips that was like nothing Canéda had ever imagined, and yet although it was so fierce and so demanding, she felt herself unaccountably responding to it.

He kissed her until she was breathless, until she felt as if the room spun dizzily round her and it would be impossible for her to stand unsupported on her feet.

Then he was kissing her neck, giving her sensations which she had no idea existed, until, as her lips parted and her breath came in little gasps, he found her mouth again.

The fire was more intense and she could feel his heart beating against hers.

Then he said, and his voice was hoarse and passionate:

"I want you! God, how I want you! Go and get into bed, my darling. There is no reason for us to wait any longer."

He put his arms round her and drew her across the room.

He opened the door; then, because there was a servant in the passage extinguishing the lights in the sconces, he took his arm from her.

"I shall not be long," he said very softly, and she could barely hear the words.

Then he went back to the Sitting-Room, shutting the door behind him.

Canéda walked almost as if she were hypnotised down the passage towards her bedroom.

Only as she reached it did she come back to reality and realise what was happening to her.

It was what vaguely she had sensed might happen, but it had in fact been very different from what she had expected.

And yet, because she had told herself that she must be sensible and must on no account take risks with a man she did not know, she had been prepared.

For a moment, as she stood inside the bedroom, she

thought she could not leave but must stay because she wanted to be with the *Duc*.

Yet, what he intended by saying that he wanted her was written in front of her eyes in letters of fire.

Because men had always treated her like a piece of Dresden china, no-one had made such demands before or expressed themselves in such a manner.

She thought the *Duc* would be the same and she would handle him as she had handled the others who had laid their hearts at her feet and pleaded with her to pick them up.

But the *Duc* had just taken possession of her, and she knew there was only one answer and that was to go, and go quickly, because she was frightened not only of him but of herself.

She went to the wardrobe and pulled out the thick cloak in which the maid had wrapped the things she had asked for, so that Ben could carry them on his horse without getting them dirty.

Canéda had in fact been surprised to see it, expecting instead a shawl or a linen cover.

However, the evening-cloak was just what she wanted, and there was no time to change into her riding-habit.

She threw it over her shoulders and very, very cautiously opened the bedroom door again.

There was no sign of the servant who had been extinguishing the lights, and although she was half-afraid to see the *Duc* come from the Sitting-Room, she guessed that by this time he would have gone to his own bedroom.

Swiftly she sped down the stairs in her soft satin slippers, making barely a sound until she reached the Hall. A night-watchman was nodding in a chair by the big door.

"Open the door, please," Canéda said in a voice little above a whisper in case it should carry.

He looked surprised, but he obeyed her, and as the door began to open she slipped through it and ran across the courtyard and out through the outer door which she had guessed always remained open and which led to the bridge that spanned the moat.

It took her only a few seconds to reach the other side.

Then she saw, as she had expected, that in the shadow of a tree Ben was waiting with two horses.

He was sitting comfortably on the ground and she knew that he did not expect her so soon and was prepared to wait, as she had told him to do, all night.

Then as she reached him he sprang to his feet.

"Ye be riding as ye are, M'Lady?" he asked.

Canéda did not reply, she merely put her hands on Ariel's saddle and Ben helped her up.

She rode Ariel down the steep incline towards the town.

It was dark, but there were lights in the windows of some of the houses to guide them, and it took only a short while to reach the bridge.

They rode across it, Canéda pressing Ariel on as if the Devil himself were at her heels.

She knew she was running away, not from the *Duc* but from her own heart, which inexplicably she had left behind on the moon.

CHAPTER FIVE

CANÉDA CAME UP on deck to sit in a sheltered spot out of the wind.

The sea was not rough but there was a heavy swell,

and *Madame* de Goucourt had retired to her cabin, saying that she had no intention of breaking her leg.

Canéda was relieved because it meant that she could
be alone and would not have to evade the questions
which she knew *Madame,* bursting with curiosity, was
longing to ask her.

When she had reached the Inn after riding away
from the *Château,* she had gone to her bedroom after
giving instructions to Ben.

It was impossible for her to sleep, and when she
dressed before her maid came to call her, she knew that
Madame de Goucourt would have been informed that
they were leaving and that by the time they had break-
fasted, the carriage and the out-riders would be waiting
to take them to Bordeaux.

Madame de Goucourt had been astonished at the
speed.

"What has happened, Canéda?" she asked when she
came to the private room. "Why are we in such a hurry
to leave for St. Nazaire?"

"I never intended to stay here for long," Canéda replied evasively.

Madame de Goucourt was an intelligent woman.

She knew by the expression on Canéda's face that
something had happened, but as it was obvious that she
did not wish to speak about it, *Madame* forced herself to
keep silent, even though it was difficult.

Only when they were driving in the spring sunshine
back to Angers did she say:

"When I received your note yesterday afternoon I
thought you were staying the night with friends, but I
learnt this morning that you returned very late to the
Inn."

"It was more convenient for me to do so," Canéda
replied.

Even as she spoke she could feel again that moment
when she had come down to earth from the heights of
ecstasy and realised what the *Duc* intended.

When she had finally got to bed she had lain awake

throbbing with the rapture he had evoked in her, even though she tried to deny it.

She had never believed that being kissed could be so ecstatic, so wonderful that she could cease to be herself and become a part of him.

How, she asked herself, could she have surrendered to him so ignominiously and so quickly, without attempting to struggle?

From the very first moment she had set eyes on him she had known that he was different from other men, not only different in his appearance and behaviour but different in the way he affected her.

None of the men she had met in London who had pursued her, courted her, wooed her, and proposed to her had aroused her in any way, except that she found their persistence rather boring when the first interest in having a new admirer had passed.

With the *Duc* she had been tinglingly aware of him from the moment she rode towards him in the Riding-School.

She told herself it was part of her goal and her objective in seeking revenge because of the way his father had treated hers.

But if she was honest she knew that she had forgotten the feud and even the reason why she had come to Saumac, and had been concerned only with the relationship between them, which had been dangerously attractive from the first few words they had said to each other.

Twisting and turning on the comfortable feather bed, Canéda could see in the darkness only the *Duc*'s grey eyes looking into hers and feel that surging rapture writhing in her breasts at the touch of his lips.

"How can I ever forget him?" she asked herself now as she looked out over the green sea.

She wondered what he was feeling and what indeed he had felt when he had gone to her bedroom last night, only to find it empty.

"He had no right to try to seduce me," she tried to tell herself angrily.

But she knew it had not been a question of seduction but of two people needing and wanting each other, and finding that they belonged to each other in a strange, unearthly manner that would have been unthinkable to refute.

It was impossible for Canéda not to know that she still wanted him and that her whole body ached for the feeling of his arms round her and his lips on hers.

"It is just my imagination," she tried to say to herself. "I was amused and enchanted by the *Château* and by the fantasy that I was not on the earth but on the moon, and I was carried away by the romance of it."

Then she knew that was not true. It was something much deeper and much more fundamental than that.

They were a man and a woman, Adam and Eve, finding each other across eternity and knowing that they were no longer two people but one.

As the yacht sailed on down the coast, Canéda asked herself how she could sink so low as to feel this way for a man whom, before she had left England, she had hated for what his father had done to her father, just as she hated her grandparents for their treatment of her mother.

"I came to France for revenge," she chided herself, "and I wanted to make him suffer!"

But instead, she knew that she was suffering in a manner which she had never thought possible.

How could anyone make her feel as she did now? Because she loved the *Duc*, it seemed as if she had lost something so precious and wonderful that the world would never be the same again.

It took them two days to reach Bordeaux, and to Canéda they were two days of introspection and misery.

She gave up pretending that the *Duc* meant nothing to her and that in hurting him she had achieved what she had set out to do.

There was no way of ascertaining that he missed her as much as she missed him, and she would lie awake in her cabin, thinking that by now he had doubtless

consoled himself very adequately with his horses and his
—mistress.

The last thought was like the stab of a dagger in her
heart, and she almost cried out at the pain of it.

Canéda told herself that he had insulted her by suggesting that she should hold the same position in his life.

Yet she had to admit that she had invited such a suggestion by her behaviour, not only in pretending that
she was a Circus performer but also in allowing him to
kiss her.

What else was he likely to think, except that she was a
woman with easy morals, especially as she had been prepared to stay alone at the *Château*?

"I must have been crazy to agree to that!" Canéda
whispered to herself, and prayed that Harry would
never find out what had happened.

She knew that she had been absurdly naïve in thinking that she could handle any situation that arose, and it
was both her innocence and the fact that the *Duc* did not
think of her as a Lady that had resulted in a situation of
which now she was ashamed.

At the same time, to be in the *Duc*'s arms had been the
most marvellous and perfect thing that had ever happened to her in her whole life, and she felt with a kind
of despair that never again would she be able to feel the
same for any other man.

When they sailed into the harbour of Bordeaux it was
so interesting and so different from anywhere else she
had been in the world that Canéda for a little while forgot her secret unhappiness.

They stayed the night in a comfortable Hotel, giving
the horses a chance to recover from the sea passage,
before Canéda put her second plan into operation.

First she sent one of the out-riders, resplendently
dressed in his best livery, ahead to the *Château* de
Bantôme to tell her grandparents that she had arrived
in her brother's yacht at Bordeaux and was on her way
to visit them.

She thought it would be a surprise that their

invitation had been answered so quickly, and she instructed the out-rider to inform the *Comte* and *Comtesse* of how many were in her entourage and what accommodation would be needed for the horses and attendants, besides herself.

It would have been impossible to get all her luggage into the smart travelling-chariot that she had brought with her in the yacht.

She therefore hired the most impressive and expensive carriage available in Bordeaux, drawn by four horses, to go ahead.

It carried her, her luggage, and her lady's-maid, a Frenchwoman whom they had engaged with the help of the Proprietor of the Hotel to wait on *Madame* de Goucourt.

By this time *Madame* was well aware that Canéda intended to impress her relatives, and she said with a twinkle in her eye:

"The *Château* de Bantôme is fortunately large enough to accommodate such an influx of visitors. I am still waiting, *ma chérie*, for you to tell me what happened when you met the *Duc* de Saumac."

Canéda started.

"How do you know I met the *Duc?*" she asked defensively.

"I am not stupid," *Madame* de Goucourt replied. "I realised that was why we stayed near Angers, which is not far from the *Château* de Saumac. I also guessed the reason for your disappearance."

"I do not wish to talk about it."

Madame de Goucourt shook her head.

"I am afraid the *Duc* has upset you. You have not seemed yourself since we left Angers. I warned you that he is a very strange man. I think he must loathe all women since his wife went mad."

Canéda wanted to tell her this was not true, but she could not bear to speak of him, and after a little silence *Madame* said:

"I will not plague you with questions, *ma petite*, but

you were so happy when we left England, and now you are suffering."

There was no response, and after giving a little sigh she talked of other things.

There was certainly a lot to see that was different from the part of France that Canéda had admired in the Loire Valley.

When they reached the Dordogne River there had obviously been quite a lot of rain, for it was swollen to what Canéda was sure was almost twice its normal size, as well as there being floods in the fields on either side of it.

The profusion of water made the high cliffs through which the Dordogne passed even more impressive, and there were the *Châteaux* and the Castles on the summit of them that resembled Saumac.

There also were forests and dark trees covering the hill-tops which were a background to the green valleys.

The trees were all in bloom, and with the white blackthorn, golden gorse, and beside the roads a profusion of cow-slips, the countryside had a beauty to which Canéda could not help responding.

But all the time that she was trying to remember that this was her mother's birthplace, she was conscious of a lump like a heavy stone within her breasts which would not go away.

From what she had heard and from what she had read on the map, Canéda knew that the *Château* de Bantôme was not very far from Bordeaux.

They stayed one night on the way, then they were in Périgord, and *Madame* de Goucourt was full of stories of the old Abbeys, the Cathedrals, and the *Châteaux* they passed.

They drove into wine-growing country, and it seemed to Canéda that those vineyards they passed seemed in good heart and there appeared to be nothing wrong with them.

In the afternoon of the second day, when they had

been travelling for some hours, *Madame* de Goucourt pointed ahead and said:

"There is the *Château* belonging to your grandparents!"

It was about a mile off the road, standing on a steep incline with trees behind it. Built of white stone, it was very impressive, and Canéda stared at it with a strange feeling that she had seen it before.

She knew it was because her mother had described it to her so often and had even attempted to draw sketches to explain to her children what her home looked like.

Canéda knew that the building had been started in the middle of the Sixteenth Century and added to and altered by various *Comtes* de Bantôme.

Each owner had embellished and enriched the *Château* until it looked more like a Palace than a mere nobleman's residence, and its beauty was enhanced by its gardens as well as the dark woods which framed it as if it were a precious jewel.

As they drew nearer they saw that there was a fountain playing in front of the house, and in the sunshine the water, thrown high in the air, glittered with the colours of the rainbow.

'I can understand why Mama loved it so much,' Canéda thought.

Then she steeled herself to remember that her mother had been exiled from her home and that she hated its occupants, every one of them!

She hoped her grandparents would be impressed by the magnificent horses drawing her chariot, by the outriders in their powdered wigs, and by Ben, who had taken the place of the one who had gone ahead, in a smart livery and cockaded top-hat, riding Ariel.

The coachman drew the carriage up with a flourish outside the front door, and servants appeared as if they had been awaiting their arrival.

The carriage-door was opened and Canéda stepped out, followed by *Madame* de Goucourt.

"You go first," Canéda said, but *Madame* shook her head.

"This is your family you are meeting."

"Do not forget that I hate them!" Canéda replied.

"You cannot say that," *Madame* persisted, "until you have met them, and I think, *ma chérie,* you are in for a surprise!"

Canéda raised her eye-brows, but there was no chance to answer, for as she walked up the steps of the *Château* a young man appeared and hurried towards them.

"May I welcome you, Cousin Canéda, on behalf of my grandparents," he said. "I am Armand!"

He was dark-haired and attractive, and because he was smiling at her with a very obvious look of admiration in his eyes, Canéda found it difficult not to smile back instead of being cold and imperious as she had intended to be during the whole visit.

However, she shook hands with him and presented him to *Madame* de Goucourt, who, as he kissed her hand, said:

"I have not seen you since you were six years old, so it is quite unnecessary for me to add that you have grown!"

"I have heard my family speak of you so often, *Madame,*" Armand replied, "and everything they have said was of course complimentary."

He certainly had the right sort of attitude for a Frenchman, Canéda thought scornfully. Then, turning to her, he said:

"My grandparents are waiting for you in the Salon. You must forgive their not coming to the door to meet you, but *Grand-père* has difficulty in walking."

Canéda inclined her head and they walked into a very impressive Hall and down a passage that was decorated with very fine antique furniture and paintings that were, she supposed, of the de Bantôme ancestors.

There seemed to be few servants about, and it struck her that the place looked a little dull and dusty, as if it was in need not only of cleaning but of painting and decorating.

She tried not to notice that the carpets were threadbare and the curtains at the windows were faded and in need of relining.

Armand opened a door and she found herself in a large Salon which overlooked an ornamental garden at the back of the *Château*.

Seated in the window was an elderly woman with white hair, and after one glance at her Canéda felt a sudden constriction in her heart, for the face turned towards her was that of her mother, although older and lined with age.

"Here is Cousin Canéda, *Grand-mère*," Armand announced.

The *Comtesse* held out her hands.

"My dear child!" she exclaimed. "I cannot tell you how happy I am to see you or what it meant to learn that you had answered my letter so quickly!"

Canéda curtseyed, then as she put out her hand the *Comtesse* took it between both of hers and pulled her forward.

Canéda had told herself before she left England that nothing would make her show any gesture of affection towards her hated relatives, and yet now it was impossible to avoid the kiss her grandmother gave her on her cheek.

"Sit down, my dear," the *Comtesse* said, indicating a chair beside her.

Then with an undoubted tremor in her voice she added:

"You are so like your mother, so very, very like her, and I have missed her so much all these years!"

Canéda wanted to reply that the de Bantômes had shown no sign of it, but Armand was presenting *Madame* de Goucourt to his grandmother, before he said:

"I must go and fetch Hélène. She did not expect them to arrive so soon."

"Yes, do that, dear boy," the *Comtesse* replied, "and

ask the servants to bring refreshments. I am sure they have forgotten."

"I will do that, *Grand-mère.*"

He smiled at Canéda before he left, and again she had difficulty in not responding.

She sat very stiffly and straight-backed in the chair beside the *Comtesse,* and, as if she felt her antagonism, her grandmother talked to *Madame* de Goucourt, whom she had known for many years.

"I could not believe it was true when the groom came with the message that you had arrived in Bordeaux on your yacht!" she exclaimed.

She hesitated a moment, then she asked Canéda:

"It is your yacht?"

"It belongs to my brother Harry."

"Is that what you call him? When I saw in the newspapers that he had inherited your uncle's title, I wondered if you called him Edward. It always seems a rather dull name."

Again Canéda felt antagonistically that if Harry had not come into the title, her grandmother would certainly not have written to him and she would not be here at this moment.

The door of the Salon opened and Armand returned with a very pretty girl.

Canéda could see some resemblance to herself, although of course both Hélène and Armand had dark eyes instead of her sensational blue ones.

She also accepted without conceit that Hélène was not as pretty as she was, because she resembled her mother.

"It is exciting to meet you, Cousin Canéda," Hélène cried, "and I have longed to do so because I have always thought that the way your mother ran away to be married was the most thrilling and romantic story I have ever heard!"

Canéda was astonished that her cousin should speak of it so openly, and in front of the *Comtesse,* but she did not miss the opportunity of saying:

"My mother was very, very happy. At the same time,

she missed her family, and it made her very sad that you all ostracised her for so many years."

Even to think of her mother's suffering made her angry and her voice seemed to ring out in the Salon, and for a moment there was silence.

Then her two cousins looked first at each other, then at the *Comtesse*.

"I can understand, my dear," the old lady said, "that you must feel very bitter that your mother was cut off from those she loved, and it hurt me, because she was my daughter, more than I can ever express in words."

"Then why were you so cruel?" Canéda asked bluntly.

The *Comtesse* made a nervous gesture with her blue-veined hands that was very eloquent, but at that moment the door opened and an old man came in supported on either side by servants.

They almost carried him across the room to sit him down in a chair next to the *Comtesse,* putting a fur-lined rug over his knees.

He did not speak, and the *Comtesse* said:

"François, dear, Canéda has arrived. I told you she was coming today."

"Who? Who?" the old man asked.

He had a fine head of hair and must, Canéda thought, have been exceedingly handsome when he was young.

Now his hair was white and his face was deeply lined, and yet she had the feeling that the *Comtesse* and his grandchildren were in awe of him.

"Canéda," the *Comtesse* answered. "She is here to visit us from England."

As she spoke she looked at Canéda, who realised that her grandmother wanted her to rise and go nearer to the *Comte.*

She did so, pleased that she was wearing an exceedingly expensive and very elegant silk gown with a taffeta pelisse over it and a bonnet trimmed with small ostrich-feathers that had been astronomically expensive.

259

Now she was to meet her grandfather, the relative who she was certain had been more instrumental than anyone else in treating her mother as if she were a leper because she had married the man she loved.

With her chin held high and her back very straight, Canéda moved in front of him, and as he stared at her she dropped him a small curtsey.

For a moment there was silence. Then in a voice that sounded strangled, the *Comte* said:

"Clémentine! You are Clémentine!"

"No, dear," the *Comtesse* said quickly, "this is Canéda, Clémentine's daughter."

The old man did not seem to hear her.

"You have come back, Clémentine!" he cried. "That is good! I knew you would see sense. Saumac was distraught because you disappeared. He loves you. I have never known a man so much in love. I had to tell him we could not find you, but now everything will be all right! Everything!"

He smiled and said to his wife:

"Send for Saumac. Tell him Clémentine is here. It will make him happy. Poor man, I was sorry for him. He has been so unhappy!"

Because for the moment it seemed as if the *Comtesse* had no words with which to correct her husband, Canéda took the initiative.

She went a little nearer and said:

"Look at me, *Grand-père*. I am not Clémentine but your granddaughter Canéda."

"You are not Clémentine?"

He spoke the words very slowly as if with an effort.

"No, *Grand-père* . . . my mother . . . Clémentine is . . . dead."

It was difficult to say the words, and yet her voice sounded quite clear.

For a moment her meaning did not percolate through to the old man's mind. Then suddenly, in such a loud voice that it made her jump, he said:

"What are you saying? Clémentine cannot be dead!

She is to marry Saumac. It is all arranged. Where is she? Where has she gone to? What are you keeping from me?"

His voice grew louder and more agitated, and Armand ran to the door.

The two servants who had escorted the *Comte* into the Salon and who were obviously waiting outside came quickly across the room towards him.

"Clémentine! Where is Clémentine?" the old man was shouting as they lifted him from the chair.

"Come along, *Monsieur le Comte*," one of the servants said. "There is a glass of wine waiting for you in your own room."

"I do not want any wine," the old man replied angrily. "I want Clémentine! Where is she? The wedding is tomorrow. The *Duc* will be here tonight, and how can we tell him that we cannot find her? Find her, you fools! Find her! She cannot have gone far!"

They were moving him towards the door, and as they went through it he was shouting:

"Clémentine! Clémentine! Where are you, Clémentine?"

Canéda could hear his voice echoing back as they moved him down the passage.

She stood feeling curiously shaken by what had occurred.

Then as she looked at her grandmother she saw that she was holding a handkerchief to her eyes.

"I think you should pour some wine for your grandmother," *Madame* de Goucourt said to Armand in a low voice.

As if glad that he could do something, Armand went towards the door as two servants came in carrying a silver tray on which were glasses and small *pâtisseries*.

Armand took a glass from the tray and carried it to his grandmother's side.

"Drink this, *Grand-mère*," he said, "and do not be upset."

"He has been better for the last two days," the

Comtesse said in a low voice, "and I did not want Canéda to know what he was like."

"She would have learnt sooner or later," Armand said soothingly, "and I feel she will understand."

He looked at Canéda as he spoke, as if he wished that she would support him, and she said quickly:

"Of course. I am sorry that Mama's running away upset him so much."

"He has never been the same since," the *Comtesse* said in a low voice. "Sometimes he is his usual self, but with our worries lately he has grown much worse."

"Do not talk about it, *Grand-mère*," Hélène said. "You know it always upsets you, and as this is Cousin Canéda's first visit here, we have so much to show her."

"Yes, of course," the *Comtesse* agreed, "and it is stupid of me to be upset."

As she wiped her eyes, *Madame* de Goucourt moved closer to her, while Canéda rose to walk to the window and look at the formal gardens.

They were laid out in the way that had been made fashionable by the gardens at Versailles.

But even at a quick glance Canéda could see that they were not well tended and needed attention.

Hélène and Armand joined her at the window.

Armand offered her a glass of wine. Then he said in a low voice so that his grandmother could not hear:

"I am so sorry you have been involved in a scene so soon after your arrival, but we never thought that *Grand-père* would take you for your mother."

"Is it true," Canéda asked, "that he has been like this since Mama ran away?"

"I have always heard," Armand replied, "that at first he was furiously angry, then very bitter."

"And now?"

"Now, with all the other troubles, his mind has gone back to the past," Armand said. "He often talks as if he were living twenty years ago, and that is why, if we had had any sense, we would have realised he would think you were your mother."

262

There was silence, then Canéda had to ask the questions which trembled on her lips.

"Did the *Duc* de Saumac really love Mama?"

"So my mother has always told me," Armand replied.

"Papa said he adored her!" Hélène interposed. "He was much older than she was, but Papa said he was like a young man who falls in love for the first time."

"I expect that was true," Armand said. "After all, Cousin Canéda knows that marriages are arranged in France, and it is only the second time round that we have the chance of choosing our wives rather than the family doing it for us."

"Mama thought the *Duc* only wanted to marry her in order to have more children," Canéda said.

"I am sure that was not true," Hélène answered. "It was really all very romantic."

"Tell me what you know," Canéda said.

"The *Duc* saw your mother at a party and fell in love with her, and of course in those days, as now, it was *Grand-père* who accepted his proposal, and I expect your mother was just told that she was to be a *Duchesse*."

"Yes, that is true," Canéda agreed.

"We have always heard from our parents that the *Duc* was so deeply in love with her that when she disappeared, he nearly went mad and raged at *Grand-père*, then scoured the countryside, and when finally it was known that your father and mother had married, he talked of taking his own life."

"I cannot believe it!" Canéda exclaimed.

"It is true," Armand said. "I have been told the same story, not only by my father and mother but by dozens of other de Bantômes who were there at the time."

"*Grand-père* had a terrible time with the *Duc* and he too was very unhappy," Hélène said. "He loved your mother perhaps more than his other children, and I think that was why he could not bear to talk about her or accept that she even existed because she had married an Englishman."

Canéda gave a sigh.

It was all so very different from what she had anticipated, and she knew that the sight of her grandfather, a
little mad, calling for her mother, had upset her more
than she liked to admit.

When she was taken to her bedroom she noticed
again as she walked through the house, escorted by Hélène, that much of it was shabby and in need of repair.

In her bedroom, which was very impressive and was,
as Hélène told her, one of the State-Rooms, the silk bro-
cade was peeling off the walls in places.

The exquisitely painted ceiling was damaged by
damp and the chairs needed recovering.

Hélène saw Canéda's eyes glancing round her and
said in a slightly embarrassed way:

"I am afraid there is a great deal that needs doing,
but, as you will understand, there have had to be drastic
economies these last years."

"Are you saying that the de Bantômes are hard-up?"
Canéda enquired.

Hélène looked at her in surprise.

"Of course we are! Did you not know?"

"Why should I, when we have had no communication
with you all these years, except for the letter which arrived some weeks ago asking my brother and me to
come and stay."

"*Grand-mère* wrote to you?" Hélène exclaimed.

"Yes. Did you not know?"

"We never heard her mention you until your groom
arrived to say that you were on your way from Bordeaux."

Canéda looked astonished, then Hélène said:

"I quite understand what has happened. She wants
your help."

"That is what she asked for," Canéda said coldly.

Hélène made a little gesture with her hand.

"I suppose we are in such a mess that *Grand-mère* is
clutching at any straw, although I am sure Papa and
Mama will be as surprised as I am that she actually
asked you to come here."

Canéda had already heard that her mother's brother, René, and his wife, the parents of Armand and Hélène, were in Paris.

Now Hélène said:

"Papa is trying to raise a loan somehow from the Banks or from friends, otherwise I do not know what will happen in the future."

Canéda paused before she asked what she knew was a vital question.

"You grow wine. Are the vines in fact infected with phylloxera?"

Hélène nodded.

"It started five years ago in a small way, but now it is getting worse and worse. There seems to be nothing we can do to stop it."

There was a note in her voice that told Canéda how much it mattered to her personally.

"Surely there must be some cure?" she asked.

"Only to flood the vineyards, but naturally the hill-side cannot be flooded."

"Then what will happen?" Canéda asked.

For a moment Hélène did not answer. Then she said:

"We will not be able to live here and the *Château* will have to be closed. I do not know where we shall go or what Papa will do. All our money comes from the wine."

Canéda could understand why her grandmother had been desperate and had written to Harry.

There was no need for it to be put into words for her to know that without a dowry, no Frenchman would want to marry Hélène, and Armand, even though one day he would be the *Comte* de Bantôme, would not be acceptable as a suitor in any family that could provide their daughter with an income.

It was as if she were watching something which had always been strong and stable crumbling to the ground, and she knew how distraught her mother would have been.

"It must not depress you," Hélène said quickly. "It is delightful to have you here, and you are so beautiful.

We have always been told that your Mama was the beauty of the family, and now I know it is true. Tomorrow I will show you a portrait of her."

"There is one here in the *Château?*" Canéda asked eagerly.

"There are several," Hélène said. "They are all hidden away because they upset *Grand-père,* but we will bring them out, and I expect if you ask *Grand-mère* she will let you have one to take back to England with you."

"I would like that," Canéda said simply.

"And I want you to tell me about your mother," Hélène said. "To me, as I have already said, it is the most romantic story I have ever heard, to know that she was brave enough to run away when her wedding-gown was waiting for her, her trousseau was packed, and the house was filled with guests and presents."

Canéda smiled.

"She was in love."

"I know," Hélène said. "That is what makes it so marvellous, that love made her brave enough to leave everything to which she belonged—and the *Duc.*"

Canéda smiled again.

"When one is in love, a title is not important."

"That is what Aunt Clémentine made very clear," Hélène said, "but I am sure if I were going to marry a *Duc* I would never be brave enough to run away with a plain *'Monsieur.'* "

"You would do so, like my mother, if you found a man whom you really loved," Canéda said.

Hélène smiled at her, but Canéda knew she was not convinced.

It was the ambition of every French girl to have a great *Château* of her own and a social position that was unassailable.

That was exactly what her mother had been offered by the *Duc* de Saumac, yet she had run away with a penniless Englishman without a title and without prospects of ever having one.

It suddenly struck her that if she herself had never

met the *Duc*, then she would not have really understood why her mother had given up so much.

She had known how happy she was with her father. At the same time, she had been well aware of how poor they were and how difficult it was to make ends meet; how hard it was for her father never to have suitable horses to ride.

Some critical part of her mind had made her ask as soon as she was old enough:

"Has it really been worth giving up so much, Mama?"

She had thought not only of the *Duc* but of the powerful, rich de Bantôme family with their acres of land in Périgord and their magnificent *Château*.

Sometimes, when she had seen her mother looking at a gown that was out of fashion and almost threadbare and wondering how she could make it last a little longer, she had longed to say:

"How could you, Mama, give up so much for Papa, adorable though he is?"

Now she understood, and was frightened to know that she understood only because the *Duc* had kissed her with a strange enchantment that made her forget everything except him.

It flashed through her mind that if the *Duc* had been an almost penniless younger son like her father, and he had asked her to marry him, she would have said "Yes."

That was love, and, although her mind tried to repudiate it, she knew hopelessly, irrevocably, that she loved a man whom she could never marry because he already had a wife.

The *Duc* de Saumac!

CHAPTER SIX

THE *COMTESSE* PUT OUT her hand to draw Canéda down beside her.

"I want you to tell me about your mother, my dear," she said.

Canéda paused for a moment.

Before she had arrived at the *Château,* she had planned so many things that she would say, but now her whole attitude towards her relatives was changing, especially towards the *Comtesse.*

After a moment she said:

"Mama was very, very happy with my father, but at times she felt homesick for her family, especially you, *Grand-mère.*"

She saw the tears come into her grandmother's eyes before she replied:

"And I missed her! One day, when you have children of your own, you will know how much they mean, and whether one sees them or not, one never ceases to worry over them and—love them."

There was a throb in her voice that told Canéda how sincere the words were, and after a moment, a little hesitatingly because she did not wish to be unkind, she said:

"How could you have ignored Mama all the years and never communicated with her even when she wrote to you?"

She thought that what had hurt her mother more

than anything else was that, when she had written to her own mother saying she had a son, the letter had been returned unopened.

The *Comtesse* gave a little cry that was one of pain.

"You must believe me, Canéda," she said, "when I tell you that I had no idea until a long time later that your mother had written to me or that the letter had been returned."

"How is that possible?" Canéda asked.

"Your grandfather was dreadfully upset and angry when she ran away, but I think he might have forgiven her if the *Duc* de Saumac had not been with us so much, raging with anger one moment because he had been made to look a fool over the wedding, then at the next in despair and desolate in a way I cannot describe because he had lost your mother, whom he loved."

The *Comtesse* drew in her breath, as if it was hard for her to remember how upsetting it had been.

Then she went on:

"I am convinced that the *Duc* was largely responsible for the fact that your grandfather became a little unbalanced and it was impossible for any of us to mention your mother's name without there being a scene."

Canéda was silent, thinking that her mother had imagined they had just forgotten her and wiped her out of their lives.

"Your grandfather's secretary, who had been with us for many years and who was devoted to him, was deeply upset at what was happening, and when your mother's letter came, he sent it back without telling either me or your grandfather that it had arrived."

"How could he do such a thing?" Canéda asked indignantly.

"He thought he was saving us more pain and misery," the *Comtesse* replied. "I have often thought that good-wishers do more harm than good."

"Mama wrote to tell you that she had a son," Canéda said.

"How I wish I had known!" the *Comtesse* murmured.

269

Now the tears welled up in her old eyes and ran down her cheeks.

Impulsively Canéda put out her hand to hold hers.

"I do not want you to be upset," she said, "and I promise you Mama was blissfully happy even though we were very poor. In fact, I often thought my home radiated with sunshine all the year round."

"She never regretted the social position she had thrown away?" the *Comtesse* asked.

Canéda shook her head.

"I do not think Papa or Mama would have changed their lives in any way, even if they had been offered the position of King and Queen!"

As she spoke, Canéda thought that was exactly what love meant, and she was understanding for the first time that nothing that the world could offer was more wonderful or more perfect than to be in the arms of the man one loved.

Because her whole being cried out for the *Duc,* she said quickly:

"I want to tell you about my home, *Grand-mère,* and what fun Harry and I had as children, and while I am here I want to show you the tricks my horse Ariel can do."

She then told her grandmother how her father and she had brought Ariel from the Circus, and all the time she related the story she was thinking of how she had told it to the *Duc.*

She could see his grey eyes looking at her as he listened intently, and she felt again that strange, magnetic vibration between them which had made her so tinglingly conscious of him even before she knew that she loved him.

When Canéda finished there was a smile on her grandmother's lips and she said:

"Thank you, dear child, you have told me so much that I have always longed to know. And now, what about yourself? You are nineteen. It is time your brother arranged your marriage."

"I assure you I would never marry a man I did not love," Canéda replied quickly.

Even as she said the words in the same way as she might have said them to Harry, she knew forlornly that if that was true, then she would never marry.

How could she ever feel for another man as she felt for the *Duc*? And yet how could she face a life of being an old maid, in the future an aunt to Harry's children, without any of her own?

The thought made her want to cry out in misery, and then because she wished to escape from her thoughts, she kissed her grandmother and went in search of Armand, with whom she had promised to ride later in the afternoon.

He was waiting for her, and when they set off it was inevitable that as soon as they left the Park they should come to the vineyards.

There was devastation where the vines had been uprooted because they were diseased.

This had obviously happened very recently in one place where the roots were being burnt so that there were dozens of little fires, their smoke rising on the still air.

There was something deeply depressing about it, Canéda thought, and without even looking at Armand and the men who were working on the vines, she knew that the future for them held nothing but despair.

As they rode back to the *Château* she told herself that the sooner she returned to England, the better.

She could feel the de Bantômes' worries and troubles encroaching upon her, and as they combined with her own unhappiness about the *Duc*, she had the uneasy feeling that now the sunshine had gone out of her own life and it would be hard to recapture it.

"I must tell *Grand-mère* that I have to make plans to leave," she said to Armand, "perhaps the day after tomorrow or the day after that."

"I shall be very sorry to see you go," he replied. "You have made *Grand-mère* very happy, and Hélène and I are so delighted to have met you. Surely you can stay until Papa and Mama return from Paris?"

"I promised my brother I would not be away for long," Canéda answered automatically.

Then, because she knew it was something he wanted to hear, she said:

"I know *Grand-mère* wants you and Hélène to come to London, and this evening I will talk to her about it."

She saw Armand's face light up. Then he said:

"That is very kind of you, but probably we shall not be able to afford it."

He did not wait for her answer but spurred his horse ahead, as if he was embarrassed, and Canéda had to make Ariel gallop to keep up with him.

When they got back to the Château she changed her gown, and, after telling the maid that she could begin packing, she went in search of her grandmother.

As Canéda had expected, the *Comtesse* was sitting with *Madame* de Goucourt in the Salon, with the sunshine coming through the window, and Canéda guessed by the expressions on their faces as she came into the room that they had been talking about her.

As they were both French, she was quite certain that they were telling each other that a marriage should be arranged for her, and it struck her how shocked they would both be if they knew that the only man who mattered to her was already married.

She walked towards them and the *Comtesse* held out her hand.

"You enjoyed your ride, my dear?"

"It was delightful!" Canéda answered.

She did not mention to her grandmother how horrified she had been at the sight of the vineyards, for she had the feeling that the place where the vines were being burnt was a new disaster and the tragedy had not yet been reported at the *Château*.

She wondered how extensive the de Bantôme Estate was, and although she tried not to seem too curious, she was sure that practically none of it would produce drinkable wine this year and perhaps for many years to come.

She sat down beside her grandmother and *Madame* de Goucourt, who was just starting an amusing story of what had happened to her husband the first time he was granted an audience with the Queen at Windsor Castle, when the door opened.

One of the old servants, who were all slightly deaf and therefore shouted when they spoke, announced in a loud voice:

"Monsieur le Duc de Saumac, Madame!"

For a moment Canéda thought she could not have heard him correctly.

Then as the *Duc* came into the Salon she froze into immobility.

He seemed even taller and better-looking than she remembered, and it was impossible to breathe as he walked across the room towards her grandmother.

"Leon, my dear boy!" the *Comtesse* exclaimed. "This is indeed a delightful surprise! Why did you not let me know you were in this part of the world?"

"I came unexpectedly," the *Duc* replied after he had kissed the *Comtesse*'s hand.

"I do not think you know *Madame* de Goucourt," the *Comtesse* said.

"Enchanté, Madame!" the *Duc* replied, and raised her hand to his lips.

"And my granddaughter," the *Comtesse* went on, indicating Canéda on the other side of her, "Lady Canéda Lang!"

The *Duc* bowed and there was not a flicker of recognition in his eyes.

Canéda could hardly believe it had happened, but it had!

Without even glancing again in her direction, he sat down in a chair opposite the *Comtesse* and said:

"How are you? And how is the *Comte?*"

The *Comtesse* shook her head.

"Not very well, I am afraid. But he will be glad to see you, as he always is. Will you be staying with us?"

"I am afraid not," the *Duc* replied. "I have come here especially to see the *Comte* de Menjou about his vineyards."

"Vineyards!"

The exclamation seemed to come from the depths of the *Comtesse*'s heart, and she added:

"You have a solution to our problem?"

"I believe so," the *Duc* replied.

"What is it?"

"It involves first flooding, then injecting carbon bisulphide into the earth round the roots, and grafting on to the existing roots."

"This will prevent the disease spreading?"

"I think so," the *Duc* replied, "but the treatment is expensive."

The *Comtesse* gave a deep sigh, and there was no need for her to say that if that was so, they could not afford to experiment.

"I do not want to worry you about it," the *Duc* said, "but I will discuss it with your Manager. All the vineyard-owners in this area are meeting tomorrow to decide what is the best thing to do."

"That is kind of you, Leon," the *Comtesse* said, "but please do not speak of it to my husband."

"No, of course not," the *Duc* replied. "It would be a great mistake to cause him more worry than he has already."

"I knew you would understand."

The *Duc* rose to his feet.

"I will go and see him now. I know this is a good time of the day."

"But you will dine with us?" the *Comtesse* cried.

"I would like to do that," the *Duc* answered. "I have my clothes and my valet with me, and perhaps you would be kind enough to send a groom to tell the *Comte* de Menjou that I will not reach him until after dinner."

"Yes, yes, of course," the *Comtesse* said. "You know your way to my husband's room."

The *Duc* bowed to the *Comtesse* and *Madame* de Goucourt, completely ignoring Canéda, and went from the Salon.

She felt as if she had been holding her breath all the time he had been there, and now that he had gone, she could hardly believe he had actually been sitting where she could see him.

She had heard his voice and had felt, as she always did, the vibrations emanating from him, and yet he had ignored her!

She knew he had done it to punish her because she had deceived him, or perhaps, because he was so shocked at the way she had behaved, he had no wish even to speak to her again.

Then she was sure that he must have known she was here before he arrived, otherwise it would have been impossible for him to enter the Salon and not show a flicker of surprise.

After thinking of him so much, she had now seen him again! Her heart was thumping in her breast and she wanted, as she had never wanted anything in her life before, to run after him and ask him what he had felt when she had left him, and if he had been disappointed.

She had the terrifying feeling that instead of being disappointed he had just been very angry, and now perhaps he hated her.

She had learnt from Harry how much a man disliked being made a fool of by a woman, and there was no doubt that that was what she had done when she had pretended to be a Circus performer and had allowed him most reprehensibly to kiss her.

Then, having excited him as she had originally planned to do, she had just disappeared.

"How can he ever forgive me?" Canéda asked herself despairingly.

The *Duc* had not returned to the Salon before Canéda went upstairs, and she wondered what he was talking about for so long to the *Comte*.

Perhaps her grandfather was telling him that Clémentine had returned.

Even if he did not mention it, the *Duc* by this time would know who she was and that it was her mother who had run away on the eve of her marriage to his father.

Because he was extremely intuitive, she felt sure that he would now understand why she had behaved as she had and that she had come to Saumac in search of revenge.

At the same time, she could not be certain of anything except that he was here and he obviously did not want to speak to her.

"I must talk to him! I must try to make him understand," she told herself.

Then she thought despairingly that she had behaved in an outrageous manner towards a man who was married to somebody else; she had deliberately provoked him into kissing her and had enticed him into making a proposition which he would never have made had he known who she really was.

Then she had run away in what seemed an ignominious fashion.

Because she was ashamed and also afraid, Canéda considered whether she should not go down to dinner and instead say that she was ill and retire to bed.

Then she told herself that she must see the *Duc* again, even if he would not speak to her and ignored her as he had done before.

At least she could look at him, and, perhaps for the last time, she would be near him.

She felt her love for him well up inside herself uncontrollably, and she had a feeling that by the end of the evening it would be intensified until she would suffer even more than she had suffered already.

'It is my own fault,' she thought wistfully, but that was no consolation.

She took a long time in choosing one of her prettiest gowns, but certainly not the pink one in case he thought she was deliberately trying to remind him of when they had dined together.

Instead she chose a gown that was white with a sash and little bows of velvet ribbon that echoed the blue of her eyes.

It was a gown that made her look very young, and when she regarded her reflection in the mirror, she thought that perhaps her youth might seem an excuse for her behaviour.

Then she knew she had not talked to him as if she was young, inexperienced, and innocent.

She had deliberately tried to appear worldly-wise and experienced in many things, including love.

It struck her that perhaps he would suppose she had behaved with him as she had with other men she met, and she longed to tell him that that was not true, that he was the only man who had ever kissed her and the only man whom she had ever wanted to do so.

She was so agitated by the time she was ready to go downstairs that it was hard to keep herself from trembling.

As she slowly descended the staircase, holding on to the bannisters, she saw a carriage outside the door and several people getting out of it.

It was then that she remembered that Hélène had told her there was to be a dinner-party tonight for some of the de Bantôme relatives who had come to meet her.

This, Canéda knew, would make it even more difficult to speak to the *Duc* alone, and she wished that she had gone down earlier and perhaps had a chance of talking to him before anyone else arrived.

When she entered the Salon it was to find quite a

number of people there already, and, while they were strangers to her, they all appeared to know the *Duc* well.

They sat down eighteen to dinner, and it all looked very glamorous because the lighted candelabra on the table obscured the parts of the room that needed redecorating.

The *Duc* was seated on her grandmother's right at the end of the table, and she found herself placed between two elderly but important cousins who had come especially to meet her.

She could not hear what the *Duc* said, but she watched him talking to her grandmother and to the wife of another de Bantôme cousin. She knew he did not give a single glance in her direction and as far as he was concerned she did not even exist.

When her cousins paid her compliments she found it hard to respond to them politely, and because her thoughts kept straying to the *Duc*, they often had to repeat what they had said before it percolated through to her mind and she was able to answer them.

"I must speak to him . . . I must!" Canéda told herself frantically, as in French fashion the ladies and gentlemen left the Dining-Room to proceed back to the Salon.

It was now dark and the chandeliers had been lighted.

Her grandmother had resisted putting in new forms of lighting. However, the candlelight was very becoming, and, seeing how attractive all the other women looked, Canéda was aware that she herself was looking her best.

She tried to edge her way to the side of the *Duc*, and just when she had nearly achieved it without appearing obvious, she heard him say to her grandmother:

"I know you will forgive me, *Madame*, if I say goodnight and thank you for a most delightful evening. As you are well aware, the *Comte* de Menjou is not as young as he was, and I do not like to feel I am keeping him up late."

"No, of course not, Leon," the *Comtesse* replied. "It was delightful to see you. Will you come again tomorrow or another day before you leave?"

"Tomorrow I am going to Paris," the *Duc* said.

"You are lucky!" exclaimed Armand, who had been listening to the conversation. "That is where I want to go."

"There will be plenty of time yet for you to enjoy the frivolities of Paris," the *Duc* answered.

The way he spoke made Canéda know only too well what the word "frivolities" meant to him and to Armand, who looked sulky because he had to stay at home.

The *Duc* kissed the *Comtesse*'s hand and turned to say good-bye to *Madame* de Goucourt.

Canéda held her breath.

She was next to *Madame* and she knew it would be impossible for the *Duc* to pretend not to see her.

"*Au revoir, Madame*," the *Duc* was saying. "It has been delightful to see you again, and I hope our next meeting will not be delayed for so long."

"So do I," *Madame* laughed, "and if it is, then you will not have grown taller but older."

"Which of course is something to be avoided," the *Duc* replied.

'Now,' Canéda thought to herself, 'now he will have to speak to me.'

Her hand was ready. Then to her consternation the *Duc* turned completely round to face the opposite direction.

He made it appear quite a natural movement, as if he wanted to speak to one of the de Bantôme cousins whom he obviously knew well.

But she knew it was a deliberate action on his part to avoid her.

Then he said good-bye to several other people in the Hall and the door closed behind him.

For a moment Canéda contemplated running after him, regardless of what anyone might think.

Then she knew that even so, there would be no

chance of a private conversation, for not only was Armand with him to see him off, but the servants were waiting in the Hall.

And what could she say—except good-bye?

She was quite certain that he would be as formal and indifferent as he had appeared so far.

Because she loved him she could hardly believe that her feelings had not communicated themselves to him. He must have been aware of how she had yearned for the touch of his hand and to see his eyes looking into hers.

Then she knew it was finished, finished and over— the most exciting, most thrilling, most wonderful adventure in her life.

She had met a man who was different from all the other men, and to whom she belonged, whether he wanted her or not.

He had said she was his, but he had not meant it, except as an expression of desire for someone who excited him physically.

But for her it was a spiritual union which nothing could break.

His kiss had carried her towards the sky, and it was there, in what they had called a Corner of the Moon, that she had known that she was his and he was hers and spiritually they were indivisible.

"I will never see him again," Canéda said to herself later that night, "but I shall always belong to him with my heart and soul, and that is something I can never give to any other man."

She felt she was running away again, but this time from France because it was associated with the *Duc*, and she could only pray that when she was home in a different environment she would not miss him so desperately as she did at this moment.

The stone that seemed to be in her heart was heavier than ever, and she thought she would never be free of it. It would break her and take away the joy of living forever.

All the preparations had been made for Canéda to leave, and as they had to start early in the morning to reach the town where they were to stay that night, she went to say good-bye to her grandmother in her *Boudoir*.

She had said good-bye to her grandfather. He had been quieter when she went to see him in his room, and although he had called her "Clémentine" he had not spoken of the *Duc* but talked of the vineyards and how worried he was that on one or two of them there were signs of phylloxera.

Armand had already told Canéda that they had kept from the old man the extent of the damage, and Canéda had cheered him up.

"There are some new ideas on how the vines can be cured of the disease," she said.

"Who told you this?" her grandfather asked.

Canéda hesitated a moment before she replied:

"The *Duc* de Saumac, *Grand-père*. And if he says there is a cure, you may be certain there will be. He is a very clever man."

"You will be lucky, my dear, to have such a brilliant husband."

He put out his hand to pat Canéda's as he said:

"I know how happy you will both be together."

He paused before he continued:

"I have often been clairvoyant about certain things, especially in regard to my own family, and I can tell you, my dearest daughter, as clearly as if I could see it written down in front of me, that you and the *Duc* will have an ideal marriage."

Canéda drew in her breath.

"I . . . hope you are right . . . *Grand-père*," she said in a low voice.

"I know I am right," the *Comte* insisted. "You will be very happy as few people have the good fortune to be, and do not forget—name your first son after me. That would please me."

"I will do that, *Grand-père*."

Canéda kissed the *Comte* good-bye, and as she reached the door of the room she heard him saying to himself:

"You are a good girl, Clémentine, and you will be happy as we have always wanted you to be."

Outside the door, she stood for a moment fighting for composure before she returned to the Salon.

If only what her grandfather had said was true: that she was really going to marry the *Duc* and his vision of the future was not just a part of his poor, troubled brain.

Then she told herself that she had to be brave, that life had to go on, and no amount of wishing could change the fact that she could not marry the *Duc* anyway, for even if he were free, he would not want her.

Now, as she knocked on her grandmother's door, she thought of how different her feelings were from what she had expected them to be when she had originally left England.

She had tried to avenge herself on the *Duc*, but the person who had been hurt was not him but herself.

She had come here hating her de Bantôme relatives and wanting to humiliate them, but instead she loved them.

"Come in!" she heard the *Comtesse* say, and she found her sitting dressed in a negligé, having had her breakfast before she dressed to go downstairs.

The old lady held out her hands to Canéda, saying:

"I wish you did not have to leave us, dear child. It has been such a joy to have you here. I shall miss you when you have gone."

"I shall miss you too, *Grand-mère*," Canéda said, and knew it was the truth.

"There is one thing I forgot to tell you," the *Comtesse* said, "and you must forgive me for not mentioning it until now."

"What is it?" Canéda enquired.

"Your mother had some money left to her in her own right, but when she ran away, your grandfather, quite wrongly I think, prevented it from leaving France."

"I know that," Canéda said.

"Then it makes it easier for me to tell you," the *Comtesse* went on, "that it is now yours, and of course you will understand that as it has accumulated over the years and your grandfather invested it not in vines but in Railways and other businesses which have made large profits, it now amounts to a very considerable sum of money!"

The *Comtesse* took an envelope from a table beside her and handed it to Canéda.

"There is a letter from our Solicitors which explains about the investments and what is actually in the Bank. Perhaps you will take it with you to Harry and he will understand what to do about it."

Canéda did not take the envelope. Instead she said:

"Listen, *Grand-mère*, I know that Mama, if she were alive, would want more than anything else to help you during this crisis over the vineyards."

She saw a sudden light in her grandmother's eyes and went on:

"I am speaking for Harry and myself when I say that we have been very lucky, and this money is far more important to you than it is to us. Spend it on maintaining the Estate and keeping the *Château* in existence."

"Do you really mean that?" the *Comtesse* asked in a strangled voice.

"I mean it," Canéda said, "and shall I add that it comes to you from Mama, with her love, which she never ceased to give you."

Tears ran down the *Comtesse*'s lined cheeks, but her eyes were shining as she exclaimed:

"Thank you, my dearest child, thank you, thank you! You cannot know what a weight this will be off my mind. I could not bear to have to close the *Château* and to dismiss so many old servants who would be unable to get work elsewhere."

Canéda kissed the old lady. Then she said:

"Good-bye, *Grand-mère,* and please send Hélène and Armand to London. I know that I can persuade Harry to give a Ball for them at Langstone House, and after that they will be asked to innumerable Balls, and I know Hélène will be a great success."

"How can you be so kind and so forgiving?" the *Comtesse* asked in a broken voice.

Canéda did not answer, she only kissed her grandmother again, finding it hard to keep her own tears from falling.

Then she went downstairs to tell Hélène about the Ball, and as they drove away she knew that both Hélène and Armand were tremendously excited at the thought that they would all meet again very shortly.

"I hope Cousin Harry will let me ride his horses!" was the last thing Armand said as the carriage moved away from the front door.

"I am sure he will," Canéda replied, and she was laughing as they set off down the drive and waved until the *Château* was out of sight.

As she leant back against the comfortable cushions she asked *Madame* de Goucourt:

"Do men ever think of anything but horses?"

"Sometimes they think of women," *Madame* de Goucourt replied.

"Only if they are Frenchmen!" Canéda replied "With the English, horses come first and women are a very poor second!"

"Now you are being cynical!" *Madame* complained. "Moreover, seeing you with Ariel, I have rather suspected that you love him more than you love any man!"

Canéda knew that if she told the truth she would have added: "All men except for one!" but aloud she said:

"Ariel is far more intelligent than most men, and certainly more amenable."

"I see I shall have to find you a Centaur as a husband," *Madame* said with a smile.

This instantly conjured up a picture of the *Duc* riding

.the chestnut horse over the jumps with an expertise that made him the best rider Canéda had ever seen.

There were so many things he might be, but to her he was always the Man in the Moon, and just as unattainable.

CRDCRDCRD

The yacht was waiting for them at Bordeaux, and as they sailed out into the open sea Canéda said good-bye to France.

The visit to the land to which her mother had belonged had been an experience that was quite different from what she had expected, and it was something which she would never forget.

But while she had gone to inflict wounds on other people, it was she herself who had been stricken, and she thought the scars would remain with her all her life.

It would be hard to forget her grandfather, still worried and distressed over a marriage that had not taken place twenty years ago, and her grandmother weeping for a daughter she had lost.

What was more, Canéda thought, she and Harry had lost something very precious by being strangers to the family whose blood flowed through their veins.

Still more bitter, she had lost her battle with the *Duc* and was in fact vanquished and annihilated.

The tables had been turned, and she had not wreaked her vengeance on him, but he on her.

She cried despairingly at night as the yacht sailed back towards England, slowly because the wind was against them, and seemingly reluctantly, and she became more and more convinced that she had left her happiness behind.

But more than that, Canéda thought, she had lost the enchantment she had found in the *Château* de Saumac, which she had called the Corner of the Moon.

It was something which persisted in everybody when they were young, when the world was peopled not only

by humans but by dreams, when there was the anticipation of adventure lurking everywhere and the sun rose
every morning on a new day to herald the promise of
untold rapture.

That had all gone!

Instead, there was of course a comfortable life waiting
for her, and money to spend, which she had never had
before, and doubtless a great many men to admire her.

But something was missing; something so vital, so important that without it she was only half of herself, and
the half she had lost would be forever imprisoned in the
moon until stars ceased to shine.

CHAPTER SEVEN

DRIVING ALONG THE DUSTY country lanes towards Langstone Park, Canéda did not see the spring buds in the
hedgerows, the primroses and cow-slips on the banks,
or the blossoms on the trees in the orchards.

Instead, she felt as if she was encompassed by a fog of
depression because she was leaving France behind her.

The sea had been rather rough after they had left
Bordeaux, but she had been so busy helping Ben with
the horses that she did not have a great deal of time to
think about herself.

When finally she got to bed at night she was so tired
that she slept heavily from sheer exhaustion, and the
next morning she was up early to let Ben have a few
hours' rest while she calmed the horses.

Ariel was easy, and so was Black Boy, but the carriage-horses and those that had been ridden by the outriders were frightened when the yacht pitched and tossed, and they whimpered when it rolled.

Canéda's voice, like Ben's, kept them from panicking, but still it was a relief that the sea was smoother when they reached the Channel.

Just before they sailed into Folkestone Harbour, *Madame* de Goucourt had said to Canéda:

"Are you going to Langstone Park, *ma chérie?*"

"I will go there first," Canéda replied, "but if Harry is in London I shall join him there."

Madame de Goucourt hesitated a moment. Then she said:

"Would you think it very remiss of me if I left you at Folkestone and took a train to London?"

"No, of course not," Canéda replied, "and if you are worried about looking after me, I shall be perfectly safe with Ben and the rest of the servants."

"I was reckoning that if I left Folkestone very early, I should arrive home early in the afternoon."

"Yes, of course," Canéda replied, "and if you want to go to London, of course you must."

"Actually it is my daughter's birthday tomorrow," *Madame* de Goucourt said, "and before I left I told her that there was no likelihood of my being with her. Now, if I catch the early-morning train, I can be in London for the family luncheon that is being given by her parents-in-law, and she was very anxious for me to dine with her and her husband in the evening."

"Then of course you must go," Canéda said.

As she spoke she thought that *Madame* de Goucourt's daughter was lucky to have a family.

It was what she and Harry had missed ever since her father and mother had died.

Now, having been with the de Bantômes, she realised how comforting and fun it was to be a member of a large family.

Madame de Goucourt had said good-bye affectionately

to Canéda early that morning, and, looking very elegant, she had set off for Folkestone Station.

Before she left she said:

"You did not confide in me, *ma chérie,* but I have the idea that your heart is aching. I wish I could help you, but remember, time heals everything."

Canéda did not reply, but she knew that where she was concerned, time would not heal the ache in her heart, nor would it alter her conviction that she had found the one man who mattered in her life and then had lost him.

She remembered her mother saying so often that as soon as she met Gerald Lang, she had known that nothing else mattered; her social position had been forgotten, as had the wealth and power that would be hers on marriage, and even that she must hurt the family to which she belonged.

Love had swept away everything except the knowledge that she belonged to Gerald Lang, and he to her.

"It would not have mattered," she had said to Canéda, "if your father had been a poor beggar or an insignificant bourgeois. He was the man whom God intended for me since the beginning of time, and it was impossible to deny my heart."

There was a deep note of emotion in her mother's voice which told Canéda that even after all the years that had passed and the difficulties they had encountered through having so little money, she never regretted for one moment the drastic step she had taken in running away on the eve of her marriage.

"I think you were very brave, Mama," Canéda had said, and her mother had smiled.

"Not brave, darling, it was a case of self-preservation. I knew that without your father, everything that mattered in life would be lost."

That, Canéda knew, was what she was feeling now, a feeling of loss and emptiness, and the stone in her breast seemed to grow heavier as everything round her was very English while her thoughts were in France.

As she drove down the drive towards Langstone Park, for the first time the impressive beauty of the house ceased to thrill her.

Instead of the exquisite and grandiose design by Vanbrugh of the stone steps leading up to a colonnaded front door, all she could see were the four towers of Saumac silhouetted against the sky, which she and the *Duc* had named "the moon."

The carriage drew up at the front door and a footman came running down the steps to open the door.

Canéda stepped out and paused to thank the coachman for bringing her home and to smile at Ben, who was still seated on Ariel, waiting to ride him round to the stables.

Then slowly, as if she regretted that the journey was over and she was home again, she walked up the steps.

"Welcome home, M'Lady!" the Butler said respectfully.

"How is everything, Dawson?" Canéda asked. "Is His Lordship here or in London?"

"His Lordship's at the stables, M'Lady. I'll send someone to tell him you've returned."

"Yes, please do that," Canéda replied.

As she spoke, she walked up the stairs to her own room.

Ben had sent one of the out-riders ahead of them early in the morning, so that she would be expected, and her lady's-maid was waiting for her in her bedroom.

"It's nice to have you home, M'Lady," she said, "and I'm sure you're glad to be back."

"Yes, of course," Canéda replied.

"I hopes Ellen looked after you properly."

"She did her best," Canéda replied.

She took off her travelling-clothes and put on a gown that she had not taken with her.

It was a very pretty one, but she barely gave herself a glance in the mirror.

What did it matter what she looked like, when the one person whom she wished to admire her was not only hundreds of miles away but even if he were here would refuse to look at her?

Then she told herself sharply that this was a ridiculous way to think; she had to take up her life in England where she had left it and enjoy herself as she had before.

There would be dozens of men waiting to admire her when she reached London, and she had not been surprised to notice a large number of letters waiting for her on the desk in her bedroom.

Her lady's-maid saw her glance at them and said:

"I'm sure you've been missed in London, M'Lady. Most of those letters were brought down by His Lordship when he came home two days ago, and he told Mr. Barnet that dozens of bouquets of flowers had been delivered to the house, but as Your Ladyship weren't there, they had just wilted away."

Canéda drew in her breath.

"We will go back to London as soon as His Lordship wishes," she said.

She knew it would be the wise thing to do. Nothing could be more foolish than to sit moping at Langstone Park and, worse than anything else, to be alone with her thoughts.

What was the point of remembering what she had felt when the *Duc* had kissed her? Or of recapturing in her mind the wonder and glory when he had swept her up into the sky?

She had thought that she would never come down to earth again.

Then she could see his face, stern and unsmiling, when her grandmother had introduced him, and after that he had never seemed to look at her again.

She wanted to cry out at the pain of it. Then she asked herself again—"What is the use?"

When she went downstairs, hoping that Harry by now would be in from the stables, she felt the same words repeat themselves over and over again in her mind.

"What is the use?"

What was the use of anything? What was the use of being unhappy? Of crying for the moon? For that was what she was doing.

She walked into the room where she and Harry sat when they were alone.

It was not as formal as the big Drawing-Room but was a delightful Sitting-Room known as the "Blue Room," which had long French windows opening into the garden.

The paintings were not of the more austere Lang relations but of their children.

There were children looking rather stiff and wide-eyed as they posed for the artist, there were children playing with their dolls, and one child holding two small kittens in her arms who looked, Canéda thought, not unlike herself.

She certainly had blue eyes, which were characteristic of the Langs, and Canéda had often thought in the past that she would like to have a large number of children who combined her mother's dark hair and her father's blue eyes, which were so sensational in her own face.

She thought now it would be unlikely that she would ever have any children, and if she did they would not be born of love such as her father and mother had had for each other.

"What is the use of thinking such stupid things?" she asked herself angrily.

She walked across the room to look out into the garden and forced herself to think how beautiful it was with the lilacs coming into bloom and the syringa scenting the air.

Because it was so beautiful, while at the same time she knew despairingly that it did not move her as it would have done a few weeks ago, she felt the tears prick her eyes and told herself it was because she was tired.

"It was a long journey, the sea was rough, and I have not slept very well," she excused herself.

She heard the door open and forced a smile to her lips.

"I am back safe and sound, as you see, Harry . . ."
she began, and turned round to feel the words swept
from her lips.

It was not Harry who had come into the Sitting-Room
but the *Duc*.

He was looking so familiar in his breeches, boots, and
grey whip-cord riding-coat, just as she had seen him
after she had jumped into the Riding-School, that for a
moment she thought he must be a ghost and she was
imagining him.

Then as he walked towards her she watched him
wide-eyed and said quickly:

"W-why are you . . . here?"

"I came to see your brother."

Canéda felt as if she had stopped breathing. Then,
because she was frightened, she asked frantically:

"Why? What had you to . . . say to him? You . . .
did not . . . tell him . . . ?"

Her voice died away because the *Duc* had reached her
side, and now she was palpitatingly aware of him,
acutely conscious that he was near her.

"I certainly told your brother that we had met," the
Duc said quietly.

"Why should you . . . want to do . . . that?"

"I have my own reasons for doing so."

"Harry will be very . . . angry with . . . me, if you
told him . . ."

There was no mistaking the agitation in her voice.

It swept through Canéda almost like a streak of lightning how furious Harry would be if the *Duc* had told
him how she had pretended to belong to a Circus!

Worse still, if he had told him that she had dined
alone with him and promised to stay the night!

As if the *Duc* was following her thoughts, he said quietly:

"I have not told your brother any of the things that
are making you afraid."

Canéda's relief almost made her feel weak. Then she
asked:

"Why did you come to . . . see Harry . . . and why are you in . . . England?"

"The answer to both questions is the same."

As if she suddenly remembered how much he had hurt her at the *Château* de Bantôme, she turned her face away from him to look out into the garden.

"I cannot understand why you should come here," she said in a voice which she tried to make cold and distant, "when you were so . . . rude to me when we last . . . met."

"I was punishing you," the *Duc* said, "as you tried to punish me."

Canéda was surprised but she did not speak, and he went on:

" 'An eye for an eye, a tooth for a tooth.' Was that not the reason why you came to Saumac?"

"How did you . . . find out . . . where I . . . was?"

She was not looking at him, but she knew he smiled.

"It was not very difficult," he said. "The Inn-Keeper where you stayed was very impressed not only with the two very elegant ladies who stayed in his Hostlery but with their magnificent horses."

"He told . . . you that we had gone . . . back to Angers?"

"At Angers they told me you had gone to Nantes, and from Nantes to St. Nazaire."

"Then you . . . knew who . . . I was?"

"Of course!" the *Duc* said. "Very large yachts belonging to English noblemen are not so frequent in St. Nazaire that the inhabitants are not curious about them. In fact, it was the Harbour Master who informed me you had left for Bordeaux."

"Then you guessed where I was going."

"The way your mother treated my father was, of course, something I have never been able to forget."

"And did you . . . hate Mama as your . . . father . . . did?"

"I never hated her," the *Duc* said sharply. "I was

merely aware that when he lost her, he lost the one
thing that mattered to him in his life."

There was silence, then as Canéda did not speak he
said very quietly:

"The same thing happened when you went away, and
I found you had gone!"

Canéda felt a little tremor run through her. Then, as
he said no more, she asked in a very small voice:

"Were you . . . very . . . angry?"

"I was not angry but distraught," the *Duc* replied, "I
thought I would never be able to find you again."

"And when you did . . . you were cruel and unkind."

"I am glad you felt like that."

"Why? Because you were having your . . . revenge
on . . . me?"

"No," he answered, "because if I could hurt you, it
meant that you cared."

Canéda felt that it would be humiliating for him to
know how much she cared and how unhappy she had
been.

With an effort she managed to say:

"That still does not . . . explain why you are . . .
here."

"I am prepared to do that," the *Duc* said, "but first I
want to ask you a question."

"What . . . is it?"

"I want you to look at me, Canéda, while I ask it."

It flashed through Canéda's mind that that was what
he had asked her to do once before, and because she
was afraid of what she would see in his eyes, and more
afraid of the strange feeling that was sweeping over her,
she shook her head.

How could she explain to him that now that he was
here, now that he was talking to her, it was as if she was
coming back to life?

The stone in her breast was melting away. She could
feel strange, unexpected thrills running through her

almost as if they were the green buds of spring opening in the sunshine.

She could feel him close beside her, feel the strange vibrations of which she had always been conscious emanating from him, and she wanted, she thought crazily, to turn round, to touch him, to make sure he was real.

"I told you to look at me, Canéda," the *Duc* said.

He had been speaking in English ever since he had come into the room, and it seemed to Canéda that he was giving her an order almost in the same way that she ordered Ariel to obey her.

Then she was afraid, not of him but of her own feelings, afraid that if she looked into his grey eyes she would forget everything else, and he would see how much she loved him.

Frantically, she tried to say to herself: "He is married . . . he is married," but somehow the words meant nothing.

All she could think was that he was here, that she vibrated to his voice, and whatever he asked of her it would be impossible to refuse.

"Look at me, Canéda."

Now the words were not a command but a plea, so entreating that it was utterly impossible to do anything but obey.

Slowly, because she was trembling, Canéda turned round.

She faced him, but she did not raise her eyes. Instead, they were on his well-tied, starched white stock.

The *Duc* did not speak, he did not move, he only waited until, as if it was impossible to resist him any longer, Canéda raised her eyes to his.

Then, as she had expected, as they looked at each other she thought that everything else was meaningless except the knowledge that he was here and she belonged to him.

The *Duc* looked at her for what seemed a very long moment. Then he said slowly, as if he was choosing his words with care:

"Answer me truthfully, Canéda—what did you feel when I kissed you in the *Château*? I thought, but I could not believe it to be true, that I was the first man ever to touch your lips."

"The . . . only man," Canéda whispered, and her voice was barely audible.

She saw a light come into the *Duc*'s eyes, and he said: "Your first kiss, *le premier fois*—and what did it mean to you?"

"I . . . I do not think I can . . . tell you."

"Tell me!"

Again it was a command, and because she felt shy, Canéda wished to take her eyes from his, and yet it was impossible.

He held her captive, and although he was not even touching her, it was impossible to escape.

"Tell me!" he insisted.

"There are . . . no words to describe it . . . you carried me into the sky . . . and we were no longer . . . human . . . but part of the moon . . . the stars, and the sun . . . and . . . and . . . God."

Her voice trembled on the last word, and now the *Duc* reached out his arms and pulled her against him roughly.

"And after that," he asked, "did you think I could lose you? That is exactly how I felt, my darling, and you are mine!"

As he said the last words his lips were on hers, and at the touch of them Canéda felt as if the Heavens opened and lifted her out of the misery and depression she had felt ever since she had left Saumac, and brought her into the light that had seemed to envelop her once before when the *Duc* had kissed her.

His lips were demanding and fiercely insistent, as if he forced her to acknowledge his supremacy and his ownership of her.

At the same time, she felt that he was wooing her and she surrendered herself to the wonder of his kiss as if he was the victor so that she could no longer fight against him.

Only when he raised his head did she say incoherently because the words were forced from her:

"I . . . I . . . love . . . you!"

"Say it again," the *Duc* said. "Say it so that I need not be mistaken in knowing that you are really saying it."

"I love you . . . I love . . . you!" Canéda cried, and because it was so overwhelming, she hid her face against his neck.

He held her very close before he said:

"I have been so afraid, so desperately afraid that I was mistaken, and yet, how could what we both felt that night be anything but real?"

"It was . . . very real to . . . me," Canéda murmured.

The *Duc* put his hand under her chin and turned her face up to his.

She thought he would kiss her, but instead he looked down at her, and she thought there was a different expression on his face, softer and more gentle than before.

She knew too that there was an expression of love in his eyes that she had always wanted to see.

"You are so beautiful!" he said. "So absurdly and ridiculously beautiful! How could you crucify me as you did by running away in that wicked way?"

"I . . . I was . . . frightened."

"I am not surprised! How could you do anything so outrageous, so disgraceful, as to get yourself into such a position?"

Canéda felt the blood rising in her cheeks at his words, and yet when she would have hid her face again, he prevented her from doing so.

"I am very, very angry with you," he said, but there was no anger in the tone of his voice.

"You swear . . . you did not . . . tell . . . Harry?" she asked.

"No. But I will make sure, as I know he would want me to, that you will never do anything like that again."

"And you have . . . forgiven me?"

"If I made you as unhappy as I was myself," the *Duc* said, "then I suppose we are what you would call 'quits.' "

"I was very . . . very unhappy when you would not . . . look at me . . . or speak to . . . me."

"I was afraid you might not care."

Canéda knew that in fact she had felt despairingly that there was nothing left in life because she had lost him.

Then once again she remembered, almost as if it loomed over her like a great menacing cloud, that he was married.

"I am sure it is very wrong of . . . us to talk like . . . this."

"Wrong?" he questioned.

She felt for the words in which to express the truth. Then he said, as if again he had read her thoughts:

"Suppose now you ask me why I have come to see your brother."

"I cannot . . . imagine . . . why you . . . should do so," Canéda said, "unless you wished to see his . . . horses."

It struck her that that must be the explanation.

There was a smile on the *Duc*'s lips as he replied:

"I am certainly impressed by them, but I am deeply concerned with something far more important—his sister."

"Y-you told Harry . . . that?" Canéda asked incredulously.

"Because I wished to behave conventionally in England at any rate, I told your brother that I hope to marry you."

"To . . . to marry me?"

Canéda was so astonished that she moved away from his encircling arms to stand staring at him wide-eyed.

"B-but I was told . . . I understood . . ."

"That I had a wife. That was true until three years ago."

"She is dead?"

"She died," the *Duc* said quietly.

"But . . . no-one knew . . ."

"Why should they?" he asked. "I have never discussed my private affairs with anyone, not even my relatives. Ever since I was first married I have been embittered by what I suffered, and I consider it my business and my business alone."

He spoke sharply. Then he said in a different tone of voice:

"I had decided never to marry again. I thought myself completely self-sufficient with my horses and Saumac, until—I met you."

"Is that . . . true?" Canéda asked.

"I think you know it is true without my saying any more," the *Duc* said.

"I wanted you to love me," Canéda said. "I do not wish you to feel now that because I am who I am, you are being pressured into marriage. After all . . . you asked me something . . . very different."

"That was entirely your fault," the *Duc* replied, "but I knew when I kissed you that I would never let you go, and that to make sure you did not leave me I must make you my wife."

"Did you . . . really feel . . . that?"

"I swear it," the *Duc* answered. "But that still does not make me any less shocked at the risks you ran in behaving as you did."

Canéda smiled.

Because of what he had told her, because he had said that he loved her and had asked her to marry him, she felt as if there was music playing all round her and the air was sparkling with light.

"It may have been outrageous . . . and you may have been . . . shocked," she said, "but if I had not let you . . . kiss me that night . . . on the moon, you might never have known how much . . . we loved each other or that it was . . . impossible to forget."

"You are twisting yourself out of a very difficult situation," the *Duc* said accusingly.

But as he spoke he moved towards Canéda and put his arms round her.

"How soon are you going to marry me?" he asked. "I do not intend to wait long."

"I have not yet accepted your proposal," she replied provocatively.

"Are you trying to refuse me?" he asked.

As he spoke his lips moved over the softness of her cheek. Then they outlined the top of her mouth, then her small pointed chin.

It gave her a strange feeling. Then as she longed for him to kiss her, her lips ready and yearning for his, he sought the softness of her neck.

He felt the quiver that ran through her as strange sensations made her feel wildly excited yet weak and submissive.

Then as her breath came quickly from between her lips, he kissed her and once again they were in the light coming from the Heavens and it was impossible to think of anything else but that she was his, and they were one person in mind, heart, and soul.

Only as Canéda felt as if the wonder of it was almost too great to be borne did the *Duc* say in a voice that he tried to keep steady:

"Now tell me when you will marry me."

"Now! This . . . moment!"

He laughed, and it was a sound of triumph.

"That is what I wanted you to say, my precious one."

He held her close once again, as if enfolding her protectively against the world and against anything which might hurt her.

"I love you! I adore you! I worship you!" he said. "Will you be happy with me on my corner of the moon?"

"I would be happy with you . . . anywhere . . . anywhere . . . in the . . . world," Canéda replied, "but especially happy on your . . . moon, as long as we can be . . . together."

"You may be sure of that," the *Duc* answered, "and I am not returning to France without you, just in case you are, as you told me when we first met, a shooting-star whom it is impossible to capture."

He kissed her forehead as he spoke. Then he said:

"On your first visit to France you not only found me but discovered your mother's family, whom you love even though your brother tells me you went there prepared to hate them."

"I love them and I feel so . . . sorry for . . . them."

"Before I came to England," the *Duc* said, "I talked with the Manager of your grandfather's Estate and with the other Landlords in the District. We evolved a plan for the future which will not make the loss of the vines quite so bad as it appears at the moment."

"I am so, so glad!" Canéda cried. "What can they do?"

"It is a question of a different sort of farming," the *Duc* explained. "The land is good, and I think they could produce a continuous succession of crops, rather different from those in other regions. Tobacco is one, strawberries are another, besides accelerating the sales of what is a particular luxury in France—truffles."

Canéda gave a little cry of joy.

"If the de Bantôme Estate can do all that, then they will not be so hard-up and will not feel so desperate over the loss of their vines."

"It will mean a lot of hard work and imagination," the *Duc* said, "but your Uncle René, whom you have not met, is prepared to make every effort, as I think Armand will be, when he settles down."

Canéda gave a little sigh.

"You are so clever," she said, "and with you to help them I know they will be all right."

"We will help them together," the *Duc* said, "just as, my precious little love, we will do everything together, you and I, especially schooling our horses."

"I thought I was barred from the Riding-School," Canéda teased.

"You will certainly not be allowed there when the young officers are having their lessons," the *Duc* said. "Not only would you make it impossible for them to concentrate on what I am telling them, but I shall be an extremely jealous husband."

His voice deepened as he said:

"If I see you looking in that provocative way from under your eye-lashes at any other man, I shall most certainly lock you up in the dungeons—and you will never, my adorable one, never again wear a pink riding-habit!"

Canéda laughed.

"I wanted to attract your attention."

"You did that, but I will not allow any other man to notice you in the same way."

Canéda looked at him with a little smile on her lips. Then he said:

"Of course I am mad to give up my quiet, well-organised life for you! I am well aware of the tortures you will inflict on me!"

"You do not . . . *have* to . . . marry me."

"You are not suggesting any other relationship, I hope?"

Canéda blushed and said quickly:

"No, of course not! I was only saying that if you wish to be free, you can go . . . back to Saumac and . . . leave me . . . here."

"And if I did, what would you feel?"

As if the *Duc* frightened her, Canéda held on to him.

"I could not bear to be so unhappy again. I love you . . . I love you! Please, do not . . . leave me!"

"I will never do that," the *Duc* replied. "You are mine, now and forever, and, my naughty one, whether you like it or not, the moon will be a prison from which you will never escape."

"I will never want to," Canéda tried to say, but his lips were on hers. She only knew that once she was in the moon and in the *Duc*'s arms, all her dreams would come true.

BRIDE TO THE KING

Author's Note

✦

During the Franco-Prussian War in 1870 negotiations were pushed ahead for the unity of all Germany outside Austria. A conference of Prussia, Bavaria, and Würtemberg met at Munich to discuss the terms of unification. There was the question of the name for the new State, and Bismarck wished to revive the title of Emperor. On January 18, 1871, King Wilhelm Freidrich I was proclaimed Emperor, in the Galerie des Glaces at Versailles.

The new Reich consisted of four Kingdoms, five Grand Duchies, thirteen Duchies and Principalities, and three free cities.

The rest of Europe was appalled and frightened.

CHAPTER ONE

❧

1875

"Zosina, wake up!"

The girl addressed started and raised her eyes from the book she had been reading.

"Did you speak to me?" she asked.

"For the third time!" her sister Helsa replied.

"I am sorry. I was reading."

"That is nothing new," Helsa exclaimed. "*Fraulein* says that you will ruin your eyes and be blind before you are middle-aged."

Zosina laughed a soft, musical laugh with an undoubted note of amusement in it.

"Although it is *Fraulein*'s job to teach us," she said, "she always finds marvellous excuses for us not to learn anything."

"Of course she does," Theone remarked, who was painting one of the fashion magazines with watercolours. "*Fraulein* knows so little herself, she is afraid that if we show any intelligence we will realise how little she can tell us."

"I feel that is rather unkind," Zosina said.

"Kind or not," Helsa replied, "if you do not hurry downstairs, since Papa wants you, you will be in trouble."

"Papa wants me?" Zosina said in surprise. "Why did you not tell me so?"

"That is just what I have been trying to do," Helsa replied. "Margit came in just now to say Papa wanted you in his Study. You know what that means!"

Zosina gave a little sigh.

"I suppose I must have forgotten something he told me to do, but I cannot think what it is."

"You will learn quickly enough," Theone remarked. "I am thankful it is not me he has sent for."

Zosina rose from the window-seat on which she had been sitting and walked across the School-Room to look in the mirror over the mantelshelf.

She tidied her hair, quite unaware that her reflection portrayed a lovely face with large grey eyes which at the moment were rather worried.

She was in fact concentrating fiercely on trying to remember something she had done wrong or something she had omitted to do.

Whatever it was, she was quite certain her father would make it an opportunity to be extremely disagreeable, a thing at which he excelled these days, when he was suffering from gout.

Without saying more to her sisters, Zosina crossed the room to leave, and as she did so, Katalin, who had not spoken until now and who was only twelve, looked up to say:

"Good luck, Zosina. I wish I could come with you."

"That would only make Papa more angry than he is already," Zosina said with a smile.

Leaving the School-Room, she hurried down the long passages, which were extremely cold in the winter, until she reached the front staircase of the Palace.

The Arch-Duke Ferdinand of Lützelstein lived in considerable style, which impressed the more distinguished of his subjects but was criticised by those who suspected that they had to pay for it.

But he did not give his family much comfort or consideration, and they knew it was because they had committed the unforgivable sin of being daughters instead of sons.

There was no doubt that the Arch-Duke was bitterly disappointed and frustrated by the fact that he had no direct heir.

"You are his favourite," Katalin would often say irrepressibly to Zosina, "because you were his first disappointment. Helsa was Number Two and Theone was Number Three. By the time he reached me, he disliked me so much I am only surprised he did not cut me up into small pieces and scatter me from the battlements!"

Katalin had a dramatic imagination and, perhaps because she lacked the affection of her father and her mother, was always thinking herself wildly in love with one of the younger officials in the Palace or, more understandably, the Officers of the Guard.

Zosina was in many ways very different from her sisters.

They had a practical and sensible outlook on life which made them accept the family difficulties, and the small but tiresome privations to which they were subject, as an inevitable quirk of fate.

"If I had the choice, I would rather have been born the daughter of a forester," Theone had said once, "than a Royal Princess without any of the glamour or excitement that should go with it."

"You will get that when you are grown up," Zosina had answered.

Theone had laughed.

"What about you? You were allowed to go to your 'Coming Out' Ball, but you had to dance with all the oldest and more boring officials in the country. Since then Mama has made no effort to entertain for you, unless you call it being entertained when you are allowed to sit in the Drawing-Room when she receives the Councillors' wives and they talk about their charities or something equally deadly!"

Zosina had to admit that these were not particularly exciting occasions.

At the same time, she had learnt long ago not to be

311

bored with having to listen to the stiff, desultory conversation which was all that the Palace etiquette permitted.

"The weather has been cold lately," her mother would say, starting the conversation as protocol directed.

"It has indeed, Your Royal Highness."

"I often say to the Arch-Duke that the winds at this time of year are very treacherous."

"They are indeed, Your Royal Highness."

"We will all be thankful when the warm weather comes."

"It is something we all look forward to, Your Royal Highness."

Zosina was not listening. Her thoughts had carried her far away into a fantasy-world where people talked intelligently and wittily.

Or else she was on Mount Olympus, mixing with gods and goddesses of Ancient Greece and pondering on the problems to which mankind had tried through all eternity to find a solution.

The Arch-Duchess would have been astounded if she had known how knowledgeable her eldest daughter was on the behaviour, a great deal of it outrageous, of the Greek gods.

She would have been equally astonished if she had known that Zosina pored over books written by French authors which gave an insight into the strange diversions that had invaded French literature during the Second Empire.

Zosina was fortunate in that the Palace Library, which had been started by her great-grandfather, was considered one of the treasures of Lützelstein.

It therefore behoved the present Ruler, Arch-Duke Ferdinand, to keep it up, for which fortunately an endowment from Parliament was provided every year.

New books were purchased and added to the thousands already accumulated, and the Librarian, an elderly man, was easily persuaded by Princess Zosina to put on his list of requirements those books which she particularly wanted to read.

"I am not sure that Her Royal Highness would approve," he would say occasionally when Zosina had pleaded for some author whose somewhat doubtful reputation had reached even Lützelstein.

"You are quite safe, *Mein Herr*," Zosina would say. "Mama never has time to read and so she is unlikely to criticise anything you have on your shelves."

She smiled as she spoke, and the Librarian had found himself smiling back and agreeing to anything which this extremely pretty girl demanded of him.

Zosina now reached the Hall and hurried to the door which led into her father's Study.

It was an extremely impressive room, the walls covered with dark panelling, the windows draped with heavily fringed velvet curtains, the furniture ponderous and old-fashioned.

It was a room which all four Princesses disliked intensely because it was always here that their father lectured them on their misdeeds and where they waited apprehensively for the moment when he would fly into one of his rages which usually ended in his storming at them:

"Get out of my sight! I have seen enough of all four of you! God knows why I should be inflicted with such stupid, fractious females instead of being blessed with an intelligent son!"

It was the signal for them to leave, but even though they found the relief of doing so almost inexpressible, their hearts would be thumping and their lips dry.

In some way which they could not explain even to one another, they did not feel safe until they were back in the School-Room.

"What can I have done to upset Papa?" Zosina asked herself now.

Then with an instinctive little lift of her chin she opened the door and went in.

Her father was sitting, as she expected, in his favourite high-back winged arm-chair near the hearth.

There was no fire because it was summer, and it was typical, Zosina often thought, that in this room there was no arrangement of flowers to fill the empty fireplace, so that its gaping black mouth added to the general gloom.

The Arch-Duke had his gouty left leg, swathed in bandages, resting on a footstool in front of him, and Zosina thought with a little jerk of her heart that he was looking stern and grim.

She walked towards him, still wondering frantically what could be wrong, when to her surprise as she reached his side, he looked up at her and smiled.

The Arch-Duke had in his youth been an extremely handsome man, and it was therefore not surprising that his four daughters were all exceptionally good-looking.

Zosina had long ago decided that their features came in fact from their great-grandmother who had been Greek, and some of their other characteristics from their father's mother, who was Hungarian by birth.

"We are a mixture of nationalities," she had said once, "but we have been clever enough to take the best from every country whose blood is mixed with ours."

"If we had been really clever, we would not have been born in Lützelstein," Katalin had said irrepressibly.

"Why not?" Helsa had enquired.

"Well, if we had had the choice, surely we would have chosen France, Italy, or England."

"I see what you mean!" Helsa had exclaimed. "Well, I would have chosen France. I have heard how gay it is in Paris."

"Our Ambassador told Papa their extravagance and outrageous behaviour during the Second Empire was the scandal of the world."

"That is over now!" Theone had said. "But I bet the French still have a lot of fun. We should have been born in France!"

"Sit down, Zosina. I want to talk to you," the Arch-Duke said now.

Zosina obediently seated herself on the sofa near him, and he looked at her until she wondered if he disapproved of her gown or perhaps the new way in which she had arranged her hair.

Then he said:

"I have something to tell you, Zosina, that may surprise you. At the same time, at your age you must have been expecting it."

"What is that, Papa?"

"You are to be married!"

For a moment Zosina thought she could not have heard correctly.

Then as her eyes widened until they seemed to fill the whole of her small face, the Arch-Duke said:

"It is gratifying, very gratifying, that the negotiations of our Ambassador, Count Csáky, should prove so fruitful. I shall of course reward him in the proper manner."

"Are you . . . saying, Papa . . . that the Count has . . . arranged my . . . marriage?"

"At my instigation, of course," the Arch-Duke said. "But if I am truthful, I must admit that the first suggestion of such an alliance came from the Regent of Dórsia."

Zosina looked puzzled, and, as if her father understood, he said impressively:

"You, my dear, are to marry King György!"

Zosina gave a little gasp, then said:

"But . . . Papa, I have never . . . seen him, and why should he . . . want to . . . marry me?"

"That is what I intend to explain to you," the Arch-Duke said, "so listen attentively."

"I . . . am, Papa."

"You are aware, of course," the Arch-Duke began, "that I have been worried for some time about the growing power of the German Empire."

"Yes, Papa," Zosina murmured.

As it happened, her father had never discussed it with

her, but Zosina remembered how five years ago everybody else in the Palace had talked of little else, when the outbreak of the Franco-Prussian War made the policy of the Minister-President of Prussia, Otto von Bismarck, seem to threaten their independence.

Prussia had long been preparing for that war, and Bismarck had cunningly manipulated the situation so that her enemy, France, was made the technical aggressor.

In July 1870, France had declared war on Prussia, Bavaria, and other South-German Kingdoms and small Principalities sided with Prussia.

The issue had never been in any doubt, and in January the following year, after a terrible siege of 131 days, starving Paris opened its gates to the enemy.

In the South, the small Kingdoms which had not been engaged in the war, like Lützelstein and Dórsia, had hoped that their large neighbour, Bavaria, would protect them from Bismarck's ambitions.

However, King Ludwig of Bavaria, always unpredictable, had been ill and therefore was not strong enough to stand up against the pressure placed upon him by Prussia's representative.

All this flashed through Zosina's mind, and she was not surprised when her father said:

"At this particular moment in history, it is absolutely essential that Lützelstein and Dórsia should be independent and keep the balance of power in Europe."

He paused before he continued impressively:

"We have a weakened Austria on one side of us, a limp Bavaria on the other, and Germany growing stronger every day, ready to draw us into the iron net of an inflexible Empire."

"I understand, Papa," Zosina murmured.

"I do not expect you to understand anything of the sort!" the Arch-Duke said suddenly, in an irritated tone of voice. "But listen to what I am saying, because it is for this reason that a close alliance, sealed by marriage between the King of Dórsia and one of my daughters, would strengthen the hands of the politicians in both countries."

Zosina wanted to say again that she understood, but instead she merely nodded her head, and her father said:

"Well, speak up! Do you grasp what I am trying to tell you? By God, if I had a son he would see the position quickly enough!"

"I see the reason, Papa, for the marriage," Zosina said. "But I asked you if the King . . . really wished to marry me."

"Of course he wishes to marry you!" the Arch-Duke thundered. "He can understand the situation clearly enough because he is a man and a Royal Monarch at that!"

"I should have thought, Papa, that the King and I . . . should have . . . met before everything was . . . decided," Zosina said in her soft voice.

"Meet? Of course you will meet!" the Arch-Duke snapped. "That is exactly what I am going to tell you. If you would stop interrupting, Zosina, I would be able to get to the point."

"I am . . . sorry, Papa."

"Your marriage is arranged to take place as soon as possible, as a warning to Germany that we will not be interfered with," the Arch-Duke said. "And because we must do things in a proper manner, I have arranged that the Queen Mother should pay a State Visit to Dórsia and take you with her."

Zosina's face lit up.

"I am to go with Grandmama to Dórsia, Papa? That will be exciting!"

"I am sorry I cannot go myself," the Arch-Duke said. "Both your mother and I would prefer it, of course, but, as you see, the damned leg of mine makes it impossible."

He winced as he spoke, and Zosina asked quickly:

"Is it very painful, Papa?"

The Arch-Duke bit back a swear-word and instead said hastily:

"I have no wish to talk about it. What I was saying is that you will accompany your grandmother on a State Visit, at the end of which your engagement will be publicly announced."

Zosina was silent for a moment, then she said:

"Supposing . . . Papa, the King . . . dislikes me and I . . . dislike him? Would we still have to be . . . married?"

Her father glared at her before he answered:

"A more stupid, idiotic question I have seldom heard! What does it matter if you like or dislike each other? It is a political matter, as I have just explained if you had listened!"

"I did listen, Papa. At the same time . . . political or not, it is I who have to . . . marry the King."

"And think yourself extremely lucky to do so!" the Arch-Duke stormed. "Good God, I have four daughters to get off my hands one way or another. You cannot imagine that I am going to find available Kings for all of them!"

Zosina drew in her breath.

"I suppose . . . Papa, you would not . . . consider Helsa . . . going instead of . . . me? She is very . . . anxious to be . . . married, while I am quite . . . happy to stay here with . . . you and Mama."

Her question, spoken in a somewhat hesitating voice, brought the blood coursing into her father's face.

"How dare you argue with me!" he raged. "How dare you suggest you will not do as you are told! You ought to go down on your knees and thank God that you have a father who considers you to the extent of providing you with a throne, which is not something to be picked up every day of the week!"

His voice deepened with anger as he went on:

"You will do exactly what I tell you! You will go to Dórsia with your grandmother and you make yourself pleasant to the King—do you understand?"

"Yes, Papa . . . but . . ."

"I am not listening to any arguments or anything else

you have to say," the Arch-Duke roared. "It is typical that after all I have done for you, I find that I have been nurturing a viper in my bosom! You are ungrateful besides apparently being—half-witted!"

He coughed over the word, then continued:

"There is not a girl in the whole Duchy who would not jump at such an opportunity, but not you! Oh no! You have to complain and find fault! God Almighty! Who do you expect will ask to marry you—the Archangel Gabriel?"

The Arch-Duke was really carried away in one of his rages by now, and Zosina, knowing that nothing she could say would abate the storm, rose to her feet.

"I am . . . sorry you are . . . angry, Papa," she said, "but thank you for . . . thinking of me."

She curtseyed and left the room while he shouted after her:

"Ungrateful and half-witted to boot! Why should I be afflicted with such children?"

Zosina shut the door and was glad as she went down the passage that she could no longer hear what he was saying.

"I should have kept silent," she told herself.

Her father had taken her by surprise and she knew that she had been extremely stupid to have questioned in any way one of his plans. It always annoyed him.

'He is also annoyed,' she thought, 'because he cannot make the State Visit himself. He would have enjoyed it so much. But it will be fun to go with Grandmama.'

Queen Szófia, the Queen Mother, was both admired and loved by her four granddaughters.

Because she had an abundance of traditional Hungarian charm, she had captivated most of the population when she reigned in Lützelstein.

But there had been a hard core of Court Officials who found her frivolous and too free and easy in her ways.

Now, when she was well over sixty, she still appeared to laugh more than anyone else, and life in the small

319

Palace to which she had retired, five miles away, always seemed to Zosina a place of happiness and gaiety.

She reached the Hall and was going towards the stairs when out of the shadows emerged Count Csáky, the Ambassador to Dórsia.

He was an elderly man whom Zosina had known all her life, and as soon as she realised that he wished to speak to her, she went towards him with her hand outstretched.

"How delightful to see you, Your Excellency!" she exclaimed. "I did not know you had returned home."

"I only returned two days ago, Your Royal Highness," he replied, bowing over her hand. "I imagine His Royal Highness has told you the news I brought him?"

"We have just been talking about it," Zosina replied, hoping that the Ambassador had not heard her father raging at her.

He smiled and said:

"In which case I have something to show you."

She walked with him into one of the Ante-Rooms where distinguished personages usually sat when they were awaiting an audience with her father.

The Count went to a table on which she saw a Diplomatic-Box. He opened it and drew out a small leather case.

He handed it to her and before she opened it she knew, without being told, that it contained a miniature of the King of Dórsia.

He was certainly good-looking, with dark hair and dark eyes.

He was wearing a white tunic resplendent with decorations and he appeared very impressive.

"I thought you would like to see it," the Ambassador murmured, standing beside her.

"It is very kind of Your Excellency," Zosina said. "I had been wondering what the King looked like, but actually, although I did not say so to Papa, I thought he was too young to marry."

"His Majesty comes of age in a month's time," the

320

Count replied. "He will then be able to reign without the Regent, and the Prime Minister and the Privy Council consider it very important that when his uncle retires, he should have a wife to support him."

"His uncle has been the Regent for a long time?" Zosina asked, thinking it was expected of her.

"Yes, for eight years. The King was only twelve when his father died and his uncle was appointed Regent, and he has, I may say, ruled Dórsia on his nephew's behalf extremely well. It is a rich country, thanks to him. Your Royal Highness will have every comfort, besides living in what is to my mind one of the loveliest places in the world."

There was so much warmth in the Ambassador's voice that Zosina looked at him in surprise.

"I am not being disloyal, Your Royal Highness, to Lützelstein," the Count said quickly, "but as it happens, my mother came from Dórsia, and that is one of the reasons why I was so delighted to be appointed Ambassador there."

Zosina looked down at the miniature and said:

"I asked my father if the King . . . really wanted to marry me, but it . . . made him angry. I would like to . . . ask you the same . . . question."

She raised her eyes to the Count as she spoke, and he thought that any man would be only too willing and eager to marry anyone so lovely and so attractive in every way.

He had always thought Zosina was an exceptional girl and he was sure that with her intelligence, her beauty, and her inescapable charm, any country over which she reigned and any man whom she married would be extremely lucky.

Then as he realised that she was waiting for him to answer her question, he said:

"As it happens, Your Royal Highness, I took with me to Dórsia a miniature of yourself, since I thought the King would wish to see it as I have brought his portrait to you."

"And what did His Majesty say?" Zosina asked in a low voice.

"I do not know His Majesty's reaction," the Ambassador replied, "for the simple reason that my negotiations for the marriage took place with the Regent. I gave him the miniature so that there would be no mistake about it reaching His Majesty's own hands."

Zosina could not help feeling disappointed. She would have liked to know exactly what the King had said when he saw her portrait.

"I do understand," the Count said with a tact that was part of his profession, "that it is difficult for Your Royal Highness to contemplate marrying somebody you have never seen, even though you realise how expedient it is from the point of view both of Lützelstein and of Dórsia."

"I . . . accept that I have been born with a certain . . . state in life," Zosina said hesitatingly, "but at the same . . . time . . ."

She stopped because she knew she could not put into words—and if she did there was no point in it—that she did not want to be just a political pawn but something much more important to the man she would marry.

"Tell me about the King," she said, before the Ambassador could speak.

"He is, as you see, very handsome," the Count replied, and Zosina felt that he was choosing his words carefully. "He is young, but that is something which time will always remedy, and he enjoys life to the—full."

"In what way?"

She had a feeling that the Count would find this question rather hard to answer, and he hesitated quite obviously before he said:

"All young men find life exciting when they are first free of their Tutors and studies, and the King is no exception. But I think, Your Royal Highness, it would be a mistake for me to say too much. I want you to judge for yourself and not go to Dórsia with a biased mind."

322

Zosina had the idea that the Ambassador was trying to get out of a rather difficult situation.

But why it should be difficult she was not certain.

She thought to herself shrewdly:

'He wants me to like the King and he is afraid that anything he might say would prejudice me one way or another.'

She looked down again at the miniature.

The King was good-looking, and almost as if she spoke to herself she said:

"He is . . . very young."

"Two years older than Your Royal Highness," the Ambassador replied, "and I am told by those who know him that he has old ideas in many ways, which is not surprising, seeing that he has been King for so many years."

"But it is the Regent who does all the work!" Zosina flashed.

"Not all of it," the Ambassador replied. "I think Prince Sándor has gone out of his way to see that the King fulfils a great number of official duties from which he might have been excused."

"Does His Majesty resent having a Regent to run the country for him?" Zosina asked.

"That is a question I cannot answer, Your Royal Highness. Knowing Prince Sándor as I do, I cannot imagine anybody resenting his authority, but one never knows with young people. I expect, however, that His Majesty will be very glad to be free of all restrictions except those of Parliament when he comes of age."

"He might find a . . . wife restricting too."

The Count smiled.

"That is something, Princess, which I feel you would never be to any man."

Zosina put the miniature down on the Diplomatic-Box.

"I thank Your Excellency very much for being so kind," she said. "You will be coming with me and the Queen Mother to Dórsia?"

There was almost an appeal in her voice, and the look she gave him told the Ambassador that she thought it would be a help and a comfort to have him there.

"I shall be with Your Royal Highness," he replied, "and you know I am always ready to be of assistance at any time and in any way that you require."

"Thank you," Zosina said simply.

She held out her hand, then without saying any more she left the Ante-Room and walked swiftly across the marble Hall and started to climb the stairs.

Only when she was halfway up them did she begin to hurry, and ran along the corridors to burst into the School-Room.

As three faces turned to look anxiously at her, she realised that her breath was coming quickly between her lips and her heart was pounding in her breast.

"What is it? What has happened?" Helsa asked.

"Was Papa very disagreeable?" Theone questioned.

For a moment it was impossible for Zosina to answer. Then Katalin jumped up and ran to put her arms round her waist.

"You look upset, Zosina," she said sympathetically. "Never mind, dearest, we love you, and however beastly Papa may be, we will all try to make you feel better."

Zosina put her arm round Katalin's shoulders.

"I am . . . all right," she said in a voice which shook, "but I have had rather a . . . shock."

"A shock?" Helsa exclaimed. "What is it?"

"I do not . . . know how to . . . tell you."

"You must tell us," Katalin said. "We always share everything, even shocks."

"I cannot . . . share this."

"Why not?"

"Because I am to be . . . married."

"Married?"

Three voices shrieked the words in unison.

"It cannot be true!"

"As Papa has said so . . . I suppose it . . . will be!"

"Who are you to marry?" Theone enquired.

324

"King György of Dórsia!"

For a moment there was a stupefied silence. Then Katalin cried:

"You will be a Queen! Oh, Zosina, how marvellous! We can all come and stay with you and get away from here!"

"A Queen! Heavens, you are lucky!" Helsa exclaimed.

Zosina moved away to sit down on the window-seat where she had been reading before she went downstairs.

"I cannot . . . believe it," she said in a very small voice, "though it is true, because Papa said so. But it seems . . . strange and rather frightening to marry a man you have never . . . seen and know very little . . . about."

"I know a lot about him," Theone said.

Three faces looked at her.

"What do you mean? How can you know about him if we do not?"

"I heard Mama's Lady-in-Waiting talking to Countess Csáky when they did not know or had forgotten I was in the room."

"What did they say? Tell us what they said!" Helsa cried.

"The Countess said the King was wild and was always in trouble of some sort. Then she laughed and said: 'I often think the Arch-Duke is luckier than he knows in not having a son of that sort to cope with!' "

"How would she know that . . ." Helsa began, then interrupted herself to say: "Of course, the Countess is married to our Ambassador to Dórsia!"

"I have just been talking to him," Zosina said. "He showed me a miniature of the King."

"What does he look like? Tell us what he looks like!" her sisters cried.

"He is very handsome and did not look wild but rather serious."

"You would not be able to tell from a picture anyway," Theone said.

"If he is . . . wild," Zosina said slowly, "I expect that is why they want him to get . . . married . . . in case he causes a . . . scandal or . . . something."

She was really puzzling it out for herself when Katalin, who had followed her to the window-seat, sat down beside her and said:

"If he is like that, you will be a good influence on him. I expect that is why they want you to marry him."

"A . . . good influence?" Zosina faltered.

"Yes, of course! It is like all the stories: the hero is a rake, he has a reputation with women, and he does all sorts of things of which people disapprove! Then along comes the lovely, good heroine and he finds his soul."

Helsa and Theone burst into laughter.

"Katalin, that is just like you to talk such nonsense!"

"It is not nonsense, it is true!" Katalin protested. "You mark my words, Zosina will reform the rake and make him into a good King, and she will end up by being canonised and having a statue erected to her in every Church in Dórsia!"

They all laughed again, Zosina with rather an effort.

"That is all a fairy-story," she said. "At the same time, I think I am . . . frightened of going to . . . Dórsia."

"Of course you are not!" Katalin said before anyone else could speak. "While you are there you will have a good time. I have often wondered what rakes do. Is there a word for a lady rake?"

"No," Helsa said. "Besides, while a man can be a rake, you know that a woman, if she did even half the things a man can do, would be condemned for being wicked, and no-one would speak to her."

"I suppose so," Katalin agreed, "and she would be thrown into utter darkness or dogs would eat her bones as happened to Jezebel."

Even Zosina laughed at this.

"In which case I think I would prefer to be ca-nonised," she said. "But at the same time, I wish I could stay here. I did suggest to Papa that the King might prefer to marry Helsa."

Her sister gave a little cry.

"I would marry him tomorrow if I had the chance! For goodness' sake, Zosina, do not pretend you are reluctant to be a Queen! And if you grab the only King there is, and I have to put up with some poor minor Royalty, I shall die of sheer envy!"

"Perhaps when the King meets you when you go to Dórsia," Katalin said, "he will fall in love with you and will threaten to abdicate unless you will be his wife. Then everybody would be happy."

"It is quite a good story as it is," Helsa said. "Here we are sitting in the School-Room, going nowhere and meeting no men, unless you count those pompous old officials who come to see Papa, and suddenly Zosina is whisked off to be crowned Queen of Dórsia. It really is the most exciting thing that has happened for years!"

"Papa said I was . . . ungrateful, and I suppose I . . . am," Zosina said slowly. "It is just that I would like to have . . . fallen in love with the man I . . . marry."

There was silence for a moment. Then Theone said:

"I suppose we would all like that, but we have not much chance of it happening, have we?"

"Very little," Helsa said. "That is the penalty for being born Royal—to have to marry whom you are told to marry, with no argument about it."

Katalin put her head on one side.

"Perhaps that is why Papa is so disagreeable—because he did not want to marry Mama and always found her a bore."

"Katalin! How could you say such things?" Helsa asked.

"I do not know why you should be so shocked," Katalin answered. "You know how good-looking Papa was when he was young. I am sure he could have married anyone—Queen Victoria herself if he had wished to."

"He would have been too young for her," said Helsa, who was always the practical one.

"Well—anyone else with whom he fell in love."

327

"Perhaps he did," Katalin said. "Perhaps he was in love with a beautiful girl who was not Royal, and although they loved each other passionately, Papa was forced by his tiresome old Councillors to marry Mama."

"I am sure we should not be talking like this," Zosina said, "and it does not make it any easier for me."

"I am being selfish and unkind," Katalin said hastily, "and we do understand what you are feeling—do we not, girls?"

"Yes, of course we do," Helsa and Theone agreed.

"It has been a shock, but at least he is young and handsome," Theone went on. "You must remind yourself if ever he is difficult, that he might well have been old and hideous!"

Zosina gave a little sigh and looked out the window.

She was trying to tell herself that she should be grateful and that, as Theone had just said, things might have been much worse.

She knew that what was really troubling her was that she had always dreamt that one day she would fall in love and it would be very wonderful.

All the books she had read had, in one way or another, shown her how important love was in the life of a man and a woman.

She had started with the love the Greeks knew and how it permeated their thinking and their living and was to them the most important emotion both for gods and for man.

It was love, Zosina thought, that motivated great deeds, caused wars, inspired the finest masterpieces of art and music, and made men at times as great as the gods they worshipped.

She thought now that beneath her endeavours to improve herself, to stimulate her mind, to acquire all the knowledge that was possible, there had been a desire to make herself better than she was.

Secretly she believed that one day the man who would love her would want her to be different from every other woman he had ever known.

In retrospect it seemed almost a foolish ambition.

Yet it had been there; and it was difficult, in the quiet, conventional life they had lived in the School-Room, to remember that they were Royal and their futures must therefore be different from those of other girls of their age.

Although it had struck Zosina occasionally that her marriage might eventually be arranged, it had never for one moment crossed her mind it would be to somebody she had never even seen.

That it would be a *fait accompli* before she had time to think about it or discuss it, or have the chance of refusing the prospective husband if she really disliked him, had never occurred to her.

"I have been very stupid," she told herself, but she knew that even if she had been anything else, the result would of course have been just the same.

It was only that deep in her heart something cried out at being pressurised and constrained into a situation in which she could only accept the inevitable and have no choice one way or the other.

'I suppose if it is too terrible . . . too frightening,' she thought, 'I could always . . . die!'

Then she knew that she wanted to live, to live her life fully and discover the world, and most of all, although she hardly dared to admit it to herself, she wanted to find love.

CHAPTER TWO

❧

THERE WAS NOT a great distance between the Capital of Lützelstein and that of Dórsia, but the land was very mountainous and therefore the train in which they were travelling made, Zosina thought, a great to-do over it.

The whole journey, however, was so exciting that in retrospect even the long-drawn-out preparations seemed worthwhile.

She had not realised that she would require so many new clothes, until she found that they were to be part of her trousseau.

This made them less attractive than they had seemed when they were first ordered.

At the same time, because her sisters were so thrilled by the gowns, bonnets, sunshades, gloves, and of course the exquisite, sophisticated lingerie, Zosina found herself carried away as if on a tide.

Everything had to be done so quickly that she got very tired of fittings, and it was a relief to find that Helsa, although she was fifteen months younger, was a similar build to herself and could often "stand in" for her.

The only trouble was that every time she did so, Helsa was so envious that Zosina felt herself apologising humbly for being the chosen bride.

"It is not fair that the eldest should have everything," Helsa would say. "First, Papa likes you the best . . ."

"Which is not saying very much!" the irrepressible Katalin interposed.

"You get married first, and to a King!" Helsa finished.

"You might add that she is much the prettiest of us all," Theone said, "because that is the truth."

"If you only knew how much I wish this were not happening to me," Zosina said at length, when Helsa had been complaining for the hundredth time.

"The whole mistake has been," Katalin said, "that you are marrying a European. Now, if Papa had had the sense to choose a Moslem, such as an Arab or an Egyptian, he could have married off the four of us simultaneously!"

This made them laugh so much that the tension was broken, but Helsa's feelings only added to Zosina's own conviction that her marriage was not only going to be rather frightening but would separate her from her own family.

There was, however, nothing she could do, and she tried to tell herself that the gowns and the approval she was receiving from her father and mother were some compensation.

The Arch-Duchess, in fact, was so unusually affable that Theone said:

"If Mama was always in such a good mood as she is now, we would be able to suggest to her that we might occasionally have a dance or even just invite some friends to tea."

"I doubt if she would agree," Helsa said. "The sun is only shining at the moment because Zosina is to be a Queen."

It had certainly pleased her mother, Zosina thought, and she was rather surprised, because the Arch-Duchess had never appeared to be ambitious for her daughters.

Then it suddenly struck her that perhaps the real reason was that with her marriage she would be leaving home and there would be one less woman about the Palace.

Children seldom think of their parents as human beings.

So it was only during the last year that Zosina had seen her mother not as an authoritative, mechanical figure but as a woman with all the feelings and emotions of her sex.

It was then that she realised, with a perception she had never had before, that her mother loved her father possessively and jealously.

On his side, as far as Zosina could ascertain, although he was scrupulously polite and courteous to his wife in public and consulted her in private, he showed no particular affection for her.

Now that she herself was to be married, Zosina found herself considering her father and mother as an example of two people whose marriage had been arranged for them and who, as far as the world was concerned, had made an excellent job of it.

Because she was looking for signs of deeper feelings than those which appeared on the surface, she realised, by the way her mother looked at her father, that beneath her almost icy exterior she was a frustrated and unhappy woman.

Looking back, Zosina recalled that at Court functions which they had been allowed to watch from the balcony in the Throne-Room or from the Gallery in the Ball-Room, her father had always singled out the most attractive woman with whom to dance or converse, once his official duties had been completed.

At the time she had merely thought how sensible he was to waltz with his arm round a lady who had a tiny waist and whose eyes sparkled as brightly as the jewels in her hair.

Now she wondered if the reason that there were so few entertainments in the Palace these days was the fact that her mother deliberately wished to isolate him from any contact with other women and keep him for herself.

She could understand how frustrating it was for her father no longer to be free to ride alone with a groom every morning, as he had done before his gout made him almost a cripple.

She felt certain too that he was not allowed to entertain any friends he might have away from the strict protocol of the Palace.

Vaguely, because she was so often day-dreaming or engrossed in a book, she remembered little things being said about her father's attractions which should have given her an idea long ago that he had other interests in which his family did not share.

'Poor Mama!' she thought to herself. 'It must have been difficult for her to hide her jealousy, if that was what she was feeling.'

Then it struck her that she might find herself in the same situation.

It was all very well for Katalin to talk about her reforming the King, if he was a rake. But supposing she failed?

Supposing she did not reform him and spent her life loving a man who found her a bore and only wished to be with other women rather than herself?

When she thought such things, usually in the darkness of the night, she found herself clenching her hands together and wishing with a fervour that was somehow frightening that she did not have to go to Dórsia.

Most of all, she wished that she did not have to marry King György or any other man whom she had never seen.

'It is not fair that I should be forced into this position just because Germany wants to drag our two countries into her Empire!' she thought.

At the same time, she understood how desperately Lützelstein and Dórsia desired to keep their independence.

The might of the Prussian Army, and the behaviour of the Germans when they conquered the French, had made every Lützelsteiner violently patriotic and acutely aware that their own fate could be as quickly settled by a German invasion.

Zosina remembered how Lützelstein had been appalled when, nearly five years ago, King Ludwig of Bavaria had capitulated without even a struggle against the Prussian invitation to join the Federation.

Because Bismarck was so keen to have the King's approval, he had offered Bavaria an illusion of independence—she was to preserve her own railway and postal systems, to enjoy a limited diplomatic status in her dealings with foreign countries, and to maintain a degree of military, legal, and financial autonomy.

Zosina had so often heard the story of how, to be certain of the King's acceptance, it was even suggested that a Prussian and a Bavarian Monarch might rule either jointly or alternately over the Federation.

This had made the Lützelsteiners hope that things might not be as bad as they had anticipated.

Then disaster had struck.

There was talk of a Prussian becoming Emperor over a united Germany.

When the Prussian representative called to see King Ludwig, he was in bed, suffering from a sudden severe attack of toothache.

He did not feel well enough, the King said, to discuss such important matters, but somehow, in some mysterious manner, he was persuaded to write the all-important letter to his uncle, King Wilhelm I of Prussia, inviting him to assume the title of Emperor.

The fury that this had aroused in Lützelstein, Zosina thought now, must have been echoed in Dórsia.

All she could recall was that her father had stormed about the Palace in a rage that lasted for weeks, while Councillors came and went, all looking grave and disturbed.

This, she thought to herself now, was really the first step in uniting Lützelstein and Dórsia by a marriage between herself and the King.

She wondered if it had been in her father's mind ever since then, and she had the uneasy feeling that perhaps he and the Regent of Dórsia had been waiting until she and the King were old enough to be manipulated into carrying out the plan of alliance.

It was all so unromantic and so business-like in its efficiency that she thought cynically that no amount of pretty, frilly gowns could make her anything but the kind of "Cardboard Queen" who was operated by the hands of power!

'I suppose the King feels the same,' she thought, but even that was no consolation.

She could almost see them both sitting on golden thrones with crowns on their heads, just like a child's toy, while her father with his Councillors, and the Regent with his, turned a key so that they twirled round and round to a tinkling tune, having no will and no impetus of their own.

"I suppose if I were stupid enough," Zosina said to herself, "I would take no interest in politics and would just be content to do as I was told and not want anything different."

She remembered how one of their Governesses had said to her:

"I cannot think, Princess Zosina, why you keep asking so many questions!"

"I wish to learn, *Fraulein,*" Zosina had answered.

"Then confine yourself to subjects which are useful to women," the Governess had said.

"And what are they?" Zosina had enquired.

"Everything that is pretty and charming—flowers, pictures, music, and, of course, men," *Fraulein* had replied with a self-conscious little smile.

Zosina had not been surprised when soon after this the Governess, who was really quite attractive, was seen by her mother flirting with one of the Officers of the Guard.

She had been dismissed, and the Governesses who had followed her were all much older and usually extremely unattractive in their appearance.

Now, Zosina thought, it was not only the Governesses who were ugly but her mother's Ladies-in-Waiting and any other women who were to be seen frequently in the Palace.

Which raised the question that she had asked already as to whether this was intentional because of her father's interest in the fair sex.

"Surely it would be impossible for Mama to be jealous of me?" Zosina asked herself.

But she was not certain!

When she had gone down to the Study to show her father one of the new gowns that had been made for her State Visit, he had looked her over and said approvingly:

"Well, I may have been cursed with four daughters, but nobody could accuse them of being anything but extremely good-looking."

Zosina smiled at him.

"Thank you, Papa. I am glad I please you."

"You will please Dórsia, or I will want to know the reason why," the Arch-Duke replied. "You are a beauty, my girl, and I shall expect them to say so."

The Arch-Duchess had come into the Study at that moment, and when Zosina turned to look at her with a smile, she felt as if she were frozen by the expression on her mother's face.

"That will be enough, Zosina," she said sharply. "There is no need to tire your father, and do not forget that beauty is only skin-deep. It is character which will matter in your future position."

The way she spoke told Zosina too clearly that she thought that was a commodity of which she was lamentably short.

She had left the Study feeling that for the first time she had really begun to understand what was wrong with the personal relationship between her father and mother and of course herself.

Every moment that she was not concerned with choosing, discussing, and fitting clothes, Zosina spent in thinking how much the company of her sisters meant to her.

It had been hopeless to try to explain to them that she felt the sands were running out and that once she had left the School-Room things would never be the same again.

Strangely enough, it was Katalin who realised that she had something on her mind. She came into her room after the others had gone to bed, to sit down and say:

"You are not happy, are you, Zosina?"

"You should not be up so late," Zosina said automatically.

"I want to talk to you."

"What about?"

"You."

"Why should you want to do that?"

"Because I can feel you are worried and I suppose apprehensive. I should feel the same."

Katalin made a little grimace as she went on:

"Helsa and Theone really want to be Queens and they do not care what they have to put up with so long as they can walk about with crowns on their heads. But you are different."

Zosina could not help laughing.

Katalin was such a precocious child, and yet she was far more sensitive than her other sisters and more understanding.

"I shall be all right, dearest," she said, putting out her hand to take Katalin's. "It is just that I shall hate leaving all of you and I am frightened I shall have nobody to laugh with."

"I should feel the same," Katalin replied. "But once the King falls in love with you, everything will be all right."

"Suppose he does not?" Zosina asked.

She felt for the moment that Katalin was the same age as she was and she could talk to her as an equal.

"You will have to try to love him," Katalin said, "or else the story will never have a happy ending, and I could not bear you to be like Mama and Papa."

Zosina looked at her in surprise.

"What do you mean by that?"

"They are not happy, anyone can see that," Katalin replied, "and Nanny told me once, before she left, that Papa loved somebody very much when he was young but he could not marry her because she was a commoner."

"Nanny had no right to tell you anything of the sort!"

"Nanny liked talking about Papa because she had looked after him when he was a baby. She thought the sun rose and set on him because he was so wonderful!"

That, Zosina knew, was true. Nanny had been already elderly when she had stayed on at the Palace to look after the girls when they were born.

Although it was reprehensible, she could not help being curious about her father and she asked:

"Did Nanny say who the lady was that Papa loved?"

"If she did I cannot remember," Katalin answered. "But she was very beautiful, and Papa loved her so much that the people were even frightened he might abdicate."

"How do you know all these things?" Zosina asked.

She could not help being intrigued.

"Nanny used to talk to the other servants who had been here almost as long as she had," Katalin replied, "and because they never liked Mama, they used to say all sorts of things when they forgot I was listening."

Zosina could believe that.

Nanny had been an inveterate gossip. She had not retired until she was nearly eighty, and had died two years later.

"Perhaps King György is like Papa," Katalin was saying, "in love with somebody he cannot marry. In which case, Zosina, you will have to charm him into forgetting her."

"I am sure he is too young to want to marry anybody."

Zosina spoke almost as if she was putting up a defence against such an idea.

"I expect that when they said he was wild, they meant

338

there were lots of women in his life," Katalin said, "but they may be what Nanny used to call 'just a passing fancy.' "

"I cannot imagine what Mama would say if she could hear you talking like this, Katalin."

"The one thing you can be sure of is that she will not hear me," Katalin replied. "I am just warning you that you will have to be prepared for all sorts of strange things to happen when you reach Dórsia."

"It seems strange for you to be warning me," Zosina protested.

"Not really," Katalin replied. "You see, darling Zosina, you are so terribly impractical. You are always far away in your dream-world and you expect real people to be like those you read about and like you are yourself."

"What do you mean by that?" Zosina asked.

"I have looked at the sort of books you read," Katalin said. "They are all about fantasy people who, like you, are kind, good, courageous, and searching for spiritual enlightenment. The people we meet are not like that."

Zosina looked at her young sister in astonishment and asked:

"Why do you say that about me?"

Katalin laughed.

"As a matter of fact, I did not think all that up about you, although it is true. It was what I heard *Frau* Weber say when she was talking to Papa's secretary."

"*Frau* Weber!" Zosina exclaimed.

Now she understood where Katalin got her ideas, because that particular Governess had been very different from all the rest.

A lady who had fallen on hard times, she had come to the Palace with an introduction from the Queen Mother.

She had been an extremely intelligent, brilliant woman, and her husband had been in the Diplomatic Service. When he died, she had been left with very little money and, as Zosina realised later, a broken heart.

The Queen Mother, who had always helped everybody who turned to her in trouble, had thought it would take her mind off what she had lost if she had young people round her.

As her granddaughters were in the process of inevitable change of Governesses, it had been easy for *Frau* Weber to fill the post.

Zosina realised at once how different her intellect and her ability to teach was from that of any Governess they had had before, and she felt herself respond to *Frau* Weber like a flower opening towards the sun.

However, her joy in being with somebody who could tell her so much that she wanted to know, and guide her in a way she had never experienced before, was short-lived.

An old friend of *Frau* Weber's husband came to Lützelstein on a diplomatic visit with the Prime Minister of Belgium and had renewed his acquaintance with the widow of his old friend.

When he left two weeks later, Zosina learnt in consternation that *Frau* Weber was to be married again.

"Then you will leave us!" she cried.

"I am afraid so," *Frau* Weber replied, "but I know I shall be happy with someone I have known for a great number of years."

The Arch-Duchess had been extremely annoyed that as a Governess, *Frau* Weber had made so short a stay in the Palace.

"It is most inconvenient and very bad for the girls to have so many changes," she said tartly to the Arch-Duke.

"We can hardly expect the poor woman to give up a chance of marriage for the doubtful privilege of staying here with us," he replied.

"I find people's selfishness and lack of consideration for others is very prevalent these days," his wife retorted.

It was Zosina who had cried when *Frau* Weber left, and she knew, as soon as she saw the woman who was to take her place, that she would never again find a Governess who understood how important knowledge was or how to impart it.

Thinking of her now, she said reminiscently:

"I wish I could talk to *Frau* Weber about my marriage."

"She is living in Belgium," Katalin said practically.

"Yes, I know it is impossible," Zosina replied, "but it would be pleasant to talk to somebody who understands."

"I understand," Katalin said. "You just have to believe it will all come right, and it will! Thinking what you want is magic. You do not have to rub an Aladdin's lamp or wave a special wand. You just have to focus your brain."

"Now who on earth told you that?" Zosina asked.

"I cannot remember, but I have always known it," Katalin said. "I expect really it is the same as prayer. You want, and want, and want, until suddenly it is there!"

Zosina suddenly put her arms round her small sister and pulled her close.

"Oh, Katalin, I shall miss you so!" she said. "You always make even the most impossible things seem as if one can achieve them."

"One can! This is the whole point!" Katalin said. "Do you remember how Papa would not let us go to the Horse-Show, then suddenly changed his mind? Well, I did that!"

"What do you mean?" Zosina asked.

"I willed, and willed, and willed him, when I knew he was asleep at night or when I knew he was alone downstairs without anybody to disturb him, and quite suddenly he said:

" 'Why should you not go? It will do you good to see some decent horse-flesh!' So we went!"

Zosina laughed.

"Oh, Katalin, you make everything seem so easy! What shall I will for myself?"

341

"A husband who loves you!" Katalin replied without a pause.

Zosina laughed again.

It was in fact Katalin who made everything seem an adventure, even the moment when the Royal Train steamed out of the station, leaving three rather forlorn little faces waving good-bye from the platform.

"Good-bye, dearest Grandmama!" they had all said to the Queen Mother; then they hugged Zosina.

"You will have a lovely time," Theone prophesied.

"I wish I were you," Helsa said enviously.

But Katalin, with her arms round Zosina's neck, had whispered:

"Will, and it will all come right. Will all the time you are there, and I shall be willing too."

"I will do that," Zosina promised. "I do wish you were coming with me."

"I will send my thoughts to you every night," Katalin promised. "They will wing their way over the mountains and you will find them sitting beside you on your pillow."

"I shall be looking for them," Zosina said, "so do not forget."

"I will not," Katalin promised.

She waved from the window not only to her sisters but to the crowds of officials and their wives who were there to bid the Queen Mother farewell on what they all knew was a very important journey.

As the Royal Train was spectacular and, since the Arch-Duke had been confined to the Palace, very rarely used, crowds outside the station had come to watch it pass.

As she thought the people would be pleased, Zosina stood at the window, waving, until her grandmother told her to sit beside her so that they could talk.

"I have hardly had a chance to see you, dearest child," she said, "and I must say you look very lovely in that pretty gown. I am glad you chose pink in which to arrive. It is always, I think, such a happy colour."

"You look lovely in your favourite blue, Grand-mama," Zosina answered.

The Queen Mother looked pleased.

She was still beautiful, although the once-glorious red of her hair was now distinctly grey and her face, which had made a whole generation of artists want to paint her, was lined with age.

But her features and bone structure were still fine, and she had a grace which was ageless and a smile which Zosina thought was irresistible.

"Now, dearest," her grandmother was saying, "I expect your father has told you how important this visit is to our country and to Dórsia."

"Yes, he has told me that, Grandmama," Zosina answered.

There was something in her tone of voice that made her grandmother look at her sharply.

"I have a feeling, dear child, that you are not as happy about the arrangements as you should be."

"I am trying to be happy about them, Grandmama, but I should like to have some say in my marriage, although I dare say it is very stupid of me even to think such a thing."

"It is not stupid," the Queen Mother said, "it is very natural, and I do understand that you are feeling anxious and perhaps a little afraid."

"I knew you would understand, Grandmama."

"I often think it is a very barbaric custom that two people, simply because it is politically expedient, should be married off without being allowed to say yes or no to such an arrangement."

Zosina looked at her grandmother. Then she said:

"Did that happen to you, Grandmama?"

The Queen Mother smiled.

"I was very fortunate, Zosina. Very, very fortunate! Have you never been told what happened where my marriage was concerned?"

"No, Grandmama."

Zosina saw the smile in the Queen Mother's eyes and on her lips as she said:

"Your grandfather, who was then the Crown Prince of Lützelstein, came to stay with my father because it had been suggested that he should marry my elder sister."

Zosina's eyes widened but she did not say anything.

"I was only sixteen at the time," the Queen Mother went on, "and very excited to hear that we were to have a Crown Prince as a very special guest."

She paused for a moment, as if she was recalling what had happened.

"It was naughty of me, but I was determined to see him before anybody else did," she went on after a moment. "So I rode from my father's Palace down the route to a point which I knew the Prince must pass when he entered the country."

"What happened, Grandmama?" Zosina enquired.

"I bypassed the welcoming parade of soldiers lining the streets by approaching the border from a different direction," the Queen Mother answered. "I had learnt that the Royal Party from Lützelstein, who had been travelling for several days, were to stop at a certain Inn just inside my father's Kingdom for refreshment, and of course to tidy up and make themselves look presentable before they entered our Capital in state."

Zosina was entranced by the story; she sat forward on the seat, her eyes on her grandmother's face.

"I often wonder how I had the temerity to do anything so outrageous," the Queen Mother said, "but I waited by some trees until I saw the Prince and his entourage come out of the Inn. They were laughing and talking, and their horses all stood waiting to be mounted."

"Then what did you do?" Zosina asked.

"I rode down to them at a gallop," the Queen Mother said. "I remember I was wearing a green velvet habit with a little tricorn hat, which I thought very becoming, with green feathers in it. I pulled my horse up right in front of the Prince. 'Welcome, Sire!' I said, and he stared at me in astonishment."

"It must have been a surprise!" Zosina cried.

"It was!" the Queen Mother replied, laughing. "Then I made my horse go down on his knees as I had trained him to do, and bow his head, while I sat in the saddle, holding my whip in a theatrical posture like a circus performer!"

Zosina was delighted.

"Oh, Grandmama! They must have thought it fantastic!"

"It was fantastic!" her grandmother said with a smile. "Your grandfather fell in love with me on the spot! He invited me to ride with him back to my father's Palace."

"And did you?"

"No. I was far too sensible to do that. I knew what a lot of trouble I would be in. I rode back alone, except of course for the groom who was waiting for me by the trees."

"And what happened after that?" Zosina wanted to know.

"When he reached the Palace, my sister was waiting for him and he said to my father:

" 'I understand Your Majesty has another daughter.'

" 'Yes,' my father replied, 'but she is too young to take part in our celebrations to commemorate Your Royal Highness's visit.'

" 'Will she not think it rather unfair to be left out of the celebrations?' your grandfather persisted."

"So you were allowed to take part," Zosina said.

"My father and mother were extremely annoyed," the Queen Mother replied, "but at the Crown Prince's insistence I came down to dinner. I remember how exciting it was, and even more exciting when, before the Prince left, he told my father that it was I he wished to marry."

"Oh, Grandmama, it is the most thrilling story I have ever heard!" Zosina exclaimed. "Why have I never been told it before?"

"I think," her grandmother replied, "your mother thought it might put the wrong sort of ideas into your head."

"It is the kind of story Katalin would love," Zosina said. "I do wish I could tell her."

"Katalin knows already," the Queen Mother replied.

As Zosina looked at her in surprise she explained:

"Apparently she heard her Nurse gossipping about what had happened, and she asked me to tell her the true story."

"So you told her."

"Yes, I told her, but I made her promise to keep it a secret. I had to respect your mother's wishes in the matter."

"I am glad you have told me now," Zosina said, "and perhaps . . ."

She had no need to finish the sentence.

"I know what you are thinking—that perhaps King György will fall in love with you the moment he sees you, as happened to me," the Queen Mother said. "Oh, my dear, I hope so!"

"But suppose I do not fall in love with him?"

"Never think negatively," the Queen Mother advised. "Be positive that you will fall in love, and that is what I am quite certain will happen."

She did not wait for Zosina's reply but put her hand against her granddaughter's cheek.

"You are very lovely, my child," she said, "and you will find that a pretty face is a tremendous help in life and in getting your own way."

Zosina laughed.

"Katalin told me I needed will-power to get what I wanted, and now you tell me it is being pretty."

"A combination of the two would be irresistible!" the Queen Mother said firmly. "So you have no need to worry, my dearest."

There was not much chance of further talk with her grandmother, because when they crossed the border from Lützelstein into Dórsia the train stopped at every

station so that the Queen Mother could receive addresses of welcome from the local Mayors.

When they continued their journey there were
crowds to wave and cheer when she and Zosina appeared at the windows of their carriage.

"The people are very pleased to see you, Grandmama," Zosina said.

"And to see you," her grandmother replied.

Zosina looked at her with a startled expression.

"Are you saying they know already that I am to marry
their King?"

"I am quite certain the whole of Dórsia is speculating
as to why you have come and drawing their own conclu-
sions," the Queen Mother replied. "In fact, if you had
listened to that last address, which was an extremely
dull one, the Mayor kept harping on the great possibili-
ties that may come from this 'auspicious visit'!"

The way her grandmother spoke, which was a combination of irony and amusement, made Zosina laugh.

"Oh, Grandmama," she said, "you make everything
so much fun! I love being with you! I only wish that you
rather than I were marrying the King of Dórsia."

"There is a slight discrepancy in age to be considered," the Queen Mother remarked, "and as you well
know, dearest, if it were not the King of Dórsia, it would
be the King of somewhere else, or perhaps someone far
less important."

"That is what Helsa is afraid she will get," Zosina said.

"We will do our best to find her a reigning Monarch,"
the Queen Mother said, "but they are rather few and far
between, unless she has a partiality for one in the German Federation."

"None of us want that," Zosina objected.

"No indeed," the Queen Mother agreed. "Those
small Courts are very stiff and starchy and one cannot
breathe without offending protocol in one way or another. I am sure you girls would all hate it! I must say
that the visits I paid there with your grandfather would
have been absolutely intolerable if we had not been able

347

to laugh, when we were alone, about everything that happened."

"Grandpapa must have been so glad he was able to marry you," Zosina said. "Do you ever wonder what would have happened if you had not been brave enough to go and meet him in such a manner?"

"Yes, I have often thought about it," the Queen Mother replied. "Someone else would have been Queen of Lützelstein, and perhaps, dearest, you would not all be so charming and so vital without my Hungarian blood in you."

"I have often thought that," Zosina agreed, "and I am sure it is why we all ride so well."

"Hungarians are born equestrians," the Queen Mother said. "I often teased your grandfather and said it was not me he fell in love with, but my horse, especially as he could do such splendid tricks."

"And what did Grandpapa reply?" Zosina asked.

The Queen Mother's eyes were very soft before she said:

"You are too young for me to tell you that, but one day you will learn what a man says when he tells you what is in his heart."

There were more stations, more crowds, and the country with its mountains, its valleys, its distant snowy peaks, and its silver rivers had made Zosina know that the Ambassador had been right when he said it was one of the most beautiful places one could imagine.

There were lakes and Castles which made her think of the warring history of the early Dórsians, and then as the countryside became more populous she knew they were coming into the Capital.

She felt her heart begin to beat in a manner which told her she was frightened, and as the Ladies-in-Waiting began to fuss round the Queen Mother, giving her her gloves and her hand-bag and asking if she needed a mirror, Zosina thought almost for the first time of her own appearance.

She knew that her pink gown was exceedingly

becoming, but somehow she suddenly felt gauche and insignificant beside the majesty and elegance of her grandmother.

"I must not make any mistakes," she said frantically to herself.

Then the train began to slow down and she saw that they were moving slowly into position at what appeared to be a crowded platform.

"Are you ready, my dearest?" the Queen Mother asked. "I will alight first, and you follow behind me. The King, and I expect too the Regent, will be waiting directly opposite the carriage door."

Zosina wanted to reply but her voice seemed to be strangled in her throat.

The train came to a standstill.

The Ladies-in-Waiting rose to their feet, and Zosina saw the Royal Party and several other gentlemen accompanying them pass in front of the window and knew they would be waiting at the door of the carriage.

Without hurrying, arranging her skirt to her satisfaction, the Queen Mother stood for a moment, determined, Zosina thought, to give a touch of drama to the moment when they would appear.

Then slowly, smiling her beguiling smile, she walked to the door of the carriage.

Zosina felt as if her feet had suddenly been rooted to the ground, and it was with considerable effort that she made them obey her.

The Queen Mother, assisted by willing hands, stepped down onto the platform; then almost without realising it, Zosina found herself behind her and a second later she heard a man's voice say:

"Welcome to Dórsia, Ma'am! It is a very great pleasure and a privilege to have you here as my guest."

She thought the voice sounded young and rather boyish. Then the next moment the Queen Mother had moved on and Zosina curtseyed deeply as she took the hand that was waiting for her.

349

For a moment it was impossible to focus her eyes or to look up, and she heard the King say again:

"Welcome to Dórsia! It is a very great pleasure and a privilege to have you here as my guest."

Now she raised her eyes.

He was good-looking, and the miniature had been an excellent likeness, but there was something which the artist had omitted and which to Zosina was very noticeable.

It was the expression in the King's eyes, and she knew as she looked at him that he was staring at her with what she thought was resentment and, she was quite sure, dislike.

It was only a quick impression; then almost before it was possible to look at the King he had turned his face towards Count Csáky, who was directly behind her, and Zosina was forced to move on.

As she did so, she heard the Queen Mother say:

"I want you to meet my granddaughter, the Princess Zosina."

Zosina curtseyed again, realising, as she did so, that she was now in front of the Regent, Prince Sandór.

It was difficult for a moment to think of anything but the way the King had looked at her and to know that her heart was thumping and she felt shocked because of what she had seen.

It was then that she felt her hand held in a firm grasp as a voice said:

"I am so very delighted, Your Royal Highness, that you are here, and I hope in all sincerity that we in Dórsia will be able to make your visit a very happy one."

There was no doubt that the voice was as sincere as the words.

As it flashed through Zosina's mind that she had no idea what the Regent looked like, she raised her eyes and saw that he was very different from what she had expected.

She had imagined, since he was uncle to the King and

had been Regent for some years, that he would be old or at least middle-aged.

But there was no doubt that the man who held her hand as she rose from her curtsey was not much over thirty-three or -four.

He was good-looking, she thought, but in a different manner from the King, and there was an easy kind of self-confidence about him which seemed to Zosina to give her the assurance she needed at the moment.

It was as if he calmed and steadied her and the expression she had seen in the King's eyes did not seem so upsetting and frightening.

The Queen Mother was greeting the Prime Minister and various members of the welcoming party and for the moment Zosina made no effort to follow her.

Her hand still rested in the Regent's, and as if he knew what she was feeling he said:

"It is always rather bewildering to meet a whole collection of new people for the first time, but I can promise you, Your Royal Highness, they are all as delighted to see you as I am."

With an effort Zosina found her voice.

"You . . . are very . . . kind," she managed to say.

"That is what we all want to be," the Regent answered. "And now I want to introduce you to the Prime Minister, who is very eager to make your acquaintance."

There were more presentations, then the King was at the Queen Mother's side and they walked together with Zosina, following with the Regent, towards the door of the station.

As they reached it, a band began to play Lützelstein's National Anthem, and it was followed by that of Dórsia.

By now they were standing four in a row, and out of the corner of her eyes Zosina could look at the King.

He was standing at attention and she thought that he was looking bored, and when the National Anthems were over and they stepped into the open carriage that was waiting for them, he yawned before he joined the

351

Queen Mother on the back seat, while Zosina and the Regent sat opposite them.

As the horses started off amidst the cheers of the crowd, Zosina noticed that there were lines under the King's eyes and she told herself he must have been late to bed the night before.

'Katalin is right,' she thought. 'He is a rake, and I expect he thinks if he marries me I shall try to stop him from enjoying himself. That is why he dislikes me already, even before we have met.'

The idea was so depressing that for a moment she forgot to bow to the crowd.

Then she realised that the women, in particular, were staring at her and waving directly at her rather than at her grandmother.

With an effort she forced herself to respond.

As she did so, she realised that the King was looking at her again and there was no doubt that the expression in his eyes had not changed.

If anything, his dislike, if that was what it was, was intensified.

CHAPTER THREE

ZOSINA LOOKED ROUND the Dining-Room and wished her sisters were there.

It was certainly very different from the sombre, rather heavy room in which they dined at her father's Palace.

The light from the gold candelabra glittered on the profusion of gold plate, and the table was decorated with orchids, which also festooned the enormous marble fireplace and a number of the marble pillars.

It was a room, she thought, that might have stepped straight out of a fairy-story. She had also thought the same of the rest of the Palace, or rather of what she had been shown so far.

When she had first seen it standing above the town, white with the sunshine glittering on its windows and what appeared to be a gold dome over the centre of it, she had drawn in her breath.

It flashed through her mind that there might be some compensation in being the wife of a King who disliked her, if she could live in such attractive surroundings.

But even as she raised her eyes to the sun-capped mountains and looked at the green woods that covered the foothills behind the Palace and the flowering trees that lined the roads along which they were proceeding, she knew that the look in the King's eyes had caused a constriction in her heart that she could not control.

Without appearing to do so, she glanced at him, sitting opposite her, and realised that his hair was far darker than it had appeared in the miniature.

His skin was dark, and sun-burnt too, and his eyes, even apart from the expression in them, seemed almost black.

It made her remember that it was a joke amongst her sisters when they were angry to say to one another:

"Do not look at me with black eyes!"

That, she thought, described exactly the way the King looked at her.

Once they had entered the Palace and climbed up red-carpeted steps lined with soldiers in colourful uniforms, she forgot for a moment everything but the beauty of the building.

It was *Frau* Weber who had made Zosina study architecture and recognise the various periods.

Of course they had started with the Greeks, and

Zosina had been so thrilled with the pictures of the Acropolis that she had felt that nothing could ever equal the symmetry and beauty of the Parthenon.

The Romans had delighted her too, and finally when they had reached the outstanding buildings erected by Robert Adam in the Eighteenth Century, she had longed, although she dared not say so, to pull down her father's Palace and erect something that she felt would be appropriate as a Royal Residence.

Here, almost like the answer to a prayer, was a Palace that embodied everything that she had ever admired.

Whoever had chosen the decorations inside had kept them uncluttered, free of fringes and tassels, and employed the vivid colours which Zosina knew always made her feel happy.

"I understand we shall be a very small party," the Queen Mother had said when they retired to their bedrooms to change for dinner. "Tomorrow there is a great Banquet being given in my honour and, although they do not say so, in yours, dearest."

Zosina did not reply and the Queen Mother went on:

"Tonight you will just meet the King's close relatives, although I expect the Prime Minister and his wife will also be there."

She had made it sound quite intimate, but there were actually, Zosina counted, looking round the table, thirty people seated in what she had learnt was the private Dining-Room of the King.

The King had the Queen Mother on his right and Zosina was on his left.

On her left was the Regent and on his other side an extremely attractive, dark-haired woman with flashing eyes, who was talking to him intimately and making him laugh.

'I must not sit here dumb and saying nothing,' Zosina thought to herself, remembering how often her father had said:

"Nothing is more boring than taking into dinner a woman who is more concerned with her food than with

oneself. It does not much matter what you say, but for
Heaven's sake talk!"

Feeling a little shy because the King had not addressed a word to her since they had sat down, Zosina
turned to him and said:

"I think, Sire, your Palace must be the most beautiful
one in the whole of Europe!"

There was a little pause before the King looked at
her, and she thought for one uncomfortable moment
that he intended to ignore her remark.

Then he replied:

"You must be easy to please. I intend to make a great
many alterations and certainly have it redecorated!"

"Oh no!" Zosina exclaimed involuntarily, thinking
how lovely it was already.

Even as she spoke, she knew she had made a mistake,
and once again the King was glaring at her with black
eyes.

"If you think anybody is going to interfere with me
once I am allowed to do what I wish," he said harshly,
"you are very much mistaken."

He spoke so aggressively that Zosina gave a little cry
before she said:

"Oh . . . please . . . I was not . . . meaning what
you think I . . . meant. I only . . . thought the Palace
was so . . . beautiful in every way, I cannot . . . imagine how it could be improved!"

Because she was embarrassed, her words seemed to
tumble over one another as she attempted to explain
herself.

The King merely remarked unpleasantly:

"You must be very easily pleased!"

He then turned deliberately to speak to the Queen
Mother.

Zosina drew in her breath.

This was even worse than she had feared, and she
told herself that she might have been tactless but she
had not meant to upset him.

Then the Regent said to her:

355

"I heard you admiring the Palace. I am so glad that you find it attractive."

"I think it is . . . lovely."

"That is what I think too."

Because he seemed kind and understanding, she said in a low voice that only he could hear:

"I did not . . . mean to . . . upset His Majesty, and I was . . . trying to explain that I could not think how, as it looks so beautiful, it could be . . . improved."

The Regent smiled.

"We obviously think the same way," he said, in a tone which she knew was meant to be soothing.

Because she thought the subject must embarrass him if she continued with it, with an effort Zosina said:

"Count Csáky told me how beautiful Dórsia was, but I think it would be difficult even for the most accomplished poet to describe adequately what I have seen so far."

"You are fond of poetry?"

"Yes, very, but I know that some people find it . . . dull."

As she spoke, she was certain that the King would be one of them.

"I think poetry is rather like music," the Regent said quietly. "It can often express our feelings or our thoughts as ordinary words would be unable to do."

"It is strange you should think that," Zosina said with a sudden warmth in her voice. "Sometimes when I look at anything very beautiful I know that it would be impossible to describe it in prose and, as you say, only music or poetry could . . . say what it . . . makes me . . . feel."

She thought, as she spoke, that there was an expression of surprise in the Regent's eyes, but she was not sure.

Then, because she thought he would understand, she asked:

"May I ask you . . . something?"

"Of course," he replied.

"While I am here, could somebody tell me about Dórsia and its people?"

She paused a moment, then said quickly:

"I do not mean just its history, I mean the real human
truths which one cannot . . . find in . . . books."

He did not speak, and, thinking he had not understood, she went on:

"It is like not being told how beautiful the Palace is
before I came, or that the flowers are so brilliant and the
people in the streets so colourful. I am frightened that if
I am not looking out for what I should see, I might miss
something important."

The Regent still did not reply, and after a second she
said:

"I . . . I thought you would . . . understand . . .
what I am trying to say."

"I do understand," he answered. "I understand very
well. It is just that such a request has never been made
to me before."

"Perhaps you . . . think it is the . . . wrong sort of
. . . curiosity," Zosina murmured.

"It would be impossible for me to think that," the
Regent replied, "because it is exactly what you should
want to know."

She had a strange feeling that he was going to add:
"But I had not expected you to do so," then deliberately
prevented himself from saying it.

"What I will do while you are here," the Regent continued before she could answer, "is to try and give you
what I believe is called a 'thumb-nail sketch' of the people you will meet and the places you will see."

He gave a little laugh before he added:

"I may not be as eloquent as some of our historical
scholars or as indiscreet as the biographers of our important citizens, but I will certainly be shorter and, I
hope, more informative."

"If you would . . . really do that," Zosina said, "I
should be very . . . grateful. But I do not wish to be a
. . . nuisance."

"You could never be that!" the Regent replied with a smile. "Now let me tell you a little about the people who are here at this table, and perhaps it would be politic to start with the Prime Minister."

He looked past Zosina down the table as he spoke, and she had a feeling that he deliberately missed out the King, who was sitting next to her.

He gave her, as he had suggested, a "thumb-nail sketch" of the Prime Minister, which not only made her laugh but at the same time made her aware of him as a man and also as a personality.

The Regent went on to one of the King's aunts, and he described her in a few words which made Zosina feel as if she were a character in a novel.

He spoke of two more people, then as he paused she said eagerly:

"Thank you, thank you, but do go on! You make everybody of whom you have spoken seem so real and also exciting to get to know. Please do not stop!"

"I am only too willing to go on," the Regent replied. "At the same time . . ."

As he spoke, he glanced towards the King and Zosina realised that she had committed a social error in talking to him for so long and not turning to the man on her other side, as she had been taught to do when at luncheon- and dinner-parties.

She was just about to say: "The King does not want to talk to me," when it struck her that the Regent perhaps wanted to talk to the very attractive lady on his left.

"I am . . . sorry," she said humbly. "I am being . . . selfish."

As she spoke, she turned her face towards the King, to find that he was sitting staring at the base of the candelabrum in front of him as if he had never seen it before.

It did not seem as if he wished to speak to her, but Zosina knew that she must make an effort, and after a moment she said in a nervous little voice:

"I was wondering . . . Your Majesty, what we will be

. . . doing tomorrow. I know there is to be a . . . Banquet in the . . . evening."

"Then you know more than I do!" the King replied disagreeably. "You do not suppose I have had anything to do with arranging all this ballyhoo, do you?"

Zosina ignored his rudeness and said:

"I suppose State Visits and that . . . sort of thing must seem very . . . commonplace to you, Sire, but as I have never been on one before, I find it very exciting!"

"Exciting!" the King exclaimed. "I can tell you it is a deadly bore from start to finish. The only event slightly amusing might be the Masked Ball."

There was just a touch of interest in his voice, and Zosina said quickly:

"A Masked Ball sounds thrilling. Does it take place here in the Palace?"

"Good God, no!" the King replied. "It is for the people, not for us. We are supposed to sit on our gilded thrones, taking no part in it."

"How disappointing," Zosina said. "I have never been to a Masked Ball but I have heard of them, and it must be fun not to know whether you are dancing with a Count or a Candlestick-Maker, a King or a Chimney-Sweep!"

As she spoke, she hoped that what she said would make him laugh, but he turned to look at her with what she thought was a different expression from the one he had used before.

"Are you suggesting that I should go to the Ball?" he enquired.

"I may be wrong, Sire, but I have a . . . feeling you have been to . . . one already," Zosina replied.

He stared at her, not quite certain how to take what she had said. Then he said:

"You are trying to trap me. I am not going to answer that question."

"Of course I am not trying to trap you," Zosina answered. "If I were King I would certainly go to a Masked Ball, if I had the chance."

He did not reply, and after a moment she said:

"Now that I think of it, in history Kings have always gone about their countries in disguise. François I, for instance, used to go out every night, wandering round the town to mix with . . . his subjects."

She was going to say: "To mix with beautiful women," which was what she remembered reading in a somewhat racy French biography.

Then she thought that to say such a thing would not only be indiscreet but perhaps somewhat improper.

"Who was François I?" the King asked.

"He was the King of France, Sire, in 1515."

"I have never heard of him, but he obviously had the right ideas."

"Are you interested in history?"

"No, I am not!" the King replied. "I found it extremely dull and boring, but then I was never told anything interesting about the Kings, and certainly not the sort of thing you have just mentioned."

"One is not taught personal details about Royalty," Zosina replied. "One has to find it out in books."

"I have not time to read," the King said firmly.

They lapsed into silence and Zosina thought he was certainly very difficult. Perhaps the only person who could have coped with him would have been Katalin.

She would chatter on regardless of whether anybody answered her and always seemed able to find a new subject.

With almost a sigh of relief she saw the Queen Mother turn from the Prime Minister to speak to the King.

Almost as if she was unable to prevent herself, Zosina turned back to the Regent.

"Do tell me about the gentleman with the huge moustache," she pleaded.

She saw the Regent's eyes twinkling as he began the life-story of the gentleman who she learnt was one of the most redoubtable Generals in the Dórsian Army.

Afterwards, when the ladies withdrew to one of the exquisite Salons, Zosina found herself sitting next to one of the King's aunts, who she soon found was an irrepressible gossip.

The Princess chatted away about other members of the family, relating some of the most intimate details of their lives which Zosina was sure the Regent would not have told her.

"The woman with the dyed red hair is my cousin Lillie," she said. "She was very pretty ten years ago but now she is married to a terrible bore. What is more, he is deaf and everything has to be repeated three times. It also makes him shout until in his presence I feel I am permanently standing in a barrack square!"

Zosina laughed, then the Princess said in a low voice:

"And what, dear child, do you think of my nephew György?"

It was a question which Zosina was not expecting, and for a moment she found it difficult to find words in which to reply.

Then because she knew that the Princess was waiting she said:

"I did not . . . expect His Majesty to be so . . . dark-haired."

The Princess raised her eye-brows.

"Has no-one told you his mother was Albanian?"

"No," Zosina answered.

"Oh, dear, I see you have a lot to learn," the Princess said. "My brother, the late King, who was the eldest of eight children, had unfortunately four daughters by his first marriage."

"Like Papa!" Zosina remarked.

"Exactly!" the Princess replied. "And very disagreeable it made him."

Zosina was about to say again: "Just like Papa!" but thought it would be indiscreet.

"When the Queen died," the Princess went on, "as you can imagine, it annoyed the Prime Minister and the Councillors when my brother announced that he intended to marry an Albanian Princess of whom none of us had ever heard."

"It must have been a surprise!" Zosina murmured.

"It certainly was, especially as we had always thought the Albanians to be a strange people, many of them being nothing but gypsies!"

There was so much disparagement in the Princess's voice that Zosina looked at her in surprise.

"However, my brother the King achieved what he had thought was an impossibility, when his second Queen produced a son and heir."

"He must have been very pleased," Zosina said.

As she spoke, she thought how thrilled her father would be if only he had a son to inherit the throne.

"You can understand," the Princess continued, "that György has naturally been very spoilt all his life. My brother doted on him until the day of his death, and his mother, in my opinion, spoilt him abominably."

The fact that the King was half-Albanian, Zosina thought, accounted for his dark hair and complexion, and it might also be the reason for his wildness.

As if the Princess followed her thoughts, she said:

"You have to be very understanding, dear, and gain György's confidence. I believe, as does dear Sándor, that if he will settle down and assume his responsibilities he will make a good King."

At the mention of the Regent, Zosina said what had surprised her since she first arrived:

"I expected His Royal Highness to be much . . . older."

The Princess smiled.

"It does seem strange, as he is György's uncle. But Sándor was the youngest of my father's large family of eight children, and my only other brother, and of course until György arrived we always expected he would be the next King of Dórsia."

Zosina wanted to ask if he had been very disappointed at finding himself no longer the heir, but then she thought it would be a tactless question.

"All I can say," the Princess said, "is that you are not

only very lovely, my dear, but exactly the sort of person we hoped you would be."

"Thank . . . you," Zosina replied, suddenly feeling shy.

Then before it was possible to say any more, the gentlemen came into the room.

The following day there were deputations of people calling on the Queen Mother from first thing in the morning until they had to leave the Palace for the Civic Luncheon that was being given for her by the Mayor and the Corporation of the City.

Once again they drove behind six white horses in the open carriage, and the crowds lining the roads seemed more enthusiastic than they had on the day of their arrival.

The Queen Mother had sent a message to Zosina by one of her Ladies-in-Waiting early in the morning to say that she was wearing pale mauve.

She suggested that Zosina should wear a white gown trimmed with lace and a bonnet wreathed with white roses.

"I look very bridal," Zosina remarked as she joined the Queen Mother in her bedroom before they proceeded downstairs.

"That is what you will soon be," her grandmother replied.

Her words sent a shiver through Zosina, who had almost forgotten, in the excitement of all that had been happening, that the disagreeable and argumentative King was to be her future husband.

Thinking over his behaviour last night, after she had gone to bed, she had told herself that he was like a rather rude school-boy and it was difficult to think of him as a man.

She had always thought her husband would be somebody who would protect her and on whom she could rely, whose advice she would seek and who would direct her life in the way it should go.

She could not imagine finding any of these qualities

in the King, and she thought that if she had to spend a lifetime trying to talk to him, that in itself was a terrifying prospect, especially if he was going to be as disagreeable as he had been last night.

However, because she wanted to do what was required of her and behave in an exemplary manner, she tried to excuse him on the grounds that they were strangers.

But she could not escape from the conviction that he disliked the idea of being married and more especially disliked the bride who had been chosen for him.

In which case, she thought, surely it would be better if he waited until he was older.

Then she remembered that the whole reason she was here was that Lützelstein and Dórsia must be united if they were to oppose the growing power of Germany.

"I wonder if anyone has explained that to him?" she asked herself; then was certain that the Regent would have done so.

'Prince Sándor is clever,' she thought, 'clever and well read. At least he will be there for me to talk to.'

Then she wondered what happened when a Regent relinquished his post.

Did he retire into obscurity, or was another position found for him in the Government?

It was a question to which she did not know the answer, and she had a feeling it would be difficult to know who to ask.

The King looked sulky and bored all the way to the Guildhall where they were to be entertained.

He made no effort to speak to the Queen Mother or to anyone else, and Zosina, waving to the crowds who were obviously excited by her appearance, told herself that the only thing to do was to ignore him.

'He puts a damper on everything!' she thought. 'I cannot think, as this is his own country, why he does not enjoy seeing his people so pleased and excited.'

To her relief, when she reached the Guildhall she found that she was not sitting beside the King but had the Prime Minister on her left and the Chancellor of the Exchequer on her right.

She found that the thumb-nail sketches which the Regent had given her the night before were very helpful, although they seemed surprised that she should know how many children they had and, in the Prime Minister's case, that his wife was French.

They were soon talking animatedly and answering Zosina's questions about Dórsia in a manner which told her that they were extremely gratified by her interest.

"Thank you very, very much!" she exclaimed as she said good-bye to the Prime Minister. "It has been the most thrilling luncheon I have ever attended and I shall never forget it."

"You have made it a memorable occasion for me, Your Royal Highness," the Prime Minister replied, "and I can only assure you that you will find Dórsian hospitality is as boundless as our affection."

He spoke with an obvious pride in his voice, and as Zosina smiled at him he told himself that she was the most beautiful girl he had ever seen in his life.

When he said good-bye to the Regent, he added:

"I can only thank you as well as congratulate you, Sire, on your choice. You were far wiser than I was. I am therefore prepared, in the circumstances, never again to doubt your judgement, especially when it concerns women!"

The Regent's eyes twinkled.

"Shall I say I am thankful not to have made a fundamental mistake in this particular instance?"

"That, I can now say categorically, is an impossibility," the Prime Minister replied.

The Regent was still smiling as he hurried down the steps to take his place in the Royal Carriage.

When they got back to the Palace the Queen Mother announced that she was going to her private apartments.

"I hope, Gyórgy, you will join me," she said to the King. "We have had no chance to talk intimately with each other since I arrived, so this is a welcome opportunity."

Zosina thought the King looked as if it was not a very welcome one to him, but it was obvious that there was nothing he could do but agree.

Having taken off her bonnet, Zosina went to the Queen Mother's Sitting-Room to find her grandmother waiting for her, and seated beside her, looking very sulky, was the King.

Zosina curtseyed and then the Queen Mother said:

"I am going to do something very unconventional, but I feel, as no-one will know about it except ourselves, we can forget protocol for a moment. I want you two young people to get to know each other and so I am going to leave you alone, without being watched by curious eyes and listened to by inquisitive ears."

She gave the King and Zosina her famous smile before, with a quickness of movement which belied her years, she went from the Sitting-Room, closing the door behind her.

Zosina, realising that the King had said nothing, looked at him nervously.

He rose and walked across the room to stand at the window looking out, and there was an awkward silence until she said:

"Grandmama . . . always tries to make things as . . . easy as possible."

"Easy!" the King replied, his voice rising on the word. "I see nothing easy about your being here or this damned marriage!"

Zosina started when he swore, because although she knew it was a swear-word she had in fact never heard a man use it in her presence.

"Do you . . . hate the idea so . . . much?" she asked falteringly after a moment.

"Hate it? Of course I hate it!" the King snapped. "I have no wish to be married. All I want is to be free—free of being ordered about, free of being told what to do from morning until night."

"I can . . . understand your . . . feeling like that," Zosina said, "but you know why our marriage has been . . . arranged?"

"I know why they *say* it has been arranged," the King answered, "but the real truth is that Uncle Sándor wants someone to take his place, someone who will manipulate me as he has always done."

"I am sure that is not true," Zosina cried, "and if it were, they would not have chosen me!"

"That is *why* they have chosen you," the King said. "It is well known that your mother bosses your father and that Lützelstein has a petticoat Government."

"That is a lie!" Zosina protested. "Whoever told you that has deceived Your Majesty with a lot of rubbish!"

The King laughed and it was not a pleasant sound.

"It is a fact, whether you know it or not," he said, "and if you think you are going to rule my country, I promise that you will be disappointed!"

"I have no wish to rule anything or anybody!" Zosina said.

She saw that the King did not believe her, and after a moment she said more quickly:

"I did not wish to . . . get married either . . . I was merely . . . told that I had to do so."

"Do you expect me to believe that?" the King asked. "Every woman wants a crown on her head."

"Then I am the exception," Zosina said. "I want to . . . love the man I marry."

The King laughed jeeringly.

"Love is a cheap commodity . . ." he said. "There is plenty of it about, but one cannot marry it. Oh no! That is arranged by one's Councillors, or in my case by my uncle."

He spoke in a manner which told Zosina that he hated the Regent.

She had been standing while they were talking, but now she sat down in a chair as if her legs would not support her.

"What . . . can we . . . do?" she asked helplessly.

"Do?" the King questioned. "What we are told to do, of course! Uncle Sándor has it all neatly tied up, while the Prime Minister and all those idiotic creatures who kow-tow to him behave as if I were a performing animal in a circus: 'Jump through a hoop, Your Majesty!' 'Turn a somersault, Your Majesty!' 'Fly on the trapeze, Your Majesty!' You do not suppose I have any chance of refusing them?"

Zosina clasped her fingers together.

"I know it seems . . . unfair . . . and perhaps cruel," she said in a small voice, "but the menace of the . . . German Empire is real . . . very real!"

"That is what they tell you," the King answered. "Personally, I do not care a damn if the Germans do incorporate us in their Empire. We would very likely be better off than we are now."

"No! No!" Zosina cried. "How can you say such a thing? We have to keep our independence. How could we be ruled by a Prussian Emperor?"

"He would leave me on my throne."

"For as long as you did what you were told," Zosina said. "If you think you are badly off now, it is nothing to the position you would find yourself in under the Germans."

"Now you are talking like Uncle Sándor," he said with a sneer. "I think it is all a lot of 'bogey-bogey' thought up by politicians who have nothing better to do!"

"Oh, it is real . . . it is true," Zosina insisted. "I read the newspapers and I have also heard what my father says about the menace of the German might. We cannot let Lützelstein and Dórsia come under Prussian rule!"

"All I want," the King replied, "is to enjoy myself and to have a good time. If I tried to interfere in politics they would soon stop me, so what is the point of my wasting my time trying to understand them?"

Zosina gave a little sigh.

The King, she thought, was more than ever like a truculent school-boy, and she had the feeling he was so

angry that whatever she said, he would never understand the seriousness of the situation or believe that she
was not trying to manipulate him in some manner.

She rose to walk across the room and stand not beside
him but at the next window, looking out as he was.

The sunshine made the snow on the peaks of the
mountains a dazzling white against the blue of the sky,
and she thought she could see the cascades of water
running down the sides of the hills.

In the distance, the river which passed through the
city flowed like a silver streak towards the horizon.

"Dórsia is so lovely," she said, "and it is yours. It belongs to you!"

The King laughed loudly.

"That is what you think, but the person who rules it is
Uncle Sándor, and everyone from the Prime Minister to
the lowest crossing-sweeper knows it."

His voice had a jeering note in it as he went on:

"Have you not been told by now that I am an unfor-
tunate 'after-thought'? The son of an Albanian gypsy
who ought never to have got into Dórsia in the first
place?"

"You are the King," Zosina replied, "and surely it is
up to you to gain the love and respect of your people.
When you have done that—and kept your country free
—you may justifiably feel very proud of yourself."

The King laughed again, and this time there was a
note of genuine amusement in his voice.

"Now you are really starting in the way you mean to
go on," he said. " 'You must be a good King!' 'Be kind to
your people!' 'They must learn to love you!' 'You must
do the right thing!' "

He threw up his hands in a gesture that was somehow
derisive.

"Uncle Sándor has done it again!" he said jeeringly.
"He has picked the right 'petticoat' to rule Dórsia . . .
and who could have learnt how to do it better than a
Princess who comes from Lützelstein?"

Zosina felt her temper rising.

"I think you are being needlessly insulting!" she said. "If I could do what I wish to do, I would go back to Lützelstein, stay with my father, and tell him I will not marry you when everything I say or do is suspect!"

"So you have got a temper!" the King said. "Well, that is better than all that mealy-mouthed preaching anyway."

Zosina suddenly realised that she was being almost as rude and angry as he was.

"I am . . . sorry," she said with genuine humility. "I do not wish to preach . . . and I promise you I do not wish to coerce you into doing anything you do not want to do."

"But you will, all the same," the King said, "and you will do it for my own good."

Again his voice was jeering before he went on:

"That is what Uncle Sándor always says: 'I am only telling you this for your own good!' If you want the truth, I am sick to death of my uncle and anyone else for that matter! I want to be left alone! I want to enjoy myself, have fun with my own friends, make love to the women I choose—and let me tell you once and for all—you are not my type!"

Zosina was tempted to snap back that he was not her type either, but she knew it would sound very childish.

Instead, she just stood staring blindly out the window, feeling that this could not be happening. In fact, the whole conversation was like something in a nightmare.

"I will tell you one more thing," the King said loudly. "If we have to marry, and I cannot see how I can get out of it, the moment I am properly a King and can send Uncle Sándor packing, I shall go my way, and you can go yours!"

As he spoke he walked across the Sitting-Room and left, slamming the door behind him.

Zosina put her hands up to her face, feeling that this could not be true, and if it was, then perhaps it was all her fault.

"How did I manage to upset him? Why did I make him angry?" she asked herself.

She could feel her hands trembling against her cheeks and knew that her whole body was trembling too.

She found it difficult to think or really to believe that the King had been so rude.

Never in her life had a man, with the exception of her father, spoken to her in a horrible jeering voice which, like a squeaking saw, seemed to set her nerves on edge.

'How can I marry anybody like that?' she thought, and felt a sudden panic sweep over her.

It was then that the door opened and a servant announced:

"His Royal Highness the Prince Regent, Your Majesty!"

Zosina put out her hand to hold on to the window-ledge.

She could not turn round. She could not face the Regent, and yet she knew that, having entered the room, he must be staring at her back, in surprise.

Then she heard the door shut and after a moment his voice, quiet and calm, as he said:

"What has happened? Why are you alone? I saw the King coming away from here."

Zosina tried to find her voice and failed. Then she was aware that he had crossed the room.

"You are upset," he said quietly. "I am very sorry if the King has done anything to disturb you."

He sounded so kind that Zosina felt the tears come into her eyes.

Then as if she could not prevent the words, she heard herself say:

"He hates me! He is very . . . angry because you . . . brought me . . . h-here!"

She felt that what she had said surprised the Regent.

"I cannot believe the King said that he hates you," he replied. "What did he actually say?"

"I . . . I c-cannot repeat it," Zosina said quickly, "but he resents having . . . to . . . to marry, and he thinks that you chose me because . . . I would . . . boss him as he said . . . M-Mama does Papa."

The words came out without her really meaning to say them, and as she spoke a tear from each eye ran down her cheeks.

She hoped the Regent would not notice, and she went on staring blindly ahead at the mountains, which now she could not see.

The Regent came nearer still and now he was standing at her side, looking at her, and she felt for some strange reason that she could not explain that she must not move; must not even breathe in case he learnt too much.

"I am sorry," he said at length in his deep voice. "Desperately sorry that this should have happened, and to you of all people."

"Please . . . can I go . . . home? Perhaps you could . . . find somebody else?"

She was afraid as she spoke the last words, and yet she said them.

"You know that is impossible," the Regent answered. "Although it seems a hard thing to say, this marriage, because it concerns our two countries, is more important than an individual's likes or dislikes."

"The . . . King does not seem to be . . . aware of that," Zosina murmured.

"He must understand it by now," the Regent said, and there was a sharp note in his voice. "The whole situation has been explained to him over and over again."

"He wants to be . . . free."

"Which is something he certainly would not be under the Emperor Wilhelm."

"That is . . . what I told him . . . but he would not listen."

The Regent sighed.

"I think perhaps he is just being difficult."

"Surely you could have . . . allowed him to . . . find his own wife?" Zosina questioned. "Perhaps he would have . . . fallen in love with . . . one of my sisters, if he had come to . . . Lützelstein."

The Regent did not reply and after a moment she turned to look at him and their eyes met.

The tears were still on her cheeks, but now she could see more clearly and there was an expression in his eyes that she did not understand.

"I am . . . sorry," she said after a moment, "but I am a . . . failure. You can see . . . I am a . . . failure."

"You are nothing of the sort," the Regent replied. "It is all my fault, but even now that I have met you, I am not certain I could have done anything different."

He saw that Zosina did not understand and after a moment he said:

"I did not expect you to be as you are."

"Why am I . . . wrong?"

There was something almost pathetic in the question, and the Regent said hastily:

"But you are not wrong! You are right, absolutely right in every way. It is just that this situation is something in which you should never have been involved. I cannot understand why I did not realise it—but then, I had never seen you!"

"What did you not . . . realise?" Zosina asked.

"That you would be sensitive, vulnerable, and far too intelligent."

Zosina's eyes widened.

"H-how do you . . . know I am . . . that?"

"You forget, we have talked together," the Regent replied.

"Then if you . . . think I am all . . . those things . . . why am I . . . wrong?"

For a moment she thought he would not answer. Then he said almost abruptly:

"I thought you would be like your mother!"

Zosina drew in her breath.

"The King said that . . . everybody knows that . . .

Mama rules Lützelstein and it is a . . . petticoat Government."

The Regent's lips tightened.

"He had no right to say such a thing."

"But it is . . . what you . . . think?"

"I have not said so."

"Is it true? I had no idea. Papa always seems so overpowering to me and my sisters that I imagined he overwhelmed . . . everybody else in Lützelstein."

Even as she spoke, it struck Zosina that perhaps the reason why her father was so disagreeable and overbearing to her and her sisters was that outside the Palace his wife forced him into making the decisions she wanted.

But even now she could hardly believe that the King had not talked nonsense.

Then she asked herself helplessly how, sitting in the School-Room, could she possibly have known what went on in the Council Chambers and what decisions her father made on the many problems that were brought to the Palace day after day by members of the Government.

For the first time it struck her that her mother always seemed to have an opinion on everything.

Because she and her sisters were frightened of her and of their father, they seldom if ever voiced an opinion of their own in the presence of their parents.

She thought now that that was what the Regent wanted to happen in Dórsia and the King was right.

He had chosen her because he thought she would be strong and determined and would force the King into doing things he did not want to do and against which he was obviously rebellious.

"I cannot do . . . anything like . . . that," she said in a whisper.

She felt, as she spoke, that the Regent had been following her thoughts and understood exactly what she was saying.

"I know that now," he said. "But it is too late."

"Why?"

"Because the Prime Minister and the Cabinet have agreed that you should marry the King. The Councillors who have met you already are simply delighted with you. They see you as somebody very beautiful, very compassionate, someone whom the country will love, which is very important."

"What . . . about the . . . King?"

It was difficult to say the words, and yet they were said.

"I will make the King behave himself," the Regent replied, and his voice was hard.

"No, no . . . please!" Zosina cried. "Do not antagonise him! He hates me . . . he resents me. If he learns I have complained to you, it will only make things . . . worse."

"Then what can I do?"

She thought that he felt as helpless as she did.

"It would be . . . better to do . . . nothing," she said. "I will try . . . really try . . . to make him . . . trust me . . . and then perhaps things will be . . . different."

As she spoke, she thought that the King was almost like a wild animal she had to tame. The first thing she must do was to prevent him from shying away at her approach, suspecting that she was trying to capture and imprison him.

Then she remembered that the King was not an animal but a man and she was very ignorant about men.

Every instinct in her body shrank from having anything to do with one who swore and jeered at her. The things the King had said made her wince even to remember them.

Her face must have been very expressive, for the Regent said:

"Forgive me, please forgive me for creating this tangle. I see now only too clearly what I have done, but I do not know how to undo it."

There was a note of humility in his voice and at the

same time a sympathy and compassion that had not
been there before.

"There is . . . nothing you can do," Zosina said. "I
am aware that it is . . . up to me . . . but please help
me and . . . if you can . . . give me courage . . . because I am . . . afraid."

Without really realising what she was doing, as she
spoke she put out her hand towards him, and he took it
in both of his.

"I do not believe that any woman could be more
brave or more wonderful!" he said quietly.

CHAPTER FOUR

❧❦❧

*F*OR WHAT SEEMED to Zosina a long time she looked into
the Regent's eyes. Then in a voice which seemed to her
to come from a long way away she whispered:

"Thank . . . you."

As she spoke, the door opened and the Queen
Mother came back into the Sitting-Room.

She looked in surprise at the Regent as he released
Zosina's hand and asked:

"Where is György? I thought he was here."

"He had an audience which he had forgotten,
Ma'am," the Regent replied.

"How like György!" the Queen Mother remarked.
"But I think that since I last saw him he is much improved. I congratulate you, Sándor. I know how difficult it has been."

As she finished speaking she glanced at Zosina in a way that made her sure that her grandmother had forgotten she was in the room.

The Queen Mother then paused and said in a different tone:

"I am sure, dear child, it would be a good idea if you rested before this evening. I want you to look your very best at the State Banquet."

"I will go and lie down, Grandmama."

Zosina curtseyed and kissed her grandmother's cheek. Then she dropped a curtsey to the Regent, feeling, as she did so, that it was impossible to look at him.

In her bedroom she found a programme of future events left on a *secretaire* and knew that it had been put there by one of the Aides-de-Camp who had been looking after them since they arrived.

It contained, besides the events at which they were to be present, a list of the important people they would meet and their positions.

Zosina picked it up absent-mindedly because her thoughts were elsewhere.

When she glanced down to see at what time she had to be ready tonight for the State Banquet, she read:

11:30 A.M. *H.M. Queen Szófia and H.R.H. Princess Zosina to inspect the Convent of the Sacred Heart.*

2:30 P.M. *H.M. Queen Szófia to open the new Botanical Gardens.*

7:00 P.M. *H.M. The King, H.M. Queen Szófia, H.R.H. Princess Zosina, H.R.H. The Prince Regent, will dine with the Members of the Order of St. Miklos.*

These, she knew, were all noblemen of Dórsia. Then an entry for the next and last day made her draw in her breath:

11:00 A.M. *Reception by the Prime Minister in the House of Parliament, where all the Members will be assembled. On this occasion the King's impending marriage will be announced.*

Zosina put down the programme and walked across her bedroom to sit on the stool in front of the dressing-table.

For a moment she saw her reflection not with her hair elegantly and fashionably arranged but with a glittering crown on her head.

This was why she had come to Dórsia; this would be her future.

She gave a little cry and put her hands up to her eyes.

How could she endure it—not being Queen of such a charming and friendly people, but being the King's wife?

She felt as if it were a trap from which there was no escape; her thoughts were going round and round like a squirrel in a cage which knew there was no way out, and she felt as if she would go on turning and turning until she died.

Then, almost as if he was again standing beside her, she could hear the Regent say:

"I do not believe that any woman could be more brave or more wonderful!"

"That is what I have to be," she told herself, and quickly looked away from the mirror in case she should see the crown again.

❦❦❦

The State Banquet was certainly impressive.

In the Banqueting-Hall of the Palace over three hundred guests sat down to a very elaborate dinner with eight courses and appropriate wines for each one.

It would be impossible, Zosina thought, for anyone to look more magnificent or more regal than her grandmother.

Wearing some of the Lützelstein Crown Jewels which she had brought with her especially for the occasion, her gown glittering with diamanté, and with five ropes of huge diamonds round her neck, she looked like every woman's ideal of a Queen.

Zosina felt that in contrast she must pale into insignificance.

Her gown, instead of being white, which she knew was being kept for her wedding, was the second most elaborate one in her trousseau.

Of very pale blue, the colour of the morning sky, it had a tulle train which frothed out behind her like the waves of the sea, and tulle encircled her shoulders, accentuating the whiteness of her skin and making her eyes seem unnaturally large in her small face.

As a concession to her impending marriage, the Grand-Duchess had lent her one of the small tiaras which had always been considered too unimportant for her to wear herself.

It was in fact a wreath of flowers fashioned in diamonds and turquoises, and as it glittered and shimmered under the huge crystal chandeliers it made Zosina, although she was not aware of it, look like the Goddess of Spring.

There was a necklace of diamonds and turquoises to match, and bracelets for her wrists.

When she was dressed she wished that her sisters could see her, especially Katalin.

Katalin had had a great many amusing things to say about her gowns before she left Lützelstein.

"You will look exactly like the Prima Donna in an Opera!" she had exclaimed. "Except, of course, you have not a large enough bosom to be a singer! But doubtless the King will be bowled over by your beauty the moment he sees you."

'Well, that at least is something that will not happen!' Zosina thought now.

She hoped, however, that the Regent would think she was appropriately dressed for the part she had to play, and perhaps if she tried very hard she could at least charm the King into being polite to her.

In a way, she could understand how he resented being under the authority of his uncle. After all, he was the King, and to have someone else, however pleasant, ruling for him must be frustrating.

She thought of how her mother had always insisted that they should take no part in any of the celebrations that took place in Lützelstein, except those which involved their going to a special Church Service or standing on a balcony to watch a procession pass beneath them.

Now that the idea that her mother was bossy had been put into her head, Zosina began to remember dozens of occasions when her mother had overruled her father's wishes or forbidden them some treat which he would have given them only too willingly.

"A petticoat Government!" she whispered to herself, and wondered how she could make the King understand that she had no wish to boss anyone, least of all him.

'I want to get to know the people,' she thought, 'and, as the Regent said, for them to love me.'

It was in fact terrifying that those who had brought her to Dórsia had done so because they thought she would keep the King in order and influence him from behind the throne.

It made Zosina feel almost panic-stricken to think that the plan was that anything that happened in the country would be done at her instigation or because she could influence the King into the right way of thinking.

"I am quite certain of one thing," she told herself. "Whatever I suggest, he will do the opposite, just out of spite."

Then she told herself that that was not how Katalin would tackle the problem.

'I have to will him into listening to me,' she thought.

She wondered if Katalin's idea of "willing" for what

one wanted could ever really be possible in ordinary, every-day life.

Then she remembered how positive Katalin had been that it would work.

"First I must will him into believing that I am not dangerous or obstructive," Zosina told herself, "but sympathetic and understanding."

Then she knew that as far as she was concerned it would be a question of praying rather than willing the King to do anything.

"God will help me," she whispered.

At the same time, she felt she was weak because she knew she would not rely on herself but only on the Power to whom even miracles were possible.

As she walked along the corridor with her grand-mother to go downstairs to the State Banquet, the Queen Mother said with her usual kindness:

"You look lovely, my dear! Everybody in Dórsia is captivated by your beauty and your charm, and I am very proud of you."

"Thank you, Grandmama."

"What was Sándor saying to you when I came into the room?"

There was an undoubted note of curiosity in the Queen Mother's voice, but Zosina thought it would be impossible to tell her what the Regent had been saying or to relate their conversation when he had found her in tears.

After an infinitesimal pause she replied:

"His Royal Highness was talking about the King, Grandmama."

The Queen Mother smiled.

"I thought it must be something of the sort, and I am sure you will find that you and György have a great many subjects in common. After all, you are practically the same age. He needs a young companion when he has so many State duties to perform."

Zosina thought that while this was true, she was not the companion he needed.

At the State Banquet she was dismayed to find that because the King was the host and she and her grandmother were the Guests of Honour, they were once again seated on his right and left.

As the dinner began, Zosina was at first so fascinated with looking at the beauty of the scene that she could think of nothing else.

Again, a profusion of exotic flowers decorated all the tables, which were also laden with magnificent ornaments of gold and silver.

Enormous crystal chandeliers which held hundreds of lighted candles sparkled overhead.

There were too, Zosina noticed, as a concession to progress, a number of gas-globes in the room, which she was sure was the regular way of lighting the enormous Banqueting-Hall except on very special occasions.

Tonight the candlelight was very becoming and she thought that the ladies of Dórsia had a beauty which certainly exceeded those of her own country.

The men too were extremely handsome, tall and broad-shouldered, with clean-cut features, like the Regent.

He was seated on her left, and as if he read her thoughts, he asked as she stared round her:

"Do we pass muster?"

She turned to smile at him and he saw that her eyes were shining with excitement.

"It is all so beautiful!" she exclaimed. "And I was thinking that the people of Dórsia are beautiful too."

"You are very flattering," he replied, "and I am sure the Queen Mother would claim it is due to the preponderance of Hungarian blood in our veins!"

"Of course that could account for it," Zosina agreed.

"Also due to our Hungarian ancestors," the Regent went on, "you will find a great many Dórsians are redheaded and fair-skinned."

Zosina longed to add: "It is a pity that the King should have inherited the Albanian appearance of his mother rather than that of his Dórsian father."

Instead she remarked:

"I have never been to a State Banquet before. I feel it is rather like taking part in the most glamorous and exciting production in a Theatre."

She remembered that Katalin had said that she looked like a Prima Donna in an Opera, and it crossed her mind that if her sister could see the Regent she would certainly think he qualified as the leading man.

Tonight, like the King, he was wearing a white tunic, but as his was a military one, it had heavy gold epaulettes and his collar was also embroidered with gold.

While the King's decorations were those traditionally worn by a Monarch, many of the Regent's were battle honours which Zosina recognised from those she had been shown when she was inspecting the Armoury in the Palace.

There was also something in his bearing and his air of authority that told her he would be a good commander in the battlefield and certainly a leader of men.

He pointed out to her one or two celebrities amongst the diners; then, because she knew she must do what was expected of her, she turned politely to the King, who sat on her other side.

For a moment it seemed impossible to think of anything to say, and she thought that if she annoyed him they might start fighting again.

Because it was the first uncontroversial thing that came into her mind, she asked:

"Do you ever give Balls at the Palace? This would be a lovely room in which to dance."

"We do have them, but they are very formal and boring," the King replied in a rather surly voice.

There was a pause, then he added:

"But I will soon change all that."

"It would certainly be fun to have a Ball," Zosina said, trying to be agreeable.

"Not if the guests are all as decrepit as these creatures!" he said, looking fiercely at the people dining with them.

Zosina was about to say instinctively: "Do be careful in case they should hear you!" then realised it would be a rebuke which the King would undoubtedly resent.

Instead she said:

"I am sure, Sire, you have a great many young friends who would enjoy dancing, as I do."

"I have," the King answered. "But you do not suppose I am allowed to invite them here? Oh no! My friends are not good enough for Uncle Sándor!"

Zosina gave a little sigh.

They were back on the subject of his dislike of authority and especially that of his uncle.

There was a pause when she could think of nothing to say. Then the King remarked:

"If you want to dance and meet my friends, you can come with me tonight."

"Come . . . with you?" Zosina asked. "Where?"

"To the Masked Ball."

Zosina stared at him in astonishment.

"The . . . Masked Ball? It is taking place tonight?"

The King nodded; then, with a note that was almost one of enthusiasm, he said:

"It will be very different from this! I am meeting my friends there when all this ceremony and pomposity is over."

Zosina looked at him wide-eyed, and he said:

"Are you sporting enough to come with me, or are you too afraid to play truant?"

There was a jeering note in his voice, as if he knew her answer without her giving it.

"What are you . . . suggesting I . . . do?" Zosina asked almost in a whisper.

"You will have to slip out when everybody has gone to bed," the King answered. "That is what I always do."

"And you will . . . take me to a . . . Masked Ball?"

"I bet you are not brave enough to come!"

It was a challenge, Zosina thought, rather of the type of "dare" in which her sisters, especially Katalin, indulged, and which had often made her afraid.

"I bet you are not brave enough to walk along the parapet!" "I bet you are not brave enough to climb over the roofs!"

They were the sort of "dares" that had always made her frightened, and yet she had often forced herself to undertake them just so that the others would not think her a spoil-sport.

But this was an even greater "dare," and she knew how angry the Queen Mother would be if it was discovered that she had left the Palace unchaperoned.

And yet, in a way, this was the chance she had been looking for, to make the King feel that she was not against him but sympathised with and understood his difficulties.

There was a cynical twist to his lips and she was quite sure that he felt she was far too cowardly and conventional to accept his invitation.

It was then that she suspected he had offered it merely as an act of defiance because he knew it was so outrageous.

Zosina made up her mind.

"I will . . . come!" she said. "If you can make quite . . . certain it is not . . . discovered. I know Grandmama would be very . . . angry, and so, I am sure, would the Prince Regent."

The King laughed.

"You bet he would! In fact, he would stop me if he had the slightest suspicion of what I was up to."

"You have done this sort of thing before?" Zosina enquired.

"Dozens of times!" the King boasted. "And nobody has ever yet caught me!"

Zosina felt a little tremor of fear that this might be the first time, but aloud she said:

"I think it is very courageous of you! But supposing you are recognised?"

"No chance of that," the King said. "You have forgotten, we will be masked."

"How can I get one?" Zosina asked.

"I will see to that," the King replied, "if you are sure you have the guts to come with me."

It was a rather vulgar way of putting it, Zosina thought, but it summed up exactly what she needed in order to do something which she was well aware could land her in a great deal of trouble and which would outrage her father and mother if they ever heard about it.

"I will . . . come!" she said, with a little quiver in her voice, "but please let us be very . . . careful and make sure . . . nobody sees us."

"If you do exactly as I tell you," the King said, "it will be quite safe, but do not go squealing afterwards, if it turns out not what you expect and you do not like being outside your gilded cage."

Again he was sneering. At the same time, Zosina thought, he was really rather pleased that she had accepted his invitation.

Then she knew the reason when he said:

"We are really putting one over Uncle Sándor! He thinks he has got your whole visit well buttoned up, down to the last detail! Well, I am ready to show you he is wrong!"

"You will . . . not tell him . . . afterwards?" Zosina asked nervously.

"And have one of his interminable lectures?" the King questioned. "I am not such a fool as to do that, but I shall feel jolly cock-a-hoop that I can outwit him."

Zosina realised that because he was obsessed with the subject of his uncle's authority, he found it impossible to talk of anything else.

Aloud she said:

"Tell me more details . . . later. I think I must now talk to the Prince Regent."

"Leave everything to me," the King said.

Zosina turned her head to find the Regent waiting to speak to her.

"I want tomorrow to show you what I think are rather beautiful pictures painted by one of the Nuns in a

Convent," he said, "which is situated high in the mountains."

"I would love to see them," Zosina replied.

"A number of extremely intelligent and talented women live in this particular Convent," the Regent went on, "and one of them is a poetess. I have had her poems bound and I am going to have a copy of them put in your bedroom. Perhaps before you go to sleep tonight you will glance through them. I am convinced you will find them very moving."

"How kind of you!" Zosina exclaimed. "You know I love poetry."

"As we have said before, poets can often say for us things that are impossible to express in any other way," the Regent remarked. "Perhaps one day—somebody will write a poem to you."

Zosina had the strange feeling that he had been about to say: "*I* will write a poem to you."

Then she told herself that she had been mistaken and there had not been a perceptible pause before the word "somebody."

She was looking again at the guests sitting at the flower-decorated tables when the Regent quoted:

> *"And bright*
> *The lamps shone o'er fair women and brave men;*
> *A thousand hearts beat happily."*

"Lord Byron!" Zosina laughed and continued:

> *"And when*
> *Music arose with its voluptuous swell,*
> *Soft eyes look'd love to eyes which spake again,*
> *And . . ."*

She stopped as she suddenly remembered the next line:

> *"And all went merry as a marriage bell."*

387

The Regent understood her embarrassment and said quickly:

"I can see you are very well read."

"I wish that were true," Zosina replied, "but because I have always had to choose my own literature, I often feel there are enormous gaps in my education, which a real Scholar would find lamentable."

"I think the education we give ourselves, because we want to know, is more important than anything a teacher could suggest."

"That is a very comforting thought," Zosina said, "but to me the real joy is knowing that knowledge is boundless and it would be impossible ever to come to the end of it."

"So you intend to study for the rest of your life?"

"As I am sure you intend to do."

"Why should you think that?"

Zosina paused to find words. Then she said:

"I have a feeling that you are always looking towards the horizon and you know that when you get there you will find there are more horizons further and further still. You remind me somehow of Tennyson's Ulysses, who longed for:

> *" 'that untravelled world, whose margin fades*
> *For ever and for ever when I move.' "*

As she spoke she was not even certain how or why the words came to her, and yet they were suddenly there in her mind and she spoke without considering whether or not she should say what she thought.

"What you have said is true," the Regent said, after a moment's silence. "But no-one has ever realised it before."

"I am glad I am the first," Zosina said lightly.

Then as her eyes met his, she had the strange feeling that there was so much more that she knew about him, so much that she could see and feel, and it was like opening an exciting new book.

And yet, once opened, it was so familiar that she already knew a good deal of what she would find there.

It suddenly struck her that if she could talk and go on talking to the Regent, he could not only tell her so many things that she longed to know but explain those that puzzled her.

'He is full of wisdom,' she thought to herself.

But she knew it was not only that; it was almost as if they thought along the same lines and she too looked towards the horizon as he was doing.

Then, as she felt that they had so much more to say, she heard the King, on her other side, remark:

"It is time you talked to me again."

"I am sorry, Sire," she said hastily. "I thought you were engaged with Grandmama."

"She has been busy telling me what I should do and not do," the King replied, pulling a grimace.

Zosina wanted to laugh.

Once again he was behaving like a naughty little boy.

As if there was no time to be lost, the King said in a low voice:

"I have worked it all out. When you say goodnight, go to your room, but do not undress."

"What shall I say to my maid?"

"Get rid of her somehow, or else . . ."

He paused and looked down at her gown.

"Perhaps you had better change into something not so elaborate, and certainly without a train. If you are going to dance, somebody might tread on it."

"I will do that."

"Then wait until there is a knock on the door."

"Do I open it?"

"Yes. You will find one of my Aides-de-Camp outside. We can trust him. He is a jolly good chap who would never betray me. I am going to give him a very important position at Court, once I have the authority."

Zosina nodded and the King went on:

"He will bring you to me, and then we will get out of

389

the Palace without anybody being aware that we have left."

"How can we do that?" Zosina enquired.

She remembered the sentries who were posted at every door through which she had entered the Palace so far.

"You will see," the King replied.

There was a note of satisfaction in his voice, and Zosina knew he was really quite pleased that she was going with him.

'That will be my only excuse if I get into trouble,' she thought.

It struck her that however plausible the excuse of doing what the King wanted, the Regent would be disappointed if she behaved in a reprehensible manner after all the flattering things he had said to her.

Then she told herself that it would be foolish of her not to do what the King wanted, when so much depended on their being friendly.

'If I refuse him this time, he might never ask me again,' she thought, 'and we would be back to hating each other and fighting.'

She stopped.

'I mean,' she added, 'the King will be hating me.'

At the same time, she had the uncomfortable feeling that what she had thought first was nearer to the truth.

The dinner-party seemed interminable.

When the long-drawn-out meal was finished there were speeches, first by the Prime Minister, welcoming the Queen Mother and Zosina to Dórsia, then one from the Regent, which managed to be both sincere and moving, witty and amusing.

After him the Lord Chancellor droned on for over a quarter-of-an-hour.

As he did so, Zosina was acutely aware that the King was not only fidgeting restlessly in his chair but also signalling to the footmen to fill and refill his glass.

'He is so young, of course he finds this rather boring,' Zosina thought, and at that moment felt immeasurably older than the man who was within a few weeks of being three years older than herself.

There were several other speeches, none of them saying anything that had not been said before, and all of them should certainly have been shorter.

Zosina realised they were all made by people who had to be heard because of their position in the country, and it was with relief that she saw the Queen Mother rise and realised that this would be the last speech of the evening.

There was tremendous applause.

Then in her musical voice, speaking clearly and with a diction that her granddaughters had always admired, the Queen Mother thanked them all for her welcome to Dórsia, and said how impressed she and her granddaughter had been with everything they had seen and all the charming people they had met.

"We are only halfway through this delightful visit," she said, "and I cannot tell you how much I am looking forward, as I know the Princess Zosina is, to all we shall see tomorrow and most of all to our last engagement, in the House of Parliament."

This remark, and the way her grandmother said it, Zosina thought, was a direct reference to the fact that it was there that her engagement to the King would be announced.

She knew by the expression of those listening and the way they looked at her that they too understood what her grandmother had not explicitly said in so many words.

She felt the colour coming into her face and almost instinctively she turned to look at the King.

He was lying back in his chair, quite obviously bored and completely indifferent to what was being said.

In fact, Zosina knew he had missed the point which her grandmother had implied.

She wanted instinctively to nudge him into an awareness that he should show himself pleased and smiling at the prospect of his engagement.

But once again she realised that he would think she was interfering and correcting him, and instead she forced a smile to her lips, as if she, at any rate, was delighted at what lay ahead.

The Queen Mother's speech came to an end with everybody in the room rising to their feet and not only clapping but calling out:

"Bravo! Bravo!"

"Thank God that is over!" the King said as at last the Queen Mother sat down.

He drank what wine remained in his glass, then rose to his feet to show that dinner was at an end.

The top table left the room first, and when they were outside the Banqueting-Hall, the Queen Mother said to the King:

"A delightful party, György! Thank you so much for giving it for me and Zosina. The food was delicious and I enjoyed every moment of it!"

The King did not reply and after a moment the Queen Mother went on:

"I must admit I now feel rather tired, and I think, Zosina, we should retire to bed. We have a great many engagements tomorrow."

They all said good-night, and as Zosina curtseyed to the King, he said, barely moving his lips:

"Be ready!"

She gave him an almost imperceptible nod to show him that she understood.

At the same time, when after saying good-night to her grandmother she retired to her own room, she asked herself if she was being crazy to leave the Palace at midnight.

It was something even Katalin would have never thought of amongst her wildest pranks, and she could imagine that if her mother was to hear about it, she would tell her that it was her duty to refuse the King's exceedingly reprehensible invitation.

And she would instruct her also to inform her grandmother of what he intended to do.

"That is just what he would expect," Zosina argued with her conscience, "and it would antagonise him once and for all, so that I doubt if he would even speak to me again."

She felt nervous and afraid to the point where she longed almost desperately to say that after all she would not go.

Her lady's-maid, who had come with them from Lützelstein, was yawning surreptitiously, and quite obviously she was put out at being kept up so late.

"We keep earlier hours at home, Your Royal Highness," she said as she helped Zosina out of her gown.

"You must be tired, Gisela, and I do understand," Zosina replied. "Now that you have undone my gown, I suggest you slip off to bed. I will manage everything else for myself."

"I'm prepared to do my duty, Your Royal Highness!" the girl said.

"There is no need," Zosina insisted, "and as it happens, I have to write a letter to Papa so that I can give it to the Ambassador first thing tomorrow morning to go in the Diplomatic-Bag. You may leave, and you know I usually put myself to bed at home."

Gisela was obviously very tired, and with a little more pressing from Zosina she capitulated.

"Very well, Your Royal Highness. I'll do as you suggest," she said at length. "I'm not pretending these late hours don't take their toll of me. I'm not used to them and that's a fact!"

"No, of course not, Gisela. You have been wonderful to have managed the many changes of clothes that I have needed since I have been here. Good-night!"

"Good-night, Your Royal Highness!"

Gisela left the room and Zosina gave a little sigh of relief.

It had been easier than she had expected.

She went to the wardrobe and chose one of her simplest evening-gowns, managing with a little difficulty to fasten it herself.

At home, when Gisela was usually far too busy to waste much time with them, the four sisters always helped one another, and once again Zosina had an overwhelming longing to have Katalin with her.

'How she would enjoy an escapade like this,' she thought, 'and what is more, if Katalin were here, I am sure she would manage the King far more competently than I can.'

However, she knew that her wishes had not a chance of fulfilment, and once she was ready, she sat down in a rather hard chair to wait.

It seemed to her that time passed very slowly and for a moment she wondered if perhaps the King was playing a joke on her and had no intention of taking her anywhere.

Then she began to wonder what would happen if they were caught and brought back ignominiously to the Palace by the Military.

She would get a severe lecture from the Queen Mother, but worst of all, she would have to face the Regent.

She found herself thinking of the subjects they had discussed at dinner and how interesting they were.

'It would be fun to dance,' Zosina thought. 'At the same time, it would be more fun to sit reading poetry with him and trying to be clever enough to cap his quotations.'

She thought of two books she would like to ask him if he had read and, if so, what he had thought of them.

She was just wondering what his opinion would be on Gustave Flaubert's latest novel, or if he would be shocked by the knowledge that she had even read such a book, when there was a knock on the door.

It made her start, and for a moment she thought perhaps she had imagined it, because it had been so faint.

Then she jumped to her feet, crossed the room, turned the gold handle, and opened the door a few inches.

There was a man standing outside and she recognised

him immediately. He was one of the Aides-de-Camp who had accompanied the King when they visited the Guildhall.

She had thought at the time that he was much younger than the others, and he had looked at her in a manner that was not exactly impertinent, she thought, but did not show the respect that was usual amongst those in attendance.

Now, with a grin on his face, he did not speak but merely jerked his head, and Zosina slipped through the door into the passage.

He did not attempt to close it for her but started to walk very quickly ahead, obviously assuming that she would follow him.

She did what was expected, and found by the time they had reached the end of the corridor that she was almost running to keep up with him.

There was no-one about and many of the lights had been extinguished, and she noticed that the Aide-de-Camp kept to the side of the corridor and, where possible, in the shadows.

Then they were in a part of the Palace which Zosina had not seen before and she supposed they were going to the King's Suite.

Instead, the Aide-de-Camp started to descend what was obviously a very secondary staircase.

Down they went, until they were in a narrow, almost dark passageway, and again Zosina found herself hurrying to keep up with the man ahead of her.

On and on, past closed doors behind which Zosina was sure were rooms that were unoccupied.

They descended yet another staircase and this time she was certain they must be below ground-level, until as they reached the bottom of it she realised that they were in the Palace cellars.

There, in the light of two flickering candles, she saw the King waiting for her.

"You have been a hell of a time!" he complained.

"I came as quickly as I could, Sire," the Aide-de-Camp replied. "It's a long way."

"I thought you were going to rat on me," the King said to Zosina.

"No, of course not!"

"Well, put this on and we will be off," he said, thrusting something into her hand.

She looked at it in surprise, then realised it was a Domino.

She had never actually seen one before, but she and Theone had been interested in pictures of the fêtes which took place in Venice when for a whole week each year the Venetians wore Dominos and masks and moved about the place incognito, enjoying a licence that could not take place except during a Festival.

She saw that the King was already wearing his Domino, though he had not pulled the hood over his head, and the Aide-de-Camp was hurriedly getting into one.

"This is exciting!" she exclaimed. "But please, help me. I am not certain how to wear it."

"It is not difficult!" the King said scornfully, as if he thought she was being very stupid. "And here is your mask. Autal found you one with lace round it, because it is more concealing."

Zosina realised that Autal was the Aide-de-Camp, and she flashed him a glance of gratitude, seeing, as she did so, that, already masked and covered by his Domino, he was quite unrecognisable.

By this time, some of the apprehension she had been feeling began to vanish.

She slipped the mask on and pulled the hood of the Domino over her hair, and as the King did the same, she thought with satisfaction that it would be hard for anyone to suspect his real identity.

"Come on!" the King said impatiently, and now he was walking ahead, with Zosina following and Autal bringing up the rear.

They did not go far, and she was not surprised when

they stopped at the cellar door, which the Aide-de-Camp unlocked.

It swung open quietly, as if it had recently been oiled, and now there was a flight of steps.

Zosina picked up the front of her gown with one hand and held out the other to the King.

"Please help me," she begged.

With what she thought was rather bad grace, he took her hand and pulled her rather sharply up the steps until they reached ground-level.

There was a carriage standing in the shadow of a clump of trees.

The King climbed into it without suggesting that Zosina should get in first, and she followed him, sitting beside him on the back seat while the Aide-de-Camp sat opposite.

The horses—there were two of them—started off immediately, and the King, lying back, gave a laugh as he said:

"Now are you still doubtful that I can get out of the Palace without anybody being aware of it?"

"It was very clever of you, Sire, to use the cellar door!" Zosina said.

"There is to be no 'Siring' and all that kow-towing now," the King replied. "My friends call me Gyo, and that is who I am, and don't you forget it!"

"I will . . . try not to," Zosina promised.

"This is Autal," the King said, waving his hand towards the Aide-de-Camp, "and we had better choose a name for you. 'Zosina' is a bit too unusual in Dórsia for it not to be suspect."

"Perhaps you could call me 'Magda.' It is one of my other names," Zosina suggested.

"That will do," the King said ungraciously, "but I think 'Magi' would be less pompous."

Zosina thought it sounded rather common, but at the same time she was not prepared to disagree.

"Very well," she said. "I will answer to 'Magi.' Are we going to meet many people?"

"All my friends," the King answered, "and they will be wondering what the devil has happened to me. I thought those crashing bores would never stop droning on! One thing I promise you, something I shall forbid in the future will be speeches of any sort."

"Quite right," Autal said, "and pass a law that anyone who makes one should be exiled for at least a year!"

"A splendid idea!" the King exclaimed. "And the sooner that is put into operation, the better!"

"You would have to allow them to make speeches in Parliament," Zosina said.

"As long as I do not have to listen to them, they can talk their heads off!" the King replied.

Zosina, however, was not listening to him.

They had left the grounds of the Palace and were now in the open street and she could see crowds of people walking about under the gas-lights which illuminated the most important thoroughfares.

She had somehow expected, because it was so late, that most people would already have gone to bed, but the streets were crowded and she could see that a lot of passersby were wearing fancy costumes and carrying paper streamers on sticks or windmills in their hands.

"It is very festive!" she exclaimed.

"You wait," the King said. "It is far better than this where we are going."

There was a sudden explosion and Zosina started at the noise, before she saw fireworks silhouetted against the darkness of the sky.

"How pretty!" she exclaimed, as it looked like a number of falling stars descending towards the ground.

The King did not reply, and she saw to her surprise that the Aide-de-Camp was pouring wine from a bottle which he held in one hand into a glass which he held in the other.

"Autal, you are a genius!" the King exclaimed. "I was just thinking I was beginning to feel thirsty waiting in the cellar for you with everything locked up."

"It will not be long before we can see what is hidden there," Autal replied.

"No, and I bet my damned uncle keeps all the best wines for himself!" the King said. "I know he has a whole lot of Tokay secreted away somewhere!"

"Perhaps he will bring it out to celebrate your twenty-first birthday," the Aide-de-Camp said with a smirk.

"To celebrate?" The King laughed. "You know he will not be doing that, not when it means 'good-night' as far as he is concerned."

"Well, we will drink to his departure," Autal said, "and good riddance, if you ask me."

The King raised his glass.

"Good-bye, Uncle Sándor!" he said. "And here's hoping we will never meet again!"

Again the Aide-de-Camp laughed, and Zosina told herself it was not the way a King should behave and most certainly not with one of his Aides-de-Camp.

It was obvious that Autal was inciting him to be more rebellious than he was already, and she thought it was a pity that someone older and wiser was not in attendance on the King.

'I suppose,' she thought, 'the Regent thought it would be better for him to have somebody of his own age.'

The King finished his glass of wine, then somewhat ungraciously said to Zosina:

"Do you want a drink?"

"No, thank you," Zosina replied. "I am not thirsty."

The Aide-de-Camp sniggered.

"You do not have to be thirsty to drink," he said. "Come on, Magi, have a sip of mine. It will get you into the spirit of things, and that's the right word for it."

He laughed at his own joke and Zosina found herself stiffening.

How dare he speak to her in such a familiar manner?

Then she told herself that she had to remember they were all incognito and she was not a Princess and the prospective Queen, but Magi, a girl who was fast enough in her behaviour to go out after midnight escorted only by two young men.

Autal had not waited for her reply, but thrust into her hand a glass from which he had already been drinking.

As she felt it was impossible to refuse to do what he wanted and she was afraid that the King would sense her reluctance, she drank a little of the wine, which was quite pleasant but rather heavy.

"That is better!" Autal said as she handed him back the glass.

Then, putting it to his own lips, he appeared to tip it down his throat.

The King finished off what was in his glass.

"We are nearly there," he said, "and one thing is that we will have plenty to drink, if Lakatos has anything to do with it."

"If he is still waiting for us," Autal said.

"He will know I am not going to miss this party," the King said.

As he spoke, Zosina thought for a moment that he slurred his words; then she told herself that she must be mistaken and perhaps he had not swallowed all the wine he had in his mouth.

The carriage came to a standstill and Autal threw the bottle, which was nearly empty, down on the floor.

The King got out of the carriage first and Zosina saw with a little constriction of her heart that there were huge crowds outside and heard the sound of some very noisy music.

Chapter Five

THE CROWDS WERE MOVING slowly and were obviously in a mood of gaiety and excitement.

The majority of people on the street, Zosina thought, were peasants, who appeared to gape at everything and everybody.

But there were also a number of anonymous figures, wearing Dominos and masks, who were moving in through a huge doorway lit with dozens of electric globes and festooned with bunting and flags.

Because she felt nervous, Zosina moved closer to the King as he elbowed his way through the crowds to the door of what she guessed must be a Beer Hall.

She knew they existed in Lützelstein although she had never actually been in one. She had heard that dances and entertainments often took place in them.

When she got through the door, holding her Domino tightly round her and afraid, because the King was moving so quickly, that she would be left behind, she found herself first in an Entrance-Hall.

There were a great number of people standing about, apparently waiting for new arrivals.

They were very noisy and the Band that was playing inside seemed almost deafening.

Then Zosina heard a cry of:

"Gyo! Gyo! Here you are!"

A moment later several men hurried towards them,

holding out their arms towards the King, and when they reached him, they shook his hand effusively and slapped him on the back.

"We'd almost given up waiting for you," they said. "Come on, Gyo! Everyone's here but you."

They started up some stairs and Zosina and Autal followed.

She wondered where they were going and a few seconds later they opened a door off a wide corridor and she realised that they were entering an enormous box.

With a sigh of relief, she knew that she would not have to cope with the crowds on the dance-floor beneath them and would be able to watch without immediately taking part in the dancing.

Then as she saw who was waiting for them she felt her eyes widen in surprise beneath the velvet mask.

A lot of the men had pulled their masks from their faces, letting them hang round their necks, and she could see that they were all young but a very different type from the sort of gentlemen whom she would expect to find in the company of Royalty.

She told herself not to be censorious, but there was something which she thought was rather common and coarse about the men, which made them different from those she had met before.

"Gyo! Gyo!" they cried triumphantly as the King appeared. "We thought you were never coming!"

"Nothing could have prevented me from being here tonight," the King replied.

"Have a drink. Lakatos has brought us some champagne—what do you think of that?"

"I bet you are several bottles ahead of me already," the King exclaimed, "but give me time, and I will catch you up!"

Somebody handed him a glass, which he filled to the brim, and he drank deeply before he said:

"Give Autal a drink, and Magi. She is with me."

He jerked his thumb at Zosina as he spoke, but she was at the moment looking with astonishment at the women, whom she had not noticed at first because they were leaning over the box, waving and shouting to their friends on the dance-floor.

Now, as if they had just realised that the King had arrived, they turned towards him with cries of delight, and she knew that if the men were different, it was impossible to find an adjective to describe the women.

Most of them had removed their masks, if they had ever worn them, and their eyes were heavily mascaraed and in striking contrast to the gold or red of their hair, which was so vivid that Zosina was certain it was dyed.

They all had crimson lips and their faces were powdered and rouged. One or two of them looked like a Dutch doll which had been Katalin's favourite when she was a little girl.

The Dominos they wore were open and beneath them Zosina could see that they wore gowns cut very low; in fact one or two were so revealing that after one glance at their bulging bosoms, she looked away in embarrassment.

"Gyo! You're here! We've been waiting for you."

Their shrill, uncultured voices raved out, all saying the same thing.

Then they were kissing the King and Autal, leaving smears of lipstick on their faces and on their lips.

Zosina stood to one side, feeling as if she were invisible. Then one of the men, with a bottle of champagne in his hand, said to her:

"Have a drink, Magi. You look far too sober, which is a mistake."

The way he pronounced his words told Zosina that he was definitely the reverse.

But because she thought it better to agree to anything that was suggested, she took a glass from him and held it as he poured the champagne into it.

"Now enjoy yourself," he said. "What do you look like behind that mask?"

He reached out his hand as if to remove it, but Zosina nervously edged away from him.

She thought he would persist in unmasking her, but at that moment the King shouted:

"Hey, Lakatos, I am dying of thirst. Are you out of wine already?"

"You need not be afraid of that, Gyo!" Lakatos replied. "I've enough bottles to float a battleship!"

"We'll need it," one of the blond women, who had her arm round the King's neck, replied. "He's no fun unless he's full to the brim, are you, my pet?"

She kissed the King's cheek as she spoke, but he appeared to be more concerned with having his glass filled than with appreciating her attention.

Because Zosina had no wish for Lakatos to notice her again, she moved along the side of the box and edged her way to the front of it.

Now she could look down at the dance-floor, which was certainly different from anything she had seen in her life before.

At one end there was a huge Band of what must have been nearly a hundred players. At the other end was a Bar which stretched right across the Hall from one wall to the other.

Behind it, barmaids in national costume were filling china mugs of beer, which were being passed over the heads of those waiting six deep to be served.

On the floor itself, the dancers were either gyrating wildly about or dancing close to each other in a manner which Zosina felt was very improper.

There were also a number of men whom she knew were drunk, because they were staggering about with or without partners and often falling down as they did so.

If the women in the box looked fast and vulgar there were far worse specimens below, and Zosina felt a little tremor of fear in case her grandmother or, worse still, the Regent should know where she was.

At the same time, in a way it was a fascinating spectacle that she had never imagined she would see, and because it was unique she thought she must take in every detail.

As she watched, a voice beside her said:

"Finished your drink? If so, we'll go down and dance."

It was the man called Lakatos who spoke, and she started nervously before she replied:

"I think I had . . . better stay up here with . . . Gyo!"

"You can't do that!" Lakatos replied. "He's already dancing. Come on! That's what you're here for."

He spoke almost roughly, and now Zosina was certain that he had had far too much to drink and she thought that he might make an exhibition of himself as some of the other people were doing.

"I think perhaps . . ." she began.

Before she could finish what she was going to say, he had seized her by the hand and jerked her towards the door of the box, so roughly that she upset most of the champagne she was holding in her other hand.

She wondered wildly to whom she could appeal to save her from what she was sure would be a humiliating performance.

Not only the King had vanished but also Autal, and the only men left in the box were drinking and laughing uproariously over something one of them had said.

There was nothing she could do but allow Lakatos to drag her out into the corridor, having with difficulty put down her almost-empty glass on a table at the back of the box as she passed it.

Then they went down the stairs, Lakatos holding on to the bannister, Zosina noticed.

The noise seemed even worse when they started to mingle with the crowds, and there was also what Zosina thought was an unpleasant smell of beer, cheap perfume, and what she was sure was sweat.

However, once they had taken to the dance-floor, it was impossible to think of anything except how to keep in time with Lakatos.

The Band was now playing a Viennese Waltz and he swung her round, but not in the graceful prescribed fashion that Zosina had learnt with her dancing-teacher, but violently, as if he wished to sweep her off her feet, frequently staggering as he did so.

Only by holding tightly on to his arm could Zosina keep her balance.

They kept bumping into other couples, who shouted at them to look where they were going—an instruction which Lakatos completely ignored.

It was all a very unpleasant experience, and before they had circled even a quarter of the room Zosina was wishing that she had never said she was fond of dancing and had not agreed to come with the King on this wild escapade.

As if to think of him was to conjure him up, the next couple they bumped into was Gyo with the fair-haired woman who had kissed him.

"This is jolly good fun," the King said as he danced beside Lakatos and Zosina, "but it is damned hot!"

"It always is," Lakatos replied, "but there's plenty of champagne to keep you cool."

"You are a sport, Lakatos, I will say that for you!" the King said. "One day I will repay you, make no mistake about that."

"I'll remind you of your promise," Lakatos said.

There was something in the way he spoke, even though he was drunk, which told Zosina that he was making use of the King for his own ends.

It struck her that what might have been just a boyish prank on the King's part, in coming to a place like this with people with whom he should not associate, could have far-reaching repercussions which would affect the country itself.

She had not read history so avidly without knowing that Monarchs always had "hangers-on" who would so-licit their favours for personal advantage, and she won-dered how many of these drunken and rowdy young men were already scheming what they could get out of the King, once he had complete power.

It was frightening to remember that this would be after his birthday, in two weeks' time.

She could understand why the Regent, who would then have no more authority over him, wished to replace his own influence with that of a wife.

But, Zosina thought helplessly, there would be nothing she could do to prevent the King from preferring friends of this sort to those Courtiers who had always served their Monarch and treated him with the respect they considered was due his position.

The Band began to play a faster tune and the King said to Lakatos:

"Come on! We will race you to the end of the Hall!"

Zosina did not at first realise what he meant, until he started off in a wild gallop towards the Bar at the far end, knocking people out of his way as he and his partner charged directly at them.

To her consternation, Lakatos followed the King's example, and they set off crashing into the dancers while both he and the King shouted and yelled to warn people of their approach.

It was not only difficult for Zosina to move in such a rough manner but it was also extremely painful.

She felt her whole back being bruised by those against whom they cannoned, and her hand, clasped in Lakatos's and held out ahead of them, struck those who were in their way with a force that Zosina was sure would bruise her knuckles.

"Please . . . please . . . you are going too . . . fast!" she managed to say with a gasp.

But Lakatos paid no attention until he reached the King, who by this time was prevented from going any farther by the crowd waiting at the Bar to be served.

"A beer, that's what I want!" the King's partner said. "A beer! I'm thirsty after all that exercise."

"That is what you shall have," the King said. "Come on, Lakatos."

He turned towards the Bar, and as he did so, several of his other friends who had been in the box joined him.

"What are you doing, Gyo?" one of them asked.
"There's champagne upstairs."

"Kata wants a beer," the King answered, "and so do
I."

"And so do we!" his friends chorussed. "Beer! Beer!
And mind we're served first!"

"We will see to that," the King said. "Come on, boys,
clear a passage for me!"

They obliged, moving forward on either side of the
King and deliberately knocking those who had been
waiting out of their path.

Because the onslaught came from behind, most of the
men did not realise what was happening until they
found themselves pushed over or deliberately knocked
down or punched on the back of the head.

It was all happening so quickly that Zosina could only
gasp, while the women who had been in the box
laughed delightedly and shrieked encouragement.

"Knock 'em down! That's right! Get us what we want!
Beer! Beer!"

It was then that the first row of those waiting at the
Bar realised that something was happening behind
them and turned round.

Zosina saw the expression of one man who was taller
than the rest and realised that there was going to be
trouble.

He put up his fists and struck one of the King's
friends, and his action incited several other men to follow his example.

Before Zosina could realise what was happening, a
fight had started that seemed to escalate every second.

Some of the men who were knocked over fell against
others, and, not certain who was the aggressor, they
struck out at whoever was nearest to them.

Soon there were a large number of men fighting for
no apparent reason except that the majority had had
too much to drink.

The noise was stupendous, and, to make things
worse, Zosina saw one of the King's friends snatch a

beer-mug from somebody who had already been served and throw it with all his strength at a long row of bottles that were stacked on the shelves behind the Bar.

There was a resounding crash and the barmaids screamed.

As if it incited other men into a desire for destruction, beer-mugs started to be thrown by a number of those who had not previously taken part in the fight.

A large mirror was cracked across the centre, and the barmaids began to run to the sides of the Bar and away from danger.

As soon as they realised that it was unattended, men climbed over it to snatch at any bottles that had not been broken; one of them, as he did so, received an empty beer-mug in the face, which cut his cheek.

It was all very frightening, and yet because she was surrounded by so many people who were watching or only just becoming involved in the fight, Zosina found it impossible to move.

Then suddenly, as she was trembling with fear as to what might happen next, a man picked her up in his arms.

She gave a terrified gasp and started to struggle before he said:

"It is all right! Keep quiet! I will get you out of this."

She looked up and saw a face covered by a mask, and as she did so, most of the lights in the Beer Hall went out.

There was a sudden shriek from the crowd, which echoed and re-echoed up to the ceiling, but there were still a few lights left, by the aid of which the man carrying Zosina found his way to the side of the dance-floor.

He had only just reached it when above the noise of screaming and shouting there was a report of gunfire.

Shots rang out one after another, and as Zosina started nervously she found herself put down on her feet.

A door was opened and she was pulled into a place of complete darkness.

409

As the door shut behind the man who carried her, there were several more shots, and she put out her hands to find him close to her.

"What is . . . happening?" she asked, her voice shaking with fear.

She raised her face instinctively as she spoke, because she knew he was so much taller than she was, and he must have been bending towards her, for, without her having any intention of doing so, her mouth touched his.

She stiffened into a sudden stillness, and then before she could move, before she could even finish what she was saying, his arms went round her and his lips made hers captive.

For a moment she was too surprised to feel anything but a sense of shock. Then a streak of lightning seemed to run through her body. It was an indescribable rapture beyond expression and different from anything she had ever imagined she could feel.

It was so wonderful, so rapturous, that she knew that this was what she had always thought a kiss would be like, and yet it was beyond her wildest dreams in its ecstasy and glory.

His arms tightened and it flashed through her mind that if she could die at this moment she would not mind because nothing could ever be so marvellous again.

She felt herself quiver all over, and it was as if the lightning which had run through her whole body had moved into her throat and was held there by a magic that was the enchantment that came not from this world but from the very stars in the sky.

The kiss might have lasted for a few seconds or a few centuries.

Zosina only knew that when the man who held her raised his head, she was bewildered and bemused to the point where, without thinking, without even realising she was speaking, she said:

"I . . . love . . . you!"

Even as she heard her own voice say the words, she knew it was true.

This was love! This was what she wanted! This was what she had prayed she would find, and it had happened when she had least expected it, when she had been afraid to the point where her whole body was trembling.

She was trembling still, but it was now not with fear but with a rapture which made her say again:

"I love you . . . I love you!"

There was no answer, but as he held her very close she felt his heart beating as tumultuously as hers.

Then suddenly she was standing alone and she gave a little cry.

"Do not . . . leave . . . me!"

"Do not move. I have to find a way out."

She stood still because he had told her to, and she knew he was feeling his way through the darkness until a door opened on the other side of what she thought must be a small room.

There was still a pandemonium of noise coming from the Beer Hall. Then there was a faint light and she could see the Regent's head and shoulders silhouetted against an open door.

He left it and came back to where she was standing.

"We can get out this way."

He put his arm round her shoulders as he spoke, and she felt herself quiver because he was touching her.

He drew her forward and out through the door, and she saw that they were in a narrow passage lit only by one gas-globe.

It was light enough for her to see, however, that the walls were dirty and not gaudily painted like the rest of the Beer Hall.

With his arm round her, the Regent drew her quickly in what she thought must be the opposite direction from which they had entered the Hall.

All the time they were moving, Zosina could hear the

noise of screams and shouts and above it all, the bursts of gunfire.

Then there was a door in front of them that was bolted, and the Regent drew back the bolts and they stepped out into the fresh air.

There was no gas-light here but the stars in the sky were bright enough for Zosina to see that they were in a yard where there were piles of refuse, empty bottles, and a huge pile of wooden barrels.

A few more steps and there was an iron gate standing ajar, through which they stepped into a road with apparently a wasteland of shrubs and trees on the other side of it.

The Regent looked to the left as if he was expecting what he saw—a closed carriage. A few seconds later he helped Zosina into it and got in beside her.

It was then, as if she knew there was no need for further pretence, that she pushed her Domino back from her head and pulled off her mask.

She saw that the Regent was doing the same thing, before in a strange voice that she hardly recognised he said:

"Forgive me! I can only beg your forgiveness!"

"For . . . what?"

"For behaving as I did just now," he answered. "You tried me too far, and I can only apologise humbly, and if you wish, on my knees, for losing my head."

"There is . . . no need . . . to apologise," Zosina said shyly.

She realised that he was referring to the fact that he had kissed her, and she knew that as far as she was concerned it was the most wonderful and perfect thing that had ever happened in her whole life.

"But there is!" the Regent said sternly. "I thought I was a controlled, civilised person, but I find instead I am little better than those brigands who are firing wildly as they always do when they are excited."

"Brigands!" Zosina exclaimed with a little shiver.

"You are quite safe," he said. "They would not hurt

you. It is just exuberance that makes them fire off their pistols, especially when there is a fight!"

He spoke in the sensible voice in which he had talked at dinner, and because she felt that he had gone away from her, that he had left her after they had been so close, she turned to him and, trying to see his face in the darkness of the carriage, said:

"I . . . love you!"

"You must not say such things."

"Is it . . . wrong?"

"Very wrong, and I have nobody to blame except myself."

"I know . . . now, I have . . . loved you ever since I first . . . came to Dórsia . . . it seems a very long time ago . . . and I wanted so much to talk to you . . . to listen to you. . . ."

The Regent made a sound that was almost a groan of pain, then he said:

"You must not talk like that. You must not torture me."

"Why? Why?"

"You know the answer," he replied, "and my only excuse is that when I learnt tonight where you had gone, I thought I should go mad with fear and anxiety lest something should happen to you."

"It was . . . very frightening . . . until . . . you came."

"How could you have been so foolish as to let the King take you to such a place?"

"It was the . . . only way I felt I could . . . gain his confidence and . . . trust . . . as you wanted."

"You were thinking of me?"

"I . . . wanted to . . . please you," Zosina said simply.

Although she could not see him clearly, only in fleeting glimpses from the gas-lights on the streets down which they were driving, Zosina knew that he was clenching his fists together.

He did not speak and after a moment she said:

"You . . . kissed me . . . and it was the most wonderful thing that had . . . ever happened to me. Did it mean . . . nothing to you?"

"I am not going to answer that question because I dare not. Oh, my dear, this should never have happened."

"You are . . . sorry that you . . . kissed me?" Zosina persisted.

"Not sorry, but ashamed."

"Of . . . me?"

"No, of course not. Of myself."

"There is . . . no need to . . . be."

"There is every need."

There was silence. Then Zosina said in a small voice he could barely hear:

"Now that I . . . love you . . . must I marry . . . the King?"

"You not only have to marry the King," the Regent answered roughly, "you have to forget me."

"I could . . . never do that . . . never . . . never! It would be . . . impossible. I know now that you are the man who has . . . always been in my . . . dreams . . . the man I thought perhaps . . . one day I would . . . find."

"We have found each other, but it is too late."

"It is . . . not too . . . late. I am not . . . married to the . . . King."

"But you have to marry him."

"Why? When I . . . love you?"

"Because our love can have nothing to do with it."

"*Our* love?" Zosina asked. "Do you . . . love me a little?"

The Regent did not reply and after a moment she said:

"Tell me . . . I have to . . . know."

"Of course I love you!" he said as if the words broke from his lips. "How can you expect me to feel anything else when everything about you is perfect?"

He drew in his breath before he went on:

"It is not only your beauty which made my heart beat from the moment I first saw you, but your sweetness, your charm, your clever little brain, and above all because we understand each other."

"That is why I love you!" Zosina cried. "You understand as . . . no-one has ever . . . understood before and as no-one ever . . . will again."

The Regent did not speak and after a moment she said in a voice that trembled:

"I cannot . . . marry the King! You do not . . . know what he was like tonight . . . he drank too much . . . and those friends of his . . ."

"I know, I know!" the Regent interrupted.

"You know he is like that? You know about them?"

"Of course I know."

"He thinks he is deceiving everybody when he goes out of the Palace. . . ."

"I know everywhere he goes and everybody with whom he associates," the Regent replied, "but there is nothing I can do about it, because in two weeks' time he will be free to behave as he likes and with whom he pleases."

"Do you . . . really think I can . . . stop him?" Zosina asked in a whisper.

"Not now that I have seen you," the Regent answered. "I was such a fool, I imagined that you would be a very different type of woman, who would be able to control him and make him do the things he ought to do."

"I would . . . not be able to . . . do that . . ." Zosina began.

"It is no use," the Regent said. "Things have gone too far. The Prime Minister and the Cabinet know why you are here, and so more or less does the whole of Dórsia. Every newspaper has pointed out the advantage such a marriage would be in stabilising the independence of our two countries."

Zosina clasped her hands together.

"I understand . . . everything you are . . . saying," she said, "but . . . I want to . . . marry you."

The Regent put his hands over his eyes.

"Would it be . . . possible if we were just . . . ordinary people? Would you then . . . want to . . . marry me?"

"Do you really need to ask me that question?" the Regent asked. "You know if it were possible and we were ordinary people I would take you up in my arms and carry you away where we could be alone together and I could tell you how much I love you."

His voice was deep and broken and Zosina knew how much he was suffering, and she said very quietly:

"I shall . . . always remember that you . . . said that to me."

"It would be easier for you if you forgot me and everything about me," the Regent said.

"Will you forget me?"

"That is different."

"Not . . . really. I can never . . . forget you, because, in a way it is difficult to put into words, I not only . . . belong to you, I am . . . part of you."

She hesitated a moment before she added:

"Perhaps we can be together in some . . . other incarnation . . . I do not know . . . all I do know is that I have been . . . looking for you all my life."

"As I have been looking for you," the Regent said. "Oh, my darling, why did this have to happen to us?"

He gave a laugh that had no humour in it before he went on:

"I thought my life was so complete with my work for Dórsia. I thought at my age I was past falling in love in the accepted sense of the word. Then when I saw you step out of the train . . ."

He paused.

"What happened?" Zosina asked.

"I felt as if my heart had turned several somersaults, and then you came towards me in a blaze of light."

"Did you . . . really feel like that? I wish I could say

the same. All I knew was that when I touched your hand I felt as if you protected me and gave me courage."

"God knows it was what I wanted to do," the Regent said. "And ever since then I have fallen more and more deeply in love, until your face is always in front of my eyes and all I can hear is your voice."

Zosina put out one of her hands and slipped it into his.

"Please . . . will you take me away with you?" she begged. "Could we not go and . . . live in another country where no-one will know us . . . and we can just be . . . together?"

The Regent's fingers closed over hers until they were almost bloodless.

"I could be with you anywhere," he said. "We could reach Heaven. But you know as well as I do that we are both too important to disappear, and Germany would take full advantage of any scandal that might affect the situation."

'He has an answer for everything,' Zosina thought helplessly.

The mere fact that the Regent was touching her made her thrill, and she felt, because they were so near to each other and because of the things he had said, that her breath was coming more quickly between her lips.

Then through the window of the carriage she saw the lights from the Palace ahead of them, and she said hastily:

"I have to see you alone . . . I have to go on . . . talking to you."

The Regent shook his head.

"There is nothing to talk about, and nothing to say except good-bye!"

"I cannot do it . . . I cannot!"

"I shall go away," the Regent said sadly, "and when you return to Dórsia for your marriage I shall not be here."

Zosina gave a cry that was like that of a wounded animal.

"Where will you . . . go?"

"Anywhere!"

"No . . . I cannot let you . . . you must help me. . . ."

"Do you think I could stay and know that you were married to somebody else?" he asked.

There was a raw note in his voice that told Zosina how much he was suffering.

"But how . . . can . . . I . . . manage without . . . you?"

"You will manage," he said, "because you are intelligent and because you have an instinct which will always guide you into doing what is right."

"It is not enough!" Zosina said wildly. "It is not enough! I want you . . . and I want to be with you . . . I need your love . . . and I want to give you mine."

They were nearer the Palace now and in the lights from it she saw him shut his eyes as if in agony.

Then he lifted her hand to his lips.

"Good-bye, my love—my only love!" he said very quietly.

The way he spoke made the tears come into Zosina's eyes and she could only feel as if her voice had died in her throat.

The carriage did not stop at the main door but drove round the great building to a side door which Zosina had never seen before.

It stopped and she realised that there were no sentries.

The Regent stepped out of the carriage, drew a key from his pocket, and, having opened the door, waited for Zosina to pass into the Palace in front of him.

Then when they stood inside a small, attractively furnished Hall, he drew her Domino from her shoulders.

"Go straight along the passage in front of you," he directed. "You will find a staircase which will lead you to the first floor and you will know your way from there. We must not be seen together."

Zosina turned to look at him.

There was only one light burning in the Hall and she could see quite clearly the pain in his eyes and the sharp lines on either side of his lips.

They stood looking at each other, and as if she knew there was nothing more she could say, no appeal against what they had to do in the future, she began helplessly to walk away from him, thinking that he was sending her into a darkness that would always deny her the light.

She had almost reached the passage when suddenly in three steps the Regent was behind her.

He turned her round and pulled her into his arms. Then as she felt her heart leap with the wonder of it, he was kissing her, kissing her wildly, passionately, demandingly.

At first his lips hurt hers, and yet even the pain he inflicted on her was a wonder and a glory that made her vibrate to him with a rapture that was almost an exultation.

Then his kisses grew more tender and there was a gentleness that was more compelling, more insistent than she had ever known before.

She felt as if not only her body but her whole spirit and soul were aroused until, as she had said, she became a part of him and they were indivisible.

It was a love that was divine, so spiritual, so perfect that Zosina felt as if God blessed them and had given them to each other.

She knew that love was even mightier and more majestic than she had ever imagined. It was all-enveloping.

There was love in every breath they drew, in every thought in their minds, in every beat of their hearts, just as there was love in the way her whole body quivered because she was close to him.

"I love you! I love you!" she wanted to say.

Yet there was no need, because she knew he was feeling the same, and however much fate must force them apart, they were still one person rather than two.

419

Then, as if the reality broke under the strain of what they were feeling, the Regent suddenly took his arms from her, and when she would have clung to him, he turned her round and pointed her in the direction of the passage down which she had been facing when he had stopped her from leaving him.

For a moment she could not think what she had to do, because she was pulsating with the celestial feeling that he had awakened in her and it was impossible to come back to life.

Then she heard a door open and close and knew that he had left her.

Alone, but because she loved him doing what he had told her to do, she started to walk slowly down the dark passage towards the staircase.

CHAPTER SIX

$\mathcal{T}$HE VISIT TO THE HOSPITAL, which was in a Convent, had been a very moving experience, and as they walked through the quiet, high rooms with the sweet-faced Nuns, Zosina learnt that it had been the Regent's idea that the women who were dedicated to the relief of suffering should actually take their patients into the Convent.

Because she loved him she felt that she was seeing everything in Dórsia in a different way from how she had before, and finding his influence everywhere.

The wildness and irresponsibility of the King had

made her realise, as she felt everybody else must do, that it was the Regent who had made the country not only prosperous but well ordered and in fact happy.

There was no need to hear the Mother Superior telling her that due to his foresight, the sick and elderly of Dórsia were better looked after than those of any other country in Europe and that the mortality rate of new-born babies had dropped dramatically.

It was the Regent whose thoughts and care for the people extended over every aspect of their life, and Zosina was sure, without having to ask, that there was little unemployment in Dórsia and modern methods were being introduced into their factories.

Having met the Prime Minister, she was sure that he was a good man politically, but she felt that outside Parliament he was not strong enough personally to have a great impact on the people.

It was the Regent who for the last ten years had done everything, but in the King's name.

It was the Regent too, she told herself, who was trying to ensure the stability of the country when he had gone.

When she looked at what had been achieved, and when she thought what might happen when the King gained control, she wanted to cry out at the injustice of the Monarchical system which put a man on the throne not because he was fit for the position but because it was his right by birth.

But what alternative was there?

The idea of a country where there was no King or Queen to rule over it was unthinkable.

When in Lützelstein she had heard that the King was wild, Zosina had had no idea what that entailed.

She had never met men who were described as "wild" and her reading had given her only a superficial idea of what any man could be like.

Now as she thought of the way the King had behaved at the Masked Ball, the friends who had treated him so familiarly, and the women who had kissed him, she felt helpless and apprehensive of the horror that being married to such a man might entail.

Last night when she had gone to her room she had been able to think of nothing but the Regent and the ecstasy his kisses had given her.

Because he had swept her into the sky, because he had aroused in her emotions and sensations which she had not known she was capable of feeling, she could not for the moment take in the full impact of knowing that she must lose him.

All she could think of was that she loved him and he loved her, and that in itself was a wonder beyond wonders, a glory beyond words.

When she entered her bedroom she saw a book lying on the table beside her bed and knew then how the Regent had learnt she had left the Palace.

It was the book of poems, written by a Nun, which he had promised to give her.

She was sure that what had happened was that he had forgotten it until he went to bed, and then because he thought she would not be asleep he had sent his servant to give it to Gisela.

Gisela would have said that Her Royal Highness was writing a letter that had to be carried in the Diplomatic-Bag back to Lützelstein the next day.

It would have been then that the Regent's servant, intent on pleasing his master, would have asked Gisela, late though the hour was, to take the book to her mistress.

Zosina knew that although the old maid-servant would have grumbled, she would have done as she was requested, only to find the bedroom empty.

She could imagine all too clearly the panic which must have ensued: Gisela would have sought out the Regent's servant to tell him what she had discovered, and his master, knowing where the King had gone, would have guessed.

Zosina could only hope that the Regent had made Gisela promise to keep silent, and when her maid came to call her the next morning, she learnt that this was what had happened.

"You gave me the shock of my life, Your Royal Highness," Gisela said reproachfully. "Why didn't you tell me you were going out last night?"

"The King invited me to accompany him to a party," Zosina answered. "But please do not tell Her Majesty. She might think it was too late for me."

"His Royal Highness told me to keep my mouth shut," Gisela replied. "But if I was doing my duty, I should report such goings-on when I gets back to Lützelstein."

Because Gisela was really fond of her, Zosina knew that this was an idle threat.

"You have never been a sneak, Gisela," she said, "and as you see, although I was late, I have come to no harm."

As she spoke, she knew it was no thanks to the King that she had not been knocked down or cut by the flying glass.

She wondered if he had worried about her when she disappeared, but she had an uncomfortable feeling that by that time he was already too drunk to remember that he had brought her to the Ball.

It was an inexpressible relief to learn that His Majesty was not to accompany them to the Hospital, though Zosina was certain that even if he had been expected to do so, he would not have felt well enough.

She was, however, not quite sure how a man would feel after such a riotous night, and she wondered whether, as the King had said that he had left the palace in such a surreptitious way dozens of times, a drunken riot was the inevitable end to his evenings out.

As she thought over what had occurred, it seemed to her incredible that the King and his friends should wish to behave in such an aggressive manner and—there was no doubt about it—deliberately start a fight.

Recalling the sequence of events, she had the feeling

that they had all behaved as if in accordance with a pre-arranged and familiar plan of action.

She remembered reading somewhere that students in Munich were accustomed to rioting in their Beer Halls, and perhaps this was the general behaviour amongst the young men of that age.

If that was true, she was quite sure that their bullying tactics would be greatly resented by the quieter and better-behaved members of the population.

Supposing the people of Dórsia ever learnt that their King was one of the ring-leaders of such a troublesome gang?

The whole thing seemed to Zosina beyond her comprehension, and as she walked round the Convent, smiling at the children, saying the right things to the Nuns, and praising everything she saw, one part of her mind was still preoccupied with and shocked by what had happened last night.

In the last ward there were babies who had just been born and one was an orphan, as it had lost its mother, who was an unmarried woman, at its birth.

"How sad!" Zosina exclaimed when she was told what had happened.

"It is such a lovely baby, too, Your Royal Highness," the Nun said.

As she spoke, she lifted it out of its cot and held it out to Zosina, who took it in her arms.

She looked down at its pretty face and wondered, as it was an orphan, what would happen to it in the future.

"It will be all right," the Nun said, as if she read her thoughts. "We will get it adopted. There are always women who are childless and longing for a baby, or others who, having a large family, do not mind having one more."

"I am glad it will not have to go into an Orphanage," Zosina said.

She remembered that she had once visited one with her mother and thought it a cheerless place which lacked love.

As she held the baby in her arms she suddenly real-ised that one of her duties as a Queen would be to pro-vide the throne with an heir.

She loved children and she and her sisters had always planned to have large families, but she had always thought that the man who would be the father would be her dream-man, the man whom she would love and who would love her.

Now the idea of having a family with the King as the father was so horrifying that for a moment she could only stare blindly at the child in her arms, knowing that every instinct in her body shrank from the intimacy such an idea conjured up.

She was very innocent and had no idea what actually happened when a man and woman were married, but she knew it would be something very secret between them.

How, she asked herself, could she contemplate any-thing like that with the King?

Last night when the Regent had kissed her and she felt as if she would be content to die with the happiness he gave her, she had known that anything he did would be sanctified because of their love.

To have his child would be a rapture beyond words. But to have one with any other man, and especially the King, would be a degradation from which she shrank with every nerve in her body.

"I cannot do it . . . I cannot!" she told herself in a panic.

She handed the baby back to the Nun with a look on her face which made the elderly woman say quickly:

"Does Your Royal Highness feel unwell? You look a little pale."

"I am all right, thank you," Zosina replied. "It is very hot today."

"That is true, Your Royal Highness."

The Nun smiled and added:

"I feel this baby has been especially blessed because Your Royal Highness has held it in your arms. As it is a little girl, would it be presumptuous of me to ask if it might bear Your Royal Highness's name?"

"I should be delighted!" Zosina replied.

She gave one more look at the child and wondered if it would ever suffer as she was suffering, if it would ever have to sacrifice everything that was beautiful and perfect in life for the good of a country.

Then, as the Queen Mother was waiting for her, she turned away, feeling as if she left the last tattered remnants of her dreams with the child who was to be named after her.

They had a quiet family luncheon at the Palace, which did not take long, because in the afternoon the Queen Mother was to open the Botanical Gardens, which Zosina had learnt had been laid out by the Regent.

It was a new endeavour for the country and had brought Dórsia recognition from other countries, not only all over Europe but other parts of the world as well.

Zosina learnt that the Regent had written to each country in turn, asking for contributions in the way of plants and shrubs which would extend the knowledge of horticulture amongst the ordinary people.

"In Britain they have Kew Gardens," Zosina had heard the Regent tell the Queen Mother, "and I was so impressed with what was being grown there and exported to other parts of the world that I thought we would try the same experiment here in Dórsia."

"It was a brilliant idea, Sándor!" the Queen Mother had said. "But then, your ideas are always original and progressive."

It was the kind of flattering remark which the Queen Mother made to everybody, but Zosina knew that she was now speaking with sincerity combined with undeniable admiration.

When they found the Regent waiting for them in one of the Salons before luncheon, Zosina had at first been too shy to look at him.

When she did so, she saw that there were dark lines

under his eyes and knew that after she had left him he had been unable to sleep.

He appeared to deliberately avoid speaking to her before they went into the Dining-Room, but because the King was not present he sat at the top of the table with the Queen Mother on his right and Zosina on his left.

His self-control made him seem at ease, and yet because she was so closely attuned to him, Zosina knew that he was as tense as she was and at the same time aware, despairingly, that time was passing and tomorrow her engagement to the King would be announced in Parliament.

The idea seemed to hang like a dark, menacing cloud over her head and even made the Dining-Room and every other part of the Palace seem less attractive than it had before.

Almost as if she could look into the future, she felt she could see the rooms in the Palace filled with the King's vulgar friends, and see the tasteful decorations changed to the kind of gaudy display that they admired.

And nowhere in the picture could she see herself except as she had felt last night—an outsider, neglected, forgotten, or perhaps, worse still, embroiled in the reprehensible behaviour of the young men and women with whom she had absolutely nothing in common.

"I cannot do this . . . I cannot!" Zosina told herself.

She thought that even to please the Regent and gain his respect she could not go on with this farce, which she knew would be the crucifixion of every ideal she had ever had.

But somehow both she and the Regent behaved at luncheon as if everything was quite ordinary and they were in fact nothing more than the future bride and the uncle of the King.

'Perhaps, as he can act so well, he does not feel what I am feeling,' Zosina thought despairingly.

She looked round unexpectedly to find that the Regent's eyes were on her, and she knew before he could look away that he was suffering as she was and his agony was that of a man who is drowning and has no idea how to save himself.

From that moment, some inner instinct and a desire to help the man she loved made Zosina not try in any way to draw his attention to her own feelings.

She knew without words that his love for her made him want to protect and comfort her, and because she loved him in the same manner, she would not add to his agony but try to alleviate it if possible.

Nevertheless, every beat of her heart, every breath she drew, seemed to be saying over and over again:

"I love you! I love you!"

She almost felt as if the clock on the mantelshelf ticked the same words and the murmur of the voices at the table repeated and repeated them, until Zosina was almost afraid that she herself was saying them aloud.

At last the meal was finished, and she and the Queen Mother put on their bonnets, collected their gloves and sunshades, and went downstairs to where the carriages were waiting.

For the first time the Queen Mother seemed to be aware that there was no sign of the King.

"Is not György coming with us?" she asked the Regent.

"No."

"Why not? It is on our programme that he is to make a speech at the opening of the gardens."

"I know," the Regent replied, "but he has cried off."

"Why do you let him?" the Queen Mother asked sharply. "I should think the people will think it very strange that he should not be there when these gardens, thanks to you, already have a world-wide reputation."

The Regent lowered his voice so that those who were to accompany them could not hear what he said.

"György says that as this is his last day of freedom, he intends to spend it as he wishes."

For a moment the Queen Mother did not understand. Then she said:

"You mean because the engagement is being announced tomorrow? Most men do not have their stag-party until just before the wedding."

"I told him that," the Regent replied, "but he was adamant that his time is his own until tomorrow morn-ing."

The Queen Mother gave a little shrug of her shoul-ders.

"Oh well, we must just make do without him, but I shall tell him I think it is very rude not only to me but to you, Sándor."

Zosina could not help thinking that that would not worry the King in the least. If he could be rude or ob-structive to his uncle he would be only too pleased.

She could understand that the Queen Mother was perturbed because she thought the foreign representa-tives who would be present would undoubtedly report the King's absence.

She wondered why the Regent had not forced the King to put in an appearance. Then it struck her that perhaps the excesses of last night were still affecting him and making it impossible for him to come with them to the Botanical Gardens.

Anyway, it was too late to do anything but get into the carriage, and now in the King's absence Zosina sat be-side the Queen Mother on the back seat, while the Re-gent sat opposite them.

The Ladies-in-Waiting and the Court Officials came behind in three carriages, and on the way Zosina learnt that they were to be received not only by those who were concerned with the gardens but also by the Prime Minis-ter and the Ambassadors of every country which had contributed plants and shrubs to it.

She had already seen that the flowers in Dórsia were particularly beautiful, but she was not prepared for what could be done with them when they were cultivated by experts.

The Alpine Section was particularly beautiful, and in the huge glass houses that had been erected for the more exotic plants she saw orchids from the Far East and azaleas from the Himalayas.

Just for one moment did the Regent come to her side when they were in the Orchid House.

She felt a little quiver run through her before he spoke, and she knew as she looked at him that he felt the same.

"You look like a flower yourself," he said in a low voice.

She felt as if time stood still as everything vanished except him and the expression in his eyes.

It was impossible to reply, impossible to find words to tell him of her love.

She knew, before he turned away to speak conventionally to the wife of a Mayor, that for the passing of one second she had been close to him as if he had held her in his arms.

'We belong . . . we still . . . belong,' she thought, and tried to understand what one of the Horticulturists was telling her, but for all the sense he was making he might have been speaking Hindustani.

The gardens were beautiful and a delight to the senses, but to Zosina they contained only one person— she could see nothing but the Regent, hear nothing but his voice.

As they drove back she thought that the day was nearly over. Tomorrow she would leave Dórsia and perhaps she would never see him again.

The King had said that he would get rid of him as soon as he came of age, and the Regent himself had said that he would not be present at her wedding.

"Where . . . will you be? How shall I . . . find you? How can I . . . live without . . . you?" Zosina wanted to cry, but her training and self-control stopped her.

She curtseyed to him when they reached the Palace and walked up the stairs behind the Queen Mother without looking back to see if he was watching her.

She thought that either the King or the Regent was bound to be present at the dinner-party that was being given for them by the members of the Order of St. Miklos.

But when she and the Queen Mother descended the stairs again at a quarter-past seven, there was nobody waiting for them in the Hall except a Lady-in-Waiting and the Lord Chamberlain.

"Surely His Majesty is coming with us?" the Queen Mother asked.

"His Majesty sends his regrets, Ma'am, but Prince Vladislav is your host tonight, and His Royal Highness the Regent will meet you at the Prince's house," the Lord Chamberlain explained.

The Queen Mother raised her eye-brows but said nothing, and only when they were driving off in the closed carriage did she say, almost as if she spoke to herself:

"I find His Majesty's behaviour incomprehensible. Prince Vladislav, as I am well aware, is a great land-owner and one of the most important noblemen in Dórsia. I only hope he will not be offended that the King is not present on such an important occasion."

"I am sure His Royal Highness will make His Majesty's excuses very eloquently," the Lord Chamberlain replied.

He was an elderly man who, Zosina had already learnt, had been at the Palace for many years and in attendance on the previous Monarch.

The Queen Mother smiled as if to take the sting out of her words as she said:

"When the Prince Regent retires, you will have your hands full."

The Lord Chamberlain shook his head.

"I too am retiring, Ma'am, as are most of my colleagues."

"Retiring!" the Queen Mother exclaimed. "Is that wise?"

"It is wise from our point of view," the Lord Chamberlain replied, "to leave before we are dismissed."

The Queen Mother looked shocked, but Zosina

thought she was actually aware of the King's intention to have his own friends about him.

She could only think once again, in horror, of the chaos they would create everywhere.

The outside of Prince Vladislav's house was almost as magnificent as that of the Palace, but inside it was a conglomeration of good and bad taste, ancient and modern.

It was, however, difficult for Zosina to notice anything, because as they entered the huge Reception-Room, already crowded with guests, she saw the Regent standing beside their host and her heart turned over in her breast.

If he had looked magnificent on other occasions, she thought now that he looked like a mediaeval Knight, wearing the uniform of the Order and a wide blue ribbon across his heart, from which hung the decoration of St. Miklos, which was worn by all the other men in the room.

But none of them was as handsome and outstanding as the Regent.

Zosina only hoped as she walked behind the Queen Mother that she looked like the flower with which he had identified her.

She had taken a great deal of trouble in choosing her gown with this in mind, and it was of a very pale leaf-green tulle decorated with bunches of snowdrops.

The same flowers were arranged in a wreath on her hair instead of the flower tiara she had worn on other occasions.

She looked very young, very innocent, and very pure, but she did not know that to the Regent it was like being struck by a thousand knives to see her eyes looking shyly at him and to know that he could never again hold her in his arms or touch her.

The dinner was superlative, the company was intelligent and amusing, and the speeches were very short.

Afterwards there was soft music as a background to the conversation, and it was with a sincere feeling of regret that at eleven o'clock the Queen Mother rose to leave.

"Our last evening in Dórsia," Zosina heard her say to the Prince, "has been more enjoyable than any other. I can only thank Your Highness for a most delightful time, and I know my granddaughter has enjoyed it as much as I have."

"It was a great privilege to have you here, Ma'am," the Prince replied, "and may I say that for the Princess I hope this will be the first of many such visits."

"I hope so too, Your Highness," Zosina replied.

She could not help knowing that the King would think the Prince's hospitality dull and boring. She was also sure that he would, as he had tonight, refuse his invitations if it was possible to do so.

Zosina wanted to ask the Regent what she should do in such circumstances.

Should she be strong-minded enough to go without the King, or should she just agree to confine herself to being his wife and associate only with the people who amused him?

It would be intolerable to endure the impertinence and familiarity of the King's friends night after night!

Then she told herself reassuringly that at least he could not have them at the Palace, not all of them, at any rate. That would be too outrageous even for him to contemplate.

Perhaps gradually she could have her own friends, men like Prince Vladislav, who, although he was old, was charming and interesting.

Her whole being cried out at having to make such decisions on her own, and after what the Lord Chamberlain had said tonight, she wondered apprehensively if there would be anybody stable and sensible left in the Palace.

To her relief, when they were escorted to the front door she found that the Regent was accompanying them home.

The Lord Chamberlain therefore changed to another

carriage, and as the Regent sat opposite her, Zosina felt that if she was not careful her hands would go out towards him and she would be unable to prevent herself from holding on to him.

"I am frightened!" she wanted to say. "Frightened of tomorrow, of having my engagement to the King announced to the world, of knowing that then there will be no going back, no escape, and when I return to Dórsia it will be as a bride."

She felt her heart crying out to the Regent with an irrepressible agony, and although he did not look at her but only at the Queen Mother, she knew that he was feeling the same.

There were huge crowds outside the Palace and the Regent said:

"I thought we would not go in by the main entrance, Ma'am, but once we are in the Palace, if you and Her Royal Highness would appear on the balcony, it would give very great pleasure to the people who have been waiting for hours for a glimpse of you."

"Of course we will do that," the Queen Mother replied.

Zosina thought it was a sensible idea that instead of the crowds seeing only their backs walking up the steps to the Palace, they would see them waving and smiling from the balcony on the first floor.

Inevitably her mind told her that the King would never think of greeting the people in that way, then she rebuked herself again for being critical.

They stepped out at the side door which in fact was very impressive and was used on formal occasions for those being entertained in the Throne-Room.

There was a wide passage covered with a red carpet, and as the Queen Mother walked ahead, followed by Zosina and the Regent, a second carriage drew up to the door.

The Lord Chamberlain and other members of the Prince's party staying at the Palace began to alight.

By this time the Queen Mother had reached the huge

painted and gilt doors which led into the Throne-Room itself.

As she did so, there was a sudden loud noise of voices and laughter, followed by several pistol-shots.

It was so unexpected and so startling that the Queen Mother stopped and looked back to the Regent.

"What can have happened, Sándor?" she asked. "Who can be shooting inside the Palace?"

As if the Regent was perturbed, he quickly walked forward and opened one of the Throne-Room doors.

Both the Queen Mother and Zosina followed him to look inside.

What she saw made Zosina draw in her breath.

The gas-lights were lit but not the huge chandeliers which, as in the State Banqueting-Room, hung from the centre of the ceiling.

On the throne sat the King, and at her first glance Zosina realised that he was very drunk indeed.

His white tunic, open to the waist, was stained with wine, his legs were thrust out in front of him, and seated partly on his knees and partly on the arm of the throne was the same girl who had been with him last night, who was even drunker than he was.

Her skirt was up above her knees and her bodice had fallen from one shoulder to reveal her breast.

On the floor in front of them were the King's friends, and Zosina saw that they were lying on the red velvet cushions from the gilt chairs and stools which stood against the walls.

She recognised most of the men who had been with the King the night before and the same women who had surprised and shocked her with the dyed hair and crimson lips.

Even in her innocence Zosina was aware that the men and women on the velvet cushions were behaving in a grossly immoral manner, the majority of the men having discarded their coats and in some cases their shirts.

She seemed to take in everything in the passing of a

second; then the King lifted his hand that was not encircling the woman on his knee, and there was a pistol in it.

He shot at one of the gas-lamps and the glass from it crashed down on the polished floor, and this shot was followed by two more, while the men who were not too engaged with the women in their arms shouted encouragement.

As another gas-bulb crashed to the ground there was a yell of triumph. It was a sound, Zosina thought, like that of wild animals baying at the moon.

Then sharply the Regent shut the door.

"His Majesty is entertaining his friends privately," he said, but he was unable to repress the anger in his voice.

They went on down the corridor in silence.

The Lord Chamberlain escorted the Queen Mother and Zosina to the Reception-Room on the first floor, footmen opened the huge centre window, and gas-lamps illuminated them as they stepped out onto the balcony.

A great roar of sound like the breaking of waves on a rocky shore went up as the crowds saw them, and hats, flags, and handkerchiefs fluttered in the air as the Queen Mother and Zosina waved.

It would have been an inspiring and exciting sight if Zosina had not felt as if someone had struck her on the head.

By the time she reached her own bedroom she felt physically sick.

All she could think of was the scene in the Throne-Room. She had had no idea that men and women could look so degraded and so utterly disgusting.

Last night had been bad enough, but tonight, with the King's friends behaving in a manner that she had never before been able to imagine, let alone see, she was disgusted to the point where she herself felt degraded because she had witnessed their behaviour.

She only knew, when at last Gisela had left her and she was alone, that she wanted to hide because she could no longer face the world, or rather the people in it.

"How can he be like that? How can any man, let alone a King, think that sort of behaviour enjoyable?" she asked herself.

The King's puffy face and half-closed eyes, his mouth slack and open, his soiled and crumpled clothes, and the woman on his knee were vividly pictured in her mind and would not be erased.

It seemed as if in that split second of time when the Regent had opened the door, the whole scene had become fixed in her memory so that she would never be able to forget it.

She tried not to think of what she had seen, the women half-naked, the men's bare backs, with overturned bottles of wine rolling about on the floor.

It was all horrible, disgusting, and vulgar, and she was ashamed.

Ashamed for the King, ashamed that any man could so debase himself when he was the Monarch of a country as beautiful as Dórsia.

Then her own personal involvement was there to frighten her even more than she was already.

"His wife!" she whispered to herself. "Oh, God. How can I be his wife when I loathe and despise him?"

Because there was no answer to the question, she buried her face despairingly in the pillow and felt that even God had deserted her.

⚜️⚜️⚜️

All through the night, unable to sleep, Zosina tossed and turned and tried to escape from her thoughts.

No exercise of will-power, she thought now, despairingly, could change the King, and it had been only a child's idea culled from Katalin that anything she could say or do could improve him.

Zosina was in fact so deeply shocked by her first encounter with impropriety that it was impossible for her to think clearly or be certain of anything except the longing to escape.

437

The hours were ticking by and she told herself that soon it would be the morning of the day when her engagement would be announced to that foul creature whom she had seen sitting on his throne.

After that it would be only a short time before she became his wife and would be competing for his interest, if that was the right word, with the women he obviously preferred, women unashamedly naked, who would debauch the Palace as he was doing.

"What can I do? What can I do?" Zosina asked, and again there was no answer.

Finally, because she could not sleep and felt as if she could not breathe, she walked to the window to pull back the curtains.

It was still very early and the mountains were silhouetted as the first faint glow of dawn rose behind them. There were still stars in the sky.

There were no longer crowds outside the Palace, only a deep quiet while the city slept.

It was then that Zosina felt as if the Palace was closing in on her, the walls crushing her so that like a rat in a trap she was slowly being suffocated by them.

"I must think! I must think!" she told herself.

But her brain seemed a jumble of impressions and nothing was clear except wherever she looked she saw the King's drunken face.

Hardly aware of what she was doing, driven by a wild desire to leave the Palace and the man she loathed, she went to her wardrobe.

The first thing she saw was one of the riding-habits she had brought with her to Dórsia, which she had not had the opportunity of wearing.

She was so used to dressing herself at home without the help of the overworked Gisela that it only took her a short time to put on her habit and find her short summer riding-boots, her hat, and her gloves.

She glanced at the clock and saw it was only a little after four o'clock.

The sky was lightening every moment and the stars were receding until few of them were visible.

Zosina opened the door of her bedroom and went down the passage.

She knew there would be a night-footman on duty in the Hall, just as there would be sentries outside the main doors.

She knew in which direction the stables lay, and rather than ask for a horse to be brought round for her, she intended to choose one for herself.

The side door was heavily bolted, but the key was in the lock and with some difficulty Zosina managed to pull back the bolts.

She found herself in the garden and saw in the distance the roofs of the stables. She walked there quickly.

As she expected, everything was very quiet.

Then as she opened the double doors of the main stable building a young groom appeared, rubbing his knuckles in his eyes and yawning.

When he saw Zosina he stared in surprise and she said:

"I am going riding. Please saddle me a horse."

He was obviously too astonished to speak, but he hurried away and she heard him calling for somebody who she suspected was one of the Head Grooms.

Realising that she had caused a commotion but still intent on riding away from the Palace, she inspected the stalls close to her, and in the third one in which she looked, she found a magnificent black stallion.

It was the finest horse she had ever seen, and she had opened the stable door and was patting him when the young groom came back with an older man.

"Good-morning!" Zosina said before he could speak. "I am the Princess Zosina. I wish to go riding."

"Certainly, Your Royal Highness," the elderly groom replied, "but I think that stallion would be too much for you."

Zosina smiled.

"This is the horse I wish to ride," she said firmly.

"Very good, Your Royal Highness, but any groom I send with you will find it hard to keep up with Samu."

"That is his name?" Zosina asked. "Then your groom must do his best. I am sure Samu will give me a most enjoyable ride."

The old groom looked doubtful but he was too well versed in his duties to argue.

He sent the boy to fetch somebody called Niki and began to saddle Samu quickly and with a deftness which came from long practice.

Zosina went out into the yard.

She wanted to breathe the fresh air, and it was an effort to speak, even to give her orders to the groom.

In a surprisingly short time Samu was brought out to her, and from elsewhere in the yard a groom appeared on another stallion, which was by no means as magnificent or, Zosina was sure, as fast as Samu.

The old groom helped her into the saddle.

"Your Royal Highness will remember," he said, "that Samu is the fastest horse in the stable. He belongs to His Royal Highness the Regent, and he says he has never owned such a horse before in his life."

Zosina thought she might have guessed that the Regent would have found a horse to which she had been drawn instinctively.

She did not reply to the groom, she merely moved forward, aware that Niki, on the other horse, was following her.

She had some idea of the direction in which she wanted to go, and as soon as there was room Niki drew alongside her.

"I'll show Your Royal Highness a good ride!" he said eagerly. "We cross the river, then you'll be in the wild country below the mountains. They tell me it's like the Steppes in Hungary, but I can't believe there's a better place for horses than you'll find here in Dórsia."

The groom led her in the direction he described, and as he chatted on, talking of the rides there were round the city and the horses they had in the stables, Zosina did not listen.

She was back with her own problem, feeling that it was pressing in on her and worrying at her brain like a dog with a bone, so that she could not escape from it, could not force herself to understand anything else that was happening.

In one detached part of her consciousness she was aware of the excellence of Samu and the manner in which he moved obediently to her wishes.

Niki was still talking when they reached the open country, and she felt she could bear it no longer.

She had to think, she had to!

An idea came to her and, without really considering it, she acted.

She drew a lace handkerchief from her pocket and as they were moving at a trot it floated away from her in the wind.

She drew Samu to a standstill.

"My handkerchief!" she said. "I have dropped it!"

"I'll fetch it for Your Royal Highness," Niki said.

Zosina reached out to take the bridle of his horse as he slipped to the ground.

When he started to run back to the handkerchief, lying white against the green of the grass, she spurred Samu forward, taking the groom's horse with her.

She deliberately moved very quickly so that he should think she had lost control, and only when she had broken into a gallop for nearly a quarter-of-a-mile did she release the reins of the other horse.

Then, spurring Samu again, she settled down to ride at an almost incredible speed over the soft grass, which was fragrant with flowers.

She rode until Samu himself slowed the pace, and when she turned to look back, not only were Niki and his horse out of sight but so was the city.

She was in what seemed to be an enchanted land, the mountains peaking high above her and the green valley in which she was riding empty save for the flights of wild birds which rose at her approach.

"At last I can think," Zosina told herself. "At last I can consider what I can do."

She brought Samu down to a trot and tried to make her mind work clearly, as it had been unable to do in the Palace, but the confusion was still there.

The impossibility of marrying a man like the King, and the equal impossibility of refusing to do so, was an unanswerable dilemma.

Round and round, over and over and up and down, it seemed to Zosina that her brain considered every aspect of the situation in which she found herself, but instead of the problem becoming clearer it seemed only to become more involved.

There was the threat of the German Empire, the hope not only of Dórsia retaining her independence but also of her own country, Lützelstein.

She visualised only too well her father's fury as well as her mother's if she should go back home having refused to accept the duty that had been imposed upon her.

Even if she tried to refuse, she had the feeling that her father, or rather her mother, would force her into obeying them.

And apart from that, how could she bear to lose the respect and admiration of the Regent?

He might love her, but he had given his whole life to his country, on behalf of the King, in a manner which she knew now was exceptional and was admired by all other countries which were aware of the progress Dórsia had made.

The British particularly, Zosina knew, would want Dórsia and Lützelstein to remain independent, because Queen Victoria, more than any other Monarch in Europe, had tried to maintain the balance of power.

"How can I fight all those people?" she asked herself.

Once again the picture of the King was in front of her eyes and she could almost see his coarse friends inveigling themselves into positions of power, and in doing so ruining everything that the Regent had built up in the last eight years.

'They must be stopped!' Zosina thought. 'But how?'

She felt as if she were trying to hold back an avalanche with her bare hands but being crushed and smothered in the process.

She rode on and on. Suddenly, after many hours had passed, she found that the sun was high in the sky, it was very hot, and she was thirsty.

She pulled off her riding-coat and laid it on the front of her saddle.

She looked for somewhere to drink and thought if she drew nearer to the mountains there might be a cascade of cool, pure water running down from the snows.

The mere thought of it made her lick her lips, and she turned her horse's head, riding towards the great fir-covered foot of a mountain on whose peak there was still snow.

"It is such a beautiful country," she told herself, "but the man who will rule it is ugly and horrible!"

She felt that if the Regent was with her she would say: *"Every prospect pleases and only man is vile,"* and he would understand.

Then she was back repeating over and over again:

"I love him! I love him!"

Chapter Seven

*I*t grew hotter still and she was beginning to think that she would have to try to find her way back to the river which she knew flowed through the valley a long way away.

She was now in the foothills of the mountains and there were huge boulders and also a lot of scattered stones which might have come from an avalanche.

But, although she kept looking, there was no cascade of clear water as she had hoped to see.

She told herself that what she ought to do was return to the Palace, but every instinct in her body fought against facing the problems that awaited her there.

She was still finding it hard to think; she only knew that somehow, somewhere, there must be a solution, and yet if there was one, it escaped her.

"I cannot go . . . back," she whispered beneath her breath.

And yet she was aware that time was passing, and although she had no idea what hour it was, soon the groom she had left behind would report that she had ridden on without him, and she supposed that the Regent would send a search-party.

'He will be . . . angry with me,' she thought, and felt a little tremor of fear go through her.

But even to endure his anger would be better than to

be without him and know instead the indifference of the degraded and drunken King whom she hated.

She felt as if her dislike and abhorrence of him, which was very foreign to her whole nature, was degrading her so that she was losing her self-respect and becoming a reflection of him.

"I cannot live such a life, nor can I become like the women he admires."

She was back with the same problems which had beset her all night and had taunted and haunted her so that she had been unable to sleep, and inevitably as she asked herself the same questions over and over again, she could find no answer.

Her lips were so dry and she was so thirsty that her need for water seemed for the moment to sweep away everything else.

And yet she was not certain whether the reason for her thirst was the heat of the sun, the hard riding, or just fear.

Then as she rounded a huge boulder she saw just ahead of her smoke rising on the warm air.

Instinctively she urged Samu forward, thinking that perhaps she would find a party of wood-cutters.

Then as she drew a little nearer to the smoke, she saw a fire and round it were seated a number of gypsies.

It was not difficult for Zosina to recognise who these people were, for there were always a large number of gypsies in Lützelstein and she and her sisters had been interested in the Romany people, Katalin finding them very romantic.

Zosina had at one time tried to learn a little of the gypsies' language but had found it too difficult.

Frau Weber had taught her their history and had pointed out that as they had originally come from India, much of their language was derived from Hindustani.

Moving nearer to the gypsies, Zosina thought of what she had learnt and was sure that as Dórsia marched with Hungary, their customs would be much the same as

445

those of the Hungarian gypsies who were the predominant tribe in Lützelstein.

When she reached the gypsies she saw that they were poorly dressed, but in other ways, with their dark hair and eyes, they were much the same as those she had seen at home.

As she rode up to them they looked at her in astonishment, and she thought too that the men who rose slowly to their feet were nervous.

To put them at their ease, she greeted them in one of the few sentences she had learnt which meant "Good-day."

"Latcho Ghes!" she said.

Instantly the gypsies' apprehension was replaced with smiles as they replied: *"Latcho Ghes!"* and a great deal more that she did not understand.

She dismounted from Samu's back and, holding his bridle, went nearer to the fire, saying slowly in Dórsian:

"Would you be kind enough to give me a drink?"

To make it clearer, she mimed the act of drinking, and the gypsies gave a cry to show that they understood; then a woman hurriedly brought a goat-skin bag from which they poured out water into a rough cup made of antelope-horn.

It tasted slightly brackish but Zosina was too thirsty to be particular, and she drank all the cup contained and the woman refilled it.

Then she pointed to Samu, feeling that he must be as thirsty as she was, and again the gypsies understood; one of the older men, whom she thought must be a *Voivode,* or Chief, took Samu by the bridle and led him to where their own horses were tethered by a large gourd from which they could drink.

Zosina stood watching the stallion move away, and then one of the women, speaking a mixture of Dórsian, Hungarian, and Romanian, which Zosina could just understand, offered her food.

She saw then that they were all eating from a great pot of stew which was cooking over the fire.

It smelt delicious and Zosina was certain that she recognised the savoury fragrance of deer or young gazelle
and perhaps that of other wild animals which the gypsies could hunt in the mountains.

She accepted the invitation eagerly because she was
no longer thirsty but was very hungry.

She had missed her breakfast, and although she had
no watch on, she guessed by the height of the sun in the
sky that it must be getting on for midday.

A thick stew was ladled onto a wooden plate, and
while the gypsies ate with their fingers, mopping up the
gravy with a rough brown bread which the peasants ate
in every country in that part of the world, for Zosina
they produced an ancient silver spoon.

It bore, she noted with a smile of amusement, an elaborate crest which she was certain must have belonged to
some nobleman.

She presumed it had been stolen, but she was not
prepared to challenge her hosts' possession of it.

She ate what was on her plate, finding it excellent, the
meat seasoned with herbs which she was sure had been
known to the gypsies for centuries.

She wished fervently that she had persevered with the
study of their language, but unfortunately she could
communicate only in broken sentences and with a great
deal of mime.

Zosina understood that they were travelling East and
she presumed they would be leaving Dórsia because it
was their nature to wander and never to settle anywhere.

The women were attractive, their huge dark eyes re-
minding Zosina of their Indian ancestry. The children,
small, dark, and full of high spirits, were adorable.

Only the men seemed rough and surly, and she
thought they regarded her suspiciously, as if they could
not understand why she was alone and not accompanied
by grooms or soldiers.

As they looked at her and whispered amongst them-

selves, she wondered if they suspected that she was trying to trap them in some way.

To set them at their ease she tried to explain that she
had ridden from the city and now was about to return
home.

She thought she had made them understand, but to
show her good will, she lifted one of the gypsy babies
onto her lap and let it play with the pearl buttons on the
coat of her habit.

One of the gypsy men whispered to the woman who
had first invited her to eat with them, and she smiled
and nodded. Then he strolled away, still looking at her
with what Zosina thought were suspicious eyes.

She was just about to say that she must ride on, when
the gypsy woman produced a cup, poured some boiling
water into it from a very old kettle, and brought it to her
side.

"Tea," she said in Dórsian. "Tea."

Zosina took the cup from her. She remembered reading that the gypsies were famous for their special herb-
teas, and when she sipped the tea, she thought the taste
was strange but delicious.

However, the herbs were impossible to recognise, because honey had been added, although not enough to
destroy the aromatic flavour.

"I wonder what herbs they have used?" Zosina asked
herself.

She thought of the different herbs that were to be
found in Dórsia, but it was impossible to translate them
into any language which the gypsies were likely to understand.

She realised they were delighted that she was pleased
with the tea, and when she had finished her cup they
offered her more, but she shook her head.

"I must be leaving," she said.

She looked for Samu, thinking that it suddenly
seemed a very long distance to where he was tethered
with the gypsies' horses.

In fact, she felt disinclined to move, even to make the effort to rise to her feet.

Then she was aware that all the gypsies were watching her, staring at her in a different manner from the way they had done before.

She wondered why, and the answer seemed to flash into her mind.

Then before she could hold it, before she could formulate the idea it presented, their faces became blurred and receded as Samu had receded into a strange and indistinct distance.

"I must get up! I must go!" Zosina tried to tell herself.

Then to do so was impossible, and she felt herself sinking away into an infinite darkness in which there was no thought. . . .

❦❦❦❦❦❦

"Wake up, wake up, Zosina!"

She heard a voice calling her from far away.

"Zosina!"

The call came again, and because she knew who it was, she felt her love rise within her and sweep over her in an indefinable happiness.

"Zosina!"

Now the voice was louder and more compelling, and because she knew who was there, close to her, she smiled and with an effort opened her eyes.

She could see his face, close to hers, and the outline of his head against the light. Then because she was conscious only of an irrepressible happiness, she murmured:

"I love . . . you . . . I love . . . you!"

"My precious, my darling!" the Regent said in a low voice. "I thought I should never find you, but you seem all right. They have not hurt you?"

Because he was speaking to her, because he was so near, she could think of nothing but him and nothing else made sense.

449

"I love . . . you!" she said again.

Now, as if he could not help himself, she felt his lips on hers, and her heart leapt and she felt as if her whole body was swept toward him by the impetus of her love.

She wanted him to hold her closer and to go on kissing her, but he said in a strangled voice:

"I thought I had lost you! How could you do anything so reckless, so mad, as to ride alone?"

It was then that Zosina remembered, and she said a little incoherently:

"The . . . gypsies! They . . . gave me . . . something to . . . drink . . . I think it was . . . drugged!"

"It was!" the Regent agreed. "And if we had not met them with Samu, we might never have found you."

"Samu?"

It was a question, and he answered:

"They had stolen him, but fortunately I recognised him the moment I saw him with them."

Zosina put her hand up to her forehead in an effort to think.

As she did so, she realised that she was in a cave, lying on a pile of dried grass, and the Regent was beside her on one knee, which was why she had seen his head silhouetted against the light which came from the mouth of the cave.

She looked round her in bewilderment.

On the ground near her was Samu's saddle and bridle, and as if the Regent realised how hard it was for her to clarify her thoughts, he explained:

"The gypsies have admitted to giving you what they call 'sleeping-tea.' They left Samu's saddle and bridle behind, and, hoping it would not be possible to identify him, they then started off on their journey. Luckily we encountered them—otherwise, if they had not led us here to you, my darling, it might have been days before you were discovered."

"I . . . I am . . . sorry," Zosina murmured.

"When the groom returned to the Palace and told me how you had gone on alone, I was frantic," the Regent said. "He thought Samu had bolted with you, but when he described what had happened, I had a feeling that you intended to ride alone."

"He . . . kept talking . . . and I wanted . . . to think."

Her eyes pleaded with him to understand, and when he smiled she felt as if the sun had come out.

"I understand," he said, "but it was wrong of you to take such risks with yourself."

"But . . . you have . . . found me."

"I found you, and I thank God for it," the Regent replied. "And now, if you are strong enough, I will take you home."

"Home?"

For the first time since he had found her, she saw by the expression in his eyes that all their problems and unhappiness had returned.

"I . . . I cannot go . . . back."

"You have to," he replied. "There is no alternative."

He spoke gently, with a sadness that was far more convincing than any other tone he could have used, and she knew that he spoke the truth. There was no alternative.

As he had said before, the well-being of their countries was more important than individuals' feelings.

"How can I do . . . what you . . . ask me to do?" Zosina whispered, and he knew she was thinking of the King and his outrageous behaviour.

"I will make him behave," the Regent said in a hard voice.

"He will not . . . listen to you."

The Regent's lips tightened and after a moment he said:

"I will think of a way."

He spoke positively, but Zosina knew that whatever he might do or suggest, the King would pay no attention.

Once he was free of restraint, once his uncle was no longer in a position of authority, he would order him

451

not to interfere, and in the circumstances there would be nothing that the Regent could do.

As if he followed the train of her thoughts, Zosina saw an expression of pain in the Regent's eyes, and in that moment she understood as she had not understood before what this meant to him.

He loved his country, he loved his people, and he understood their needs and more than anything else their overwhelming desire to be independent of Germany.

She knew he would give his life willingly in the field of battle for such a cause, but it was harder to live without even fighting a battle on Dórsia's behalf.

And yet in a way, that was exactly what it was—a battle against his instincts, his intelligence, and, most of all, his love.

In that moment Zosina grew up, and she knew that she could not add to the agony he was suffering by complaining or clinging to him.

"We will go back," she said, and now her voice was not hesitating or frightened but courageous.

For one moment they looked at each other, then as if there was no need for words the Regent just raised her hand and kissed it.

Then he rose to his feet and, going to the mouth of the cave, called one of the soldiers who were waiting below to collect Samu's saddle and bridle.

Zosina rose from her bed of dried grass.

She shook out the skirts of her habit, picked up her riding-hat with its gauze veil which lay on the ground, and walked towards the opening of the cave, carrying it in her hand.

When she emerged into the sunlight she gave a little start, for she saw that the gypsies had carried her quite a long way up the mountainside to hide her in a cave where, if the Regent had not awakened her, she might have slept for the rest of the day and into the night.

She still felt muzzy in the head, but there was a touch of wind in the air and as she drew several deep breaths it cleared her brain and she knew how fortunate she was to have been found so quickly.

There were six soldiers with the Regent, and amongst them Samu with his black and shining coat looked very magnificent, especially when his silver bridle was restored to him instead of the one of rough rope which the gypsies had used.

Zosina put on her riding-hat; then, as she saw the girths of Samu's saddle being fastened, she asked:

"Where are the gypsies?"

The Regent smiled.

"When they brought us here, I let them go."

"You let them go?" Zosina asked in surprise.

"To take them back for trial would cause unnecessary talk and speculation," he replied. "We would have had to explain why you left the Palace so early and why, even if Samu had bolted with you, when you had got him under control you did not turn back."

"You are very . . . wise."

"That is what I try to be," the Regent said with a little sigh. "The gypsies were lucky, when I first learnt what they had done to you, that I did not punish them as they deserved."

"Perhaps you should . . . punish me instead. I thought I would never find you. I had no idea that a flower-filled valley amongst the mountains I have loved all my life could seem so menacing."

"I am . . . safe now," Zosina said reassuringly with a little smile.

Then as she spoke she realised that that was not true —she was very unsafe, and perhaps in a more dangerous position than any the gypsies might contrive.

Yet what was the point of saying so?

At least, she thought irrepressibly, she would have the joy of riding with the Regent for the next hour, perhaps longer.

She had no idea how far she had come from the Palace.

As they rode side by side, the soldiers dropping behind so that they were out of ear-shot, Zosina said:

"This is something I have always wanted to do . . . to ride with you."

"There has been so little opportunity to do the things I wanted," the Regent replied. "I have wanted to ride with you, to dance with you, and above all to show you my own house."

Zosina looked at him with a question in her eyes and he explained:

"I have a house of my own, which belonged to my father, and to me it is very lovely, which is why I wished to show it to you and to see you in it."

The expression in his eyes said more than his words, and Zosina asked quickly:

"Where is it?"

"In a valley rather like this," the Regent replied, "with mountains all round it. It is built on the side of a warm lake."

"Warm?" Zosina questioned.

"There are hot springs beneath it," the Regent replied. "I can swim in the winter as well as in the summer."

"How lovely!" Zosina exclaimed. "I would adore to do that."

For a moment their eyes met, and she thought nothing could be more exciting or thrilling than to swim with the Regent in a lake where they would be alone, the blue sky above them, the sun reflected on the water.

They rode for a little while in silence, then Zosina said:

"Perhaps one day I will be . . . able to come to your home."

Even as she spoke, she knew that it was a forlorn hope.

It would be the last place the King would wish to go, and as Queen she could hardly visit the man whom her husband hated and who would, if he had his way, be exiled from the Palace.

As she knew the Regent would be feeling as sad and frustrated as she was, Zosina said quickly:

"I shall . . . dream about your . . . house near the . . . warm lake, and that way I shall feel . . . near to you as I felt just now when you . . . woke me."

"I shall be dreaming too," the Regent said. "At least nobody can take that from us."

"Nobody!" Zosina agreed firmly.

She thought she had ridden a very long way when she had left the Palace, but all too soon she could see the spires and the towers of the city ahead of them.

She looked at the Regent and knew he was thinking, as she was, that now their troubles would begin all over again.

There would be explanations to be made to the Queen Mother and doubtless to all the officials who had been perturbed and surprised by her disappearance.

"Leave everything to me," the Regent said. "Samu bolted, you lost your way, the gypsies befriended you, and they would have shown you the way back if we had not found you first."

"Will the soldiers tell the same story?" Zosina enquired.

"They are my own body-guard from my Regiment," the Regent replied.

There was a note of pride in his voice and Zosina knew she had been right when she thought he would be a good commander in battle and a leader whom any soldier would be proud to follow.

"I am glad that you are protecting the gypsies," she said after a moment.

"I am protecting them," the Regent answered, "because I do not want the people of Dórsia to be frightened of gypsies or to persecute them as has been done in our neighbouring countries."

Zosina, remembering the terrible persecution of the gypsies in Hungary, said quickly:

"I could not . . . bear that."

"That is how I knew you would feel," the Regent said.

"I have always worked for peace and comradeship for all our people, and that includes the gypsies."

"As I said . . . before, you are very . . . wise."

While he smiled at the compliment, she knew that they both were thinking that the King would be very unwise.

Already he was antagonising so many people—the Courtiers in the Palace, the owners and workers in the Beer Halls, and in fact anyone who wanted sanity and decorum amongst his people.

'I must try to make him see that it is desirable,' Zosina thought to herself.

But once again she felt helplessly that it would be impossible to convince him that anything was desirable that did not concern his own pleasure.

Because the Palace ahead of them was overpowering, they rode in silence, and the soldiers drew nearer as they entered the streets of the city.

There was only the sound of the horses' hoofs and the jingling of their bridles, and, Zosina thought, the beating of her heart.

She was nervous, apprehensive, and afraid of what lay ahead.

But one thing, she thought, had been worth every difficulty, every question, and every problem she had to face—the fact that once again the Regent had kissed her.

His lips had taken possession of hers and she had known the incredible ecstasy and wonder of being close to him, of knowing they belonged, of feeling that nothing else was of any consequence except the glory of their love.

She wanted to tell him how much he meant to her, how wonderful she thought he was!

But because that was impossible, Zosina just turned her head to look at him, and as his eyes met hers, she knew that he too remembered their kiss.

They entered the Palace grounds by a back drive

where there were only two sentries on guard, who came smartly to attention as their party appeared.

Then they were riding between flowering shrubs where the pink and white blossoms from the trees were scattered on the ground in front of them.

It was then, as if the last remnant of the drug that had precluded clear thinking was swept from her mind, that Zosina asked in a very low voice that only the Regent could hear:

"What will . . . happen, now that I have . . . missed the . . . ceremony in Parliament?"

"I imagine it has been postponed," he replied. "Leave everything to me."

"That is what I want to do . . . always," Zosina replied.

But she thought, as he did not reply or turn his head, that he had not heard her.

They dismounted at a side door of the Palace, and as they entered, Zosina had an irrepressible impulse to slip her hand into the Regent's.

She felt that if she could hold on to him, nothing else would matter, even the scolding she anticipated from her grandmother and doubtless the Prime Minister because she had disappeared when she was most wanted.

There was one slight consolation in that the King would not be in the least perturbed.

But she knew now how rude it would seem to the Members of Parliament, and she thought humbly that she must make abject apologies to everybody concerned and never again do anything so wrong and reprehensible.

They walked down a long corridor until they reached the main Hall of the Palace.

An Aide-de-Camp hurried forward to meet them.

"A guard on the roof spotted you in the distance, Sire," he said to the Regent. "The Prime Minister is waiting in the Salon."

As if she knew, without being told, that she could not escape the repercussions of her behaviour, Zosina walked towards the Salon as two flunkeys opened the double doors.

As they entered, she saw the Prime Minister and the Queen Mother at the far end of the room.

Feeling rather like a naughty school-girl, Zosina walked towards them.

Then as the Regent moved beside her, the Prime Minister came to meet them.

Zosina drew in her breath, trying frantically to find words in which to express how sorry she was.

But to her surprise, as they met in the centre of the Salon, the Prime Minister was looking directly at the Regent.

As if he too was surprised, he stopped moving, and Zosina did the same.

"It is with deep regret, Sire," the Prime Minister said in a low voice, "that I bring you bad news."

"Bad news?" the Regent questioned.

There was no doubt, by the way he spoke, that this was not what he had expected.

"We learnt a few hours ago," the Prime Minister went on, "that His Majesty was involved in a riot which took place last night in the centre of the city."

The Regent stiffened but did not speak.

"A piece of flying glass from a bottle or a glass struck His Majesty in the jugular vein," the Prime Minister went on. "It happened apparently very late last night, and when His Majesty's body was discovered this morning, he had bled to death!"

There was a silence in which it seemed that neither the Regent nor Zosina could move or even breathe.

Then the Prime Minister said in a loud voice:

"The King is dead! Long live the King!"

He went down on one knee and kissed the Regent's hand.

Zosina walked across the room to the window, then gave a little cry of sheer delight.

She was looking out on a panorama of high mountains and both they and the valley beneath them were white with snow. The lake on which the huge house was built reflected the steel blue of the winter sky.

From it arose a transparent mist which she had already learnt was the heat rising from the water into the chill of the atmosphere.

It gave a fairy-like quality which made it seem not real but part of the magic which she felt in herself.

Her husband came to her side and she turned to him to say:

"It is lovely . . . even lovelier than you said it would be! Oh, Sándor, is this really true?"

"It is true, my darling," he answered. "Have you forgotten that we are married and you are my wife?"

"How could I . . . forget that? I felt as if the months we had to wait would never pass and perhaps you would . . . forget about me."

He smiled.

"That, you know, is impossible, but I felt the same. I thought that seven months was like seven centuries, but I dared not make it any shorter."

Zosina gave a little laugh.

"As it was, Papa was shocked that it was not the conventional twelve."

The King smiled.

"I was very eloquent on the fact that stability was more important than conventional protocol, and as Parliament in both countries agreed with me, your father was, as you know, overruled."

"You mean . . . Mama was!" Zosina said mischievously. "But that was because she was delighted to be rid of me."

"I cannot believe that."

"It is true," Zosina insisted, "and Katalin said I had grown so pretty, because I was so in love and so happy,

459

that it was more than Mama could bear to have me
about the place."

"And why were you so happy?" the King asked in his
deep voice.

"You . . . know the answer to that," Zosina said. "It
was because I was in love . . . madly, crazily in love
with the man I was to marry!"

There was so much passion in her voice that the King
put his arms round her and held her close.

Then when she thought he was about to kiss her, he
pushed back the hood, edged with white fox, which covered her hair and unfastened her ermine-lined cloak,
which was also trimmed with white fox.

She had worn it when they had driven through the
streets, filled with cheering crowds, to the railway-sta-
tion where the King's special train was waiting to carry
them on the first part of their journey to his house on
the lake.

For the last part there had been a sleigh drawn by two
magnificent horses which had travelled over the snow at
breathtaking speed and which Zosina said was like being
in a chariot of the gods.

Leaning back against silken cushions and covered
with fur rugs, she had held tightly on to the King's hand
beneath them and felt that everything that had happened since she had arrived in Dórsia had been a
dream.

When she had returned to Lützelstein with the
Queen Mother, it had been hard to pretend that she was
sad that King György was dead.

The manner of his death had been presented to the
outside world in a very different fashion from what had
actually occurred, and only a very few people knew that
the King and his friends had gone from the Palace,
drunk and aggressive, deliberately to smash up a Beer
Hall where the people were enjoying a quiet evening.

When the Queen Mother and her granddaughter returned to Lützelstein, Zosina was quite content to wait,

knowing that her future was suddenly and miraculously golden.

Her sisters Helsa and Theone had asked apprehensively:

"Now that the King is dead, what happens?"

It was, of course, Katalin who knew the answer.

"There will be another King of Dórsia and Zosina will marry him."

She did not miss the radiance in her sister's face, which she could not suppress, or the fact that she was encircled with an aura of happiness that was inescapable.

"You are in love, Zosina!" she said accusingly, as soon as they were alone.

"Yes, Katalin, I am in . . . love!"

"With the man who will be the new King?" Katalin questioned. "Then everything I prophesied will come true. You love him and he loves you, and you will live happily ever after."

"It cannot be quite as . . . easy as . . . that," Zosina said, as if she herself could hardly believe that the nightmare was over.

At the same time, she was sure that Katalin was right. She would live happily ever afterwards. It was only a question of waiting.

The newspapers proclaimed the King's death, and, Zosina was certain that at first Germany thought it would be a good opportunity to press Teutonic claims on Dórsia.

Then the speeches from the new King, proclaiming their independence and dedicating himself to the service of Dórsia, were so impressive and meant so much in Lützelstein that the Ambassador looked glum.

"Everything will be all right now, Papa," Zosina said delightedly to her father.

"What are you talking about?" he enquired.

"Sándor will stand up to Germany in a way that György would never have been able to do. We shall be safe, both Lützelstein and Dórsia. Germany will never coerce or force us into the Empire."

"What do you know about such things?" the Arch-Duke asked automatically, as if he felt he must assert his authority over his daughter.

Then he added unexpectedly:

"Perhaps you are right. I always thought that György was too young to be King, and from all your grandmother tells me, Sándor is an excellent chap in every way."

"He is, Papa!" Zosina said.

Then, because she felt she must share her happiness with her father, she put her hands into his and said:

"I am so lucky, Papa. He is everything a King should be, I love him, and I shall try in every possible way to help him."

For a moment the Arch-Duke seemed too surprised to answer, then he said:

"You are a good girl, Zosina. It is a pity you were not a boy; at the same time, I have a feeling I shall be proud of you in the future."

"I want you to be, Papa."

She bent and kissed her father on the cheek; then, hearing her mother's voice outside the door, she moved quickly away from him to the other side of the room.

⚜⚜⚜

From the moment Zosina stepped out of the train at Dórsia to find the King waiting for her, she had known that she had come into a special Kingdom of her own which was like reaching Heaven.

Once again, because her father and mother were unable to travel to Dórsia, the Queen Mother accompanied her, and also in the train were Helsa, Theone, and Katalin, the latter in a wild state of excitement from the moment they had left Lützelstein.

There was to be one night spent at the Palace before

the wedding, and the King had arranged a State Dinner Party.

But this time there were no speeches except the one he made, and it seemed to Zosina as if everything glittered and glistened with happiness as they walked into the candlelit Banqueting-Hall.

The flowers were just as lovely, the candelabra shone on the table, and there was a very gay Band playing Viennese Waltzes in the Musicians' Gallery.

But there was too, she thought, a happiness she had never seen before on everybody's face, including the older Councillors, who, she learnt, had all been persuaded to stay on.

It was as if they knew that everything would be all right for their country because they had the right King to rule them and he would also have the right Queen at his side.

"Promise me one thing," Katalin said as they went up to bed.

"What is that?" Zosina asked.

"That when you are married, you will find Kings just as handsome and just as charming as Sándor for Helsa, Theone, and of course for me!"

Zosina laughed.

"That may be impossible, but I will try, although you will have to wait a little while."

"Only four years," Katalin said. "Grandmama was married at sixteen."

"Four years is a long time," Zosina replied, "and Helsa must be married first."

"We will go through the *Almanach de Gotha* as soon as you come back from your honeymoon."

"I may have something more important to do," Zosina teased.

"The family comes first," Katalin objected. "That is, until you have one of your own."

Zosina felt that if Sándor had been there she would have blushed.

But when she was alone she thanked God with all her

heart that she was to marry the man she loved and that she was not afraid, miserable, or apprehensive as she had been when she had last slept in the Palace.

The wedding in the big Cathedral had been as beautiful and inspiring as any bride could have wished, and what made it different from any other Royal Marriage was that few Queens had ever braved being married in December.

"You are not going to look very becoming if you have a red nose from the cold," Katalin said, when Sándor had first told Zosina he could wait no longer and was arranging for their wedding to take place before Christmas.

"I do not care what I look like," Zosina replied, "all I want is to be with Sándor. I would marry him in a tempest at sea or in a thunderstorm, as long as I could be his wife."

The snow had made Dórsia more beautiful than it was already and Sándor had said that the huge stoves in every room of the house by the lake would keep them warm whatever the temperature outside.

"Actually the hot springs underground keep the house warm too," he explained, "and you can be prepared to swim even on Christmas Day."

"Mama would be shocked at the thought of my swimming at any time of the year!" Zosina replied.

The King turned her face up to his.

"It is not what your mother says now, it is what I say," he said, "and I want you to swim. I promise I will look after you whether it is winter or summer. Perhaps I should prefer the winter, because I can hold you closer in my arms to keep you warm."

There was a note of passion in his voice which made her heart turn over in her breast, and as she looked into his eyes she knew how much he wanted her, as she wanted him.

Now they were married, they were in the house by the lake, and they were on their honeymoon.

It was Sándor who had planned everything, the early

wedding, the Reception, which did not go on for too long, and the manner in which they could slip away, leaving their guests to enjoy themselves.

They had left the three girls thrilled and excited because Zosina had asked them to act as hostesses in her absence.

"You must keep everybody happy," she said, "so that they do not think it rude of Sándor and me not to be there. But we do want to reach his house by the lake tonight."

"Of course you do!" Katalin said, "so you can be alone and tell each other of your love."

She was speaking dramatically as usual, but Zosina knew it was the truth.

That was what she wanted, to be alone with Sándor, and now that she was, she felt herself thrilling because she was close to him.

Now that she was married, she felt, in some way which she could not quite explain, that he was more masculine, more overwhelming, and more exciting than he had ever seemed before.

"I love . . . you!" she said as he looked down at her, his eyes searching her face.

"And I adore you, my precious!" he said. "I have a great deal to teach you about love, and I think it is a subject about which you are not as knowledgeable as I am."

"But I am a very . . . willing pupil," Zosina whispered.

"You are so sweet—so perfect!"

He kissed her until she looked round in surprise to find that the sun had sunk and it was already dusk.

Later, from the windows of the Dining-Room, which overlooked the lake, Sándor explained how in the summer they could sit on the terrace outside to have their meals and watch the wild birds.

Now in the candlelight they wanted only to look into each other's eyes, and there was really no need for words, because they vibrated to each other in a way which told Zosina that her thoughts were his thoughts.

When dinner was over she thought that Sándor would take her back into the Salon, where she had not yet had time to look at the exquisite paintings on the walls and the furniture which his father had collected and which she had learnt were the envy of Museums all over the world.

Instead, with his arm round her shoulders, he took her up the carved staircase and along the passage which led to their private apartments.

She had already learnt that her room opened into a *Boudoir* which connected with his, but before dinner there had been no time to explore because she was in such a hurry to change her gown and be with him again.

Now he opened the door of the *Boudoir,* and as she stared round her, she gave a little cry of sheer delight.

She saw that it had been decorated with Christmas-trees, silver tinsel, and witch-balls.

It was lit by tiny candles on two Christmas-trees and they blazed bravely like little tongues of fire against the background of green fir. Beneath them were piles of presents done up in silver paper tied with red ribbon.

"It is lovely!" Zosina cried. "You have done this for me?"

"You are my Christmas bride," he said, "and I knew when you saw it you would look as you do now, like a child seeing a fairy-tale coming true."

There was a tenderness in his voice which made her press her cheek against his shoulder. Then he said:

"Tonight, my darling, you are only a child, and not yet a woman, and that is why I want you to think that I am the Prince of your heart, just as you are the Queen of mine."

"That is what I . . . want to be," Zosina said. "Oh, Sándor, this is so lovely . . . so magical that I am afraid I shall . . . wake up and find it is . . . all a dream."

"You will never wake up," he said in his deep voice. "This is the happy ending we neither of us expected to have, but we should have had more faith. Fairy-stories always end happily."

He pulled Zosina into his arms as he spoke, and kissed her until she felt that the little candles swung round them, and yet their light was in her heart, flickering through her body.

"I love you! I love you!" she wanted to say, but his lips held her captive.

"Can I open my presents?" she asked when she could speak.

"Tomorrow."

"There are so many . . . I wish I had more for you."

"You can give me the one present I want more than anything else in the world."

"What is that?"

"Yourself."

She blushed and hid her face against his shoulder. He kissed her hair and said:

"I love you! God, how much I love you!"

She heard the passion in his voice and saw, as she looked up, that there was fire in his eyes.

For a moment they were both very still. Then he said hoarsely:

"I adore you! I worship you, my lovely one, but I also want you unbearably! I have waited a long time."

"I . . . want you . . . too," Zosina whispered.

He pulled her fiercely against him, then checked himself to say:

"I will be very gentle, my adorable, innocent little bride—but you are mine—mine, as you were meant to be, for ever and eternity."

"I want to be yours. . . . Oh! Sándor . . . love me and make me . . . love you as you want to be . . . loved."

He could barely hear the words but they were said, and with his arms round her he opened the door of the *Boudoir* and drew her into the bedroom.

Here too there were no large candles as there had been when she dressed for dinner, but only tiny Christmas ones on the mantelpiece and on the table, and the light from them made the room, with its huge carved and canopied bed, seem enchanted.

She looked at Sándor, feeling that he was waiting, and he smiled as if he understood and said:

"No lady's-maids tonight, my lovely, precious little wife—just you and I."

He was kissing her again, kissing her as he took the necklace she had worn at dinner from her neck and the diamond stars from her hair, then the large brooch from the front of her bodice.

He undid her gown and as it fell to the ground in a froth of tulle he said:

"You are so beautiful, so perfect. I am afraid I too am dreaming—you are not real."

"I am . . . real!"

It was hard to speak because of the wild excitement that was coarsing through her. It was like little tongues of fire flicking in every part of her body.

Yet because he was looking at her, she felt shy and tried to cover her breasts with her hands. He understood and said:

"My angel—I would not frighten you, but there can be no barriers between us, no shyness, because you are mine and I am yours. Tell me that is true."

Zosina pressed herself against him, crying:

"I . . . am yours . . . all . . . yours!"

The King made a sound of triumph and lifted her up in his arms.

She felt as if he carried her into a very special fairy-land, a land which contained a radiant and unbelievable happiness, where there was no darkness, no fear, but only him.

"I love . . . you!" she whispered as her head fell back on the soft pillows.

Then she thought that he had left her, but a moment later he was beside her, holding her close in his arms, then closer and still closer until they were no longer two people but one.

She was the bride not of a King but of the man whose heart was her heart, whose soul was her soul, and who would rule forever a world which belonged only to them both.

A world of love.

About the Author

BARBARA CARTLAND, the world's best known and bestselling author of romantic fiction, is also an historian, playwright, lecturer, political speaker and television personality. She has now written over five hundred and sixty-one books and has the distinction of holding *The Guinness Book of Records* title of the world's bestselling author, having sold over six hundred and twenty million copies all over the world.

Miss Cartland is a Dame of Grace of St. John of Jerusalem; Chairman of the St. John Council in Hertfordshire; one of the first women in one thousand years ever to be admitted to the Chapter General; President of the Hertfordshire Branch of the Royal College of Midwives, President and Founder in 1964 of the National Association for Health, and invested by her Majesty the Queen as a Dame of the Order of the British Empire in 1991.

Miss Cartland lives in England at Camfield Place, Hatfield, Hertfordshire.